MIRACLE PLAY

Other Books by Susan Richards Shreve

A FORTUNATE MADNESS

A WOMAN LIKE THAT

CHILDREN OF POWER

Juveniles

THE NIGHTMARES OF GERANIUM STREET

LOVELETTERS

FAMILY SECRETS

THE MASQUERADE

MIRACLE PLAY

a novel
by
Susan Richards Shreve

William Morrow and Company, Inc.
New York   1981

Library of Congress Cataloging in Publication Data

Shreve, Susan Richards.
  Miracle play.

   I. Title.
PS3569.H74M5   813'.54   81-1481
ISBN 0-688-00482-2   AACR2

Printed in the United States of America

First Edition

1   2   3   4   5   6   7   8   9   10

BOOK DESIGN BY MICHAEL MAUCERI

for Porter

I am grateful to the John Simon Guggenheim Memorial Foundation for its support, to the Corporation of Yaddo, to Marian Seldes and to Mary Tonkinson for special gifts.

CONTENTS

MIRACLE
PLAY

THE BIRTH OF JULIA

The first entry in the Howells family Bible was made by Caleb Howells in 1820 and said in an awkward hand:

THE BIBLE IS FOR KEEPING THE TRUE AND IMPORTANT STORIES OF THE HOWELLS FAMILY IN THIS NEW LAND, THAT IN THE YEARS AHEAD OUR CHILDREN WILL HAVE A HISTORY.

In between Genesis and Exodus and Leviticus were sheafs of unlined paper for the Howells family to record their own testaments. For generations, the Howells children left home in Bucks County, Pennsylvania, armed with stories sufficient for combat in the world and sustained by the wonderful belief that they could always come home.

"Caleb Howells was a Quaker from Wales," John Howells told his only child, Nathaniel, when he was old enough to learn about the family. "He came to Pennsylvania to escape religious persecution."

"He was a criminal, darling," Rachel Howells said. "He came to America to escape prison."

"He was a conscientious objector, Bam," John insistĕd crossly, "like all good Quakers."

"All of the Howells are objectors of one kind or another," Rachel Howells said, clearing the supper dishes. "He made up being a Quaker for convenience."

Rachel liked Caleb Howells. She, after all, had made up her own history. She was born in Detroit, Michigan, of German Jewish parents of the working class. In 1914, after she finished high school, she went to New York to be an actress. To support herself she was a secretary in John Howells' advertising firm, one of the first businesses of its kind in New York, and before she had a chance to audition even once, John Howells had fallen in love with her. They were married in a civil ceremony by a Bucks County judge in late October and wired their families of the event.

"I expected this kind of bad news when you went to New York," her father said.

"I won't tell your grandmother," her mother said. "It will kill her."

Her brother, Isaac, asked her on her first visit back to Detroit if John were circumcised. He had overheard an argument between his uncles in which the conclusion had been that John was not.

It was clear to Rachel as the new wife of a fifth-generation Quaker with a university education that it was easier among the people with whom they would be associated in New York to seem to be Anglo-Saxon and wellborn. She collected calyxware and Wedgwood, decorated her apartment in spare and understated good taste, perfected a round eastern clip in her vowels, developed a gentle social humor and was believed to be, in the public world in which they lived, entirely appropriate as the young bride of a Christian gentleman at the beginning of the twentieth century.

"I wanted to be an actress," Rachel said when John protested that she was pretending to be someone she was not. "And then I fell in love with you before I had a chance to try."

When Rachel returned to the dining room after clearing the supper dishes, John was still talking to Nat about the family.

"The original Howells were gentle and freethinking Quakers, for Chrissake," John said to Rachel, anxious to settle these matters for his son without confusion.

"Bullshit," said Daniel Howells, John's father, United States senator from Pennsylvania, retired, still at eighty-five full time in his pursuit of young women, considered dangerous alone.

"They were warmhearted and bad-tempered fighters," Rachel said. "Like you. There is no other way they could have kept this crazy place."

The place Rachel Howells referred to was about one hundred acres of land in Bucks County, Pennsylvania, on which four generations of Howells had lived and still lived.

Caleb Howells had a hope as old as the family Bible which sat in the library bookcase. He wanted a place for his family, large enough for generations to build on the same land, a place to return to in bad times, as America had been a place to come to for Caleb Howells. So he built a house and his son built a house, and his son's son, now ex-Senator Daniel Howells.

In 1937 there were five houses, including the Main House, where John and Rachel now lived, three barns, one studio, a child's play-

house and four families who lived on the land purchased from the
original deeded land of William Penn. A three-foot wall of native
stone surrounded the Howells land, high enough to suggest what
Caleb Howells had dreamed of building, a small fortress to sustain
his family against the invasions of changing times in a new land.

When the telephone call from the obstetrician at the University
of Pennsylvania Hospital came on a Saturday afternoon in 1937,
John was in the library checking the stories in the family Bible for
boys' names.

"I called your son last night," the physician said, "and he left
Cleveland this morning very early. But I thought you'd want to be
here, too, in case of complications."

In case your son, still more your son than any child's father, cannot meet his obligations. John Howells heard that in the physician's
voice as well.

"Of course," John said. "I'll take the next train."

"It won't be an ordinary birth," the physician said.

"As if I didn't know," John said to Rachel, who watched him
change to city clothes, his small, tightly wired body moving with
quick grace. He was startling-looking for a small man, with carefully
detailed bones, considered beautiful when he was a boy. Now he was
in his mid-forties and his thick black hair had turned white as a
swan's. Even as she watched him dressing, Rachel wanted to detain
him.

She was taller than he was, slender, though thickening at the
waist, with deep-set Semitic eyes and black hair she wore in braids.
She dressed in costume without inhibition. In New York she was
considered sufficiently well-born to get away with eccentricities.

"Imagine," John would say to her, "little Rachel Schoenberg,
daughter of a meat-packer from Detroit," and he'd kiss her on the
lips.

"Shut up," she'd say and nudge him gently in the crotch with
her knee.

"I would like to come with you to Philadelphia," she said.

"I know," he said and brushed his lips across her cheek.

"Because of Cally," she said.

He nodded.

Cally was Caroline Howells, the daughter that Rachel had wanted
and never had, Nat's wife, the eighteen-year-old child whom Nat

had taken with the wonderful high-sailing lust of boys which accounts for nothing but its own great moment. Certainly nothing so permanent as a baby.

Rachel and Cally did not get along.

"She has a will of steel," Rachel said to John when she and Cally first met.

"Nat is accustomed to a will like that," he said and kissed his tall wife on the neck until she folded to the bed they shared where they had always seemed to be the same size.

John was quiet driving to the station in Doylestown. He and Rachel sat in the car in the early September afternoon, waiting for the train, Rachel's hand across his neck, tugging gently against his preoccupation.

"She could die, I suppose," Rachel said.

"Of course," John said. "No one knows. There's no precedent for a birth like this."

He kissed Rachel on the lips when the train came, lingered as the old locomotive struggled to a stop.

"I love you," he said in her ear.

"Call as soon as you know," she said.

"If ex-Senator Howells gives you any trouble at supper, give him a yank," John said, brushing a strand of hair off her forehead. "I bet you'll find there's nothing left and he's smooth as a girl."

Very early that same day, September 13, 1937, Nathaniel Howells got up and went immediately to the Ohio State Penitentiary, where he spent fifteen minutes with Bessie Mae Frame ex-Birdsell ex-Cummings ex-Smith etc. etc., who was scheduled to be executed for the murder of six former husbands at 5:30 A.M. Central Time in the company of one guard and Nat Howells.

As he left, she took his face in her hands and kissed him.

"Sweet boy," she murmured. "Sweet boy." Strutting back to the main reception room where the rest of the press had gathered, he felt three times his normal size, the deliverer, a messiah, the last kiss on earth given to a "sweet boy."

The company of seasoned journalists was not friendly to Nat Howells. He was a boy without a hard line of trouble on his face, an easterner from Yale and rich, no doubt, who didn't know a thing, and this was his story. He'd scooped a big one at twenty-one. One year out of Yale he was by-lined on the *Cleveland Plain Dealer*

—as if for decades he'd haunted the back bars of lower Cleveland waiting for stories.

"Old Bessie thought he was pretty," one journalist said.

"She always had an eye for young ones and couldn't resist."

"What were the last words from the old cow?" another one asked Nat in the corridor.

Nat pulled his hat down square over his eyes as he'd seen it done by the older men and shrugged with the splendid indifference acquired for defense in eastern schools. "See ya in heaven," he said jauntily, misunderstanding their intentions as good, having been excessively loved all his life.

"Write that in your story," the journalist said.

Nathaniel Howells had been hired as a crime reporter straight from Yale, where he'd been editor of the *Yale Daily*. He was twenty-one years old and free and flying on winged feet. Immortal. Everything he imagined was possible.

He met Bessie Mae at Cavanaugh's bar, where she went regularly. There were stories and he'd heard about her. A woman doesn't lose six perfectly healthy husbands without arousing suspicions. She was feeling smug. After all, six undiscovered murders were no minor accomplishment for a small, cherubic woman with an average mind. She thought Nathaniel Howells was "cute" and so she hinted from time to time when they drank together about her successes.

Shortly thereafter she was arrested by the police, who had been alerted to Bessie Mae long before Nat had met her. Once in prison, she made a special request that Nat follow her story to the trial.

At five-fifteen, Nat was summoned by the guard from the main room where he milled with other journalists. He followed him down a long corridor through several institutional offices and into a small closet, where he stood next to the guard who would throw the switch for the electric chair, visible in front of them through a one-way mirror. The guard was gloved and hooded. At five twenty-five, two guards brought Bessie Mae, also hooded, into the adjoining room, strapped her into the chair and left.

Bessie Mae had asked permission for Nat Howells to witness her death.

At five-thirty, the gloved guard standing at Nat's right pulled a lever on the wall above his head and Bessie Mae Frame convulsed three times in a wild dance and died.

Nat Howells didn't take his eyes off her. He had promised to watch.

By the time he got to his office at the *Cleveland Plain Dealer* he was sick. He wrote the final story on Bessie Mae Frame, handed in the copy and caught the eight-thirty train to Philadelphia, where it was hoped that his young wife would give birth to a miracle baby that day.

Someplace in Pennsylvania, watching the green rolling hills in the center of that state shimmy by his window, Nat Howells lost control.

The conductor heard him sobbing in the bathroom and sat down on a seat to listen. It occurred to the conductor that the boy might injure himself, but the good man didn't want to invade his privacy. He determined that as long as the boy kept crying, he had not slit his wrists.

Afterwards Nat sat on the floor with his head against the toilet, recovering from weeping which had been like a swift raging illness.

"Are you all right?" The conductor knocked, bothered by the sudden silence.

"Yes," Nat replied, not trusting his voice further.

He blamed the execution of Bessie Mae. He was, however, too young to understand that Bessie Mae Frame ex-Birdsell ex-Cummings ex-Smith etc. etc. had been a fine shield against the serious reversals in his own life this past year. Now she was eight hours dead, burned to crumbling, the last story on her done, and Nat Howells was left unprotected.

Caroline Bouché literally took Nat Howells' breath away. After he danced with her at the Martins' party Christmas vacation his first year out of Yale, he had to sit down because there was such a commotion in his stomach.

At the bar, everyone was talking.

"Cally," as they called her, was from New Orleans, the Martins' houseguest, Sally Martin's niece. She was only seventeen years old.

"Imagine," Tom Boatwright said, clapping Nathaniel on the back, "a child."

"I'm not interested," Nat said.

"Liar," Tom replied. "Two bits she's never been kissed anyplace but on the hand."

"I have no intention of correcting that," Nat said without humor.

"I do," Tom said and poured himself a bourbon. "We'll send that poor girl back to New Orleans scarlet."

Nathaniel walked away, unable to listen to such talk. Already Caroline Bouché was consecrate.

She was not beautiful in a conventional sense, but haunting with the cool, deceptive stillness of watercolors. There was something fragile about her as well; like watercolors, she could be washed away imperfectly. The memory of her slender hand in his, of her slight body moving like velvet under his right hand possessed him. He had not talked to her, although her head, her thick, black, sweet-smelling hair were next to his face. Only afterwards did he find out her name.

"Caroline Bouché," he said over and over to himself as he watched her dancing. "Cally."

Nathaniel was twenty-one and he thought he loved Ellen McCay. Even this evening, stunned by the proximity of a seventeen-year-old southern child, he was supposed to be loving Ellen. Presumably they had fallen in love in his junior year. It was all right to be in love with Ellen, nothing spectacular, but predictable, one of the things you accomplish in your four years away from home, like making the first-string hockey team and majoring in history. You fall in love and take the girl home to meet your parents.

Rachel was dressed in a yellow terry-cloth turban and baggy pants the weekend Nat brought Ellen home.

"Oh, dear," Rachel said, whirling Ellen off to the kitchen. "Come. We've got to talk." Nat sat in the living room reading the *New York Times* and keeping his grandfather company until he got drunk. At eight the Bucks County Volunteer Fire Department arrived for supper.

"I had forgotten to tell you, darling," Rachel said to her son. "I hope she doesn't mind firemen," she said, referring to Ellen. Rachel considered her house a refuge for the community and often invited groups when she and John spent weekends at the farm. "I think of us as a kind of church," she told Ellen. "Nondenominational, of course."

At the table, Daniel Howells wore a napkin on his head because, he claimed, there was a leak in the ceiling and he was tired of getting plaster in his hair. Rachel changed into a new costume for supper, more appropriate to the occasion, but she continued to wear her yellow terry-cloth turban. "Because of my hair," she said to Ellen.

"What's the matter with her hair?" Ellen whispered to Nat before supper.

"Ask her," Nat said. "Perhaps she's shaved it off."

"Jesus," Ellen said. .

But for once, Nathaniel did not object to his mother and even forgot to tell his father the next day that Daniel had eaten supper with a napkin on his head and could something be done about them both.

He should have known then that whatever he had with Ellen McCay had to do with convention and not love.

Ellen spent the night and Nat crept into her bedroom late as they had planned and did with her what they had planned. She moaned and sighed. She said it hurt a lot. But on the whole the evening with Ellen was disappointing and Nat lay beside her wondering what he had expected. He wanted to sleep in his own bed, where there was more room.

Nathaniel watched Ellen, now dancing with Tom Boatwright, and wished she would disappear. He couldn't remember her middle name. He couldn't remember whether or not she believed in God or communism or having children, discussions they had had many times together.

"I feel ill," he told Ellen McCay when she sat down beside him after dancing with Tom Boatwright. "Maybe Tom could take you home."

"Love-sick," Tom whispered, and Nathaniel had the good judgment to disregard him.

The next day he asked Caroline Bouché to go walking in Central Park. It snowed and they fed pigeons an entire loaf of bread they bought at a market off Park Avenue. Ellen McCay called at five to say her father had tickets to *The Children's Hour* and would he like to come.

"No," he said. He wouldn't be able to do that.

"Why?" she asked accusingly.

"I've seen it already," he said feebly, which was neither true nor relevant because she wanted to see him that night whatever they did.

"I have to go to the country with my parents," he lied.

That night he took Caroline Bouché to a French restaurant which cost him more than he had in his pocket, so the maître d' had to call his father in Bucks County and exact a promise that a check for the remaining six dollars would be in the mail the next morning.

The first time Nat kissed Cally Bouché was December 28 just

before midnight on the corner of Eighty-sixth and Park, outside the circle of a streetlamp. Next to her, he was enormous, he thought, with hands the size of a giant's and legs too powerful for making ordinary love. And so he kissed her gently.

"I thought we were getting married," Ellen McCay said on the telephone, which was as close as Nat allowed her to come to him that Christmas. "It was not even my idea," she said coolly. "You brought it up in the first place last July."

"Things change," Nat said apologetically. "It's entirely my fault." He couldn't remember Ellen's face or whether she wore lipstick. Her voice was unfamiliar on the phone.

"It is fortunate I found out in time that you have a weakness for children," she said just as he hung up.

"What do you see in her?" Ellen asked another time. She pleaded with him to come to Wellesley after exams, to work things out, to reconsider.

"What did you see in me?" Nat asked. "What sense does it make, this seeing something in another person?" he said, carried away. "It's as though we can be looked at through peepholes like scenes inside those stupid Easter eggs you get at Bonwit's." He was becoming a poet, he thought, pleased with the deep resonance of his voice, wasted on the silly Ellen McCay.

"What's happened?" Ellen begged with the desperation of a failed woman, twenty-one in 1936, who would have to return to Wellesley College unattached.

"I'm sorry," he said. "I can't help it."

He couldn't help it. His love for Caroline Bouché consumed him. He couldn't breathe properly. Occasionally he felt huge and still growing, succumbing to an irregular virus that makes elephants of men. Light-headed, he believed he had ascended to a position high enough above the earth that the people gathered below him were dark fields of poppies, indistinguishable one from another. Drugged, he had been wonderfully banished from earth. He could only court angels. It was like a long illness from which he might never recover; a delicious, languorous illness from which he never wished to recover.

When he had fallen wildly in love with the fleeting, childlike Cally Bouché, he had fallen in love with himself as well. He couldn't imagine a more stunning and compelling man than the one he had become. At night before he fell asleep, he watched himself waltz like Fred Astaire across the ceiling of his room, transformed, a young man with unimagined possibilities, falling in love again and again, hour after hour with a watercolor portrait of a child from the South, a French Catholic whose deep passions were diffused in the grace and respectability required of her upbringing.

"She is a pretty girl," John Howells said.

"She'll wilt by the time she's twenty-five," Rachel replied crossly.

"I expect you're jealous." He wrapped his arm around her waist, pinched the underside of her breast.

"Nat is mentally ill," she said, pulling away from John's advances, angry as a provocative woman can be at the foolishness of men, at her own husband's pleasure in their son's acquisition.

"He's not mentally ill," John said. "It's simply that nothing has ever happened to him before."

Nothing had ever happened to Nathaniel Howells. He was the only child in a family whose sense of themselves as a family was as sacred as God. John Howells had been the youngest, the favored child of his mother, and had stayed on in Washington with her during his father's terms in the Senate until his mother's death. He was the one child of Daniel Howells to return to Bucks County, where he spent weekends and summer holidays with his family at the Main House. John and Rachel raised their only child with humor and gentle criticism and such unequivocal love that Nat did not understand that a world outside his own family expected something of him.

So he was ripe as early summer berries for the risk of Caroline Bouché.

"Something terrible is going to happen," Rachel said to John one night in their bed after the lights were out. "I can feel it."

"You always expect the worst, Bam," he said.

"It's a good thing I do," she said, "in this family of dreamers."

Something terrible did happen, but not immediately, as Rachel had expected it to, and not directly to Nathaniel.

Nat made love to Cally Bouché three nights before she went back to New Orleans. They went to his parents' apartment on East End Avenue since his parents were in Bucks County for the holidays, and he took Cally back by midnight to the Martins'.

"No one would guess," he said.

She never spoke about their lovemaking at all; Nat suspected she thought it was sacrilege to name it.

He had not planned to make love to her. She was sitting against the headboard of his parents' bed, going through recipes for sweets, reading out the ingredients like birdcalls: cinnamon, nutmeg, crushed cloves, powdered ginger. Impulsively Nat rolled over on the bed, lifted her velvet skirt and kissed her knee. She didn't talk. She seldom talked, certainly not like the girls he had known in college who talked all the time, believing words sufficient for everything. And as he kissed her knee, she threw her other leg over him. He was taken with an urgency to have her, to take her, to swallow her whole.

He expected that she loved him mightily as he loved her, although she never told him anything.

Rachel met Nathaniel at the train station in Doylestown the evening that Cally Bouché returned to Louisiana. She was wearing a raccoon coat and fishing boots, a red bandanna tied like a kerchief under her chin, an imitation immigrant who touched her face to his with both cheeks in the distant Latin gesture that avoids the lips.

"Gerte Belinsky," he said wryly, making a false bow.

She laced her arm through his.

"Honestly, Mother," he said with exasperated affection. "When I think of you while I'm away I try to remember a reasonable woman of good taste."

"Well?" she asked, ignoring his comments on her dress.

"Well, what?"

They got into the jeep, which she drove fiercely down the main street of Doylestown.

"The little girl has gone home?" she asked.

"When I am sixty, Mother, the little girl will be fifty-six," Nathaniel said, lighting a cigarette, clouding the window on his side with smoke.

"Did you use our bed?" Rachel asked with an edge. She had not planned to intrude. She had planned to wear a proper English tweed suit to the station to meet her son, to be lighthearted and full of stories so he'd be happy to be home, so he wouldn't miss the infant from New Orleans at all. Sometimes she astonished herself.

"Yes," he answered, surprised at his mother's invasion, but unoffended, even pleased for the opportunity to tell her. "I used your bed."

It made her weep. She was not a sentimental woman. She seldom wept. She parked the jeep by the Main House and took Nathaniel's face in her hands.

"Jesus, Mother," he said with honest irritation. "You'd think there'd been a death."

"I feel as if there has been," she said simply.

"I was awake all night with your tossing and turning," John said. "I wish you'd worry when something happens to Nat instead of worrying about what might happen."

"Then it's too late," Rachel said.

Already it was too late and she knew it with the unspecific sensitivity of animals that smell danger in the woods.

In early March Cally Bouché called Nat from a phone booth in downtown New Orleans with the news she was having a baby.

It was an extraordinary stroke of luck.

He had written her daily and received three unimpressive and disposable letters with the only promise of requital in the closing, "Love, Cally."

Now this. And he'd begun to doubt his splendid powers. He took the first plane from New York to New Orleans and met Dr. and Mrs. Michael Bouché straightforwardly and without apology, like a man.

"You are Jewish." That was the first thing Mrs. Bouché said that Nat could remember. She was a very beautiful woman, cold as a medieval virgin in stone.

"I am," he said.

"Of course you are," she said. "We checked."

Dr. Bouché nodded in approval. Nathaniel would learn that Dr. Bouché always nodded in approval.

"The baby will be Jewish," she said. "It's very upsetting. You're a terrible young man."

He was pleased to be terrible. It seemed sufficiently extreme and dangerous. He didn't know whether to be grateful to his Jewishness or his wondrous powers of conquest or the fact that he was northern and had gone to Yale.

But he was glad of it, glad, too, that the baby growing like crazy inside their precious daughter's belly was his.

Arrogant, they called Nathaniel, and certainly at this moment of heroic conquering, they were right. He had not imagined that sex could yield such splendid dividends as that small jewel, Caroline Bouché, now his own for a lifetime.

The wedding was planned for early June. Cally was five months pregnant and her belly stuck out exactly as though she had put a basketball underneath her skirt.

"No one in New Orleans is to know she's pregnant," Mrs. Bouché announced before Nathaniel returned home. "Or that you're Jewish. Promise me that."

He promised nothing.

Nat took a weekend off from the *Cleveland Plain Dealer* for the wedding in New Orleans. He planned to move Cally into a small house he had found in Shaker Heights. Meanwhile, he had a room in a boardinghouse downtown.

Later, when he thought back to that time, he remembered particularly the reflection in the long walnut mirror in the hall which he examined every morning before he left for work. It was a fine man he saw there—good-looking, almost wise, to whom he was justifiably certain the world shuffling beyond the boardinghouse door would be generous.

The train from Cleveland arrived in late afternoon at Thirtieth Street Station, Philadelphia, and Nathaniel took a taxicab along the familiar route down Market to Thirty-fourth and across to Spruce, where the University of Pennsylvania Hospital spread two blocks, a low brick building without character.

Caroline Bouché turned her head on the pillow so she couldn't see herself in the automobile rearview mirror placed above her head at one end of the iron lung. For the four weeks since August 14, a Sunday, she had lain there on her back, reading a book parallel to her head, held in place by a metal contraption. She could turn the pages with a stick in her mouth, but often she turned too many pages or the book fell out of its contraption. Otherwise, she could look at her face in the mirror until it grew as unfamiliar as the faces of the hospital staff which routinely pressed in on her. It was an ordinary face she saw, strangely pale, more the face of a child than she sensed it should be. But not beautiful. Not beautiful, and beautiful was what she had expected of herself since childhood, what she had been told, what she needed now as a small dividend in return for the investment of this last month.

Growing up, she had been taught to be quiet and gentle and attentive to men, but cautious, honest only with women, to hide her intelligence like the growing body of a young girl, provocative, if not properly concealed. She had been taught to be beautiful.

It had not worked. Wrongheaded teaching: she'd been cautioned to look both ways before she crossed the street only to find that cars dropped from the sky; she'd been promised sweets for good behavior after the adults had emptied the box of chocolates.

"Your husband is here," the doctor said. He stood by her for a moment and brushed his hand over her forehead.

"Hot," he said.

"I know," Cally said.

"I'm going to check now," he said. "All right?"

He had been kind that way. Always coming to her head first, where she could see him, brushing her hair back like a father, not like her father—and then examining her. It was a real invasion without warning, because she could not feel his hands, but she knew he was examining her.

"Coming," he said. He closed the iron lung and returned to stand by her head.

"How long?" she asked.

He took a cloth and wet her lips, wiped her face.

"Not too long," he said, "but it's difficult to know. I've never attended a birth like this."

He kissed her forehead. He had never kissed her before. She wished she could remember his name.

"Your husband is here," he said again.

"You told me," Cally said. "I don't want to see him."

"Not at all?"

"Not before."

She called to the doctor as he was leaving. She had in mind to ask him if she might die.

"Could it be a boy?" she asked instead. She didn't want to know any more than that, although she expected that death was very much the same as what she now knew as life.

"Of course it could be a boy." He laughed. "It could also be a girl."

She daydreamed of boys. She daydreamed of a perfect blond baby boy, of presenting it to Nathaniel and Nathaniel's father and her own father like a gift. She imagined them clapping and cheering for her and this baby boy, as she used to imagine her parents in the school auditorium cheering for her when she won prizes for good behavior or beauty, but those were just imaginings, for she never had won prizes.

Sometimes she daydreamed about acting alone on a stage with a houseful of people, weeping because she'd made them weep, laughing because she'd made them laugh. When her parents were away, leaving her with Melvina, her nanny, and Lila, Melvina's daughter, Cally would play to the mirror in her bedroom, captivated by her own face in the glass. Occasionally, when they were very young, she'd play to Lila and afterwards they'd lie together, giggling quietly, on her organdy canopied bed, furtive as thieves, her white hand sometimes holding Lila's black one, daring the footsteps of Melvina on the stair.

She wanted wonderful congratulations for this baby; only her special gifts could have arranged for its remarkable birth.

Besides, it was probably the only child she could have. The doctor whose name she could never remember had told her that. Even if she recovered.

More than once the same doctor had told her about sex. That he did not know whether it would be possible for her again. She had understood what he was saying in the first place, but her upbringing did not permit such discussion and so he thought he must tell her several times.

It was true that she had not exactly understood the first time Nathaniel Howells had made love to her. She remembered lying on his parents' bed, reading recipes and wanting something, not specifically Nathaniel Howells. He had come over to her, had unbuttoned her blue silk blouse professionally, as Melvina used to, had lain beside her and she remembered also her embarrassment when she threw her leg across him. He undressed her quickly then. She did not resist. She lifted her back while he took off her panties. She opened her legs instinctively when he touched her and she knew, lying there with the view of rows of New York City apartments, that she wanted something to happen. Although it was painful, she was pleased to feel him grow inside her, as if she had unmentioned powers, and she was surprised at the wildness of this young man's body.

But the vague wanting was left after it was over. Again and again when they made love, she lay with Nat's head on her breast wanting something and saddened by what had happened between them.

When the doctor came in the next time, she asked if it would be possible for him to call Lila to tell her about the baby when it came and gave him the number in New Orleans. She wanted Lila there, standing thick and strong beside her iron lung.

In August of 1937 the worst recorded epidemic of infantile paralysis spread through the South, killing hundreds of children, mostly infants, paralyzing many others. Cally, round with child, was living with her grandparents in Memphis, sent out of New Orleans right after the wedding until the baby came and she could move with Nat to Cleveland. She had gone to Bucks County to visit the Howells the weekend of August 12 and on Sunday she woke up with a high fever, unable to move, finally unable to breathe sufficiently. She was awake when they wheeled her into the room where she still remained at the University of Pennsylvania Hospital. In the center of the room was a brown cylindrical box on wheels that opened to a bed. She was lifted onto the bed and the top of the box closed down on her, leaving her head, like Houdini's, outside on a pillow. She would have to learn tricks to escape.

Rachel Howells called the Bouchés.

"Polio," Mrs. Bouché said in horror. "I can't imagine she has polio. That's a servant's disease. You get it from filth." Apparently Dr. Bouché, whose medical proficiency had to do with hearts, not viruses, agreed. The Bouchés came to Philadelphia and stayed a week. Afterwards Mrs. Bouché wrote notes on linen stationary and kept in touch by phone. They said that when the baby came, they would visit again. They were inexplicably and deeply ashamed. One would have thought Cally had contracted syphilis or leprosy.

"Cohabiting with Jews," Rachel said to Nathaniel when he was home.

While John was in Philadelphia waiting for Cally's baby, Rachel cooked. She took the peaches she'd put up that summer and made peach pies, rolling pastry thin as paper. She sliced apples kept in barrels in the basement and mixed dough for bread, sweet raisin bread with nuts and dates which she kneaded and kneaded with the heel of her hand to a tight shiny ball. She made bean soup for Sunday supper, enough to serve a battalion. At seven, she called her little brother, Isaac, in Detroit, who sold used cars to poor Jews in the old neighborhood. They talked about her mother. They always talked about her mother and the conversation always ended when

Isaac said with assurance, "She never forgave you for marrying John Howells."

Upstairs in her bedroom, waiting for the pies, Rachel changed clothes, putting on black silk pants with puffed legs. She tied a long scarf, rose and turquoise with thin gold threads, around her midriff, flattening her full breasts. She wrapped her black hair in a turban and applied eye makeup and white powder.

Then she made a fire in the dining room fireplace and waited for old Daniel to come for supper.

Men had always wanted Rachel Howells. She knew that without a sense of victory. She was a woman with secrets who promised rewards in her distance and containment. Her gentle touch, which accompanied all relationships, would linger on an arm, the back of a neck, without embarrassment. To come to her was to come into the warm comforts of her house rich with the smell of baking peaches and apples with cinnamon and red wine.

Old Daniel, eighty-nine, with a pecker dried as apricots and panting when he walked from his house to his son's, could not resist her. She allowed him licenses, his gnarled old hand slipping from her waist.

"For Chrissake," John would say to her. "The damn goat's had his day."

Rachel would shrug, withdraw in spirit. It was the only anger between them and Rachel was not certain whether she allowed Daniel liberties because of unspecific grievances against his son or whether fundamentally, in her unthinking self, she believed her body was an ornament and not exactly hers.

After supper Daniel followed Rachel into the kitchen and sat down at the table. While she was lining up the loaves of bread, he grabbed her waist and pinched her.

"You're getting plumpy-dumpy, Bam," he said.

She moved away from him without breaking the pattern of her work.

"You remind me of Hannah," he said of his dead wife, as though that would make Rachel compliant.

"You are a crock of shit, Daniel," Rachel said. "I'm not a bit like Hannah."

"Oh, dear." Daniel banged his forehead with his fist. "Such a tongue for a lovely woman."

She raised her eyebrows at him in warning. "My tongue," she said.

"So you remember Hannah," he said, letting his eyes fill with the skill of an old politician, an artful persuader without conscience, which was what he had been in the twenty-four years he had represented Pennsylvania in the Senate. That and admired as well for being a hard-nosed practical man with gumption who could be counted on not to be swayed. In spite of herself, in spite of the old raccoon's clever fingers pulling at her apron just now, Rachel was fond of Daniel Howells.

"Hannah was dead when I met John," Rachel said. "You remember that."

"She was a wonderful woman," Daniel said in a far-off, cracking voice, mythic in resonance, the voice of a storyteller inventing the truth as it ought to have been, making mockery of history. "I adored her," he said fervently, and it was almost possible at that moment for Rachel to believe he had not been responsible in the least for her suicide.

"If it's a girl," he said, "I wish that Nat would name her Hannah."

The first time the phone rang Rachel was conscious with an awful sense that she wanted to hear from John that the baby was dead.

The call was not from him but from Mrs. MacDonald in New Hope about the Citizens' Association. When Rachel hung up the phone, she sat in a chair, stunned at her shameful wishing.

She was not really hoping for the baby's death. She knew that. She had wanted babies, girl babies especially, and lost them, half-formed, sightless, with tiny teeth in their skulls. She wanted this baby, her own flesh once removed, so much she could taste it. But she wanted something to happen to Caroline Bouché worse than what had happened, bad enough for Cally to give in to Rachel Howells' terrible need for a daughter.

When the telephone rang the second time, she knew it was John.

The attending physician misunderstood as he watched the Howells, father and son, huddled together in the hospital waiting room like conspirators, comical pirates, laughing and laughing. In fact, the doctor spoke about it to the residents and interns, other obstetricians and internists, even a specialist in pulmonary diseases who had come to witness this dangerous birth.

"The husband," he said with some distaste, referring to Nat

Howells, "and his father are telling stories as if this is some kind of cocktail party they've come to. I don't believe they understand the seriousness of the case."

Under the circumstances, the physician felt that it was necessary to tell Nat Howells that Cally or the baby or both could die, that the situation was as serious as any he had lately attended.

"I know," Nat said with such gravity, such visible fear and confusion, that the physician knew he had been mistaken about these people and simply did not understand the odd machinery of families who survived emergencies by telling stories.

The doctors gave Cally nothing but oxygen. She kept her face turned to the side against the hand of a young resident.

"You can bite if you wish," he said with great kindness.

The only thing she asked for, and that very late, minutes before the baby, was that someone cover the mirror please so she didn't have to see herself.

The attending physicians, a white-uniformed battalion, grave-faced and oddly anxious, gathered around the iron lung, which was opened like an Egyptian sarcophagus to reveal the young woman's swollen body.

When the baby came with such force that Cally was knocked out by the revolution of her body, there was a cry of surprise from the physicians because an ordinary baby was born between the lifeless legs of this young mother.

A girl. It was a girl.

"It is a girl," the regular physician said as though it were not obvious by looking at the small wet child lying across its mother's belly where he had laid it after birth.

"What good luck," he said to the intern immediately on his left. "There's less risk with girls," he announced to the rest of the young doctors. "They're stronger at birth."

"A girl?" Cally asked when she woke. "I thought it would be a boy."

But when the nurse brought the child, cleaned and swaddled, Cally, who had been brave for months, wept freely. "I'm glad it's a girl," she said truthfully.

Nat and Cally had not chosen names. In the visits Nat had had with his wife since she was ill, they had not mentioned the baby as a fact, only as a trial, like a major operation Cally had to go through in the future. With Cally's illness the world had turned on them unexpectedly and they no longer anticipated good fortune.

"Her name is Julia," Cally said matter-of-factly to her doctor. "Tell Nat he can choose the middle name."

The physician called Nat and his father into the corridor outside the waiting room. There was no reason to believe, he told them, that this new child would not have an ordinary development. But at the same time, the circumstances were unusual. She might have lacked oxygen at birth. Cally's illness might have affected her, or the iron lung or the medication. Anything was possible. Although the baby seemed to be perfectly normal, he would make no promises.

The room where Cally was resting was nearly dark and by the small gold light that made her face seem even paler than it was, she looked to Nat like a china-faced doll, beautifully crafted, even lifelike, but unreal.

When he kissed her, he was surprised at the heat of her skin.

"Are you cross?" she asked.

"Don't be silly," he said. He put his hand through her hair. "I'm proud of you." It seemed the right thing to say for a grown man whose wife has given miraculous birth to a daughter.

"Are you?" she asked, smiling slightly.

"Oh, Cally," he said, kissing her face, her lips, her hair as she lay there unable to move. "I feel terrible about you."

John Howells linked arms with his son and they walked Thirty-fourth Street to Market and right on Market to Thirtieth Street and the train back to Doylestown. It was eleven o'clock on the night of the thirteenth of September and beginning to rain.

"Julia," John said. "That's splendid."

"I like it, too," Nat replied.

"What middle name?" John asked.

"Daniel?"

"Absolutely no," John said. "His immortality is assured." They crossed Market Street against the light. "What about Walker? For Uncle Walker. Remember?"

"Daniel's brother who died when he fell drunk in front of a streetcar."

"My mother told me when Walker died that good men die ignominious deaths."

"Julia Walker Howells. I like that," Nat said.

At the station, John Howells took his son's face, feeling the sharp stubble of tomorrow's beard on the face that he had not held like this since it had belonged to a little boy, soft-skinned and resisting the touch of his father's cheek against his own. Now Nat kissed his father without shyness.

"Thank you for coming," he said.

Nathaniel went back to the hospital. Cally was sleeping, so he did not go in her room but stood by the door and watched her in semidarkness through the window. In his excessive tiredness, the iron lung plugged into the wall, sustaining by invisible electrical wires Cally Howells' young life, became the chair in which Bessie Mae Frame had that morning been charged to a swift and violent death.

When the resident on night duty found Nat, he was sleeping on a couch that was too small. Occasionally his leg or arm would quiver, then wildly shake. Like Cally and Bessie Mae, he was connected to wires of high intensity.

Rachel had eaten half a peach pie. She was running her fore-finger around the circumference of the pie plate, planning to suck the thick juices, when she heard the front door.

"Mmm," John said when he kissed her. "Is there any left?" She put her finger, wet with nectar, in his mouth.

"Half. I ate the other half while I was waiting. Already I'm get-ting fat," she said. "Appropriate for grandmothers." She put a piece of pie on a plate for John. "So, how are they?" she asked.

"Nat is fine," John said. "Cally is better than they had expected her to be. And Julia seems to be wonderful. Did you call the Bouchés?"

Rachel followed her husband through the living room into the library.

"I did," she said. "They didn't like the name Julia, they said. They had hoped the baby would be a boy and in any case that it would be named Jervais. Cally had told her mother yesterday that boy or girl, she'd name it Jervais." She sat down on a rocker. "Do you want supper?"

"Just the pie, love," John said.

The Howells family Bible was kept on a shelf of the bookcase beside a collection of Dickens, a number of signed volumes of

Hawthorne, three identical editions of *The Odyssey* and some skulls that had belonged to Daniel's father, who had been a doctor. John took down the Bible.

"Did Father have supper with you?" he asked Rachel.

"Yes," she said. "I walked him home an hour ago and he was weepy for your mother."

"Jesus," John said, flipping through the pages of the Bible, through Job and Psalms and Ecclesiastes, to the blank sheets of paper after the entries of the birth and childhood of Nathaniel Howells, which had been written in the wide, scrawling hand of his grandfather, the senator, now eighty-nine and in his cups, full of false sentiments. "Poor, terrible liar."

"He's worse than that," Rachel said, kissing the top of John's head. "I'll make coffee and then we'll have to go to bed before I drop."

John sat in the chair and listened to her soft shoes on the linoleum floor.

His own birth was recorded by his father in his customary flat prose on the page designated for births:

AUGUST 1, 1893, JOHN HOWELLS WAS BORN IN WASHINGTON, D.C., IN THE BACK BEDROOM OF OUR HOUSE ON P STREET DURING MY SECOND TERM IN THE SENATE. HE IS OUR FOURTH SON.

Underneath Daniel had recorded Nathaniel's birth on November 12, 1915:

NATHANIEL HOWELLS WAS BORN IN THE MAIN HOUSE IN THE MIDDLE OF THE NIGHT, THE FIRST CHILD OF JOHN AND RACHEL HOWELLS. RACHEL DID NOT DO WELL AND WHEN THE DOCTOR CAME THIS MORNING BEFORE THE SUN WAS UP, HE SAID IT LOOKED TO HIM LIKE SHE SHOULDN'T HAVE MORE CHILDREN.

Although Daniel Howells was still alive, John now wrote the entries in the Bible; his father did not like to write because his hands shook. And John was glad for the chance to record the family history in his own philosophic, even romantic words.

JULIA WALKER HOWELLS [John Howells wrote], BORN SEPTEMBER 13, 1937, AT 9:15 P.M., BLUE AND BALD, WITH FINGERS THIN AS BIRD'S FEET AND EYES SET WIDE ENOUGH APART TO SEE CLEAR ROUND HER HEAD. CHILD OF NATHANIEL HOWELLS AND CAROLINE BOUCHÉ, THEIR FIRST, NAMED FOR HER GREAT-UNCLE

WALKER HOWELLS, WHO LEFT NO PROPER HISTORY EXCEPT THAT HE DIED DRUNK FALLING IN FRONT OF A STREETCAR. THE BIRTH OF JULIA WAS EXTRAORDINARY, ATTENDED BY PHYSICIANS IN ALL DEPARTMENTS OF THE UNIVERSITY OF PENNSYLVANIA HOSPITAL, INVITED TO WITNESS THE FIRST AMERICAN BABY ON RECORD BORN IN AN IRON LUNG.

John Howells dried the ink, closed the Bible and put it back on the shelf where it had been kept since Caleb Howells built the Main House before the Civil War.

A
MULTITUDE OF SEEDS

THREE DAYS BEFORE CHRISTMAS NAT CAME HOME FROM THE WAR FOR GOOD [John Howells wrote on Christmas Eve, 1945]. "SAFE AND SOUND WITH US," JULIA SAID TO HIM THE FIRST NIGHT HE ARRIVED, AND NAT AND I LAUGHED, KNOWING, AS YOU DO AT HIS AGE AND AT MINE, THAT FOR SAFETY THE WAR IN EUROPE WINS OVER THE DANGERS OF LIFE IN THIS FAMILY.

Since 1942, when he had left as a correspondent for the war in Europe, Nat had been home twice on leave because of difficulties with Cally, resulting not from the polio but from psychological complications after the births of two more children, both sons.

"It's the one thing I do well," Cally said once to John Howells.

"It's in bad taste to have children like rabbits," Mrs. Bouché said to Cally, "especially under the circumstances."

"What circumstances?" Cally challenged. She had grown sharp-edged in the eight years since Julia's birth, living on the Howells family compound with Nat in Europe, battling Rachel in fettered silence, guarding her children from everyone, especially Rachel, like a jungle cat, merciless with her claws.

"The circumstances of your affliction," Mrs. Bouché said, cautious with her daughter since she had become an unfamiliar young woman whose old friends in New Orleans decorated society like bougainvillea, their children turned out in handmade French clothing. Cally, paralyzed below the waist and in a wheelchair, wore blue jeans and Nat's shirts, her hair in a single braid down her back. She had not been to a social occasion since she and Nat were married, except parties of Rachel's for the Volunteer Fire Department or the Society for the Improvement of Conditions for the Elderly held at the Main House.

There were two other houses on the Howells land called the

43

Cousins' Houses for relatives of Daniel's who had lived in them at one time. Since John had moved to the Main House and Daniel to a smaller house on the property, those houses had been rented, often at merely nominal sums, to distant relatives or friends in difficulty. During the thirties both houses were always occupied. But because they were two-story affairs built in the 1850's with small rooms and narrow passageways and would not have been convenient for Cally in a wheelchair, John built a one-story glass house for his son's family. It looked like a shoebox and people driving on the road between Solebury and New Hope could see Cally and her brood there— three small children, two mongrel dogs, one burro ordered from an ad in the back of *Town and Country,* a large number of related cats.

"Which affliction?" Cally asked her mother, although she knew which one her mother had in mind. She imagined bridge parties in New Orleans, the ladies in organdy, their hands, holding the cards, soft and freckled.

"Another grandchild?" they'd ask and inquire about the name and size at birth and express amazement to each other that these grandchildren could be made one after another in a body dead below the waist. These proper ladies playing bridge, listening to Chopin on the Victrola, would wonder how Nat Howells managed to get these babies going, how an active man made love to half a corpse.

In the time after Cally was released from the University of Pennsylvania Hospital they had made love often. She would lie on her back, her legs propped like water-soaked logs on pillows, and want him for the babies he could give her. Just that. But the wanting was as strong as desire and satisfactory because of her great need.

"I want as many children as I can have," Cally told her mother.

"You are twenty-six now," her mother said without grace. "With Nat around when the war is over, you could have twenty or so more."

"I don't want to talk about it," Cally said.

"You can begin to name them from the billboard advertisements like the colored do," her mother said. "Lucky Strike or Quaker Oats."

Rachel understood the babies, but Cally spoke to Rachel only in the code of distant relations.

In the week before Christmas, 1945, John Howells spent his

waking hours waiting for a call from Nat saying that his plane had arrived from England.

On the evening of December 21, when Nat did arrive, John was in New York. He called Rachel in Bucks County to tell her and asked to speak to Cally.

"Only the children came for dinner tonight with Lila," Rachel said. "Cally stayed home."

"Is she all right?"

"Lila has gone back to check on her."

"I expect she's upset because Nat is coming home for good."

John understood Cally's state of mind. For the eight years since Nat and Cally had met, there had been impediments. Their love, their marriage, in fact their whole lives, like debris on hazardous waters, had been kept afloat by turbulence: an unsanctioned marriage, Cally's illness and Julia's birth, the war and other babies. Now that the war was over, there would be only Nat and his young wife, and their babies; no buffers against the hard fact of the union of their independent lives.

John Howells wanted to handle this new life for his son. "Find a reasonable job as a reporter in Philadelphia or Washington," he'd say. "Leave the farm for Cally's sake. No more babies. And send Lila back to New Orleans. Make something of yourself, Nat. Be the best reporter you can. Work harder than anyone else. Work longer hours."

Nat had been thirty on November 12, 1945. At thirty John Howells remembered himself as middle-aged. He had been ambitious, generous, honest, but aggressive as a small black bear on the prowl for dinner. He had grown up the youngest child of a senator who ran for office every six years and won and won and won amidst the hoopla, the wild celebration, the innocent declarations of elections in America before Roosevelt. John Howells had wanted to win, too. In fact, until he was the father of Nathaniel, he didn't know there was a choice. He went into advertising because it was brand-new at the beginning of the century, attended by the energy of competition, an expansionist economy, an intramural fight. Besides, the Howells had no patience with repeated careers.

"Be a man of your time," Daniel Howells had said.

John Howells had been and it had made him rich, although the money did not interest him except as a convenience. It seemed easy to come by and therefore unimpressive. But he loved the process, the strategy, the sport of selling something, Casey's Gin or Langer

Oats or Archers Coffee or Roberts Tobacco, in which he could out-distance his competitors. He loved the game, each fight more splendid than the last. By 1937 John Howells had one of the largest advertising agencies in New York and it sailed through the Second World War undisturbed.

Nevertheless, he didn't entirely approve of his work. It was satisfactory like making love or intercepting a pass, but not sufficient to the anxious spirit of a largehearted man.

John Howells wished impossible victories for his son. He wanted him to be excellent and original in his work; whatever the work, the best possible. He wanted him to be generous and wise.

"I want to be a good father," Nat had said the last time he was home on emergency leave for Cally. They were driving to the airport in March of 1944 after the birth of a second son, Nathaniel, called Bumpo. "If I put the rise in sales of Post Toasties next to the three inches Julia Howells has grown, she's got it, hands down," Nat said.

"Of course," his father said. And because he loved his son, because he had given him everything, every imaginable protection, denied him the chance to fail, John Howells tried to understand that it could be, with a war and serious difficulties with a young wife, sufficient to be a father.

"I know you're disappointed," Nat said, "but I simply can't do anything about it." He loved his father deeply and with little complication, but he did not have the energy to please him. He had never been interested in winning as his father was.

"He hates to fight," Rachel had said of Nat.

"He has to fight," John said.

"You're always afraid to let him, John, in case he loses. Besides, what you really want is an accomplishment for the damned Bible. It's like a man joining clubs so they'll be listed in his obituary."

The soldiers who returned from Europe in 1945 to inherit the opportunities of a postwar economy set about in haste to make up for lost time. For their presence at home with their families, they substituted the material things that were abundant and were gathered as expressions of well-being in America.

"I have never understood Nat," John Howells said to Rachel years after the war. "Even the failures among the Howells were driven by temperament to make original contributions, to go against the tide."

"Nat did," Rachel said. "When other men came home from Europe to make money, Nat became a father."

Nat's plane was due to leave England the morning of December 20, 1945. The soldiers boarded once, prepared for takeoff, and then were taxied back to the hangar because of engine trouble. There wasn't enough food and Nat missed breakfast and dinner. He was bad-tempered. The general excitement among the soldiers turned inward and they sat in the airport, silently waiting for the plane to be repaired. They had too much time to think about the world they were leaving in Europe and the one they would find in the United States. They had grown accustomed to war.

As the hours passed with no information about leaving, Nat decided he was afraid to fly. He expected, as he watched the other soldiers around the waiting room, concealed in their private worlds, that the plane would crash at takeoff. All engines open and charging and the plane wouldn't lift off the ground, or the engines would fail, first one, then the other, over the Atlantic. Or worst of all, having made it out of London, across the ocean, "safe and sound," as Julia would say, the pilot, exhausted by years of service, would miss the runway.

He'd go by ship, take the long route, be sensible and safe. He'd make arrangements.

"Hey, buddy," the soldier next to him said, putting an arm on Nat's. "Take it easy. We'll be out of here soon." And Nat realized he had been biting the cuff of his shirt.

"Yes." He turned, half smiling, to the soldier and said, "I have a daughter at home." It sounded like the beginning of a confession and Nat was surprised at himself, concerned that he was in a state of mind to tell this stranger personal stories. He was not familiar with unreasonable fears, this making up of air disasters.

"I know," the soldier said kindly. "It's the last leg and you can't believe you're going to make it home for that daughter of yours." He took Nat's wrist with the frayed cuff and shook it playfully.

FOR JULIA, WITH LOVE, DADDY. Nat imagined himself boxed up for the flight over, wrapped in lamb's wool in case of turbulence in the air, marked FRAGILE, HANDLE WITH CARE. His own life, this body which he'd seen a few short years ago as the splendid and capable body of a lover, had become the brittle bones and weak joints of a father who must protect himself with great care to survive the childhood of his daughter.

"Listen, buddy," the soldier said. "I got gum and cigarettes if you get tired of chewing khaki." Nat laughed.

After Julia's birth, Nat had returned to the *Cleveland Plain Dealer,* but he got only the small stories: petty thieves, bank robbers, street beatings, gang warfare on the Italian side, bar fights, fraud. He moved into the house he had rented in Shaker Heights without Cally and bought a bed and dresser from Goodwill. Weekends he went home to Bucks County, where his father had started building the shoebox house.

Cally got better. She could spend hours at a time out of the iron lung.

"I'll move to Shaker Heights with you by March," she said.

"The doctor has told me you'll be out of the iron lung for good before then."

"Does the house in Shaker Heights have windows all around?" she asked. "Is there a garden?"

They'd spend hours imagining the house they would make, the furniture they'd find for it and the colors they'd paint it, although they both knew that Cally would never move to Cleveland.

Nat came home for Christmas in 1937, and the house for Cally was nearly finished; already Rachel had attacked it, armed with colors and printed fabric. When Nat saw it for the first time with his mother, who was dressed for this occasion in a rabbit fur hat and coat, a long-legged snow bunny, matching exactly the blanketed fields of the Howells farm, he lost his temper. The bathrooms and kitchen were incomplete, but the rest of the house had rugs and pictures on the walls, lamps and chairs and beds, two matching chintz couches in the living room, an antique washstand, a spool crib for Julia in a room done in sunshine yellows with tiny hand-drawn flowers across the ceiling like a field of daisies. There was nothing left to do. Even the dresser in Cally's room had a silver hand mirror with her new initials and a wedding picture in a carved wooden frame.

"For Chrissake," Nat said to his mother, collapsing on one of the couches.

Rachel took off her hat and put it on the mantel. She took off her rabbit fur coat and threw it on a chair. Stalling for time to recover, she ran her fingers through her thick hair to comb it and wiped off the coral lipstick, which she could feel was smudged on the corner of her mouth. She rearranged the pine cones in a huge glass bowl of pine cones and baby's breath. She dusted the cherry coffee table between the couches with the palm of her hand and moved up an old federal rocker that had belonged to Hannah Howells, and which she had re-covered in smoke blue velvet with clay ribbon, and sat down across from Nat. "I'm so sorry, Nat," she said.

He knew, in spite of the limitations of his youth, the clear confession of error in his mother's deep and generous eyes.

Then, with characteristic resilience, she brushed her hands together and with that gesture eliminated the decorated house. "I will simply undo it," she said brightly.

"No," Nat said. "Don't. It'll be all right. It looks lovely. Cally probably wouldn't have the energy to fix it up herself."

"It simply didn't occur to me," Rachel said, walking across the south fields from the new house to the house where Nat had grown up.

But Rachel could not help herself. When the bathroom was finished, she papered it in Swedish ivy, and she painted the kitchen white with red maple trim which would match the maples in the side yard every fall. The day that Cally moved with Julia to Bucks County for good was a cold gray day in late February, and Rachel filled the house with tulips she had forced to early bloom in the greenhouse that Hannah had built.

Nat was fired from the *Cleveland Plain Dealer* on Groundhog Day, 1938. In fact, he had a feature story in the third section of the paper that morning on groundhogs which, as an assignment, had been the last straw. It had been downhill ever since Bessie Mae. The end of his career may have come before Thanksgiving, when he covered a raid on a southwest city bar. He'd had too much to drink with an old college friend before he went on assignment and the copy editor complained to the city desk. He had received only a warning, but the editor of the city desk suggested that he was not sufficiently interested to pursue a career in journalism, that perhaps the old newspapermen who had complained about him during the trial of Bessie Mae were right and he was too privileged, soft at the center.

He never brought up Cally or Julia because it wasn't in his temperament to make excuses or tell his personal stories. Besides, he had come to know, through Bessie Mae for one, bad times are prevalent in everybody's life. He was not soft at the center, he told the city desk editor. He simply wanted to go home.

"Go," the editor said.

"No," Nat replied. "I'll stick it out and do a better job."

He stuck it out, but he didn't do a better job. When he returned to Cleveland after Christmas, he had been switched from news to features and it was clear to him that his stay in the Midwest was a matter of time. He did a story on a striptease dancer and found it difficult, finally impossible, to leave Brown's Hotel, where she lived, without a token of her gratitude. He did a story on the Girl Scouts, which was thrown out because it could have been written, according to the features editor, by a twelve-year-old Girl Scout. He moved out of the house in Shaker Heights in early January and into another rooming house near the paper, renting a room by the week, prepared to leave town quickly, which, as it turned out, he did.

Hitler was on the march in Europe and the *Inquirer* in Philadelphia was satisfied to have a young news reporter from the area, a graduate of Yale, because the editors of the paper had faith in Yale and in local boys. In 1942 Nat was sent as a correspondent to Europe with the generous promise from the paper that he could return in case a serious problem developed with Cally while he was out of the United States.

But Nat's real work, the work that required the energies of a young man bound to inherit the riches of an energetic land, was finished when Bessie Mae Frame ex-Birdsell ex-Cummings ex-Smith died in Nat's company in Cleveland, Ohio. His stories even from Europe betrayed the sad misgivings of a young man whose youth had been snatched from him.

Lila arrived on February 24, 1938, by train from New Orleans. It was snowing and Nat met her at Thirtieth Street Station. He had been told by Cally that Lila was distinctive, very tall and very black. That he couldn't miss her. But Cally was too gentle a woman, too quiet in her ways to prepare Nathaniel for the astonishing self-possession, the vivid and unsettling beauty of Melvina's daughter, Lila, who had come at nineteen years of age to care for Cally, to help raise Julia, to live in the one-story glass shoebox at the south end of the Howells land.

It was Lila who carried Caroline Howells wrapped in blankets and a red cape across the threshold of her new home amid the blaze of yellow tulips from Rachel, promising spring.

In the next four years, before the United States entered the war, Nat raised Julia, bathing her, feeding her, playing games by the hour in the kitchen, reading her stories, telling her stories until she fell asleep against his arm. She grew strong and, despite Nat's attentions, self-sufficient, with the dark and angular features of Rachel. Although very small for her age, she looked older than a child.

"Because she's thin," Rachel said. "And dark."

"It's her eyes," John said. "They put people off."

She had dark blue eyes, wide-set and invasive. Her ordinary look was an investigative stare and people accustomed to guilelessness in children were disturbed. She would say anything.

"Julia is not polite," Mrs. Bouché remarked when she came for a visit.

"She's truthful and observant," Cally said, "and sweet. She's really very sweet."

"That may be," Mrs. Bouché said. "But she's not polite." And her husband, growing irritable with middle age, agreed.

Julia was fiercely protective of her mother. By the time she was five she knew how to help Cally in and out of chairs, how to help with the marketing, pushing Cally's wheelchair down the aisle of Lincoln Market in Doylestown, how to call the doctor or Rachel in the event of an emergency if Lila was out. She and Cally did not play together as she played with Nat, although Cally would often sing to her and teach her keys on the piano, but Julia always brought her toys to the room where Cally was resting and played there on the floor, conscious as a mother is conscious of any alteration in Cally's state of mind.

"How has Mother been today?" Nat would ask Julia at night before she went to sleep. "A little funny?"

"A little," Julia might say. And she'd touch her head, making flapping bird's wing of her fingers to show her father that Cally's mind had been flying, as it sometimes did.

Cally wanted another baby.

"No," Nat said at first. "It's crazy. You have all you can do to handle Julia, even with Lila."

"That's not fair," Cally said, and he had to admit that it was unfair. She had been a fine mother, gentle and unimposing with a quality of grace. Children were different around her. Her quiet spirit discovered the angel in them and let it temporarily free.

"I'd be fine if we had another baby," Cally said. "Just one more before Julia gets too old."

The doctor said Cally was strong enough. She went everywhere in her wheelchair, across the south fields of the farm, down the driveway to the mailbox. She drove a car especially built by General Motors and operated entirely by hand. She took in animals from the Humane Society and had a garden. Her shoulders were like the shoulders of a swimmer. She cooked, although Lila was always there to help her. She made beds and swept the floor. In fact, she did everything an ordinary wife and mother at the beginning of the forties did except dress herself. She could have, but Lila did that.

Every morning after Nat was up and dressed, Lila came in the room, undressed Cally and carried her to the bath she had drawn for her. She'd put down the toilet seat and sit on it, watching Cally bathe, laughing and talking as they used to do when they were young, locked in Cally's bedroom with Melvina banging on the ceiling below with the end of a broom to warn them that Mrs. Bouché was coming home. Often Cally would lean back in the tub and rest her head against the curved edges of porcelain, the ends of her long hair skirting the water. "Would you?" she'd ask Lila, and Lila would kneel on a bath mat and bathe Cally with a soft cloth, her long strong fingers moving with authority across Cally's back and shoulders, over her bare breasts and stomach, her legs.

"Can you feel that?" Lila asked once, touching Cally's legs.

"Yes," she said. "But it feels as if my legs are wrapped in cotton."

Lila rubbed the soapy cloth on Cally's thighs, across her pubic bone.

"And that?" she asked, her black eyebrows raised, an odd, almost challenging expression on her face.

"You mean, when you touch me?"

Lila shook her head, rinsed Cally's shoulders with clear water.

"You mean, with Nat? Do I feel it when Nat's there?" she asked.

"I didn't say that," Lila said with haste. "You did." And they both laughed, like the young exploring women they were. Lila lifted Cally onto the toilet seat and dried her with a large, soft towel.

"Have you ever?" Cally asked. "You know. With a man?"

Lila shifted her shoulders in an exaggerated shrug that meant, as it always meant, that the talk had gone as far as she would let it.

Nat was bothered by the laughter between Cally and Lila because he was left out of it. At the same time he was grateful to Lila. She allowed him a sense of satisfaction in his marriage, taking some of the responsibility for it on herself, that he could not have felt without her.

Cally and Nat didn't share the same bed. No one knew that Nat slept on the couch in the window of the bedroom, often watching Cally sleep across from him in the huge four-poster, where, if they slept together, she would roll unyielding as a grain sack on his much heavier body. Lying on the couch, he would often think of Lila at the end of the hall, imagining her naked, sleek as a panther with legs that gripped his buttocks as they made love. She'd be wild like an animal on the stalk; she would bite and kiss him with her tongue. Occasionally he put himself to sleep with thinking of Lila.

There was nothing that Nat did or thought about in his daily life that disturbed him as much as his desire for Lila.

Now that Cally wanted another baby, was desperate for it, making love had to do with sperm. Night after night he mounted Cally as if she were a pillow, hoping this time, this night, some lucky swimmer would reach the mark, tie the record, and this crazy lovemaking, baby-making, this frantic sex that sometimes made him impotent at twenty-three could stop. Then he wouldn't dream of Lila while he lay on the couch watching his wife in the silver light, wondering if tomorrow the cells in that pretty head would cease fire, retire from their foolish civil war.

"Perhaps," the doctor said, "polio has created a hormonal change and pregnancy is necessary for her mental well-being."

"She should be pregnant forever in that case," Nat said annoyed.

"Have one more child," the doctor said, but Nat expected that the doctor was filtering out the bad news a little at a time. Twenty years from now, when his house was bursting with children like a dandelion with seeds in June and Cally's belly had gone slack as unstarched curtains, the doctor would say, as if it were a remedy that had just occurred to him, "Have one more."

Cally discovered that she was pregnant with Peter on Julia's birthday and Nat took her to supper in New Hope in celebration.

"I'm so happy," she said to him, and he was pleased, of course, and held her hand underneath the table. But he felt the awful burden of responsibility for a job he had not elected to take and whose final accomplishment was beyond his control.

When Nat's plane from England arrived on the night of December 21, 1945, it was too late to go back to Bucks County and John Howells was grateful for a chance to be alone with his son. They went to a bar at Forty-fifth and Lexington and drank until 3:00 A.M., sang and told stories until the last man was shoved out the door. Arm in arm, they walked down Lexington until a taxi stopped and took them to the Howells apartment. There, on East End Avenue, where John had continued to live weekdays throughout the war, he celebrated his son's return. They drank to the Americans, the English and the French, to Rachel and to Cally, to Peter and Bumpo, and finally to Julia.

They undressed sloppily and climbed into twin beds in the guest room so they could spend Nat's first night listening to each other's breathing.

"What will you do now that you're home?" John asked, hoping for an outline of serious plans.

"I'll be a father," Nat said. "Tomorrow I'll screw my wife and hope for healthy swimmers to keep her sane and pregnant forever."

Rachel had moved to Bucks County in 1941, sometime after the fate of the Jews in Europe was clear. She left New York to take care of Daniel, who was not in poor health. The plan was that John would spend weekdays in the city and weekends with Rachel in Bucks County. The first week she settled in the Main House for good she canceled delivery of the *New York Times* and read only the local paper, which covered briefly national and international news. She listened to classical music on the radio and switched the dial when the newscaster came on at the hour. She didn't want to hear about the war. The careful eastern cultivation of her tone and accent gave way to the high sweeps and rises of Yiddish. Mostly she cooked, all day long, taking special cakes and tarts to Cally and the children, to the families in the other two houses on the Howells land, to old Daniel, who finally had the good sense to get sick and take advantage of Rachel's need to nurse. She was an energetic woman and a day's cooking, even dealt out among so many, left plenty for Rachel to eat alone in the kitchen weekdays. Even before

Nat had gone to Europe in 1942, she had grown fat. Her clothes no longer fitted so she made saris out of heavy white cloth and wore baggy pants underneath the dresses.

"White for peace," she told Julia.

She wore her hair long. Occasionally she put a red dot in the center of her forehead with a tube of lipsitck which, by evening, after she had spent hours over the stove working with flour and butter, baking, would be streaked like blood across her head.

"The people in India use white for funerals," she told Julia.

She made a sari for Julia, who once dotted her whole face with red raspberry from Rachel's old lipstick drawer.

"I'm an Indian with measles," she told her.

Many evenings Rachel called Isaac in Detroit.

" 'Don't tell me the bad news,' she says," Isaac would mimic. "It's horrible," he'd say. "It's a nightmare. You wouldn't believe what I heard tonight on the radio about the Jews in Holland. And that's censored. There's a regular office in Washington fixing the news for us so it sounds better. We don't even know the worst."

"I know the worst," Rachel would reply.

Rachel expected absolutely that Nat would die in Europe.

Every time a telephone call came to the Main House, she prepared herself for notification of Nat's death. When she met John's train in Trenton or Doylestown on Friday afternoon, she'd examine his face for signs.

John was patient for a long time. Finally he told her. "You have got to stop it. It's driving me crazy."

"There is a good chance," Rachel said.

"There's a chance that every United States soldier in Europe, every correspondent and photographer, could be blown up this afternoon," John said, "but there's also a good chance that our son won't be."

Rachel sat down that evening on the couch next to John, by a fire cracking like hunting guns in the fireplace.

He put his hand on her soft and ample belly. "You are paying too much for pretending not to be a Jew, Rachel," he said to her sadly. "Look at yourself. I don't need to turn you inside out to see your unhappiness. You were a very beautiful woman."

The Christmas of 1943, when Nat had not been home for several months, John lost his temper with Rachel.

"Perhaps you want him to die, Bam. So you can pay your dues."

"Shut up," she said.

That night he made love to her with a kind of angry passion she had never known with him before, even hurt her. Then she knew that she had been sacrificing him as well for the destruction of the Jews. "I'm sorry," she said, cradling his head in her arms next to her bare breasts.

Daniel died dutifully on May 1, 1944, in his sleep. When Rachel went to his house to cook breakfast, as she sometimes did that year, he was dead and the physician estimated that he had been dead for five hours. It was, according to John, the only unselfish act in his father's life.

"You think he made the decision to die last night?" Rachel said.

"There's not a question in my mind," John said.

From his father's first illness, John was not sympathetic and Daniel knew that. So weekends, when John was home, Daniel came for supper at the Main House dressed in tweeds, woolen shirts and ties, the senator emeritus at home in the country. Weekdays with just Rachel, and Julia as she grew older, coming to make breakfast, bathe him and walk the south fields with him, old Daniel was impossible. He peed everywhere, opening the drawers of the buffet where the best linen was kept and peeing on the Belgian lace mats, on the crocheted chairs in the dining room done by a desperate Hannah Howells in the last year of her life, and once he shot his urine like a child with a water pistol at the painting over the mantel, a bull's-eye at the breast of Lucy Tanner Howells, his mother, a dark beauty who had borne an illegitimate daughter by a Confederate soldier during the Civil War. The four cats, tabbies, unaltered brothers, called Taft, Roosevelt, Hoover and Wee Willy Wilson, followed suit and began to pee right after Daniel with a loyalty surprising in cats. He hid food, fruit, cheese, puddings made by Rachel in drawers and in the backs of closets, inside his shoes until the food rotted, and the house with urine, cat and man, and rotting food was intolerable for anyone but Rachel and Daniel. He got up early in the morning and knocked over tables and chairs, threw his clothes out of the closet, broke lamps. He blamed robbers and natural disasters for the mess in the house, but on weekends, with John home, he would be as clearheaded as possible for a sharp-minded man just ninety. He talked to his son about the war in Europe and Japan, about Churchill's leadership qualities and unanticipated trouble with the Russians. Now and then he'd grip the large soft buttocks of his son's wife with a veinless hand resembling driftwood.

Rachel didn't complain. She welcomed trouble with Daniel and convinced herself with an uncharacteristic belief in a reasonable universe that trouble with Daniel was a protection from greater and unimagined trouble, just payment for her betrayals.

She began a game with herself that lasted throughout the last year of his life: that Daniel was her father, Samuel Schoenberg, who had died of a heart attack when she was forty. She had not seen him for two years, had talked to him, of course, but her life, stuffed with incidentals like a Christmas stocking full of junk, had not seemed to have room for a trip back home. She made no excuses. She was ruthless in her blame of herself.

So she pretended Daniel was her father and he pretended dementia with childish pleasure and only on weekdays. For Rachel it was a misplaced act of love, like making love with the memory of some other face than the one you are with, more satisfactory than not pretending, but incomplete.

When Daniel died, after the doctor had signed the death certificate and ordered an ambulance from Doylestown to collect the ex-senator from Pennsylvania, Rachel filled a basin with water, undressed the old man and bathed him in the ancient Jewish manner to prepare him for burial. She knew it would have pleased Daniel to have been a Jew for a moment in death, an exile, God's chosen son.

Rachel was unprepared for John when he came home early on the afternoon of his father's death. There was an unfamiliar look about his face and she stepped aside to let him pass her, through the hall and up the stairs to his room. He didn't even kiss her hello, a gesture so automatic that it could persist through serious arguments.

"I can't talk to anyone," he called down from the second-floor landing and shut the bedroom door. From time to time Rachel slipped quietly upstairs and listened, was satisfied to hear the sorting through of papers, a soft hum of life, but she stayed close at hand, checking often from the top stair, unsettled by an odd sense that she had wrongly predicted John Howell's response to his father's death, that worse than this silent retreat was possible.

She prepared for the ceremony of mourning with only Julia's help. Throughout the next day the house filled with flowers and telegrams from Washington and from around the state. There were telephone calls, even one from President Roosevelt, which John did take, and one from Secretary of the Interior Ickes, a special friend; food from neighbors in Solebury and relations on the farm. By three o'clock that day, when people began to come by, Julia and Rachel had ruined a whole chocolate cake by pinching the icing and Cally's retriever had eaten the beef casserole brought by neighbors for the Howells' supper and thrown it up on the Oriental rug in the living room.

"My great-grandfather is dead as a doornail," Julia told Mrs. Hayes Biddle matter-of-factly when she arrived with a bouquet of flowers from the Biddle family.

"I'm so sorry," Mrs. Biddle said solemnly, shaking Julia's hand.

"That's all right," Julia said. "It wasn't your fault."

By five the house was full of people and Rachel, impatient with greeting, knocked on John's door.

"Please," she said, and John did come down, to mingle stiffly with the guests, making small, mannered bows.

Lila arrived with Cally and would not wear the dress and apron Rachel had brought out of the pantry for her. She didn't say no; she simply didn't say anything and made a face at Rachel when her back was turned.

"I'll kick Lila for you if you'd like me to," Julia said earnestly after Lila had left the kitchen.

Instead, Cally's burro kicked Mrs. Biddle in the leg as she prepared to leave. It wasn't a bad kick, but Mrs. Biddle insisted she had a tendency to blood clots. An ambulance was called and Rachel ended up following the ambulance with John in Mrs. Biddle's car, leaving the house in Cally's hands. When John and Rachel came back from the hospital in the volunteer ambulance, the guests had left except for ex-Congressman Sellar, who was full of sherry and asleep on the living room couch.

"Dead as a doornail," Julia said, satisfied with her new and profound knowledge of death.

That night John Howells found what he had been looking for ever since his father's death in an ordinary dresser in a guest room at the back of the house, unheated for years.

Photographs. Stacks of photographs of his parents' children, the four sons of Daniel and Hannah Howells, John and his three brothers. They were wrapped in tissue paper, yellow and brittle with time, like lace wedding veils, accruing worth with age, preserved intact for the next generation.

John opened the package his mother had wrapped forty years before, requiring him now to repeat with his father's death that of his mother, whose death had shaken him beyond acknowledgment.

John Howells was ten the spring his mother died. It was April 22, 1903, when he found her sitting almost upright in her bed. She had shot herself. It had been her intention, he knew, to kill herself when no one was there so the parlormaid would be the one to find her when she arrived at eight. Senator Howells had left early for the Senate, the cook was in Tennessee for the month with her mother who was ill, and the temporary cook did not live in. John had left for Sidwell Friends School downtown at seven-thirty and could have been in the classroom by eight o'clock had he not forgotten his Latin book. He let himself back in the house, picked up his Latin book on the sideboard and called to say good-bye again to his mother. He thought it odd when she didn't answer. It was her custom to stay in bed until the parlormaid came. Often she read. John went upstairs. The door to her bedroom was closed and he knocked twice, even though he knew after the first knock that something was amiss.

He did not stay long in his mother's bedroom, but what he saw remained absolutely clear in his memory until he died.

Hannah Howells was dressed in a scarlet velvet gown he had never seen her wear, open and very low at the neck. Her breasts, pressed together by corsets and stays, were round as oversized peaches. She had on a huge velvet hat turned up jauntily on one side with a feather, turquoise and rose. When she had shot herself, the hat had fallen forward and only her chin beneath the feather was visible. On her arms, on every finger, around her neck were jewels, necklaces and brooches, rings, bracelets, covering her arms to the elbow. Beside her hand there was a single long-stemmed rose from the arrangement in the dining room.

Years later, after John was married and Nat was born, he created a final scene to accompany his startling memory of his mother and came to believe in it.

He imagined that when he had left that morning for Sidwell Friends, Hannah had gone downstairs and taken a rose from the centerpiece on the dining room table. Upstairs she had dressed in the scarlet gown, put on all of her jewelry, a daring hat which couldn't possibly have been worn by the restrained and aristocratic wife of the senator from Pennsylvania. He believed she might have stood in front of the full-length oval mirror on her closet door at the final curtain of a play created in her head, a play in which an imaginary character to the left of the mirror handed her a single long-stemmed rose. She must have killed herself quickly while the applause was still ringing in her ears.

Once when John was at college, his father met him for dinner and they talked for the first time about Hannah's death, easily at first, until John brought up the extraordinary dress his mother had chosen to die in.

"She was mad," Daniel Howells said. "Suddenly. Just that morning. It happens with women."

"I don't think it was sudden," John said. "She told me you drove her children away from home."

"She was only interested in the children. Don't bring it up. There's nothing to be gained speculating on the reasons a woman went mad."

Now John spread the photographs of his family out on the desk. The top photograph was one taken for the newspaper after Senator Daniel Howells had been reelected for a second term and showed John at five or six, leaning against his mother's knee. One brother, Anthony, was twelve and the other two, twins, their father's size, stood next to Daniel, behind Hannah, and looked about eighteen. John could remember nothing about them except their names, Matthew and Oliver, and the fact that they were twins, sent off to Harvard.

There was once an argument between Hannah and perhaps Matthew, or else Oliver, during which the brother said he would never come home as long as Daniel was alive, and Hannah wept. John remembered it for Hannah's weeping and not for the threat, thinking in a child's way that she would die of weeping; only children are allowed to weep.

John knew Anthony better because he stayed on at the house in Georgetown, a sickly child requiring his mother's constant attention. John felt terrible but was relieved when Anthony died at fifteen of meningitis. Once he told his mother that he'd been glad for Anthony's death and asked her to forgive him, to promise him it was reasonable to have such jealousies. But she lost her temper.

"You're jealous like your father is jealous, allowing me no one but himself."

To repent and because he loved her, John spent the four years after Anthony's death with his mother. He talked with her after lessons, sat in the room while she sewed, stood beside her at occasions required of the wives of senators at the turn of the century, trying to fill the space of his brothers.

Of course he failed. By the time he was a young man, wiser than many young men his age, he had long understood that a son cannot sustain his mother without her help. When Hannah died—"murdered by Father," according to Oliver, who returned at the time; "ruined by him," Matthew said—John knew her death had been more complicated than that. It was a death she might have chosen as the wife of any man in the late 1800's, an inevitable death which pained him now with her lost life, lost sons, reproduced in black-and-white photographs in his hands.

After Hannah was buried in the rich, brown soil of southeastern Pennsylvania, Matthew and Oliver Howells left home for good. Matthew to Canada and Oliver, with an English friend down on his luck, to New Zealand. Daniel never mentioned their names, referring to them only as the twins, anonymous as oak seeds blown by a cold wind to unfamiliar soil.

There were, however, listed in Daniel Howells' address book under *H*, their names, first Matthew and then Oliver, and addresses—only one for Matthew in Toronto, but many for Oliver, the last in Australia.

"You're going to contact them after forty years?" Rachel asked.

"He was their father," John said.

"I doubt they remember his name," Rachel said.

"I found Daniel's letter passing on the Bible. It was among the papers in the desk," John said.

"Did you read it?"

"No, love," John said. "There is, as you can imagine, a formal ritual for the occasion. There are instructions at the front of the Bible which tell me exactly what to do. I must notify all the relations and then they must gather at the Main House and my father's letter, which has been sealed, God knows how long, is opened."

"Of course," Rachel said. "Your family can't even die without trumpets."

She took the letter which John was holding and held it up to the light. "He must have written this years ago," she said.

"I expect when Mother died."

"I'm sure your father left the Bible to you, darling," Rachel said.

"Daniel was an odd, philandering billy goat," John said, "but he was a constitutional lawyer. He followed the rules."

And John was right.

On May 2, 1944, the family, including Lila and Cally's children, gathered in Daniel Howells' living room, where his ghost deviled the corners like a naughty child, to hear the letter written by Daniel Howells, which, according to tradition, passed the family Bible to the next generation, to the eldest male member of the family. It was a dry, legal document, unsalted by the lusty and earthbound mind of its author. "The responsibility for keeping the history of the Howells family is entrusted to my eldest son, Matthew Howells, firstborn of the twins, if he can be located in Toronto, Canada, and is willing. Second to my second son, Oliver Howells, in Sydney, Australia, if he can be found and is willing. Finally, in the event that the aforementioned are neither available nor willing, the Bible is left to my third living son, John Howells, with my blessing."

"Christ," John Howells said quietly. But he found them both, forty years gone, and pulled them back for the occasion of their father's death, making capillary threads of telephone wires, slender but actual lines of blood in the modern world.

Matthew, a professor of astronomy at the University of Toronto, said, "Bullshit," as Daniel used to say for every ceremony, and John was amused to hear it repeated with the inflection that his father had used. Matthew promised to visit sometime, but he absolutely refused responsibility for the Bible. Oliver, found in San Francisco, was very drunk and wept about Hannah's death as though it had reoccurred with the death of Daniel. Oliver said he didn't want the goddamned Bible. He didn't believe in Bibles, never had even as a boy. He had married a Japanese woman, they had had no children, and he had a miserable headache and would have to hang up.

If John lay down, his head spun. So he sat up with his hand in Rachel's. She put it against her cheek.

"It's not just to blame Daniel," John said to her that night. "Not for Mother's death or for the twins leaving home."

"Your family has this crazy need to believe in justice," Rachel said.

"Order, Bammy," John said. "I need for things to make sense."

"All I know is that Daniel was often a terrible man and I loved him a great deal." She rolled over on her back, keeping John's hand next to her cheek. "And that makes perfect sense, doesn't it?"

At Christmas dinner, Christmas Day, 1945, at Rachel's house, two days after Nat's permanent return from Europe, Nat wore a linen napkin on his head in honor of Daniel.

"To keep the plaster out of my hair," he said and toasted his grandfather with stories.

"The Howells haven't the sense to let a man die properly," Rachel said. "Everyone hangs on in stories. Perhaps Daniel doesn't want to spend another noisy Christmas at this house. Perhaps after ninety-three years, he'd like a taste of anonymity."

"Ah, Bammy," John said. "You know better. The Howells have no interest whatsoever in anonymity."

The Howells family honored celebrations. They believed in rituals, in the holiness of birth, the necessity for funerals, the sacrament of marriage, in honoring moments to fix in memory the illusion of a grand design.

Cally was at Christmas dinner between Nat and Lila, like a daughter, and Lila arrogant as a dancer except with Cally, who leaned from time to time against her. Peter threw his dinner on the floor in a temper and Bumpo, sitting next to his grandfather, fell asleep during the stories, so Rachel finished his dinner and Julia's as well as her own. The families from the other houses on the farm were there and a small group entertained with excerpts from "A Christmas Carol." They sang songs out of tune and Julia told the story of the birth of Jesus with special attention to the toys he received from the wise men, who numbered in the hundreds. One of Cally's cats, with a remarkable sense of ceremony, gave birth to four matted tiger kittens in the hall closet, likely fathered by her own tiger son and destined to cat's Down's syndrome, but God's own creatures nevertheless, honoring the triumph of birth in the Christmas season.

And finally, as anticipated, John Howells stood at the head of the very long table of relations and toasted his son's return from the war to the cheers of Howells. "Welcome home," he said, "to the splendid and unshakable order of your family."

Nat laughed, a full, untroubled laugh. "Bullshit," he said. Daniel's lines, and Nat spoke them for his grandfather, raising his glass with the rest.

* * *

Only Rachel noticed the dark look in Cally's face, gathering like storm clouds, and she wanted to reach out to this adopted daughter, take her in like an abandoned animal, but Rachel had no access to Caroline Bouché. She simply felt the darkness settling and knew, better than anyone else in the room, even Lila, that trouble was afoot.

That night or perhaps the next, surely Christmas week, one fine swimmer, survivor of the war in France, uncomplicated soldier in splendid form, claimed his territory and the second Caleb Howells began like a silly fish to grow suitable for the world.

The first Bible entry made in 1946 by John was in honor of children and read:

NAT HAS RETURNED FROM THE BANG BANG BANG OF THE WAR IN EUROPE TO THE BANG BANG BANG OF OUR ORDINARY LIVES, GRACED, IF WE ALLOW THEM TO BE, BY A MULTITUDE OF SEEDS.

BOXING DAY

John Howells began in red ink, December 26, 1950. And Julia must
have entered at that moment, running from the glass shoebox without a proper coat, scrawny as a goose, with black hair like wet
feathers around her face. She must have entered the back door
shouting for John Howells' help because the next entry in the
family Bible was made in ink of another color. It recorded a day
exceptional not for the beauty of the weather but for the permanent
alterations it made in the Howells' lives.

Boxing Day was actually a British holiday, the first weekday after
Christmas, set aside for giving gifts to employees, government
workers, sanitation engineers. None of the Howells knew the origin
of Boxing Day except perhaps for Nat, who had spent a Christmas
in England, or Rachel, who had gone about memorizing things
English in her wellborn years before the war. As the language had
been borrowed and translated to a raw and ungovernable land, the
Howells had borrowed only the name from the British and made up
the occasion to suit themselves. According to their tradition, Boxing
Day was the day after Christmas when all the members of the
Howells family boxed up the dispensable accumulation of the past
year and burned it in a bonfire at the front of the property. Through
the years it had become a village celebration and families came
from Solebury, sometimes New Hope, occasionally old friends from
New York or Philadelphia, and tossed unwanted letters and bills,
history tests and compositions, court reports, briefs, rolls of useless
wallpaper, drawings on cardboard, old checks into the bonfire on
the Howells farm. Afterwards they joined the family's celebration with baked ham and biscuits and hot wine in the Main House.

67

Among the entries on Boxing Day there were stories of wonderful occasions in which the Howells seemed to capture the spirit of magazine advertisements for Bell Telephone—a large family with smiling cats in front of an energetic fire. But there were as many stories of accidents and high passion. The expectations of Christmas and the chance on the following day to burn the disappointments and incidentals of the past year sometimes collided in a conflagration like the bonfire which rose, with the loading on of boxes, above the heights of the families gathered around it.

Even Daniel, who courted danger like a mercenary, had said, "Perhaps next year we should do away with Boxing Day." He was thinking of what had happened with Hannah, a story which he entered in the family Bible, truthfully and with surprising humility.

The Boxing Day before Hannah died, after Anthony's death and the departure of her sons, the family had gone from Washington to the farm in Bucks County for the holidays. Daniel, some distant cousins, the townspeople were gathered about the fire, all boxes being tossed one by one to the accompaniment of cheers, when Hannah walked down the hill from the Main House alone, carrying a medium-sized box, taped shut. The custom was that the men threw the boxes on the fire, considering it a dangerous task for women, but this evening Hannah stepped up beside Daniel, and before he had an opportunity to take the box from her, she had tossed it herself and it fell at the edge of the fire. As it burned, Daniel recognized the ivory velvet dress that Hannah had worn to their wedding twenty-five years before. When he looked at her, after the box had burned and the people dispersed, her face was impassive, cast in wax. He never mentioned the dress to her, nor she it to him. The entry recording the event was not made until after her death.

On an earlier Boxing Day, Lucy Tanner, Daniel's wild mother, had lit a ball of cloth on fire and raced around after Thomas, her physician husband, to light a decent fire beneath him, she shouted. The town told stories about her drinking, but Lucy didn't need to drink to misbehave like that.

Nat tossed Ellen McCay's letters in the fire the Christmas after he'd met Cally and they didn't all burn. At the party afterwards some friends read the ones they had retrieved from the fire to shouts of laughter leading to discussions of sexual postures and ways to satisfy the urgent eighteen-year-old boy while leaving the Wellesley virgin intact.

Later Rachel would take the blame for the events of Boxing Day in 1950, for insisting on Thanksgiving at the Main House, for inviting the Bouchés to come from New Orleans for a family holiday against Nat's wishes. Just before the fat brown turkey was taken from the oven, Cally, so Lila said, went crazy as a June bug.

"Nothing would have happened if Nat hadn't been worrying over Cally," Rachel said to John, full of self-reproach. But John simply raised his eyebrows without a word, indicating that any conversation about the events of Boxing Day was unproductive.

Rachel had wanted Thanksgiving at the Main House that year to show off her new enterprise. When two of the houses on the farm had become vacant, Rachel decided to rent them, and in her characteristic way she chose as tenants two welfare families.

"I am supporting an infantry right now, Bam," John said.

"Rent, darling. We'll collect from them."

"I bet," John said. "That's why they're on welfare."

"I didn't know you were becoming so thoroughly middle-class."

"I have always been," he said, but he agreed to have the Cares and their three children and the Volpones (whose name, it turned out later, wasn't Volpone at all) move into the vacant houses for one hundred dollars a month plus chores on the farm.

"We live in a different time from the one in which we grew up," Rachel said. "We can't afford to live here the way we always have or expect our children to stay here always. Either we sell the remaining houses . . ."

"Or give them away," John said.

"The reason Mr. Care is on welfare, darling, is that his leg was smashed by a machine in Reading."

"Then ask him to do work that doesn't involve machines," John said.

But on the whole, the welfare families worked out very well on the farm until Mr. Volpone, whose picture appeared in post offices throughout the country, was discovered and the police were sent in, leaving Mrs. Volpone and her two children, who stayed until she met a mechanic from Flourtown.

Even Nat said that the welfare families had given Rachel a sense of life she had given up when the war broke out. She lost weight because she had people for the food she cooked endlessly in her warm kitchen. She put away her saris and wore more conventional pants and dresses. She even went to dinner and the theater in New York.

But Thanksgiving, 1950, the Volpones were still in residence and Rachel wanted to include them and the Cares, who had moved into Daniel's house, in the family dinner.

"Wonderful, Mother. A first-rate idea," Nat said, following his mother to the barn, where they collected a bushel of apples recently harvested. "Mrs. Volpone and Mrs. Bouché at dinner together. I can imagine, for example, Dr. Bouché and Mr. Care discussing medical problems in a personal way at the table."

"Sometimes you astonish me, Nat, and just at the time that I have the most confidence in your generosity."

"It sounds like a terrible Thanksgiving."

"Well, when Thanksgiving is at your house next year, you're free to invite the Junior League."

Two days before the Bouchés arrived for Thanksgiving, Cally found out about Lila's boyfriend.

She had been up with bad cramps after Nat was asleep, unable to get comfortable sitting in her wheelchair or lying in bed. When Lila came home with her friend, she heard them both laughing, as she and Lila laughed, outside the front door. She heard Lila's low voice and then a silence that would not quit.

When Lila came in the door, Cally was sitting in the living room in the dark. Lila waltzed in, not seeing her at first, snapping her fingers, tilting her head so she could see the car which had brought her home go down the driveway. Then, as her eyes grew accustomed to darkness, she saw Cally.

"So what are you doing out here this time of night, Caroline Bouché?" she asked, and Cally knew she expected trouble. "Spying?"

Cally didn't reply.

"Well?" Lila asked too quickly, betraying what already Cally knew.

Lila flopped on the couch.

"You don't own me, Miss Caroline," she said with an edge, a kind of meanness in her voice. "That war, in case you missed some information in your history books, been fought and lost, my sweet girl." She put her feet up on the coffee table between the couches.

Cally moved her chair over so she faced Lila. In the dark Lila was black as night with white teeth that shone pearly. An instinct for survival, resisting her own desires, brought her mother's words to mind. But only to mind. "You please to stand in our living room, Lila, and not put your feet anywhere but on the floor," or to Dr. Bouché, "The young colored girls are letting independence go to their heads," or to Cally, "Lila is no more to be trusted than the rest of them."

"Who were you with?" Cally asked quietly.

"Jimmy," Lila said, drawing the word through a thin pipe.

"Did you meet him at work?"

"I met him at the bus stop," Lila said, smiling.

"Tonight?"

"Last week, Caroline." She threw a stockinged foot over Cally's knee, a gesture at once comic and provoking. "On Thursday at six P.M., while I was standing on the corner waiting for the last bus to Solebury, Jimmy stops me and says . . . well, no difference what he says." She closed her eyes.

"Tell me."

Lila opened one eye and looked at Cally. "You sure you want to know?"

Cally nodded.

"Hello."

"Hello?"

"He said to me, 'Hello,' and I said to him, keeping my head down with a mannerly, ladylike look which would have pleased your mother and mine, 'Hello.' And he said, keeping his distance, mind, but standing on one foot with a jaunty look in his eye, 'What's your name?' And I said, letting my head tilt just a pinch in his direction, 'Lila.' "

"Shut up," Cally said.

"Why, Caroline Bouché." Lila took her feet off the coffee table. "I never heard you say 'shut up' before. There must be something under your skin this evening."

"I don't feel well," Cally said.

"In your head?"

"My head is fine," she said. She pressed her stomach. "There."

"Wanting." Lila shook her head, dared Cally to meet her black eyes directly. "I know the feeling. It can drive a woman crazy."

Ordinarily they would have laughed the way they used to when they were young. Ordinarily a remark like that from Lila would have set off a string of naughty stories, one after another, but Cally, surprised by unfamiliar tensions in her brain, confused by them, was in no mood for laughter. What she thought she wanted was

Melvina, Lila's mama, lovely Melvina, as gentle in her touch as soft bread, warm and spongy from the oven, who used to hold Cally on one knee and Lila on the other and sing the blues to them until Cally burned, her insides set aflame.

"I like the colored," Cally said to Mrs. Bouché once.

"Of course, darling," Mrs. Bouché replied. "I like the colored, too."

"I mean," Cally said intensely, the usual caution with her mother tossed aside, "I love the colored."

"Well," Mrs. Bouché said, put off.

"White people are so boring," Cally said.

Later Mrs. Bouché suggested to Dr. Bouché that Cally go to boarding school a year early to get away from Lila, and Dr. Bouché inevitably agreed.

"I was keeping Nat up," Cally said.

"He's awake now?"

"Not now," Cally said. "It's just that I had cramps and was going to keep him up if I stayed in the bedroom."

Lila stood, picked up her coat and swung it over her shoulders. "Well," she said, "I'm beat."

She ran her fingers through Cally's hair. "Sweet dreams."

"Did he kiss you?" Cally asked.

Lila raised her eyebrows, shook her head.

"You're lying," Cally said.

"You going to bed or not, Caroline?"

"I thought," Cally began carefully, "I'd sleep in the twin bed in your room so as not to wake Nat."

"Please yourself," Lila said.

Cally followed Lila to the back of the house behind the kitchen, where Lila had a bedroom with twin beds and a small sitting room, painted taupe with white woodwork by Rachel. Lila bent down and picked Cally up, laying her on the bed.

"Don't cover me," Cally said as Lila started to draw up the bedcovers. Cally lay in darkness and watched Lila undress by the closet light, taking off her sweater over her head. She wore no bra and Cally guarded her temptation to know why not; was it for the freedom of Jimmy's hands? Her breasts were high, like a girl's breasts, unaltered by the round mouths of babies, and full like Melvina's, but Melvina was plump and her breasts were followed by rolls of flesh around the ribs and belly and hips so there was no distinction between breasts and other flesh. Lying on the twin bed in Lila's room, Cally remembered sleeping against Melvina's breasts and thinking with wonderful satisfaction what a lucky child she was that Melvina could read to her at night instead of her mother, whose chest was exactly like the chest of a man.

Lila took off her skirt and hung it in the closet. She undid her garters and pulled off her stockings, one by one. She stepped out of her panties and set the pile of underthings at the bottom of her closet. She stood in the closet door naked for a moment and she must have known what was going on in Cally: the years they'd been together as children, these last years in the same house, Lila caring for Cally as Melvina used to do and not like Melvina at all, for there was a girlishness about it. Their odd duet required improvisation. Now Lila stood in the doorway of her closet in no hurry to find her gown.

"I've never seen you naked before," Cally said.

Lila faced Cally in the dark, standing on one foot, her bare arm against the doorway, understanding with dark wisdom her future in flesh.

Cally didn't know what was happening to her, but what happened, what she said and did, was automatic.

"Lila," Cally said, and the words came without warning. "I want you to kiss me."

Lila slipped her gown over her head, pulled the cord of the closet light and moved over to the bed where Cally was lying. She sat on the bed beside her, put her long, slender hand against Cally's cheek and, with a knowledge of inevitable developments, leaned over the small white face and kissed Caroline Bouché on the lips.

That night in Lila's room, Cally had lain in the bed next to Lila's listening to the wonderful abandonment of Lila's breathing. She was bewildered. Still awake when the night began to change to silver, she pulled herself out of bed into the wheelchair and went to her own room, where Nat was sleeping on his couch, his back to the dawn. He looked like a small boy whom she had wronged, the way his knees drew up, his brow furrowed perceptibly even in sleep, and she felt a love for him she had never felt before, had felt only for her babies; they were honestly part of each other in ways she had resisted absolutely for dignity and because she had altered his life.

"Where were you?" he asked in the morning when he got up.

"I couldn't sleep," she said.

"I called you."

"I didn't hear you." She wanted to tell him where she had been, and for a moment before the sun lit their bedroom, she believed he would understand or perhaps that he could make her understand.

By daylight that morning Cally was bewildered again.

She didn't understand what had happened to her when Lila came home with Jimmy, what surfaced that had been swimming beneath her vision of herself like secrets of a tropical gulf, that leaped, unannounced and unexpected above the water. And if she thought about it, thought about herself, southern girl, a sweet southern girl gently reared in a world without sharp edges—if she thought about herself with a woman, with a colored woman, she was confused, not with shame because she didn't feel shame. She felt inverted like one of those dual rag dolls who, turned upside down, its skirt turned inside out, is another doll with another head quite different from the first.

The Bouchés arrived Wednesday for Thanksgiving. The following morning, while Cally was dressing, she looked at her face in the mirror. She was aging in tiny, half-inflated balloons around her eyes and under her chin—not well, she thought. The face she used to live with in the mirror above the iron lung flashed before her in scenes of increased confusion. She felt her mind begin to slip like a glass bowl held in buttered fingers.

On Thanksgiving afternoon, just before dinner at the Main House, Nat was not having an easy time. Caleb wouldn't wear a white shirt and wool shorts.

"For babies," he said, putting on his cowboy shirt and corduroys.

"For Bam," Nat pleaded, "and Grandmother Bouché."

"Nope," Caleb said.

"Even Johnny Care has a suit on," Julia said to him.

"Johnny Care is a baby," Caleb said. "He looks like a baby rabbit."

"Jeez," Nat said. "Four is the worst age. You can stay home," he said to Caleb.

"Good," Caleb said. "I want to stay home. I don't like Grandmother Bouché."

"You already said that, Caleb, while Grandmother Bouché was in the kitchen, and she heard you. I don't think she likes you very much either," Julia said.

"Good," Caleb said with his usual fine sense of justice. "We're even."

Bumpo and Peter had a fight that Bumpo, as usual, lost badly.

"I'm telling," Bumpo said.

"Daddy thinks you're chicken," Peter said.

"I'm not telling Daddy," Bumpo said. "I'm telling Mama." And he ran into the back bedroom where Cally was, so everyone thought, putting on a dress and fixing her hair for dinner at Rachel's.

At that moment Peter was sitting in bad-tempered victory on the living room couch. Caleb was in his room, playing *Peter and the Wolf* full volume on his Victrola, and Julia, with Nat, was covering the pies in foil to take to Rachel's for dessert.

"Peter," Bumpo called Peter first in a high-pitched voice. "Julia," he shouted, rushing to the kitchen where Nat and Julia were. Julia went after Bumpo with Nat. Only Caleb in his room, pretending he was the wolf after the silly duck did not hear the commotion.

Cally was in her wheelchair and her back was to the door.

"Look at her," Bumpo said motioning to Nat and Julia.

"Mama?" Julia said.

"Wait," Nat said, but Julia rushed forward, throwing her arms around her mother.

What Nat saw when he looked at Cally was a department store mannequin dressed in a bright red wool dress, her long hair piled on her head, her plaster body fixed and her eyes staring sightless at an empty room.

"Daddy." Julia let go of her mother and stood back. "Touch her."

Nat didn't touch her. He looked at her carefully like a painting in which he was examining the painter's method.

"Cally," he called softly.

"Is she dead?" Peter asked.

"No," Julia said. "Is she, Daddy?"

"No, she's not," Nat said. "Cally?" He knelt down beside her, put his arms on her shoulders, pulled her frozen body towards him. Nat slapped her cheek.

"Daddy," Bumpo cried.

"I'm trying to wake her," Nat said.

"Is she sleeping?" Peter asked.

"I'm calling Bam," Julia said.

"No, Julia," Nat said. "Call an ambulance. The number is beside the telephone." He turned to Peter. "Get blankets." Together they covered her. Rachel and John arrived before the ambulance.

Caleb stood in the door to his bedroom and watched the men carry his mother out on a stretcher. Then he put on his gray flannel shorts, his white, round-collared shirt and knee socks and oxfords, his coat with a velvet collar which had been Julia's and Peter's and Bumpo's before him, took Julia's hand and walked with the Howells children to Thanksgiving at the Main House.

"I'm sorry," Peter said on the walk over. "I'm getting meaner every day."

"Okay," Bumpo said. "You didn't hurt me on purpose."

The hospital in Doylestown sent Cally to the hospital in Swarthmore, Pennsylvania, where she had been twice before while Nat was a correspondent in Europe and there had been too much time between babies. She had stayed there a month, requesting on Christmas Day not to come home. "It would undo me," she told Nat. "Though I hope doing the dinner on Boxing Day won't be too much work for you."

"I don't mind," Nat said, knowing Cally had never been fond of his family's celebrations, especially Boxing Day.

Nat Howells woke up before the sun on Boxing Day, 1950, woke with a start when the hot urine of his youngest son sleeping beside him soaked the back of his pajamas.

"Caleb," he had told the child again and again, "I'm tired of dreaming of rivers and waking up wet. Sleep with your sister."

"She's too bony," Caleb said. "I won't wet my bed *ever* again," he declared without a question of a doubt.

"My bed," Nat said. But Caleb didn't promise that and this morning Nat got up and let Caleb sleep.

He felt light-headed. The atmosphere seemed thinner when he stood. In the bathroom mirror he looked unwell, the image of a boy gone suddenly old with deep lines and eyes painted flat blue, as if the mirror had tricks, a mercurial substance just beneath the surface of glass to make middle age of children. He still felt faint when he had washed his face, and he sat on the edge of the toilet seat waiting for the dizziness to pass.

He was sitting there when Julia knocked and came in, fully

dressed in hiking boots and jeans with bright purple lipstick done
to make a fat bow of her lips.

"What's the matter?" she asked her father quickly, expecting
the worst as she was temperamentally inclined to do. "Are you
having a heart attack or something?"

"No, darling," Nat said. "I haven't had a heart attack for weeks."

"Good." She leaned over to kiss him.

"Not with those clown lips," he said, pulling back.

"I forgot." She looked at herself in the bathroom mirror. "It's
Lila's. Isn't it awful? She has matching nail polish and silver stars
for her cheeks."

"You're not supposed to go in Lila's room, Julia."

"She's away," Julia said, making faces in the mirror with her
bow lips, drawing them up like a small purple sourball. "See."

She tilted her head for her father, widened her eyes like bright
gumdrops. "Clara Bow."

"Stay out of Lila's room, Clara," Nat said, pulling her down on
his lap.

She was small and fine-boned with black hair made of Oriental
silk and blue-black eyes set wide apart on a planed face like a grown
woman with little hint of girl. She was surprising, like a rare bird,
striking to look at, with an energy boiling just below the surface,
ready to escape.

"I hate Lila," Julia said to her father, getting up from his lap.
"She's like a witch."

"We don't hate," Nat said automatically, still sitting, light-
headed, slightly unwell. It was tension, he decided. He had been
under a lot of pressure since Cally had gone into the hospital. Her
illness had been a surprise. She'd been fine for months, and then
something in her mind went, as though the tracks of her brain
serviced trains that had missed switching to the appropriate con-
necting track and crashed head-on.

"I do hate mystery," Nat said. "I want facts. It's a fact your
mother had polio. It's a fact that she can't walk. It's even a fact
that she's happier when she's pregnant and has a small baby. It's
perfectly all right to hate mysteries, Julia; we just can't hate people."

"Are you sure nothing is the matter?" Julia asked, looking at
him carefully.

"Nothing is the matter at all, Jules. Not cancer of the colon or
gallbladder attacks or brain tumors." And they both laughed,
trying to be lighthearted about the fact that in Julia's vision of

the world, everything was major. "It's just that your baby brother peed on me this morning and sometimes when I get up too fast, I get dizzy in the head."

Julia followed him out of the bathroom.

"Speaking of that," Julia said. "Someone let Roger in last night."

"Jesus," Nat said. "Where?"

"The blue rug."

"A fact I didn't know before I married your mother is that burro pee is worse than cat pee." He opened the curtains to the beginning of morning over the edge of the farm. "It's also permissible, if you're interested, to hate animals and I hate Roger."

Downstairs Julia had set the table for the buffet that afternoon, had dressed the ham with cloves and honey and made breakfast for Peter and Bumpo, who were sitting at the kitchen table engaged in a battle of Rice Krispies when Julia and Nat came down.

"Ready for Boxing Day?" Nat asked, kissing them both on the top of the head.

"I have a boxful of papers from Mrs. K's class and a broken airplane and four old soldiers that can't be fixed," Peter said.

"They're mine," Bumpo said. "My broken soldiers."

"Nope," Peter said absolutely. "I'm burning them. The box is taped with my name on it. I packed it up last night."

Bumpo's eyes filled.

"Peter," Julia said. "You're so mean. They are Bumpo's."

"Dumb toy soldiers without arms or legs. Paraplegic warfare."

"But they're Bumpo's."

"It would hurt their feelings to be burned," Bumpo said.

"Jesus," Peter said. "They're plastic. They don't have souls, Bumpo. Don't you understand?"

But Bumpo didn't understand. Peter untaped the box and gave the broken soldiers to Bumpo, who laid them on his bed, covered with pieces of toilet paper for blankets.

"They're plastic, Peter," Nat said later. "We can't burn plastic."

"But he's so dumb," Peter said. "He should've been a girl."

"Sometimes I think you don't have a soul, Peter Howells," Julia said. "Maybe you're plastic, too."

Nat put them all to work. Peter gathered wood for the fireplace and Julia made pumpkin pies and Bumpo picked up the laundry and cleaned the rug where Roger had peed and fed the cats.

Caleb had leftover turkey for breakfast when he got up and fed the dressing to the dogs. He packed his own box for Boxing Day while the other children were working and included his wet pajamas, all of the books he'd inherited from Julia about fairy princesses and training pants like a girl's, which stupid Lila made him wear to nursery school. He liked to pee through the hole in his big boy pants even though he usually missed. When he was finished packing, he put half a roll of masking tape on the box so no one could untape it, got dressed in regular big boy underpants, a cowboy shirt and jeans and boots without socks.

"I'm done," he said, carrying the box downstairs.

"What did you pack?" Nat asked.

"Trash," Caleb said evasively.

"Like what trash?" Julia asked.

"Regular trash," Caleb said with confidence.

"No clothes, did you?" Nat asked. "Nothing you've outgrown. We may have another baby, you know."

Julia asked about the baby, so everyone forgot about Caleb's box except Caleb, who remained wisely quiet and dutiful all day.

Julia and Nat were in the kitchen when Julia brought up the subject of a baby again. They were making pies from mince Rachel had put up, rolling the dough for the crusts on a large wooden table in the center of the room.

"You'll make someone a fine wife," Nat joked with Julia.

"You too, Daddy." She laughed. "Mine. You're the perfect wife for me."

"No, mine," Nat said, laying the circle of dough in the pie plate. "I can't imagine a better wife for me than you."

"Daddy's married already, dummy," Caleb said from underneath the table where he was making a family of bears out of dough snitched from Julia's bowl. "Aren't you, Daddy?"

"I am, Caleb."

"See," Caleb said triumphantly.

But through the years, since Nat had returned from the war to be a father, which is what he had done except for an occasional free-lance article for the *Inquirer*, sometimes the *New York Times*, Julia had been as much a wife for him as Cally had been, depending on Cally's state of mind. At thirteen, Julia had the accomplishments of a wife at the beginning of the fifties. She could cook and care for small children, clean if absolutely necessary, sew on buttons, sew up rips and mend hems. She did all that, especially on the days that Cally was off "on vacation," as Rachel called it, though they both knew it couldn't have been much of a vacation because all Cally did was sit in her room at the window and stroke one or two of the cats that lay in her lap. Lila often went out in the evenings, and as the children grew older, she had a job in New Hope, but Julia noticed that Cally was happier when Lila was at home.

"I know Lila loves Mama," Julia told her father, "but she doesn't love children too much."

"I used to think about sending her back to New Orleans," Nat said, "but your mother needs her."

"I can help Mother just fine," Julia said, "and so can you."

"It's more personal than that," Nat said, but he didn't go into it with Julia, although he talked to her about most things, always the boys and their troubles, Rachel and why Rachel and Cally were at odds, even his own decision to stay at home and how he'd come to it.

"Who makes the money for us?" Julia asked once.

"Your grandfather," Nat answered truthfully.

"When I grow up, I want to make my own, not tons of it or anything, but my own so I can buy silver dresses and plastic high heels if I want them without asking. I hate to ask."

"So do I," Nat said.

Sometimes he made a gesture to his father to repay him and John dismissed it. Only once, with a perceptible edge in his voice, John Howells had asked, "How will you repay me, Nat? With Dr. Bouché's money when he dies?"

For weeks afterwards Nat refused the check sent automatically by John Howells, Inc., returned it unopened to his father's secretary, until finally John Howells came over late one night and begged him to take it and the subject of money wouldn't come up again.

"You have to live, Nat," John said. "I'd rather you take it from us than go to the Bouchés. You don't want that kind of debt. Of course, you're needed more at home than most fathers. I'm honestly glad to be able to do it."

But money did come up again and in the fall of 1949 John set his son up in business to settle the question.

"He could have been a columnist," John told Rachel. "Syndicated. A good one."

"Well, he's not," Rachel said.

"I wonder how many sons of my generation of fathers have been ruined by money easily got."

"It's not that, John," Rachel insisted. "It's Cally and the war and Nat himself who isn't suited to the competitive system."

"Bullshit," John said with honest irritation, and Rachel knew he was right.

"Perhaps we should have adopted some children," John said.

"What difference would that have made?" Rachel asked.

"To spread around our hopes."

"They're spread around now, darling—in Julia and Bumpo and Peter and Caleb."

"Caleb wets his bed and Bumpo, for Chrissake, is afraid of everything, even the frogs in the pond behind the barn."

"I've never known you to be so gloomy about the future," Rachel said. "Why don't you do something? That's always your approach, lamb. Action."

John Howells established a small advertising agency in Philadelphia, an independent representative of Howells, Inc., in New York. He hired a secretary in the hopes, not great ones, not out of line, that Nat would make a small success of it.

"So you can say he goes to an office every day," Rachel said.

"Perhaps," John answered.

But Nat, accustomed to the business of fathering and working around the farm, preferring it, didn't go to the office every day. He had won and lost four accounts by the end of the winter. The subsidiary company in Philadelphia cost John more out of pocket than he had paid before Nat worked because he added to Nat's salary the salary of a secretary, the cost of office rental and supplies, etc. etc. He never mentioned it to Rachel and finally, in a kind of personal desperation, he asked his accountant to handle the expenses and not bring the matter up to him except in the event of an emergency.

"If we have another baby," Julia said, setting the oven to bake the pies, "you'll have to stay home from the office even more."

"True," Nat said.

"I'm the baby of the family," Caleb said from under the table.

"So I've noticed," Nat said.

"I don't think you really want a baby," Caleb said. "Babies wet their pants, y'know."

Nat picked Caleb up, put him in a hat and coat and sent him out to gather twigs.

"Is Mother having a baby now?"

"No, she's not," Nat said, "but she's begged for one since Caleb was two. Always when her last baby is two and eating by himself and walking, not willing to cuddle in her lap any longer, she wants another. And then you've probably noticed she goes farther and farther away from us."

"I thought the doctor said she was getting better."

"She's always better with the doctor," Nat said, taking the ham out of the oven, basting it with honey and wine.

"She seems to just get sick with us," Julia said and knew immediately by the stricken look on her father's face that it had been the wrong thing to say.

"That's inappropriate," he said.

"I'm sorry." She hugged him. "I really am. I think we have a splendid family, better than any I know with regular mothers and fathers who go to work. It's a wonderful family and just proves that you don't have to be ordinary."

"Occasionally it would be nice," Nat said, kissing her hair, "but I suppose no family is ordinary. Others simply have better luck at pretending."

By ten on Boxing Day everything was almost ready for the party. The day was so tinsel bright that the bare trees, even without snow, sparkled, and the air had the dry cold of the mountains, rare for Pennsylvania. Nat took the children for a walk through the woods behind the Main House, over the fields planted in season, to Daniel's house.

"I hate walks," Bumpo said, taking his father's hand, "especially in winter."

"Pretend you're an Indian," Caleb said, making an evil face at Bumpo, attacking his back with an invisible tomahawk.

"You are an Indian," Peter said.

"I know," Caleb said, hopping on one foot, letting out a war cry.

"I mean a real Indian, dummy," Peter said exasperated.

"I know, dummy," Caleb said, unperturbed. "Pure-blooded red man and I'm gonna kill you," he added, attacking Peter with his invisible tomahawk.

"Stop him," Peter said to his father. "He's driving me crazy."

"What Peter means, Caleb," Julia began, taking her small brother's hand, "is that we are really part Indian, not make-believe, because Lucy Tanner was half Indian and she was your great-great-grandmother."

"Is that true?" Caleb asked his father suspiciously.

"Of course it's true," Julia said. "Daddy's father is John, your grandfather, John's father was Daniel, your great-grandfather, and Daniel's father was Thomas, who was boring, and he was married to Lucy Tanner, who was part Indian and not boring a bit."

"I can tell Bam told you this story," Nat said. "Her prejudices."

Julia nodded.

"Is my Indian grandmother dead?" Caleb asked. "Was she hatcheted to death?"

"Sure," Peter said. "Hatcheted in little pieces and her head was shrunk."

"I want to go home," Bumpo said. "This is a creepy story."

There was a true story. Rachel had told it to Julia one afternoon that summer when they were gathering wild berries by the family cemetery at the far north end of the property, land which connected to the cemetery of St. Mark's Episcopal Church and seemed from the road to be an extension of it. The two-foot fence which Daniel had put up when he was old, and which ran a crooked line to separate, as he said, the heathens, who invented a religion to justify divorce, from the Quakers, was invisible from the road.

The grave of Lucy Tanner was several hundred yards outside the family cemetery, beneath an old oak tree, and the plain marker read:

LUCY TANNER: 1830–1870

It didn't say that she was the beloved wife of Thomas Howells. It didn't say that she was a Howells at all. Thomas himself was buried in the main cemetery next to his second wife and second cousin, Eliza, called "Beloved wife of Thomas Howells," smug in death beneath their granite slab, as if even as bones they took pleasure in the banishment of Lucy Tanner from blessed ground.

Beside the plain marker on the earth which flowered above the body of Lucy was another marker, smaller than Lucy's and undated, which read simply:

LUCINDA, daughter of Lucy, age 6

"Illegitimate," Rachel had said to Julia.

"What does that mean?" Julia asked.

"It means Dr. Howells wasn't the baby's father." Rachel got down on the ground and pulled away the vines growing over the child's grave.

"What does that mean?" Julia asked, but Rachel was onto another train of thought, still on her knees, clearing the growth around the graves.

"You see," Rachel said. "Lucinda was born in 1865 or 1866. Of that I'm certain because her father was a Confederate soldier. We have proof in letters that Lucy kept. Your grandfather has them somewhere. Lucinda died right after Lucy, a year or two."

"She died of sadness," Julia said with confidence.

Since their visit to the graves Julia had played Lucy Tanner, both in her bedroom and on the hill behind the house, with a doll re-named Lucinda with whom she played only when she was imagining herself to be Lucy Tanner. Or she made herself up as an Indian, staring at herself in the mirror over her dresser and sucking in her cheeks so that her cheekbones were distinct, practicing various ex-pressions with her eyes until she seemed to be a woman in her twenties, capable of being bad and very brave.

She put herself to sleep with dreams of Lucy Tanner in modern dress. Joan of Arc, she told her friends at school when they were studying saints, didn't hold a candle to her great-great-grandmother Lucy, either alive or in her martyred death.

"I bet they were all murdered," Caleb said, leaving the graveyard with his hand firmly in his father's.

"Why did we have to go to the graveyard?" Bumpo asked. "I mean, it's so stupid to go to the graveyard the day after Christmas. It spoils all the presents."

"They weren't murdered," Nat said, ignoring Bumpo. "Lucy Tanner died in childbirth when she was over forty, which was too old in those days to have a baby. God knows what Bam suspects happened to Lucinda, but I'm sure if you want to hear terrible stories about the Howells, Bam will happily provide them."

After their walk Nat stopped at the Main House and left the children with his father for the afternoon while he went to visit Cally. He promised that he'd be back by four, in plenty of time to start the bonfire in daylight.

Cally, in the hospital, waited in a sunny room with Mary Cassatt reproductions of mothers and chlidren on the walls and curtains in windows that overlooked thin woods. She waited as a boat waits in the locks of a canal for the water to fill beneath her so she can sail on through the open waterway to the next lock. She waited as a woman waits for dinner to cook in the oven, for the rinse cycle on the machine, for the end of the day when the house is again awash with children—waiting without thinking so the mind's view of the world seems at once cut off and complete.

Often Cally thought about her children, imagining days with them playing happily in the kitchen, telling stories in front of the living room fire, singing with them in the evenings, true days which they had had together and would have again. Whenever she looked ahead, it was for her children. She couldn't look ahead for herself.

When Nat came on Boxing Day, Cally was available to him in ways she had never been before, and full of decisions.

"I want to move," she said. "Someplace where you can have a job, a real, honest-to-goodness job like the one you had when we met and one that hasn't been purchased by your father."

"Where?" Nat asked, surprised.

"Anywhere," she said. "It doesn't matter. Just not Louisiana or Bucks County, but anywhere else in the whole world."

"It's Bam, isn't it?"

"Some," Cally said as Nat wheeled her through the large grounds of the home in Swarthmore. "Bam's like the goddamned iron lung," she said. "She breathes for me." And Nat laughed with great pleasure because Cally had never said "goddamned" before. It was a good sign and he kissed her on the lips in the open spaces of the hospital grounds, in full view of windows of patients and nurses. He felt she was his, not in splendid triumph as he had felt when he was eighteen, but in gratitude as though he had been rescued in the midst of a long fall. He sat down on a wooden bench, holding her cold and gloveless hand in his, meeting her eyes, which, he noticed for the first time, had changed since she was eighteen and lay beneath him on his parents' bed with an animal look of surprise and fear and detachment.

"The doctor thinks I'm not so sick after all," she said, "and I've simply felt terrible because I had polio."

Later they talked about a baby, giddy with their plans as if it would be their first and they still believed in plans.

"One more," Nat said. "We're still very young."

"This is the only time we've ever decided to have a baby," Cally said, "both of us."

When he left Cally that afternoon, driving back to Bucks County, he was cautious of trucks and passing cars and the speed registering on the speedometer. Once the dizziness he had felt that morning came over him, but it slipped away when he stopped the car for a moment by the side of the road and he made it home to the Howells' farm by four.

Julia was playing Lucy Tanner in Rachel's sitting room, but none of her brothers would agree to be the Confederate soldier except Caleb.

"I won't be a soldier," Bumpo said, coloring in a book on the floor. "I hate to fight."

"I'll say," Peter said. "I hate girls."

"I'm not a girl," Julia said. "I'm a woman with a baby and you're the father," she said to Peter.

"Not me," Peter said, collapsing on the couch, putting a pillow over his head. "I'm never getting married."

"We're not married, stupid," Julia said. "The Confederate soldier was the father of the baby and Lucy Tanner was married to Dr. Howells, which is why she's in trouble."

"I'll be the Confederate soldier," Caleb said. "What do I do?"

"You sit there," she said, indicating a stool, "and put your head in your hands."

Caleb did.

"Good."

"Then what?"

"Then, when you see my husband coming, you run, saying, 'Here comes your husband!' and then Peter, you're my husband."

"Not me."

"I'd rather have Bumpo anyway," Julia said indignantly. "I wouldn't marry you if you begged me."

"What a break," Peter said.

"Okay, Bumpo. This is a terrific part. After I finish my speech, you walk over and ask who that man is who ran away and then you lock me in my room and say I can't come out or see anyone but you for the rest of my life."

Julia picked up a doll wrapped in a pillowcase, checked her face in the mirror for the proper tragic expression and took her place.

"There you are, William," she said to Caleb, extending her doll wrapped in a pillowcase, while he peered out beneath his elbow. "Your daughter. Look."

Caleb looked.

"Made out of plaster," Peter said.

"Lucinda. I call her Lucinda and she's the child of my heart and my love for you."

"Great God," Peter said.

"Look at her, William."

Caleb looked again.

"Same old plaster doll, Caleb," Peter said. "Don't get excited."

"Shut up," Julia said. "Take me away with you." Julia whispered to Bumpo, "Hurry up." She touched Caleb, whose head was still buried in his arms. "Say it."

"Here comes your husband!" Caleb shouted dutifully at the top of his lungs.

"Run," Julia said.

Caleb jumped up and ran to the other side of the room.

"Who was that?" Bumpo asked.

"Caleb Howells, you dummy," Peter said.

"No one," Julia said to Bumpo. "I don't know who you're talking about."

"Your boyfriend," Bumpo said.

"Not boyfriend," Julia said. "They didn't have boyfriends in those days."

"You have to go to your room," Bumpo said.

"Pull me," Julia whispered. "Be very rough."

"I can't," Bumpo said.

Julia twisted and thrashed, pretending to be forced into the closet.

"There," Bumpo said. "I'm locking the door."

"Don't," Julia shouted. "Don't, please. You can't leave me here. Please."

"BRAVO," Peter shouted. "BRAVO. ENCORE. ENCORE."

"It's not over," Julia said.

"BRAVO, BRAVO," Peter continued.

"What is this?" Rachel asked, coming to the door.

"Julia is playing Lucy Tanner," Bumpo said.

"And I'm her boyfriend," Caleb said.

"And Bumpo's the father," Peter said.

"I hate Peter," Julia said to Rachel. "He ruins everything."

"I need your help, lamb," Rachel said, taking Julia. "You boys stay here and do your play or go to the study with your grandfather while we're gone."

"We don't do plays, Bam. Julia does," Bumpo said. "We play."

"Then play, lambs. It will soon be time for the party."

Rachel had a small room to herself in the back of the house. It had been at one time a maid's room and was located at the top of the kitchen stairs. Now she used it as a study, but for a number of years, during the war and even later, George Katz, a German Jewish boy, a refugee from Hitler's Europe whom Rachel had met at a party in New York where he was tending bar, lived in that room. At the party Rachel had invited him to her New York apartment for tea, and the afternoon he came for tea, she invited him to come to Bucks County for the weekend. He did, and stayed four years in the maid's room above the kitchen.

Rachel's kindness to George Katz was, like her nursing of Daniel, a small repayment for living a false life. That George was not worth such generosity was incidental to the fact that he was German and Jewish, a refugee without a family and available when Rachel needed him. He left in 1948 to marry a waitress from New Hope, taking only a few possessions, leaving in the room at the top of the kitchen stairs all of the gifts Rachel had given him through the years, and until this Boxing Day, Rachel had worked in his room without disturbing anything.

"You understand that I love Lucy Tanner," Rachel said to Julia as they climbed to the top of the kitchen stairs.

"You didn't know her," Julia said.

"I didn't, but I know about her and love her for the stories I've heard." She took Julia into her study and sat down beside a box of letters and old papers she was packing to be burned that evening.

"I don't think she was wrong to have that baby," Rachel said. "Even though it's not accepted to love a man when you're married to another, women do."

"You thought I was making fun of Lucy Tanner in that play," Julia said, understanding Rachel's concern. "I wasn't," she insisted. "I play Lucy Tanner all the time because she was brave."

"I'm glad, Julia," Rachel said, taking Julia's face in her hands and kissing her. "Sometimes our lives don't turn out the way we expect them to and we must live the best we can."

Rachel was sorting the drawers of her desk, putting much of their contents into boxes. "Do you remember George?" she asked.

"Yup," Julia said.

"Do you remember when this was his room?"

"Yes," Julia said. She watched her grandmother busying through the drawers, confused by Rachel's request for her presence, wondering if perhaps she was expected to contribute conversation while Rachel sorted and packed. "I didn't like George," Julia offered as a beginning.

"No?" Rachel asked without looking up. "Why not?"

"He was mean," Julia said. George had worked in New Hope at a bakery, but weekdays, when John was in the city, he drove John's car around Bucks County, going very fast, and sat in the living room after work, smoking a pipe in front of the fire Rachel had built and waiting for the supper Rachel would cook. If the Howells children came in while he was there, George requested that they leave him alone to read uninterrupted.

"How was he mean?" Rachel asked. "I know he didn't like children."

"I thought he was mean to you," Julia said.

"Was he?" Rachel asked. She couldn't remember. She remembered the deep hurt when he left with the waitress, but that was mixed with a kind of exhilaration that he was gone; his presence had been a physical weight on her. She remembered also the pleasure, almost a sexual pleasure, and that was another complication, of serving him, cooking for him, cleaning for him, doing his laundry, making herself essential to his sense of well-being. So when he left, unannounced and in a hurry, she knew what, of course, she had known all along, that she was not essential to his well-being at all. She had to be satisfied that George had been important to her, that, finally, their odd union had nothing to do with either of them, but only to do with the fact that Rachel was a Jewish woman who remembered German from her father's house and that George was a Jewish boy who had learned English in Rachel's house —a simple dispensable union which, when it was over, left her with a sadness beyond its worth.

"He treated you like a mop," Julia said absolutely.

"Like a mop?" Rachel asked.

"That's what Daddy said. He said you were a beautiful woman behaving like a mop."

"Honestly," Rachel said.

"He said it to Granddaddy when we were in town getting ice cream cones. Caleb was a baby and Granddaddy got furious and said he didn't want to hear about mops again."

"You certainly do have a fine memory," Rachel said quietly.

"I do," Julia said with great pleasure. "I remember every conversation I hear. Granddaddy also called George a bastard. I remember the whole thing because Mother asked him not to say 'bastard' in front of Peter, who would say it in kindergarten to the teacher, and Granddaddy said how sorry he was and for Peter certainly not to and of course Peter said 'bastard' to the kindergarten teacher the next day."

"I expect Granddaddy often used 'bastard' in reference to George."

"Daddy said George was a leech." Julia made a face and sucked her wrist. "Bloodsucker," she said, beginning to enjoy this conversation with Rachel, misunderstanding its complications.

"Granddaddy said that, too," Rachel said, finishing one box, taping it, going through the drawers on the other side of the desk.

She remembered one night just after Nat had returned from Europe, John tossing in the bed next to her unable to sleep.

"Come here," he said and pulled her over. "Goddammit, Rachel Schoenberg, come here."

"I'm here, John," she said, pulling away. "You're hurting me."

"Aha," he said. "You can feel that." And he pulled her against him. "You're not here, Bammy. You're never here anymore since George moved into the maid's room."

"I am," Rachel said.

"Not really here. Your mind is always floating down the hall to the top of the kitchen stairs."

And another night John asked her if she loved George.

"In what way?" she asked with caution.

"Any goddamned way at all," he said, sitting against a pillow with the reading light on.

Rachel thought honestly about loving George and after a silence said that no, she didn't, in any way at all.

"That's wonderful," John said, slapping his knee in mock joy. "Splendid news, Bammy, because honest to God, if you searched New York City top to bottom, you could not have come up with a more terrible human being than George Katz."

Rachel was weeping and he took her hand.

"I know why, Bammy," he said. "I understand. It just makes me very sad that he is the recipient of your lovely generosity."

John did not understand what happened in the last year of George's residency at the Howells place and whether he knew or not, Rachel was never sure, but she guessed that he did.

George was restless. The dinners, the evenings by the fire, the gifts and English lessons and quiet conversations had become tire-some, and one evening, in an act Rachel recognized later as a des-perate move to deflect his restlessness, she touched his lips with her finger when she kissed him good-night on the cheek, left her finger there in an unmistakable gesture, and then, with the instincts of a woman who knew without hesitation the bedding of men, ran her finger over his tongue.

He was a terrible lover. Like a jack-in-the-box, Prussian by design. And Rachel did detain him for one last year of instruction in lan-guage, teaching him also, on the nights that John stayed in the city, with her hands and her lips the pleasure of the senses, so he could leave her, technically perfect, softer, gentler, occasionally a lamb, for the silly waitress in New Hope.

Julia heard Nat's car pull up in front of the Main House while she was taping boxes.

"Daddy's back from seeing Mother," she said. "I better get the boys. People will be coming by six."

"You'd better, lambie," Rachel said, lifting one box and handing it to Julia to carry. "Take that to your father's car. And Julia," she said, "not a word about George."

"Secrets, Bam," Julia said. "You're worse than a child."

"Julia," Rachel said in warning.

"Not a word," Julia said. "I promise."

Nat took Caleb with him to start the bonfire.

Peter set up the bar in the living room, and Bumpo helped Julia with the food in the kitchen.

"Girls' work," Peter said with confidence.

"Don't listen to him, Bumpo," Julia warned. "He loves it when you're angry."

But Julia saw that Bumpo was crying. "Filling the butter plate with salt water," she said and hugged him.

The day was gold in the last hour of sunlight, and it rested on the edge of the farm. With great seriousness Caleb helped his father pile kindling, loose twigs that they had gathered from that morning in their walk through the woods, and larger logs from the woodpile.

"It'll burn higher than you," Caleb said.

"Higher than the houses." Nat smiled.

"It'll burn high enough to catch the sun on fire."

"The sun is on fire already, Caleb," Nat said. "Look at it." And he put his hand under Caleb's chin, lifting it, so the boy squarely faced the setting sun.

"I'm going to light the fire now, Caleb," Nat said, kneeling down, packing the newspaper and kindling more closely than Caleb had. "Stand back."

Caleb moved back behind his father.

"No, farther," Nat said. "There's a wind."

Caleb stepped back. He counted ten giant steps backwards and then forgot what came after ten. He went backwards a few more giant steps, guessing twenty. When his father fell, he wasn't even aware the fire had started because he was looking behind him. And then he heard Nat's shout and the sharp crackle of the fire burning thin dry wood. When he looked around, his father was lying face-down on the ground and the fire, high as a man, higher, shot above him like a fountain.

"Daddy," Caleb screamed and ran towards him.

"Get Julia," Nat said. And by then he had jumped up and Caleb could see his pants were on fire, but Caleb couldn't move, either towards Nat or towards the glass shoebox, where Julia was with Peter and Bumpo.

"Get Julia, goddammit," Nat shouted, and then he did a very strange thing, as Caleb told it later. He dove on the ground and rolled around and around and around.

By the time Caleb got Julia, so white and frightened that he couldn't speak when he found her in the kitchen, by the time Julia ran down to the bonfire, which burned in glorious competition with the bright orange sun, Nat's pants were not burning but charcoal and he lay on his stomach, not unconscious but not conscious either, in such great pain that he couldn't speak to Julia or to Bumpo, who ran his hand through his father's hair, or to Peter and Caleb, who stood beside him, holding each other's hand.

Later Peter would remember himself with contempt at that moment and return to that evening as the time in his growing up when he decided to be a doctor.

Later Nat's accident would be used as evidence against the manufacturer of highly flammable materials and finally his case would be among those on which the Pure Food and Drug Administration based its requirement that manufacturers use flame retardants on synthetics.

Later Nat would tell the story of kneeling down beside the pile of kindling, of telling Caleb to move back, then farther back, of lighting a match, leaning over so his arm could reach more or less into the center of the kindling and light the pressed newspaper. At the very same moment the dizziness he had felt that day and other days came up like smoke. He fell and the fire caught his pants or else the fire had already caught his pants and then he fell. One or the other, he couldn't remember which.

It was after four in the morning when Rachel and John returned to the Main House with Julia, who had insisted that she go to the hospital with them. The boys were asleep, all three of them in Nat's old bed in his parents' house. And Mrs. Care, who had come immediately when Rachel called her, was sitting up in the living room.

"How is he?" she asked when the Howells arrived.

"He has third-degree burns over the lower half of his body," John said. "A fifty percent chance of living, whatever that means."

Julia and Rachel went upstairs to Rachel's room. Julia put on her grandmother's nightgown and climbed into her grandparents' bed.

"We'll sleep together," Rachel said, "until Granddaddy comes up."

But John didn't come up. When Rachel went downstairs at seven that morning, rising with the sun, there was evidence that John had spent the rest of the night in the living room. There were coffee cups and an ashtray full of emptied pipe tobacco. There were red coals in a fire that must have burned all night and a plate with half a piece of pumpkin pie. There was a note on the library table which said, "At the hospital, John," and the family Bible was closed on a wing chair by the fireplace with a black-ink ball-point pen between the pages. On a page headed "Boxing Day, 1950," John had written a sentence which he crossed out, and now Rachel crossed it out again so no one could ever read it.

She could imagine in what spirit of great love and anger and confusion, with what irreverent challenge to a world busily inventing its own destruction, he had written:

NAT CAUGHT FIRE BUILDING THE BONFIRE FOR BOXING DAY LATE THIS AFTERNOON AND BURNED HIS BALLS OFF.

MIRACLES

I DON'T ORDINARILY BELIEVE IN MIRACLES [John Howells had written on August 30, 1954], BUT WE HAVE HAD A MIRACLE THIS LAST YEAR AND I'D BE A CYNIC NOT TO RECOGNIZE IT.

He was astonished by his own high spirits, by the remarkable capacity a man has to readjust his mind and heart and by the general tenor in the rooms of the Main House beyond the library where he was writing.

When Rachel had called Cally in Swarthmore the morning after Boxing Day, Cally had dressed quickly, packed her suitcase and asked a nurse in the main building to call a taxicab.

"Cally has needed a reason to get well," Rachel told John, some weeks later, not bitterly, but with a fundamental understanding of her own need to nurse. "She'll be fine."

Cally was fine. She arrived at the Howells farm as though she'd simply been to the market. She called Rachel at the Main House to send the children, whom she greeted with a wonderful calm which didn't hint at her absence from them or their father's grave condition. After their initial surprise, standing back and looking at her to see if she fulfilled their memory of her face, after the fluster of stories about the fire and the ambulance, the household settled like trees after a heavy wind. Too still.

"It's as though everything is fine," Julia said to Rachel the first night that Cally was home.

"It's Cally's way, Julia," Rachel said, getting ready to go with Julia to the hospital, "and look how well it works with the boys."

"Maybe with them," Julia said.

"We have to wait to see what happens," Rachel said.

"I don't think it's occurred to Mother that he could die."

"I think it has, Julia," Rachel said. And they stood vigil in the

hospital corridors for days in intensive care, then weeks of recupera-
tion, then months, through several operations and recoveries.

It had occurred to Cally. John had taken her to the hospital the
first day and she had seen Nat, although it wasn't possible for her
to go in the room because of the danger of infection. But their eyes
had met and it was clear to her in the strange distance of Nat's eyes
that he was half out of the world already.

"It's a matter of will," John said, containing his own fears by de-
ciding in favor of will.

That night she read to the boys—even Peter wanted a story—
kissed them good-night and went to her own room. She sat up reading, and heard Julia get up, move around her bedroom, turn on
the light in the living room.

"Go to bed," Cally called to her.

"I can't sleep," Julia said. She came in her mother's room, lay on
the bottom of her bed, on her back, resting her head on her arms.

"If anything happens to Daddy, I'll die," Julia said with her eyes
closed.

"No, you won't," Cally said.

"You're supposed to say nothing's going to happen to Daddy,"
Julia said. "You're supposed to make me feel better."

"It already has happened, Julia," Cally said. She reached down
and brushed Julia's hair out of her face. "You need a haircut."

"Why are you so calm?" Julia asked. "You'd think this was just
a regular family night at home."

"I don't honestly know."

"You're so calm, even the boys think Daddy is going to be fine.
It's deceitful." And she fell asleep at the end of her mother's bed
in a taut ball, ready to spring at the slightest touch.

"I've decided to wear my hair very long," she said just before she
fell asleep.

Cally didn't think Nat would die, but this strange peace was
more than intuition. She lay in bed, a novel open across her belly,
the night-light on, and thought about herself. When Rachel had
called her in Swarthmore that morning, she had not reacted pre-
dictably. Her blood hadn't raced or her stomach tightened or her
throat dried or her heart pounded or anything at all, but there was
a confirmation in Rachel's call of what she had been sitting in her
room in Swarthmore expecting, as if she were a witch with special

perceptions. Now, in her own bedroom, she thought perhaps she was in shock. If so, she should be cold and clammy, her pupils dilated. Her hands were warm; her arms, uncovered in winter in a glass room, were the comfortable temperature of arms. She loved Nat, she thought, but maybe she didn't know what love was, raised in a family in which love had been formalized to decorum, arranged like rose dahlias in a vase. Maybe she was passing the years like a ghost, unencumbered by feelings. She was simply a representative of her moment in time, a woman who is married and has children and dies, or else her husband dies first and that, in the course of things, satisfies the order of history. Perhaps the only thing that had mattered to her was herself and now, if Nat lived, if he came home to this house, this couch in the window across from her bed, she would be in charge of his fragile life. With that terrible thought forming in her mind, Cally pulled herself out of bed, into the wheel-chair, rolled into the kitchen and called the Main House, where Rachel, to her relief, answered the telephone.

"Bam," she said, and out of the blue, Cally wept. She put the phone down on the counter, and when Rachel, in John's bathrobe and boots, ran across the fields with a flashlight, opened the kitchen door and took Cally in her arms, the phone on the counter was still connected to the Main House.

Altogether Nat was in the hospital six months. He had skin grafts that took and others that didn't, secondary infections, kidney trouble that recurred and couldn't be traced either to antibiotics, which were suspected, or to the burns themselves, but the doctors were concerned about kidney failure and didn't want to release him, even after the burns had healed for the most part, until they were confident his kidneys were working. Nat lost interest in living. The quotidian of the hospital routine, the operations and the long re-coveries, the endless visits from his family, the same questions and answers bored him with their repetition. He began to sleep after breakfast, promising himself that he'd get up by the time the sun was mid-window and walk around, which the doctors said he must do or his legs would stiffen, but often he slept until lunch and fell asleep reading after lunch, waking only for the visits from home. By March, when the trees outside his window were beginning to bud with the promise of an early spring, reminding him of his own dying, of his bad luck, he became angry at his family.

"Haven't you anything better to do in the afternoon?" he asked

Julia crossly one day during her spring vacation from school.

"What do you mean?" she asked, alarmed.

"Most girls your age have friends over during vacations," he said. "They don't spend all their time in the hospital with their father."

"They don't have fathers in the hospital," Julia said simply.

"That's exactly what I mean," Nat said. "Leave. I'm in no mood for visitors."

"Do something," Julia said to her mother when she got home from the hospital that afternoon.

Cally did, but it took time, and meanwhile, Nat refused to see all visitors.

Julia wouldn't play with anyone spring vacation. She sat in her room and wrote plays, four of them, one in which Caleb was expected to play the role of a porcupine born without quills.

"I won't," Caleb said, lying at the bottom of Julia's bed, playing cars on his stomach, vrooming the cars up and down over his rib cage road. "Peter laughs at me."

"Peter's mean," Julia said. "Peter," she called, but she didn't need to call because he was leaning against the doorway of her room.

"I don't care if you call me mean," he said, coming into the room and sitting down on Julia's window seat, "or any other wonderful name you invent."

"Sticks and stones blah blah blah blah," Caleb said.

"Play the porcupine, Caleb," Peter said. "There's nothing else to do this vacation but be in Julia's plays."

"We could go to the circus," Caleb said. "Or a parade."

"Like where do you expect to find the circus?"

"Dunno," Caleb said, vrooming his cars. "It has to be someplace or we never would have heard of it, right?"

"Right. Someplace, Caleb, but not here," Peter said. "NOTHING is here."

"You are a creep, Peter," Julia said.

"Right. I admit it. First-class and all that. Tell me about your wonderful porcupine play," he said. "Why doesn't the porcupine have any quills?"

"He was born without them," Julia said. "Born defenseless."

"Born deformed," Peter said. "He must be related to us."

"Oh, shut up."

"I'm not kidding," Peter said. And later, after Cally had left with Caleb to make a circus in the playroom, Peter told Julia what he had overheard in the library between Rachel and John the night before.

He lay down on Julia's bed, propped his head up on a pillow and closed his eyes.

"Do you know what balls are?" he asked.

"Well," she said.

"I don't mean like a softball," he said.

"No," Julia said.

"Testicles?" he asked.

Julia shook her head. "I've heard of them," she said.

"Jesus," Peter said. "Girls in my class know that. Probably in Bumpo's. You are so innocent, Julia, I don't know what will happen to you."

"So what are they?"

"Do you know what a boy looks like naked?"

"Of course."

" 'Of course,' she says."

"I have three younger brothers, stupid."

"You've never seen me," Peter said.

"Who'd want to?" Julia said. "So I know what boys look like."

"So they have a penis."

"Right."

"And two balls," Peter said. "Those two things on either side of the penis are called balls or testicles or nuts or anything you like. Okay?"

"Okay," Julia said, embarrassed.

"So yesterday at Bam's, Granddaddy got a call from the hospital. I was sitting in the kitchen having lunch and he went into the library and told Bam that Daddy's going to have to have his cut off 'cause they won't heal."

"That's awful," Julia said. "That's too awful. Don't tell me anything else."

"There isn't anything else."

"We're not supposed to know."

"I overheard, dummy. It's not exactly the kind of thing you tell a kid, right?"

"It's too personal. Daddy would kill us if he thought we knew."

"Then lie," Peter said.

"You promise not to tell a soul?" Julia said.

"I promise."

That night at supper Cally told the children that Nat was going to have another operation because he wasn't healing properly. They hoped that operation would be the last one and would get rid of the infection and even his kidneys would be fine after that.

"What kind of operation?" Peter asked guardedly.

"Similar to the others," Cally said.

"See," Peter said to Julia that night after they had gone upstairs.

"No one can ever know we know," Julia said. "Daddy would die."

Cally was hard at work. She collected all of Nat's articles from his years as a journalist, wrote letters to newspapers in Boston and New York and Washington, in Atlanta and Richmond, in Baltimore and Philadelphia because she wanted to live in a city, she wanted a new life of their own making. She didn't tell Nat about these letters, simply signed his name and sent them. When Grayson Philips from the *Washington News Leader* called the house for Nat and told Cally that he had been particularly impressed with Nat's stories on Bessie Mae as well as his stories from Europe during the war and would Nat call, Cally got in the car and drove to the hospital, racing down the corridor in her wheelchair full of their good fortune.

At first Nat shook his head with such a look of sadness that Cally cried.

"I thought you'd be so happy," she said. "I thought you'd be thrilled." She took his hand. "You've been wanting to die, Nat. You've been wanting to go to sleep and never wake up." She was surprised at the sense of wisdom which had come to her since Nat's accident.

"We can move to Washington," she said. "Just the six of us."

"If I ever get out of here," he said.

"You'll be out soon, according to the doctor. Maybe next week."

And Cally was right. By the end of the week Nat had stopped sleeping. He called his father in New York and told him about Grayson Philips; he called Grayson Philips and said he'd be down mid-June when he'd recovered sufficiently; he let the children sit on his bed and walked the corridors every afternoon with Julia or with a cane.

"Your mother is like a camel," he told Julia once. "She stores water for the dry season."

"We can sleep in the same bed now that you've lost so much

weight," Cally said to him the day she picked him up in the hospital.

"I'll stay thin forever," he said and kissed her.

By June of 1951 Nat was moving his family to Washington. His position with the *Washington News Leader* was due to begin the first of September. He rented a house in Georgetown at Thirtieth and N streets, a three-story house built as a tavern in the 1800's, with rooms which were charming but so small it was difficult for Cally to maneuver her wheelchair. She bought leg braces which she could lock at the knee so her legs, the muscles of which had long since atrophied, wouldn't collapse like paper legs beneath her.

"It's crazy," Rachel said to Cally. "You'll be exhausted going up and down those steps."

But Cally was determined to have the skinny house in Georgetown and learned to use crutches and braces without her wheelchair. It took her five minutes to go upstairs, she figured, and half a minute down if she bounced on her seat, sliding her crutches in front of her.

"Don't do that in front of my friends," Peter insisted, referring to his mother's method of descending the stairs.

She went everywhere in Georgetown in her wheelchair, taking the whole sidewalk. She walked the dogs by tying their leashes to the handles and learned to do the marketing with a wagon attached to the back of her chair by link chains. She did her own cleaning and Julia helped her cook.

Lila married Jimmy Zimmer before Nat and Cally left Bucks County. They were married in a small ceremony at the Main House and moved to an apartment in Dolyestown, where Lila worked in a drugstore and had a weekend job in New Hope at a bar. Sometimes she'd spend all night at the bar and Jimmy would come the next morning on the bus to take her home.

"Got to drinking," she'd say.

The only regular thing Lila did was call Melvina once a week in New Orleans, charge it to Cally's phone in Washington and call Cally collect on Sunday nights.

"Things are all right," she'd say. "Passable. Marriage, I'm finding, isn't all it was cracked up to be, but I should've known that since Mama always said she wouldn't marry the king of England if he turned colored and begged her on his knees."

* * *

Cally's life was her marriage to Nat, as though she were making it like spice cake from scratch with white flour and Demerara sugar ground to tiny crystals. One night in late July of the first year the Howells were in Washington, a night so hot the air had substance like cream sauce off the stove, Nat and Cally lay naked in their bed without sheets.

"We're a fine pair, Caroline Howells." Nat laughed, looking at his own checkered body, patched like old pants discolored from too many washings, at Cally's pale legs like the legs of a plaster doll, shapeless with disuse, which she had lifted with her hands and laid across his groin. "Candidates for Caleb's and Bumpo's circus."

Cally reached over and touched him.

"Only from the waist down," she said. "From the waist up, we're beautiful." And she kissed him on the lips with her tongue.

"Soupy is what they are," Peter said in late September, walking home from the streetcar with Bumpo and Julia after their first week at Friends School on Wisconsin Avenue.

"So what?" Julia asked.

"Gaze into my eyes," Peter said to Julia. "You are so beautiful, so wonderful, a jewel, a treasure."

"Oh, shut up," Bumpo said. "Daddy's never talked that way in his life."

"You'll be lucky to marry an iguana, Peter," Julia said, crossing Thirty-first Street.

"It's just that I hope my friends don't see them like that," Peter said. "It's so soupy I'd die."

By the following summer Nat was on the editorial page reporting on national news, his reputation one of wit and generosity.

"You see," John said to Rachel.

"I never said he couldn't, lamb"—she ruffled his white hair—"but I'm glad for you."

"It's not for me," John snapped, and Rachel laughed at him.

At the beginning of the second school year in Washington, Nat decided they should expose the children to a religious upbringing.

"They can rebel, of course," he said. "I'd expect them to, but we should give them something to rebel against."

He started with grace one Sunday afternoon at a midday meal with just the family.

"A moment of silence," he said.

"What for?" Peter asked. "We've never had grace before," he said. "It's creepy, like someone's gonna die."

"I don't want a moment of silence," Caleb said. "It's so boring. I want to say something like 'God is great, God is good and I thank him for my food.' "

"Say it then," said Bumpo.

"I did."

"It sounds like you're buttering up to God," Peter said.

But Nat persisted and they had a moment of silence every day for a week until Caleb, struck suddenly by the stomach flu at the dinner table, threw up on his plate. Thereafter grace had associations with stomach flu, and to everyone's relief, Nat dropped it.

"Don't feel bad," Caleb said to his father. "We have plenty of grace at school."

"You're different," Julia said to Nat one evening as they sat together in the living room after supper, after the boys were in bed and Cally was resting.

"In what way?" Nat asked.

"Peter says you're soupy with Mama. And then grace, remember? We had grace for a week until Caleb threw up. I feel funny. We are all so nice to each other, like it isn't going to last."

"Being nice to each other?" Nat took her hand, played with her fingers.

"Nope," Julia said. "Just being at all. Bumpo said if we act too nice, God might want us to join Him in heaven."

"You don't believe that, do you?"

"I don't believe in heaven," Julia said. "But it does worry me."

"Listen, babes, when your pants are burned right off you in broad daylight, things change and you are different."

In the summer of 1953 Nat went home to Bucks County, after routine surgery to remove a lump on his left kidney at the University of Pennsylvania Hospital.

"It is rarely malignant on the kidneys," the doctor told Cally before the surgery.

Nat was certain he would recover. Lying in the hospital, looking out the west window at the dreary buildings of the University of Pennsylvania, the flurry of summer school students lingering on Spruce Street, he felt like an old man. If troubles counted as a measure, he had lived double a lifetime in thirty-eight years. He had earned more years and so he believed the lump was gone, that he would get well in time.

The attending surgeon told John and Rachel that the cancer had spread to Nat's liver and was inoperable. They told Cally late the night before Nat came home.

"I know," she said. "Some things you know by instinct."

They all agreed they would not tell Nat because of his confidence or the children until it was absolutely necessary.

Nat and Cally spent the rest of the summer at the Main House in the bedroom where he had grown up and Rachel fed him three meals a day, special desserts and hot breads, tea at four with cakes.

"It's time to go back to Washington because I'm smothering in food. Look," he said to Cally, trying to zip up his jeans the morning before the family left. "One could die of attention at Bam's."

Besides, it was time to go because Julia was in trouble.

A group of actors from Bucks County Playhouse had moved into the glass shoebox for the summer, and in the month that Nat had been home recuperating, Julia had dropped her independent mind and become a hand-sewn doll, pliable as cloth.

"I might expect this of another child," Rachel said, "but not Julia."

"Perhaps it's because of Nat," Cally said once to John when Nat was out.

"Do you think she knows?" Rachel asked.

"You know how close Julia and Nat are. I think she senses something is wrong," Cally said. "The actors fill up her time."

"That's it, Cally," Rachel said with her usual conviction. "Julia is escaping."

"I want you to have the goddamned actors move off the place, Bam, tomorrow morning after breakfast," John said.

"Darling, I've made an agreement."

"The agreement didn't include the brainwashing of Julia."

"My dear," Peter said. "How splendid to see you looking so mah-vel-ous, Julia. Like a small onyx. Pure and delicate as a fern."

"Shut up, Peter," Bumpo said.

"That's honestly how they act with Julia."

"I don't care how they act," Bumpo said. "It's Julia. She's turned into a chameleon."

Peter floated across his grandfather's library, where they were playing.

"I don't know," he wailed. "I don't know what to do with my life. My mind is a tangle of wires, a hotbed of confusion, a muddy creek full of dead frogs."

"Go to your room, Peter," John Howells said, coming in from the porch. "This isn't a joke with Julia. It is serious and upsetting."

"She doesn't even talk to me anymore," Bumpo said to his grandfather. "She looks at me like she can't remember what my name is."

"I think she's gone crazy," Caleb said. "That's what the Cares say. Mrs. Care said to me this morning, 'crazy as a loon.' "

"Bam," John said that evening after the boys were asleep, "I don't want to rent the houses out any longer. It's affecting our lives together. We'll have the Cares move."

"This is their fourth year, John," she said.

"This is my ancestral ground, Bammy. I own it and I want them off."

John felt the Howells land falling away from him, as if a part of his body were changing. It was no longer the Howells land in the sense that it had been when he was growing up, but shared as spoils with welfare families like the Cares and second-rate actors who did not appear to eat regular meals. In his mind, he equated Nat's illness and Cally's, the recent difficulties in their family, with the portioning off of land to unrelated people. Instinctively he believed that he and the land were indivisible, requiring cultivation of each other, a constant regeneration by new seeds. So he decided, although he knew it was unreasonable, to ask everyone unrelated to leave.

"If you're going to be extreme, I'm not related," Rachel said.

"It's a matter of choice," John said. "I chose you. Not the Cares or the actors."

It was late August, cooler than usual for summer in Bucks County, the countryside in full green, the last splendid weeks before the leaves began to dry and turn. Julia was in the glass shoebox with the actors from the playhouse who were living rent-free in return for taking care of Roger, the burro, who had grown ill-tempered since Cally had left, and several related cats, who, unattended, had continued to reproduce variations of themselves.

Nat found Julia with the Bucks County players. She was lying in the grass, listening to them perform. It made Nat cross to watch her.

She got up when he beckoned. He was concerned about her and told her so as they wandered over the Howells farm together, past Lucy Tanner's grave, Lucinda's, which Julia had cleared of vines as she'd seen Rachel do, and by Daniel's house, where the Cares were living.

"You don't like the actors," she said.

"Not much," Nat said. "You're too interesting for them."

"Interesting. I read that, too, on my report card," Julia said, linking arms with her father. She was almost as tall as he was now, very thin, and looked the way Rachel had looked when she was young, but too irregular in her features to be as beautiful as her grandmother had been. Her eyes, wide-set just above the sharp bones of her cheeks, gave her face a look of expectancy.

"You're not dull"—he laughed—"but I never expected you to be taken in like this."

"What do you mean?" Julia asked evasively, knowing exactly what her father meant, knowing the change in herself which had come over her, an odd feeling in her stomach, a sense of falling in the brain. These actors with whom she had fallen in love, these silly actors, who drank too much and could talk only about themselves, who played to each other, staging scenes in the yard of the glass shoebox, could get Julia to do anything, to hang, batlike, upside down, to make their beds and scrub the kitchen, to fly from the balcony of her bedroom.

"I mean that however difficult you've been growing up, I've always counted on you not to do dangerous things," Nat said.

"I'm careful," Julia said.

"You've been careful."

"Except when I ate the baby aspirin. Remember? A bottle and a half, a real feast."

"Then you could have your stomach pumped."

"I'm not being poisoned, Daddy."

"All you will ever really have is yourself. I don't want you to give yourself away."

"That's not the same as being poisoned," Julia said.

"Do you know about Bumpo?" he asked.

"What?"

"Do you know he's cried every night since this thing with the actors started because you don't talk to him anymore?"

"Bumpo cries if it rains, for Chrissake," Julia said, but she pulled away from her father and did a two-step up the hill. "Let's not talk about Bumpo."

That afternoon Julia didn't go to the glass shoebox, and when Nat came in for supper, she was playing badminton with Bumpo in the front yard.

"It smells like you're cooking with wine," Cally said to Rachel, wheeling into the kitchen on the last afternoon before she and Nat were to return to Washington.

"I am," Rachel said. "Bourguignonne with mushrooms from the Bales farm and raspberries," she said, popping one in her mouth. "I don't know whether to serve them fresh with cream or in a flan. Here." She handed Cally a spoon of raspberries from the beige crockery bowl. "What do you think?"

"I think it's thoughtless to make bourguignonne when Nat got sick on the wine dish you made last week."

"He did?" Rachel asked. "He never said."

"He doesn't want to hurt your feelings," Cally said, dumping the spoon of raspberries back in the bowl. "But I told you. I came down Wednesday morning before he did and told you he had been up all night."

"I don't remember," Rachel said, a rare color in her cheeks. "I expect that, as is often the case, you simply stewed in silence and didn't tell me anything."

"As is always the case, you don't listen to me. Only to Nat and Julia," Cally said. "I could say the barn was on fire and you'd simply say, 'Now, Cally, always remember to add thyme. Don't measure. Just a pinch with your fingers.'"

"Nat loves bourguignonne," Rachel said. She wasn't going to cry, she told herself, narrowing her eyes at Cally. "Which is why I'm making it for supper."

"He used to love bourguignonne," Cally said.

"I've been his mother for thirty-eight years."

But Cally didn't wait to hear Rachel out. She wheeled into the hall, took her crutches from the back of the wheelchair, locked her braces and went upstairs. John met her halfway up.

"Don't tire yourself, Cal," he said. "We're eating soon."

"I go up and down the steps without a problem twenty times a day in my own house," Cally said, and she swung into the room where Peter slept and lay down on the bed.

She was not accustomed to temper, but when it came in a series of short internal explosions, it made her ill. Her turn of spirit gave off a kind of atomic dust dangerous to the survival of her own gentle cells.

"Close the door," she said to Peter, who was performing brain surgery with scissors on one of Julia's old dolls.

"With me in or out?" he asked.

"You can be in," she said, "but quietly. I have a headache."

"You have lots of headaches lately," Peter said.

"I have some headaches," Cally replied.

"I read about brain tumors in Granddaddy's medical book."

"I don't have a brain tumor, Peter," Cally said.

"I didn't think you did," Peter said, removing the doll's black curly hair. "I just thought you'd like to know."

"That's very helpful, Peter," she said, her eyes closed, her arm covering them to cut out the light.

"Why didn't you tell me you were sick on the chicken dish I made last week?" Rachel asked Nat as he came in the back door with Julia.

"Because Cally told you," Nat said, sitting down on a kitchen chair, taking off his hiking boots and cleaning the mud off the bottoms.

"I have been trying to fatten you, Nathaniel."

"I'm fattening, Bam," Nat said. "I simply prefer dull foods right now—plain chicken, plain eggs, junket."

"I hate junket," said Julia.

"Can you eat bourguignonne?" Rachel asked.

"I love it," Julia said from the sink, where she was washing her hands. "Mmm." She took a handful of raspberries.

"I'd honestly rather have a piece of cold chicken," Nat said.

"All right," Rachel said quietly. "And raspberries?"

"He'd rather have junket," Julia said.

"Then I'll make the damned junket," Rachel said, kissing the top of Nat's head. "I suppose you want vanilla so everything you eat for supper will be white."

Rachel made a flan. "For the boys," she said to John, who sat with her in the kitchen, drinking a scotch before supper. "The boys prefer something sweet," she insisted.

John could hear the hitch in her voice, and when she turned from the sink, he saw that she was crying. He took her by the wrist and pulled her over to him, down on his lap.

"I'm too fat," she said. "I'll break your leg and you'll have to get a driver to take you into the city every morning," she said. He kissed her breast underneath the large apron.

"Don't, John," she said. "I'm not in the humor." But she put her arms around his neck and buried her head in his shoulder. "Nat won't eat the bourguignonne," she said, and she was weeping. "I even made it with good wine and just a little garlic, the way he likes it, and wild rice from scratch with herbs from your mother's garden."

"Bammy."

"Don't discipline me," she said.

"We can't do this," he said. "If he doesn't want to eat, it won't do a bit of good."

"I know," she said. "I know." She stood up, brushed her hands through her hair, washed her face with cold water. "One of the 'yokes' of my old age, besides fatness, will be making junket out of packages in three flavors. You'll probably have a long-term illness and won't be able to eat at all, my love." She dusted his face with flour. "Nothing but glucose through the veins."

"Mother won't come down," Peter said when dinner was announced. "She has a headache."

"She's mad at Bam," Caleb said. "That's what she told Daddy and I overheard. Right, Julia? You heard, too."

"Hush, Cale," Julia said.

"Mother said no more shut up and hush in the house at all," Caleb said as they gathered in the dining room for a last family supper.

"I can't stand the fighting," Bumpo said. "Everybody's fighting, as usual."

"Except the pure at heart," Peter said. "God's own angel boy."

Julia pinched Peter in the seat as Nat came in from the side porch and everyone settled quickly into his chair.

"Say 'sorry' to Bumpo," Julia whispered to Peter.

"I will later," Peter said, "if I decide I am sorry."

* * *

In the kitchen John asked Rachel to apologize to Cally.

"This is their last dinner with us for a while," John said. "All of our nerves are on edge." And Rachel went upstairs reluctantly, intending a formal apology, but when she saw Cally lying on the bed in Peter's room with her arm over her head, her body below the shoulders like the body of a young girl, her face in repose like a child's, Rachel knelt down beside her and put her arms around her.

"We can't be this way with each other," she said.

Cally stiffened, but she did not pull back.

"I'm so sorry," Rachel said. "I'm going to make tons of vanilla junket. There won't be room in the icebox for anything else."

In the mornings Nat worked in his bedroom at a desk overlooking the walled garden behind the house which had a certain charm even in winter, full of holly and fruit trees whose branches curved with the elegance of Oriental line drawings. The winter of 1954 he was writing a series of articles for the *News Leader* on Senator Joe McCarthy and the upcoming hearings, but he worked at home, researching primarily on the telephone, still too weak to get about without tiring. Cally sat on the bed while he wrote, mending or writing letters or reading or simply looking out the window, because he wanted her there.

"I ought to feel better," he said to her one morning after the children were at school.

"You will," Cally said. "In the spring," she added, as if she knew. Often she'd rub his neck and shoulders, run her fingers lightly across his face until he fell asleep in the afternoon.

"I sleep too much," he said. "I haven't slept in the afternoon since the hospital."

Julia got the main part, the part of Abigail Williams, in the Friends School production of *The Crucible*. In the afternoons she practiced screaming for the witch trial scene in the mirror over her dresser.

"Did you hear me?" she asked Cally at supper.

"Hear you?" Peter said. "The neighbors probably think we're trying to kill you, which is a thought."

"I can see the devil in his eyes," Julia said, pointing at Peter, her eyes widening in horror. "Watch out." She covered her face.

"Do you really drink blood in the play?" Caleb asked.

"Half and half," Julia said, her eyes shining. "Half blood and half water. Peter's volunteered his blood as a prop."

Bumpo left the table. "I'm going to be sick," he said.

"I'm sorry, Bumpo," Julia said. "I'll stop. It's just made up."

"It's too late," Bumpo said, taking his plate to the kitchen and going up the back stairs to his room.

"Ever since you got to be Abigail," Caleb said, "you turned mean. It's worse than with those actors at Bam's this summer. You go around the house like this"—he widened his eyes so they started out of his head—"and this"—he narrowed his eyes to slits.

"Julia," Cally said later, "I don't want you to practice screaming at home any longer."

"Yeah," Peter said. "Daddy had such a headache he couldn't eat."

"Is that right?" Julia asked her mother.

"It's taking him a long time to get over the operation," Cally said.

The light was off in her parents' bedroom when Julia knocked. "Daddy?"

"Come in, Jules," Nat said. He sat up and turned on the light.

"I'm sorry. Mama told me about the screaming."

"I think you have that part of the play down cold."

She sat at the end of his bed. "You don't ever feel well, do you?"

"I don't tonight," Nat said.

"Not last night, either, or all week or even since Christmas."

"Mother says by spring I'll be fine. It's the winter doldrums."

Later that night, while Julia was practicing expressions of evil in the mirror, Nat came in.

"Lo and behold," he said, smiling. "My own sweet witch."

She turned around, holding the wild expression she'd been practicing in her eyes.

"Don't scream," he pleaded.

He had come for something. She could tell. He sat down in her armchair across from her and didn't talk at first. Perhaps he had forgotten what he had come for or was waiting for the right moment to make the conversation he had intended appropriate.

"You're so weird tonight," Julia said, uncomfortable.

"I was in my room finishing this piece on McCarthy and thinking about you, Jules."

"Thinking what?" she asked with caution, sensing, as she did occasionally with Bumpo, whose cells had no outer layer, a profusion of feeling in her father, an overwhelming sweetness, like lilacs in the light May wind. She was afraid of missing this moment, but its promise of intimacy was too much for her, and above all, she wanted the safety of distance.

"Would you like to see me do Abigail?" she asked casually. "From the beginning. Reverend Parris is kneeling over Betty. I am his niece, seventeen, an orphan, and I enter. 'Uncle!' You," Julia said to her father, "are Reverend Parris, my uncle. Look at me. 'Susanna Wallcott's here from Dr. Griggs.' " Julia leaned out the door to her bedroom. " 'Come in, Susanna,' " she called.

"Oh, Christ," Peter said from his room. "Will you stop it? I'm trying to finish my math."

Julia shut the door.

"Do you want the script?" she asked Nat.

"I'd rather you'd play Julia for a moment," he said. "Come here."

Julia walked over to her father, self-conscious, expecting trouble. She sat down, but he didn't speak to her, just looked at her, took her hand in his. "They're long like Cally's," he said, measuring her fingers. "I don't think I've actually looked at your hands since you were little."

"They're veiny," she said, pulling away.

"I was sitting at my desk," he said, "thinking about you and the treasure you have been in my life."

It was too personal.

" 'The wings!' " Julia said, standing automatically, looking at the ceiling above her. " 'Mary, please don't, don't—' " and then she was Julia again, not Abigail, and she looked at her father.

"I can't help it, Daddy," she said to him honestly. "It's too much when you're sweet to me."

"Well," Nat said, standing slowly, "tonight, in my prayers, I'll make a special request for mean and terrible men in your life. As you wish it, my love."

"You know what I mean?"

"I know the only difficult role for you to play, Julia, is the one you were born to."

"Daddy is furious at me," she said, flopping down on Peter's bed. She didn't come often into Peter's room. It smelled bad, full of old socks under the bed and medicine for skin problems, stale food filched from the kitchen and forgotten, but Peter, at twelve, was the only one of her brothers old enough to understand troubles without a young child's fear that any trouble has volcanic proportions.

"You are the light of Daddy's life," Peter said. "His jewel. His radiant sapphire."

"Be serious," Julia said. "I'm being serious."

"Why is he furious?"

"Because I can't stand love. I just can't stand it."

"Terrific, Julia. You can look forward to a wonderful love-free life."

"I hate you, Peter," she said, turning on her back. "You have the brain of a pygmy squirrel." But she didn't leave. She lay on her back with her eyes closed. "Why don't you ever put your socks in the laundry?" she asked.

"Listen, loveless Amanda, you don't have to lie in here smelling my socks. You're not tied to the bed. You can perfectly easily get up, go in your own room and look at yourself in the mirror until morning."

Julia didn't move. She didn't even open her eyes.

"Do you know what I mean about too much love?" she asked.

"I don't suffer from that particular problem," Peter said.

"No one loves you, right?"

Peter got up, turned on his radio to the top forty.

"Sure," he said. "Sure. Everyone does. I mean, even poor Natty Bumpo, however mean I've been to him. And you, dummy that you are. But nobody loves me like Daddy loves you."

"That's what I mean," Julia said. "It's scary."

Peter shrugged. "On the whole," he said, "I'm more scared of murderers."

"You think it's upsetting, too, Peter. I can tell."

"You know what I think?"

"What?"

"I think Daddy's sick."

"Of course he's sick. We all know that. But he's getting better."

"I think he's really sick," Peter said.

"I suppose you got that reading your stupid medical almanacs. If you had your way, Peter Howells, the whole family would be dying of something interesting like beri-beri or acute flamingo." She got up. "Remind me to get in touch with you again the next time I'm in real trouble."

That night Julia slept with Caleb in the top bunk over Bumpo's bed.

"I didn't hear you come in," Caleb said in the morning.

"I came in late," Julia said. "Don't tell anyone."

"How come?" Bumpo asked from the bottom bunk.

"Because they'll think I'm having nightmares if I have to sleep with my eight-year-old brother," Julia said.

"Or that you're lonely," Bumpo said. "I get lonely when Caleb sleeps over at someone's house."

When John and Rachel came to Washington for a winter holiday the January following Nat's surgery, Rachel brought a white cyclamen which she had started years before from a cutting of a plant in Hannah's greenhouse. Three white blooms just beginning to open were standing like brave soldiers in the middle of a circle of dark green leaves, veined black. Underneath the leaves, invisible at a distance, was a multitude of new buds, which should, Rachel said, if properly cared for, and kept in the south window, rise to full bloom and survive the winter.

During this visit John showed Julia the house where he had lived on Twenty-eighth Street, between P and O, a Victorian bay front, painted yellow. "Same as it was," John said, and the woman sweeping the light snow from the brick sidewalk in front was the same woman who had, as a young bride, purchased the house from Senator Daniel Howells, who had not wanted to return to the house where Hannah had died.

That night Julia asked her father about Hannah's death in the house in Georgetown.

"Hannah killed herself," Nat said.

"There's more to it than that, Nat," Cally said. "Rachel has told me that whatever happened when Hannah died, your father wouldn't talk about it."

"Your grandfather found his mother dead," Rachel said to Julia when she brought it up.

"Mama says you think there's more to it."

"No one in the family will talk about Hannah's death. It was something worse than suicide," she said. "Daniel put it out of his mind that she killed herself at all. He simply remembered an untimely death, and your grandfather told me once that he didn't want to talk about it because he was the one who found her."

"How did she kill herself?" Julia asked.

"She shot herself in the brain," Rachel said. "John has told me that."

Peter looked up information about gunshot wounds to the brain in the medical almanac.

"Maybe she was murdered by a robber," Caleb said. "She could've been sitting in bed with the flu and reading the paper when the robber crept in the kitchen window, you see."

"Stop it, Cale," Bumpo said.

"Wait a minute, let me finish. And then he crept up the kitchen stairs and down the hall on tiptoe, planning to steal Hannah's jewelry, when, surprise of surprises, there sits Hannah in bed with her nightgown on and the robber gets scared and shoots her in the head."

"He'd probably have raped her first," Peter said with confidence.

"Shh," Julia said. "Bumpo and Caleb don't know about rape."

"I do," Caleb said. "I know every bit about it from Susie Stone."

"I don't want to know about it," Bumpo said.

Julia asked her grandfather about Hannah and he told her the story of his discovery of his dead mother which he had not told his family.

"Do you think she killed herself because she wanted to be an actress?"

"I doubt it was as simple as that. We all hide something of ourselves which doesn't seem to suit the order of our lives."

"Do you think she was crazy?"

"Probably—at the time."

"She must have been very unhappy."

"I suppose she was, but she never let anyone know that."

"You're losing weight," Nat told Julia once in late February in the middle of rehearsals. "Don't work too hard."

"But I love it," Julia said.

"I know you love it, Jules," Nat said. "It's just not worth making yourself sick." But he understood that Julia was losing herself in work—even her grades had been outstanding this year—as a protection against the change in him which he had begun to acknowledge silently.

"You're losing weight, too," Julia said to him that same evening.

"In sympathy, Jules," he said, "so no one will mistake us as unrelated."

By the second week of rehearsals Julia had begun to feel Abigail

Williams in herself. After rehearsals she'd walk home as Abigail, a contemporary conniver, bargaining for control, and it thrilled and frightened her at the same time that she could find within her familiar self a young woman competent in destruction.

"I sure will be glad when this play is over," Bumpo said to her.

"I won't eat supper one more time with Julia," Caleb said to his father, "because she keeps doing that eye thing with me."

"Why don't you be a veterinarian, Julia?" Peter suggested. "It's a bloody but responsible job."

"I saw you conjuring in your bedroom last night," Julia said to him, pointing a slender finger at his eyes.

"That's what you think I was doing," Peter said, giving Julia a knowing look, "but in fact, I was doing something altogether different which you wouldn't know about because you are a GIRL."

In the last weeks the director took Julia aside and told her to be conscious of not taking too much space on stage.

"You are so much better than an ordinary high school actress that by simply being good, you will seem to overplay the part."

And Julia worked hard to take that cautionary suggestion.

In early February, after her grandparents had left Washington for Bucks County, Julia received a letter about *The Crucible* from her grandfather. It was the first letter she had ever received from him, and it was almost as unsettling in content as was the only other letter he wrote to her, but that was much later, when she was a grown woman.

February 14, 1954

Dear Julia,

I understand you have the role of the villain in *The Crucible* at Friends School. I'm pleased you have a leading role, for certainly you'd choose to have a leading role, and, secretly, I'm happy to learn you are a villain, believing, falsely perhaps, that you can play out the villain in you onstage, leaving for our lives together only the Julia who is pure at heart.

Primarily I'm glad you might be an actress—in spite of the fact that your father has told me he wants you to go to college now that your grades are so much better, to have a responsible career, to get married, of course, have babies—though he hasn't got the whole thing planned for you. But you have a heritage of secret actresses in your family—just look at Bam, for one—and I hope very much if you want in your heart of hearts to be an actress, you will be one.

This is a very long letter for a man in advertising, trained for one-liners, and so I will close with love and a promise that Bam and I will be in the front row opening night.

Love, G.

All of the Howells were in the front row opening night and so was Harold Markus, only Julia didn't know it at the time, and even if she had, the name Harold Markus would not have interested her. But after the first curtain Mary Warren told the cast that her uncle Hal had come from New York to see the production and was in the front row, so at the second curtain Julia took particular note of the slender black-haired man, sitting at the end of a row, his legs crossed like a woman's. He was, she thought, odd-looking.

The performance was good, not splendid, but for a school performance it was good and the director was pleased, claiming extreme success in the high excitement just after the final curtain on the first night.

But Julia had been splendid and she knew it, being hugged by the other members of the cast backstage. "Wonderful," "Wonderful," "You were terrific." In this performance at least she had been distinguished.

"You're so quiet," Mary Warren said to Julia, sitting beside her in the dressing room. "You're not upset, are you?"

"Nope," Julia said, leaning her head against the wall. "Just tired."

"You were really great," Tituba said. "Mrs. Ames says you're the only pro."

Julia smiled.

"What's the matter, Julia?" Elizabeth Proctor said, putting her head on Julia's shoulder. "You seem depressed."

"It's not that at all," Julia said.

Julia had worked hard, not surprising in itself because she always worked hard.

"You would've been a knockout Puritan wife," Peter said. "Vork vork vork vork vork."

"If she didn't do something with the energy God gave her," Nat said, "she'd drive us all crazy."

"It's 'cause she was born in an iron lung," Bumpo said.

"Sure, Bumpo," Peter said.

"That's what Mama says."

"God didn't give her too much energy," Caleb said. "She evolved like that from an ape."

She wasn't depressed as she leaned her head against the wall in the dressing room after the first night, but she was stunned by the realization that through hard work and concentration a kind of magic was possible. Sitting in the dressing room, she was Julia Howells again, but for two hours she had been Abigail, flesh and bone. That was the kind of miracle she had played with before in her years as Lucy Tanner and others, but she had never believed in it absolutely until now.

"I want you to meet my uncle," Mary Warren said. "Remember I told you about Hal Markus?"

"He's a director in New York. You could be famous," Elizabeth said.

Julia did meet Harold Markus at the front door of the theater, just as she was leaving with her family.

"Abigail," he called to her, and he was alone. No one introduced them. "Don't leave so quickly." He took her by the shoulders, holding her firmly, looking at her in the eyes. "Julia. I know your name is Julia because I read it on the program."

"Julia Howells," she said automatically.

"Julia Howells," he said. He kissed her on the cheek with ceremony. Close up, he was like a fast spinning disk whose shape was lost in movement, still an odd-looking man with eyes that pierced the surface of her skin, right into the center of her stomach.

"You are very good," he said.

"Thank you," Julia said. "I'm very glad you thought so."

"I am particularly impressed by your presence onstage," he said.

"Thank you," Julia said, uncomfortable with this insistent man, wanting to leave because the conversation was awkward, yet knowing at the same time that she would replay these moments with him, remember his face that night when she went to bed. What he seemed to say behind the formal gestures of a man who knew how he looked from a distance translated in Julia's mind as "You are mine, you are mine, you are mine."

In the car Julia wept.

"What's the matter, for Chrissake?" Peter asked.

"I don't know," Julia said.

"It's good you want to be an actress," Peter said, "you'll have plenty of chances to cry."

Bumpo took her hand.

"It's the excitement," Cally said.

"Or that awful young man," Rachel said.

"Harold Markus?" Julia asked. "Did you think he was terrible, Bam?"

"Of course he wasn't, Bammy," Nat said. "He's Jewish. You've always said that about Jewish men."

"I don't like arguments," Bumpo announced. "How many times do I have to tell you that I hate arguments?"

Rachel came into the bedroom after Julia's light was out and sat down on her bed.

"Sleeping?" she asked, putting her hand next to Julia's cheek.

"Nope."

"Too excited?"

"I guess," Julia said.

"I shouldn't have said what I did about Mr. Markus," Rachel said.

"It's all right," Julia said. "Did you think he was terrible?"

"He seemed too interested in you, like he could eat you up."

"He thought I was good, Bammy."

"You were good, lamb."

"I'll never even see him again," Julia said, kissing her grandmother's hand. "Don't worry."

"He's about forty," Peter said when Hal Markus called the next day.

"He's thirty," Julia said. She decided to wear her hair up. With her hair up and no lipstick, only mascara she'd taken from the makeup room, she looked older.

"You look a little like Frankenstein," Peter said, "except for the nose."

"Good, Peter," Julia said. "That's exactly the look I'm trying for."

Hal Markus had asked her to lunch.

"I'll never see him again but once," Rachel said, reminding Julia of their last night's conversation. But she helped her dress, selecting a suit, a simple blue one with a tie blouse and three-quarter-inch heels.

"Some rouge," Rachel said, using her own. "Otherwise, you'll look tubercular and you'll hardly be worth his time if you're dying soon."

"I thought that was the image you wanted me to have, Bam. Early death."

"No, lamb, that's much too appealing to men of his type—the early death look."

"You shouldn't worry, Bam," Nat said after Hal Markus had picked up Julia for lunch in Georgetown. "He's more high-strung than Julia. They'll destroy each other before dessert."

"I don't like him," Rachel said.

"Fortunately, darling, he hasn't asked you out for the afternoon," John said.

At first, Julia didn't talk in the restaurant. She sat across from him and their legs touched. He ordered wine and she was light-headed after one glass. She couldn't eat and scattered her food around the plate to appear to be eating. He told her funny stories about the theater. He asked her everything about herself, about her brothers and her parents and her friends and her work, and she ended by telling him that when she was growing up, she had played Lucy Tanner with her doll in her bedroom. He thought it was a wonderful story.

He touched her cheek with his fingers. "You have a distinctive face," he said.

"Is that good or bad for the stage?" she asked.

"For you, it will be good." He examined her face with his hands. He examined her hands. "It's a memorable face," he said.

No one had been that direct with her before, and when he touched her face, she felt his hands everywhere and she forced herself to look at his eyes, which were a soft green.

He wanted to try her for a new play he was doing in the fall he told her, a minor role, the role of a daughter, but she would be playing with Judith Anderson. Julia said she was going to Radcliffe in September, if she got in, that she had promised her father she would go to college, that it meant a great deal to him. Hal Marcus didn't press.

"If you ever want to come to New York," he said, leaving her at the front steps of her house on N Street, "just get in touch with me." He wrote down his number and address and she put it in her coat pocket. "It would give me great pleasure to show you something about New York theater." He took her hand in both of his and kissed her fingers. She would remember that moment always, after other men and marriage and children, after a life of astonishing fortune and success as well as reversals.

"I trust you'll make it to school in time for the second performance," Nat said to Julia at four, when she was still sitting in the wing chair by the window facing N Street where she had collapsed after lunch.

"It's enough to make me sick," Peter said.

"It makes me unbearably sad to see a woman fall in love. It seems to me it can't be done without giving yourself away like an outgrown coat, at least the first time," Rachel said. "It makes me especially sad with Julia." Rachel was fearful for Julia because she recognized these passions in herself and because Julia, like Nat, had been so much loved she would not suspect that there could be dangers in falling in love.

"He's gone away forever and ever, Bam," Julia said, "and I'm going to college in the fall like every other privileged girl my age."

Nat and Cally stayed up late every night in the spring and early summer—in the spring because, as Cally said in her soft southern voice, "You've been injected with daffodils." He had found a mysterious source of energy which lasted until late June. They lay in bed and talked and talked into the night, sometimes until dawn. It was as if they had just met and fallen in love and wanted to unfold their lives to each other. They lay together open in spirit, bravely open like petals before the autumn.

They laughed without bitterness at their diminished forms. "War veterans," Nat said. And often in the spring Nat kissed her in a place she'd never allowed him before, never imagined before, it seemed too personal, but he lay with his head between her thighs and buried his lips in the stiff brush, kissing her with his tongue until she came, always to her astonishment. For years, because of her Catholic inhibitions at first, and then because of polio, that sweet release had been Nat's and not hers, so in that spring, just thirty-five, Cally knew the secrets of her body for the first time. It gave Nat a sense of life he didn't have in daylight to feel his wife come against his lips, to fall asleep with his head on her thighs.

In mid-July, after a holiday by the ocean, Julia woke up one night to find Nat sitting in a small chintz-covered chair near the open window in her room.

"I couldn't sleep," he said. "I didn't want to wake your mother."

"It's so hot," Julia said. "That must be it."

"It is hot," Nat said. "Ninety, at least."

"Do you want a fan?"

"We have a fan."

Julia sat up in bed, propping her pillow behind her back. The lights were off in her room and she could see her father only by the streetlight on N Street. He seemed very small, sitting in the chair across from her in the dark.

"Something is the matter with me, Julia," he said.

"What's the matter?" Julia asked.

"I don't know," he said, "I couldn't sleep. I haven't been able to sleep since we went to the ocean. I'm losing weight and every time I see the goddamned doctor he says he simply doesn't know and makes an appointment for the next week, hoping I'll be better."

"Let's go back to Bam. You know the doctors there," Julia said, sitting on the edge of the bed.

"No," Nat said. "I can't bear to be around Bam. She'll kill me with her splendid care."

"We'll get a new doctor here then."

"No," Nat said. "I don't think it will do a bit of good because I think I'm dying."

He wanted to say that his body had been slipping away from him for weeks, since late June, a sense of falling, of his cells closing down in groups and leaving whole areas isolated and out of touch.

"Oh, Daddy," Julia said quietly. For a moment he thought he could move the conversation in reverse, say, "Silly of me to think such thoughts," or, "Your neurotic father is becoming middle-aged," but it was too late to make retractions and he knew it by the stricken look on Julia's face, by the knowledge that he had told the truth.

The next morning Nat was in Julia's room when she woke. He looked well. His face, although thin, had color and his hair was scarcely lined with gray.

"Julia," he said, sitting down beside her on the bed, "I don't want you to tell the boys, but especially I don't want you to tell Mother what I said to you last night."

"What do you think is the matter with you?" Julia asked.

"I expect I have cancer," he said.

"Mother will have to know."

"Sometime. I'll tell her."

Julia was doing carpentry with the Arena stage crew for the summer, but she didn't go to work that day. Instead, she walked through Georgetown and up the hill to Cleveland Park, through the Bishop's Garden and down Woodley to Connecticut, downtown to Pennsylvania Avenue, past the White House. People in courtesy looked the other way when they saw her coming because she was crying softly. She cried all day in the hot July sun, lying in Montrose Park in late afternoon, rehearsing in her mind the next scenes as she would play them, Nat dying, her brothers and mother sitting around his bed in vigilance as he got weaker and weaker, her father dead and the train home to Philadelphia, her grandfather at the station and Bam, poor old Bam, eating the contents of the refrigerator as though she were hungry. Then the funeral at the Friends Meeting with that terrible silence, the burial with the children as close to each other as possible for support.

When she got home that evening, she found Bumpo carving a small totem pole in the backyard out of a stick. She sat down next to him and wrapped her arms around his legs.

"You've been crying," he said. "I didn't think you ever cried. What's the matter? Did someone die?"

"Nope. Nothing's the matter. Nobody died, dummy."

"You aren't telling the truth 'cause your eyes are red," Bumpo said nervously, depending, as everyone did, on Julia for the truthful response to every situation.

"I am."

"You had a bad day."

"Yup."

"I have lots of bad days," Bumpo said. "Wouldn't Peter be surprised to know that you were crying and not me?"

"Thrilled," Julia said.

That night Bumpo was sick.

"Stomach flu," Cally diagnosed. "Poor Bumpo. We'll probably all get it now."

But Julia knew it wasn't stomach flu. Nat's dying was in the air, flapping like birds in their hurry south. Everyone sensed the Howells' lives were out of key, but they lived for the rest of July and into August, pretending stomach flu, which was short-term, jolly with each other at the supper table, measuring out the last weeks without acknowledging that measuring was necessary. At night Nat and Cally lay beside each other and didn't talk. In the morning Nat wrote, although he slept more and more sitting up at his desk. On Wednesday, August 25, Nat fell when he got out of bed.

"Stay in bed for the day until you feel stronger," the doctor said when he made a house call before noon.

"Poor jackass," Nat said when the doctor had left. He didn't want to eat, but Cally brought him juices and sat with him. She knew what to expect.

That night, while Nat was sleeping, Cally told the children.

Peter lost his temper. "Everybody in this family is so extreme," he said. "He's tired, for Chrissake, not dying," and just as he was leaving by the back door to see his friend who lived at the end of the alley, he added, "He almost got burned up, remember? He's going to be tired from time to time."

"Can't we do something?" Caleb asked when Peter had left.

"We can sit with him," Cally said.

"That's all?" Caleb asked.

"That's all," Cally said.

"Why didn't you tell us before?" Caleb wanted to know.

"There was no point," Cally said. "We needed to live normally."

"I knew," Julia said.

"You did?" Cally looked at her.

Julia nodded.

"How?" Cally asked.

"Daddy told me," Julia said. "Only in July, after our vacation. He guessed. He didn't know for sure."

Cally wheeled her chair to the steps, locked her braces and got up. She took her crutches and dragged herself upstairs. She undressed in the dark, sat on the side of the bed, took off her braces, put them under the bed and lay down next to Nat.

Nat was not breathing easily.

"Do you want to be propped up?" she asked him.

He turned to face her. He was smiling.

"Nathaniel," she whispered, taking his hand in both of hers.

His eyes were clouded with the kind of silk film that presages death, but they seemed to look at her directly. "Cally," he said to her thickly, "no goddamned requiems."

"I love you," she said and fell asleep holding his hand.

In the morning he was unconscious. The children sat with Cally in the bedroom. At five in the afternoon, Julia noted it on the clock, she got up from her chair beside her father's bed and left the room. Peter was standing by the bathroom door when she came out.

"He's dead," she said.

* * *

On Sunday they took the train to Philadelphia with Nathaniel in the baggage car. Rachel and John met them at the station and drove them home to Bucks County. Nat was buried on August 30, a Tuesday, just after noon, and there was a luncheon afterwards at the Main House for all the family and friends, people from Washington, distant relations.

Julia found her grandfather sitting in the library writing after lunch. She leaned on the back of his chair and read over his shoulder.

"What do you mean by a miracle?" she asked, reading the first paragraph.

"Your lives together this last year," John said.

"I wish there had been a real miracle," Julia said.

"There was," John said. But Julia wouldn't understand that miracle for a long time.

UNDER
THE DIRECTION OF...

JULIA LEFT THIS MORNING FOR RADCLIFFE COLLEGE. I PUT HER
ON THE TRAIN IN NEW YORK FOR BOSTON AT NINE A.M. AND
DIDN'T LINGER THERE TO WATCH THE TRAIN PULL OUT. I DIDN'T
ALLOW MYSELF THE LUXURY OF THAT MOMENT BECAUSE I'M
TOO OLD AND CAREFUL NOW TO WALK THROUGH PENN STATION
AND OUT ONTO THIRTY-FOURTH STREET WEEPING SENTIMENTAL
TEARS.

That entry in the Bible was made in September 1954, less than a
month after Nat's death and there were no more entries of any kind
for a year and a half.

"Because of Julia," John said simply when Rachel asked him one
evening why the Bible had been away for months, gathering dust
on the shelves with the polished skulls from Dr. Thomas Howells'
collection. It was the spring that should have marked Julia's sophomore year in college.

Julia had lasted three months at Radcliffe before she had gone
to New York to become an actress. She seldom wrote and didn't
ever come home for holidays. Although the Howells called her frequently in the apartment where she lived in New York, their conversations were unsatisfactory. She told them very little about
herself and seemed to have lost interest in them.

"Did you hear from Julia?" Rachel would ask Cally after she
saw the postman's truck leave the glass shoebox and turn left towards Solebury.

"No, not today," Cally said again and again. Finally, she promised
that she would call Rachel first thing if she did hear.

"Do something. Make Julia come home for a week at least," Rachel
said to John one night, lying in a bed which had not been made
all day, the night-light on, the *Times* scattered on the comforter.
They had not made love for months. Not since Nat, she thought,

but she didn't bring it up. She had stopped running her fingers lightly over John's face, across his back and shoulders when they lay together because he had snapped, "Don't, Bam. You're putting pressure on me."

"What can I do?" John asked, kicking the newspaper off the bed.

"I don't know," Rachel replied. "But always before, you've been able to think of something."

"There's nothing to do but wait," John said. He turned off the light, rolled on his side away from her. "It would help if you made the beds in the morning like you used to and we ate in the dining room like civilized people to give ourselves the semblance of being alive."

"Oh, shut up," Rachel said, but the bed on her side was cold, so she lay beside John, against his back, her knees fitting into the tunnel made by the bend in his.

"We have decided to pretend that Julia is dead," Bumpo announced to his grandfather one Sunday evening at supper, "or do you think it would be better if we pretended she'd gone to Africa on a long trip?"

"I certainly prefer the latter," John said.

"Otherwise," Bumpo said, "waiting for her to come back is driving me crazy."

"We're studying witches in Salem," Caleb said to Rachel, "And I think maybe Julia's possessed."

"With what?" Rachel asked.

"With the devil, of course," Caleb said. "Otherwise, why would she be acting this way?"

By the end of the first week at Radcliffe Julia knew she was not going to last in college. It was simply a question of when she would leave and under what circumstances. She lost weight. She could not sleep. She bought the texts and a spiral notebook for each course and went to classes, but she never took any notes or read her assignments.

"I have a good aural memory," she told her roommate.

In October she tried out for the part of Emily in *Our Town*.

She was the only freshman to try out and she won the part easily.

The boy who played the role of George Gibbs, who marries Emily, walked her home from rehearsals every night and she let him kiss her under the bright yellow light in the archway of the dorm. But when he put his hand inside her camel's hair coat and touched her breast, she pulled back and shook her head, saying as kindly as she could, because certainly George Gibbs was not responsible for the way she felt, that she simply didn't want anyone to touch her.

After that George Gibbs walked her home at night with the girl who played Mrs. Gibbs and Julia assumed he kissed Mrs. Gibbs good-night when they got to her dorm two blocks south.

For a while she called home on Sundays and then she called every other Sunday and then she stopped calling. They called her. Usually Rachel with the boys. Seldom her mother. Everyone wrote letters to her except John and she read some of them and kept them all. She read Peter's and Caleb's, but she didn't read Bumpo's or her mother's and only some of Rachel's, depending on the thickness. If the letter was thin, she could count on its being news and not sentimental and then she read it. It was not that she didn't think about them. She thought about them all the time, each of them, dreamed about them and tried, whenever her mind slid in that direction, not to imagine herself as a child again at the Howells farm with her father in work pants and her mother in his shirts tied in a knot at the waist.

Julia had difficulty with *Our Town* from the beginning. She thought at first it had to do with the character of Emily, a good girl, hardworking, a little smug and condescending. She was not a girl that Julia could have been. Or at least that's the way she saw it.

"You are resisting the character of Emily," the director said impatiently early in the rehearsals.

"You know what he means?" George Gibbs asked one night on the way home. "You gotta walk like Emily," George Gibbs said. "Think like her. Talk to your friends as though you're Emily and pretty soon, bango. I mean, people are beginning to think I'm a first-class dunce since I began to play poor old George Gibbs. My friends are wondering whether I've developed a brain blockage."

"I'll try," Julia said.

They had been understanding. Even the director took her aside after he had lost his temper and said that she had been his choice for Emily and he didn't intend to give up no matter what.

Julia left the play on a Friday evening nine days before the opening. They were doing the last scene in the third act after Emily has died in childbirth and has requested one last visit back to the living and chooses her twelfth birthday at home with her family.

"I feel sick," Julia said to George Gibbs backstage at the beginning of rehearsal.

"Like throwing up?" he asked.

"Worse," Julia said. The revolution in her body was unfamiliar, a tidal wave, as if she were struggling underwater to surface.

At the beginning of the rehearsal her lines spun off automatically, but halfway through the final scene, Mrs. Webb, Emily's mother, has spoken and Emily is supposed to say, "I can't bear it. They're so young and beautiful. Why did they ever have to get old?"

Julia turned to the theater as she'd been blocked to do, her arms outstretched, but the tape in her mind which had recorded her lines snapped, split and was slapping aimlessly against the inside of her skull.

" 'I can't bear it,' " the director said, cueing her from a seat in the front row of the theater.

"I can't do this play," Julia said.

She walked to the steps at the front of the stage.

"Get back in your place, Julia," the director said, choosing deliberately the absolute approach. "What do you mean you can't do this play?" he shouted.

"I can't bear it."

"Those are your lines," he said. "Now, for Chrissake, get back up there and say them."

"I can't," Julia said and walked down the steps, up the aisle and out the door of the theater. When the director found her in the dressing room, she was putting on her parka.

"Didn't your parents ever read you the story of 'The Little Engine Who Could'?" he asked. "Jesus Christ. This is the last time I'll cast an infant in a major role."

Julia said, "I feel terrible about this." And the director must have sensed that she was telling the truth because he didn't say anything more.

Julia called Peter from a restaurant in Harvard Square. Since her father had died and she had moved to Cambridge, Peter was the only member of her family she could talk to easily without betraying herself, without weeping, and she knew that at nine-thirty on a Friday night Peter would answer the telephone because he'd be the only one up.

"I'm going to New York for the weekend," she said to Peter. "With a friend named Jill," she added, lying easily. "We're going to see some plays on Saturday and Sunday night and we're staying at 555-6150. Remember the director who saw me in *The Crucible?*"

"The one Bam hated?"

"That one," she said. "We're staying with him."

"Mama's in bed. Do you want me to get her up?"

"Nope," Julia said. "Just tell her. Is she okay? Is everyone okay?"

"Okay." Peter hesitated. "I mean we've had an all-round better time in other years."

"Peter," she said to detain him, although she had nothing more to say.

"Are you okay, Julia? You sound funny."

"You probably think I sound funny because of my neck. I have a pinched nerve in my neck and it makes my voice shaky."

"Probably," Peter said. "We're all coming to see *Our Town*," Peter said. "Is it good?"

"Okay. I'm not so good in it," she said. "Peter?"

"Yeah?"

"Give everyone my love and stuff."

"Sure, Julia."

"And don't forget to give Mama the number where I'll be."

"Y'know," Peter said, "it's been terrible since you left. Bumpo and Caleb can't even get dressed by themselves any longer."

"Too bad."

"Anyway, I have to get off 'cause Roger's going to pee in the hall if I don't let him out."

"Don't lose the telephone number in New York."

"I gave it to Roger to eat, Julia," Peter said. "He's out of burro food."

Hal Markus wasn't at home when she called. His answering service took her name and said he was at the theater. She went to the bus terminal and purchased a ticket for the 6:00 A.M. bus to New York City. She slept in the bus terminal. She slept all the way to New York. It was the first real sleeping she had done since she left Bucks County. When she arrived at the Port Authority on Saturday afternoon, Hal Markus was not at home again. This time the woman had a message for Julia to call him at the Billy Rose Theater. He wasn't at all surprised to hear from her, as if he'd been expecting her all autumn.

"Come right here," he said. "Do you have money?"

"Of course," she said.

When the taxicab with Julia drove up, he was waiting outside and insisted on paying the driver. He took her bags and parked them with the young boy who was sitting at the entrance to the stage door.

"You have a lot of luggage for a weekend," he said.

"I've left Radcliffe for good, but I don't know how long I'll be staying in New York."

He wasn't surprised about that either. "You look awful," he said matter-of-factly.

"I'm tired," Julia said.

"You must have lost ten pounds."

She followed him backstage, where they were setting up for the evening performance. There were two brown paper bags on the stage manager's desk and Hal took one of them and handed it to Julia.

"Corned beef on rye and hot chocolate," he said.

"I can't eat," she said. He took the sandwich out of the bag, unwrapped it and gave her half.

"Mustard and mayonnaise. Eat it."

"I'll be sick," Julia said.

"You're sick already," he said, taking her across the stage to the other side where the light crew was. "If you want me to take care of you, you're going to have to do what I say."

"I didn't say I wanted you to."

"Yeah, you did." He took her to an empty dressing room, put the sandwich out on the dressing table and sat Julia down in front of the mirror.

"See," he said. "Look at yourself."

She bowed her head.

"Don't you dare throw the sandwich in the toilet," he said. "I'll be back and we'll watch the play from the audience. *Little Foxes.* It's very good."

He shut the door, leaving Julia alone in a Broadway dressing room for the first time. She drank the hot chocolate and flushed the corned beef sandwich down the toilet one half at a time.

Julia had no plans. For a child who had arranged each day as if it were to be performed, this state of mind was unfamiliar. She didn't know whether she would stay in New York or not, whether she would act or go to college, whether she would live with Hal Markus or find a place alone. The first evening she had supper with him and spent the night on a couch in his apartment, too conscious of his presence in the next room to fall asleep. His apartment was full of theater posters, antique couches with worn velvet seats, Oriental rugs faded to obscure designs. He had framed programs of plays he had directed, and one wall was full of pictures of children, the same children at different ages, a boy and a girl.

"My children," he told her when he found her examining them in the morning.

"I didn't know you were married," Julia said.

"I'm not married," he said. He made breakfast, beating eggs for omelets, warming fresh brioche and making very strong coffee. He set a small table which sat in a window eight floors above Central Park.

"You were married," Julia said, sitting down across from him.

"I was married to an actress who lives now in Connecticut with these two children on the wall," he said. He reached across the table and turned Julia's face to the window, examining her profile.

"I am married to my work," he said. "Eat everything." He put a second brioche on her plate. "If you were onstage this afternoon, you'd faint."

"Probably," Julia said, eating everything as he told her. "I guess I've lost weight because my father died this summer," she said suddenly. She had not expected to tell him. She had not told anyone at Radcliffe. In fact, she had never told anyone at all because it hadn't been necessary. Everyone with whom she regularly lived her life knew.

"I'm so sorry," Hal Markus said, and when he looked up at her and saw the expression on her face, the awkward gesture of her hand, his instinct for theater told him the great importance of those lines. "I'm very sorry, Julia," he said and touched the tips of her fingers with his own.

"You've come to New York to be in the theater, of course," he said, cleaning the dishes in the kitchen, talking to her while he washed them, dried them, put them away.

She nodded. She had come to New York to see him because something had passed between them at lunch in Washington after *The Crucible* that remained with her like a promise. She had come to New York because her father had died.

"I may direct a new play," he said. "It's called *Playing for Keeps* with a role for a young girl."

"For me?" Julia asked.

Hal Markus laughed. "The theater isn't that easy, my love," he said.

"I'd be very pleased to work under your direction." She was sitting on the old Edwardian sofa where she had tried to sleep, her legs folded under her, her head against the wooden back. Her hand rested between them and Hal Markus lifted it, held it for a moment and replaced it.

"You're under my direction already," he said and brushed his hand lightly across her face. "Your hair is too long. See." He picked up a piece of hair. "The ends are dry and breaking. Take a shower and wash it so I can cut it."

Julia wore his robe and sat in the window overlooking Central Park West while Hal Markus cut her long hair in a straight pageboy, shoulder length.

"There," he said. "Have you a skirt and sweater? Something simple?"

She nodded.

"Get dressed then," he said. "I've found a place for you on West Seventy-ninth, a few blocks from here with an older actress who is no longer acting and whom I admire. You can be a companion to her, cook, clean, be paid while you wait for parts. She's a little crazy, but so am I and so are you and so is everyone worth knowing at all."

"I thought I was going to stay here," Julia said, alarmed. "I don't even know this woman. I've never lived anywhere except at home and at Radcliffe."

"You can't stay here," Hal Markus said.

"Why not?" Julia asked. "Maybe I could stay with my grandfather then. He has an apartment in town and stays there sometimes during the week."

"Suit yourself," Hal Markus said, shrugging his shoulders.

"Why can't I stay here?" she insisted, surprised at her forwardness and confused by her response to this man.

"Because I like to live alone," he said. "It would be complicated if I cast you in a play I'm doing and moved you into my living room at the same time. You are a girl."

"Almost nineteen."

"Inexperienced," he said.

"What do you mean?"

"Get dressed," he said. And she did, in a sweater and skirt as he had suggested.

She wrote home Sunday afternoon, sitting in a restaurant on

Forty-fifth Street, waiting for Hal Markus to meet her. She wrote her grandfather because he had been the one to pay her bills at Radcliffe.

Dear Grandfather,

I am in New York right this minute at Bralove's on West 45th, waiting for the director you met in Washington to take me to the theater. He thinks he may try me out for a new play he's doing called *Playing for Keeps*. In fact, he's quite confident I'll get the part.

I have left Radcliffe. I dropped out of *Our Town*. If you will look at p. 46 of the paperback version of Thornton Wilder's collected plays, halfway down the page where Emily speaks to her mother, you, above all people I love, will know why I left Radcliffe because it didn't make sense to stay there. I will repay you at the end of this year when I make some money.

I have moved in with a very responsible older woman who used to be an actress, but she's very responsible, nevertheless. Honestly. My address is 140 West 79th, Apartment E. I hope you will visit.

My plan is to work hard this year and determine whether this is work I can and want to do. I will let you know everything I'm doing and promise you I'll take VERY good care of myself.

I love and miss you all.

Love and kisses,
Julia

p.s. Do you think I should take the name Lucy Tanner as a stage name or keep Howells to immortalize Daddy? What do you think of the name Julia?

Rachel read the letter several times, sitting in the library with John in early December.

"Are you trying to commit it to memory?" John asked crossly. She didn't reply.

"May I have it?" he said.

"I'm reading between the lines," Rachel said.

"Of course," John said. "I should have realized that, for Chrissake." He got up from his chair and went to the window to look north towards Daniel's house, in which the Cares still lived. Mr. Care was working under his car, which, along with two other cars, was up on cinder blocks.

"Bam," he said, "I thought we had agreed that the Cares would leave before Mr. Care turns the entire farm into a mechanic's paradise."

"You mentioned that, darling," Rachel said, "but we didn't agree."

"Well, I'm mentioning it again," he said.

"We need the money," Rachel said. "You can't support a place this size with empty houses."

"I can support it now that Julia's dropped out of college."

Rachel got up and sat beside him in the window seat. "It's Julia you're upset about, lamb, not the Cares."

"Of course," John said. "The Cares can rot in hell. My interest in them is best expressed by my desire for their immediate disappearance."

"Reading between the lines, I think she's all right," Rachel said.

"What did she say between the lines?" John asked.

"That she's better than she was at Radcliffe," Rachel said. "Her letters from Radcliffe were frantic between the lines."

"This is a moronic conversation." John walked across the room, turning off the lights. "We could afford to keep this place as other than a welfare farm if you didn't light it like a Christmas tree every evening."

"Oh, John, you're becoming an old man." Rachel followed him to the kitchen, where he warmed milk on the stove and drank it, sitting on a kitchen stool.

"She may go back," Rachel offered.

"No. She won't go back. She'll probably marry the jackass she went to lunch with in Washington."

"I doubt it," Rachel said. Leaning towards him, she ran her fingers over his lips. "Don't worry over Julia like you did over Nat."

"I don't want you to mention Nat," John said, putting his mug in the sink, going up the back stairs. "I wish you'd lose weight, Bammy, and stop wearing those Indian costumes that make you look like a sacrificial bull."

She took out a cherry pie she had baked that afternoon for Cally's family and cut a large piece. She sat down at the kitchen table, eating it with her fingers. John was sitting on the back stairs, watching her.

"You know, John," she said quietly, looking up at him with warmth and sadness, "I have wanted you for a long time, and you haven't been available."

He went upstairs to their bedroom and she sat in the kitchen,

listening to the familiar sounds of ritualistic years together. He was
in the closet getting his pajamas. He had been sleeping in pajamas
since spring. He was in the bathroom putting up the bedroom window just enough so the cold air blew on Rachel's neck, an argument
they'd had for years, that he had won for years.

When Rachel put away the rest of the pie and went upstairs, the
light in her bedroom was off and John was lying on her side of the
bed.

She opened her closet door and turned on the light. She took out
a gray tweed suit from the years right after George Katz, when she'd
been fat before, but she couldn't pull the skirt down over her bottom. She took out a camel's hair suit with a flared skirt which she
could not button at the waist. Her alligator shoes were tight. If she
wore a sweater which pulled down over the gaping skirtband and
kept the jacket on to conceal the tubes of fat around her back, she
looked handsome. Not lovely as she used to look, but she was still
a large, handsome woman. In the cold of December her feet would
contract and the alligator shoes wouldn't hurt so much.

"What in God's name are you doing?" John asked.

"Trying on clothes," Rachel said.

"At eleven-thirty?"

"At whatever time it is," Rachel said. "I'm going into the city
with you tomorrow morning to see Julia at her new place."

"You said you thought she was fine," John said. "That reading
between the lines, you thought she was better."

"I do." Rachel put her clothes for the next day on the chair.
"But of course I want to see her and the place and this responsible
old actress she's living with."

"You don't think the actress is responsible?"

"I don't know, lamb. I want to see for myself."

"I expect the worst."

"I know you do. You've been expecting the worst since June,"
she said, sitting down beside him on their bed. "Move over."

"I'm sleeping here," he said. "You sleep in my place."

Rachel crawled into the other side of the bed. "Why?" she asked.
"I've been sleeping on this side of the bed for forty years. I won't
be able to sleep."

"I thought if we changed places, it might make a difference."

"To what?"

"It's worth a try."

She turned over, pressing her back next to his, and closed her eyes.

"John," she said after a few minutes, "I can't feel the cold air from the window."

"I thought you hated the cold air," he said. "I thought you wanted me to keep the window closed."

"I thought so, too," she said.

Cally's grief was expressed in silence. The state of mind had come on her like a faint, when the face turns suddenly white and the hands go cold. She didn't speak unless it was necessary in order for things to be accomplished and then she only said briefly but pleasantly, "Tie your shoes, darling," or "Wear a hat," or "Walk home through the fields if it doesn't snow," or "I need eggs and sugar and a gallon of milk for supper." So the boys developed a dinner table conversation to substitute for the long and difficult silences at the table.

"So what did you do today, Caleb?" Peter asked.

"Beat up Dickie Atkins and ate some poisonous paint to prove I wouldn't die and jumped from the top of the jungle gym without breaking my leg."

"Terrific," Peter said. "A better day than yesterday."

"What did you do?" Caleb asked.

"I walked home over the railroad tracks with Mary Myers, who stole three candy bars from Slovers', only I got caught for it, and rode Jimmy Inglefield's horse bareback through the Inglefields' woods and I cheated in math class."

Bumpo could not be part of these conversations, which were intended to shake Cally out of silence, because he could not imagine lying the way his brothers did. But the conversations seemed to pass like smoke over Cally's head and only occasionally did she respond to the boys by saying it would be helpful to her if they did their very best in school this year. They all promised that they would and did.

Cally went about her daily life with written instructions. Every night she made a list and followed it exactly the next day, checking off the items, one by one. "Take out the trash, make the beds, bring in the milk, call the vet on Roger's eyes, call the pediatrician on Caleb's sore throat, market for supper, ask John and Bam to Sunday dinner, sew Bumpo's trousers, wash hair and cut, write a card to Julia." She wanted the time to pass as she had wanted it to pass when she was a child, but then she had wanted to be one year older, to see what changes one year would make in her face in the mirror.

Now she wanted the days to pass to be rid of them. October gone and then November—into December, a matter of days until the end of 1954. Another year and a new calendar.

It made her sick to think of Nat, so she put him out of mind. She knew she was quiet. She knew that it worried the boys, that it made Rachel crazy and that John, whose own temper filled every family occasion, blessed her silent grieving because it did not impose on his own.

Rachel met Julia for lunch on Thursday morning in early December, almost a week after Julia had left Radcliffe. Julia was waiting outside the apartment entrance when Rachel's cab pulled up.

"You're too thin," Rachel said, holding Julia in her arms.

"But I'm eating," Julia said. "I had two eggs and a piece of toast and chocolate for breakfast."

Rachel took Julia's face in her hands. "You're too serious as well," she said. "Let's go up."

"Where?"

"To meet your responsible roommate, lamb." Rachel took Julia's hand.

"I thought we were going straight to lunch," Julia said. "Honestly, Bam, we better not. Lydia hasn't been a bit well."

"We'll only stay a moment."

Julia followed Rachel into the building and punched the twelfth floor on the elevator. "You'll find her odd, Bam. I'm afraid you'll be surprised."

"After years on the Howells farm, I doubt I could find anyone odd."

"She is odd," Rachel said later at lunch.

"But sweet, don't you think?"

Rachel shrugged. "Sweet, I suppose."

They were eating at a tiny Japanese restaurant, shrimp tempura and vegetables. Rachel ate Julia's, all but the shrimp, because Julia insisted she'd had a huge breakfast and repeated the breakfast menu again for Rachel's benefit.

"She's an alcoholic," Rachel said. "I'm sure you know that."

"Well," Julia began. Lydia Hall had been an actress in the thirties and early forties, a star, but by 1940 she was more often drinking than not, drinking during performances, performing badly, finally forgetting lines, pasting them on props around the stage as a reminder and then forgetting where she had pasted them. On the opening night of *Antigone* in April 1943, she fell off the stage at the curtain call and broke her leg. Afterwards she never performed again, but she was well loved and cared for, a woman without inner defenses who found the quiet spinning of the alcoholic brain preferable to life in clear focus.

Hal Markus had explained to Julia the nature of her job at Lydia's, which was to keep the old woman from injuring herself, to make certain all the cigarettes were out when they went to bed, to cook at least two meals and sit with Lydia while they ate so she would not throw it out. For that Julia would live rent-free and earn a small stipend. He promised she would learn a great deal about acting and living in the process.

"It's difficult to accept, darling, that you have left college and moved in with a late-middle-aged drunk and want to be an actress under the direction of a man I don't trust."

"You're disappointed," Julia said.

"No, that's not true. I'm worried."

"There is nothing to be worried about. I'm safer than I've ever been."

When the cab let Julia out at West Seventy-ninth, before it went on with Rachel alone to John's office, Rachel took Julia's face in her hands and kissed her on the lips.

"If I'm disappointed, it's in the fact that this has been an artificial afternoon with you, my love, and I've never had a moment with you before that seemed untrue."

"I'm sorry you think that," Julia said.

When Rachel hugged her, she could feel Julia's anger bristling like quills against her cheek.

"Something is going to happen to her," she said to John on the train to Trenton that evening.

"I don't want to hear about it." He folded the paper and studied the national news.

"She's left us."

"Did you expect her to grow old with us?"

"She's left us in spirit, John," Rachel said. "And in that state of mind she's an easy target for that Hal Markus."

"I am sick of your Jewish melancholy, Bam," John said, tearing the paper in his haste to turn the page.

"I see." Rachel examined the scene outside the window. "I can look forward to a fat old age, padding around the empty house with a man gone antisex and anti-Semitic at sixty-one."

He folded the paper in his lap, leaned against Rachel's soft arm and whispered in her ear, "And what do you think this terrible man has in mind?"

"Teaching Julia to be an actress."

"I can imagine worse situations."

"She adores him. Stupidly. We have taken too good care of her, John. At her age I expected the worst and Julia, because we've protected her on that silly farm, expects the best."

"I think she could become a fine actress under Mr. Markus' direction, Bam. Don't worry so much."

"He's a man with a short attention span and I am worried."

Often in the next months John took a taxi to West Seventy-ninth Street, got out and walked by the apartment building like a love-sick boy hoping to catch a glimpse of his beloved but not willing to put himself forward.

They wrote often from the Howells farm.

"If she gets a letter every day from one of us," Caleb said, "then she can't forget us."

"She won't ever forget us," Bumpo said desperately. For him, Julia's departure had been almost like Nat's death.

"Maybe she will," Peter said. "Maybe she'll marry the weasel director and have her own babies. You never know."

"Don't be cruel, Peter," Rachel said.

"I'm being honest, not cruel."

"Don't be honest, then," John said, "unless it's helpful."

They called often and usually Julia answered. She said she was fine, just fine, how was everyone, good to talk to them but she'd better be going.

"Where are you going?" John asked one night, put out by these empty conversations.

"Well, you know," Julia began.

"I don't know," John said. "Are you going out? Are you going to cook dinner? Are you going to bed?"

"What I mean is that I haven't anything else to say," Julia said.

"Say it then," John said.

"All right," Julia said. "I haven't anything else to say."

* * *

At Hal Markus' insistence, Julia went to the Brattle Theater in Cambridge at the end of June 1955.

"You need to learn everything about the theater," he informed her, "and there you'll do everything: props, sets, scrub floors, play bit parts. And," he added, "you'll be away from me."

"That's good?" she asked, lying back against the couch.

"You need to breathe."

"I'm breathing very well around you," she said.

But she agreed to go to please him, and because she knew that he hoped to get a play called *The Children's Garden*, which had a wonderful part for a young girl. She wanted to be ready for that part. It never occurred to her that he wouldn't choose her.

Her life during the six months she had been in New York had been filled by routine. She got up early, fixed breakfast for Lydia Hall and ate with her. Often that winter, Lydia Hall, believing she was Medea, wore sheets without underthings and occasionally the sheets, wrapped loosely around her with failing hands, would fall off, leaving her withered breasts exposed. Not troubling to cover herself, she would wander after breakfast around the apartment, reciting the lines from *Medea* and believing herself beautiful, which she must once have been.

After the breakfast dishes were done, Julia went off to classes at the Neighborhood Playhouse and was back at four, checking first for liquor under the beds, behind the curtains. Always during the day one young actress or actor would drop in for a visit with Lydia and would be charmed into buying a bottle of sherry, which would be gone by supper. Weekends Julia was with Hal Markus, watching one of his plays or a new one which had opened that week. Most evenings they had supper together.

She was overtired, but that, she decided, was a good thing because there wasn't time to think about her family, about her father. When she went to bed at night, often after midnight, she fell asleep, too exhausted from a day of working for her sadness to have a chance to surface.

She was in love. At least she thought she was in love.

"You are my student," Hal insisted, and she'd smile, understanding him to mean something different. She believed that he loved her as well, that his cautions with her were generous, that after he directed her in *The Children's Garden*, when he went on to another play and she went on to be famous, then they could make love all day and night, then they could pledge their lives to each other.

"I'm simply another director, Julia." But she didn't believe him. He told her how to wear her hair, how to walk and speak clearly but without intrusion, how to command a room with simple gestures, how to dress, and she followed his directions exactly, convinced that he was training her for himself. Occasionally he came to the Neighborhood Playhouse and watched her, made notes, waited for her after classes. She couldn't imagine that with such careful attention he didn't love her.

She wanted him. When they were alone in his apartment, she would lie on the couch, on the floor, arranged like a photographer's model for provocation, although she didn't exactly understand what it was she wanted or why she lay on the couch with a sense of fever, unable to eat, why she turned pliable as though she'd been cut from thin paper.

Only once did Hal Markus kiss her. She was leaning against a wall of his apartment as he put on his coat, preparing to leave for rehearsals. She was wilting against the wall, the life gone suddenly out of her, when he took her in his arms and kissed her hard on the lips with his mouth open.

"Put on your coat," he said crossly after he let her go. She put on her coat and followed him out of the apartment, walking quickly to keep up as he went to the theater, where he was watching rehearsals for *Crime and Punishment.*

Another time, during rehearsals for that play, a young actress who was an understudy for the lead told Julia that she had been one of Hal Markus' actresses.

"What do you mean?" Julia asked.

"Don't you live with Lydia Hall and keep her from dying of alcohol or burning up the place?"

"Yes," Julia said cautiously.

"Well," the woman said, "so did I. And Hal trained me, taught me a great deal. He was wonderful. Two years ago he cast me in a small part in *Ondine* and since then I have always been working, which is certainly more than I had dreamed."

They were sitting in the back of the theater, their feet up on the seats in front of them. "You're very lucky Hal has chosen you," she said.

"Did you love him?" Julia asked quickly. Before she had a chance to form the question in her mind, it was out.

"Love him?"

"Oh, never mind," Julia said. "That was a silly question."

"Of course I loved him." She looked at Julia, barely visible in the darkened theater. "You mean, was I in love with him?" she asked.

"It was a silly question," Julia said.

"Don't fall in love with him," the young woman said. "He's a director first and last."

"He told me," Julia said. "He's married to his work. Of course I'd never fall in love with him."

That night, however, when he took her home after a late supper and told her that she was lovely as Amanda in *The Glass Menagerie*, which the Neighborhood Playhouse had done in part that afternoon, she knew that she was different from anyone he had chosen before and that, in time, he would know it, too.

Back in Cambridge with the Brattle Theater, Julia lived in a small room over a bakery in Harvard Square. It was spare with an iron bed and a dresser painted white with a glass top, a hard-back rocking chair, also painted, and a hooked rug, very worn, whose colors were faded to beige by the sun from the curtainless south window. Underneath the glass on the painted dresser Julia put a copy of an article in *Variety* about Hal. In the accompanying picture he was wearing Levi's and an open shirt, a pencil behind his ear. His booted left foot was on the seat of a metal chair, his arms resting on his knee.

She liked the room because it was simple and ordered. She kept her bed made, scrubbed the bathroom one flight down, shared with two older gentlemen and another summer apprentice from the Brattle. She hung up her clothes and washed her underwear. She worked hard and it gave her pleasure to work hard. She was extremely well liked by the company because she did what she was expected to do. She played small parts in every play and the other members of the company spoke of her promise. As she walked from the theater through Cambridge, through the crowded streets, the bookstores and delicatessens and bakeries, she was like a young pregnant woman satisfied by the imperceptible changes in her body day after day. She had always wanted to be an actress. And she was going to be. She was going to be the best young actress in New York for Harold Markus. He would be enormously proud because he was responsible and because he was in love with her.

Hal came to Cambridge once in July and saw her in *Alice in Wonderland*. Afterwards they went to dinner and he walked her back to her room.

"Would you like to see it?" she asked, feeling her heart lunge in the small cave of her breast.

"Your room?" He laughed, taking her chin in his hands. "I have seen enough rooms in rooming houses to last me three lives."

"You don't understand," she said. "It's a very nice room."

He pulled her towards him, hugged her and set her back against the building like a board which had fallen and would not return to its place without assistance.

"Would you like to stay?" she asked quietly into his shirt.

"No, Julia," he said, but so gently and with such understanding of the complicated nature of their association that she believed his intentions were honorable. "No, no, no."

"I'm grown-up," she said. "I can make my own decisions."

"You're not grown-up, Julia." He laid his hand against her cheek and left it there for a moment before he went, but he didn't kiss her.

She ran upstairs, touched by his invasion of her privacy. She expected him to follow her, to comfort her in the room she had kept so carefully, but he did not. From her window she watched him walk down the street away from the square and out of sight.

In August, he called her to New York to try out for *The Children's Garden*, but before that, Cally arrived unannounced at the Brattle Theater the night that Julia, who understudied Frankie in *Member of the Wedding*, was playing the part because the original lead had had a miscarriage.

It came as a surprise to Cally that she wanted to go after Julia. She had thought that the few letters of undeclared love from Julia were sufficient, that in time when one box of letters under the bed was full, she would start filling another; the substance of her relationship with her daughter would be in the counting of letters, intimacy by the size and number.

By intention, Cally still did not think of Nat. But one night Nat suddenly flooded her sleep. She saw his beautiful face rocking above her the first time they made love. Before she could arrange the image, Julia was in her place, naked, with small breasts and a mound of pubic hair, a shadow between her legs. She saw her mounted, filled with the spill of anxious young men.

"I'm going to Cambridge," she said to Rachel when she called the Main House the next morning.

"Good," Rachel said, "I'm so glad."

Although Cally was seated in the side aisle in her wheelchair when the curtain went up on *Member of the Wedding*, Julia didn't notice her mother until just before the first curtain. The first act had progressed without mistakes, gone beautifully, but when Julia walked across stage left towards the aisle where Cally was sitting and saw her mother, she lost her final lines.

Backstage Julia sat in a metal hard-back chair in the corridor beside the dressing rooms, her dark eyes set like baked ceramic.

"Goddammit," she said.

"No one noticed," the director said.

"I noticed," Julia said. "You noticed. The company."

"It happens. You left the stage with grace," he said. "Now have someone fix that braid. It's coming loose."

They ate at The Midget after the play, just the two of them, Julia still in braids and blue jeans. The waitress had to move a table into the aisle for Cally's wheelchair to fit.

"You were very good," Cally said awkwardly.

"I was okay." Julia ordered onion soup and a glass of wine.

"Do you eat onion soup?" Cally asked.

"I have always eaten onion soup."

"Not at Bam's. You never used to. Is that all you're eating?"

"I don't eat very much after a play."

"When do you eat?" Cally asked in spite of herself, knowing this conversation was poorly managed.

"I eat, Mother," Julia said.

"I'm sorry."

"Your coming here has surprised me. You never leave home," Julia said by way of apology.

"I left home once when I was your age." She nervously fingered her sandwich, no longer hungry. "Only once and I'm thirty-five."

"Where did you go?" Julia asked.

"I went away from New Orleans to New York and met your father."

Julia ordered another glass of wine and ate the other half of her mother's sandwich.

"How good were you tonight?" Cally asked uncertainly.

"Fair," Julia said. "Better than fair, I guess. Promising. There were good moments. The second act. I was good in the second act."

"You seemed wonderful the whole time to me," Cally said, unaccustomed either to complimenting her children or criticizing them.

"I dropped a line when I saw you at the end of the first act."

"I'm sorry."

"It's all right."

She wheeled her mother across Harvard Square to her house.

"I only have a twin bed," she said to Cally.

"That's fine for one night. We'll fit there together. I'm taking an early train back to New York tomorrow."

In the room Cally asked Julia for a nightgown. "It was a quick decision to come," she said. "I didn't bring anything."

In the mirror, while she unbraided her hair, Julia watched her mother undress. She was a private woman. Julia had never seen her naked. She looked with interest at Cally's large, strong torso, her shoulders freckled from working in the sun, her breasts high like the breasts of a girl. Below the waist, the skin, unbound, fell like the soft folds of cotton sheets around her hips and thighs, her legs dangled like vines. She had a beautiful face, still young, in fact, younger than Julia's own dark one reflected in the mirror beside her mother's. The years since Cally's girlhood had come not as troubles, but as surprises. She was brave, like a child learning to ride a bike, falling and falling, skinning her knee, her leg, the palm of her hand, but teetering back onto the bicycle, unabashed.

Cally, in turn, lifted herself onto the bed and leaned back against the pillow, watching her daughter. She wanted a secret with Julia, but they had never had secrets. They had never been able to talk to each other, not the way Rachel could talk with Julia, or Nat. Julia's fierce independence and Cally's quiet withdrawal, both protections against the consequences of love, had made them cautious with each other, tabby cats stalking their territory, peeing the battle line.

Cally wanted to rearrange the years and find Julia as a child again, at two or three, when her blue-black eyes first set in defiance against a world she intended to conquer.

Julia sat in the rocking chair.

"Climb in, there's room."

Julia folded her feet beneath her. "I'm not tired."

"I'm exhausted. It's after one," Cally said.

"I stay up late. It's hard to sleep after a play."

"What do you do?"

"We go somewhere and eat and talk and then I come back here and read. Usually I read."

"Alone?"

"Do I read alone? Mother," Julia said, understanding Cally's implication.

"The first time I ever went away from home, when I met your father, I was so innocent, such a little child, anyone could have done anything to me. I was just lucky it was your father I met."

"I don't honestly want to know," Julia said.

"I want you to."

"I don't want to talk about Daddy." Julia got up and rearranged her books on the dresser. "Do you need to go to the bathroom? It's downstairs. You don't want to go in the middle of the night."

"No," Cally said.

"I need to," Julia said. She sat on the bathroom floor for a long time, reading the script of *The Children's Garden* which Hal Markus had sent to her. She didn't want a conversation with her mother, who, she understood, was trying to protect her from exactly what she dreamed about every hour she was Julia and not Frankie or Tweedledee in *Alice in Wonderland* or Meesia in *Perfect Gardens* or the Tin Woodman in *The Wizard of Oz*. She wanted to be with Harold Markus in empty open fields under a clear sky so they could watch their bodies make wonderful love.

She didn't want new information from her mother or cautions or considerations—certainly, above all, she didn't want to know the love story of her mother and father. To imagine them full of the same dreams as she had now, to imagine the short life of dreams while it is necessary to believe in them, would touch her too deeply.

When Julia came upstairs, her mother was sleeping. She crawled in bed beside her, her head next to her mother's legs. Cally moaned a little, moved to accommodate Julia and wrapped her free right arm around her daughter's legs. Julia, propped against the foot-board of her bed, was awake when the early sun turned the square gray with the filtered light of dawn.

The Children's Garden went into rehearsal the beginning of September with a young woman who had been in a movie and onstage before playing Alissa, Julia's part.

"I made no promises," Hal Markus said to her shortly after she had returned from Cambridge and resettled with Lydia Hall.

"I know," Julia said.

"You can come and watch us open in New Haven," Hal said. "It might be interesting for you."

"Maybe," she said. They were walking down Forty-fifth Street to Broadway, meeting friends of Hal's for drinks before the theater.

"Is it the part you really wanted?" he asked, taking her arm. "Or were there other reasons?"

"I'm perfect for the part," Julia said fliply. "She's bright, mercurial, imaginative and difficult." She leaned against him.

"Difficult," Hal said. "That you are."

"I want to be in a play you do, to be wonderful for you," Julia said. She took his hand. She wanted to hold hands. She wanted to walk down Forty-fifth with her hand in his, so that everyone they passed on the streets would be clear about them, so that she'd be clear about them. When he took her hand, it was in a stage gesture denying affection.

"I want you to be good, too, Julia," he said, "but for yourself."

"What a bore," she said. "What kind of pleasure is there to lie in your own bed by yourself and think to yourself, I was just wonderful for myself?"

"That is the pleasure," Hal said quietly. At Forty-fifth and Broadway he hailed a cab, climbed in with Julia and gave the driver Lydia Hall's address. They rode across town in silence, Hal's arms folded tight across his chest, his face towards the window, his legs crossed at the knee.

At 140 West Seventy-ninth Hal got out of his side of the cab, let Julia out, took her wrist in his hand and looked at her directly.

"I thought we were going to have drinks," she said.

"You were going with me and two other directors as a student, Julia," he said. "You continue to mistake my intentions."

He got back in the waiting taxicab and Julia watched until it turned out of sight on Amsterdam.

She didn't go up to Lydia Hall's apartment immediately but sat instead in the lobby with her back to one wall mirror, facing another wall mirror so that she saw herself as she seldom did in the round. She didn't look at herself in mirrors as Julia Howells— only as Lucy Tanner or Amanda or Frankie, expressed by them in her blue-black eyes, the angle of her chin, the set of her full lips. As Julia Howells, doubled in mirrors in the lobby of 140 West Seventy-ninth, she was smaller than she expected to be, younger than she remembered. And touching. Goddammit, she thought. Certainly Hal Markus should be touched by her even if he didn't love her. For the first time she doubted her convictions about him. Perhaps he did not love her, as he had said he didn't. Perhaps he was interested in her only professionally as he said he was. She might have been wrongheaded all along.

She would be excellent for him, she thought as the elevator creaked the twelve floors to the top, and then he would know, of course, that he had loved her all along.

Hal Markus went into rehearsal for *The Children's Garden* and Julia went back to caring for Lydia Hall, who had become more air-headed and confused over the summer. Only Lydia's gestures were exact and expressed what she wanted to say.

On a Sunday, in mid-September, hours after Hal had asked Julia to understudy Alissa beginning the following day, Peter called from Bucks County in trouble.

"Are you ever coming home?" he asked. "Or have you changed your name?"

"Sometime I'll be home," Julia said. "I'm really busy now."

"Well," Peter said. "Everybody's fine."

"Good."

"I mean, you didn't ask, so I'm just pretending to myself you want to know."

"Of course I want to know."

"Yeah." He paused. "Do you still look the same?"

"Of course."

"Black hair, long nose, a black mole on your temple?"

"Shut up," Julia said. "I'll be home sometime. Don't try to make me feel bad."

"I'm not trying to make you feel bad. I feel bad. That's why I called in the middle of the afternoon. I feel just awful." He was crying. In her memory Peter had never cried. Not when Nat died or was burned or when Cally fell out of the world or when he was hurt.

"Peter," she said. "What's happened?"

"I was baby-sitting for the Brays in Solebury." He was tossing out his words like tiny spitballs. "For Jimmy, who's three, and he was in the front yard and I was in the house playing this game that belongs to Mr. Bray and forgetting sort of about Jimmy, though, of course, I expected he was in the front yard, where I'd left him. And then I heard a crash and a thump and a screech, and when I looked out the front window, Jimmy was lying in the road and a car was crashed into a tree."

"Is he dead?"

"No," Peter said. "Please come home."

"You're sure he's not dead."

"He's not dead. Bam said he absolutely won't die. He'll be all right, but his leg is broken in two places. The Brays are so mad they could kill me."

"How's Mama?"

"She's quiet, quiet, quiet. She hasn't said a word."

"Where is she?"

"At the hospital with Bam and the Brays."

"Why aren't you there?"

"I was there all day and Granddad brought me back here after lunch because I kept throwing up. I think I threw up my whole stomach. And Bumpo has been sitting in the living room window seat and crying like a woman. I told him he ought to get a sex change."

"I'm really sorry."

"I can't believe I was so careless. You know, it would be a good idea if you came home just for the day. This thing has really upset Caleb, especially."

"Today?"

"Yeah."

"Well," Julia said. "I don't know."

"You could take the train and be back tomorrow morning."

"Let me see if I can get out of rehearsals. I'll call you."

"I guess you're getting famous," Peter said.

"Not quite, but I may be."

She went into her bedroom and sat down on the bed. From her open door she could see Lydia Hall talking to an empty chair across from her. Curiously Lydia Hall seemed real to Julia in a way that the desolate voice of Peter had not.

She called Hal Markus, who told her that she should go home, but she had already made up her mind.

"I'm not coming," she said to Peter.

"I didn't think you would."

"Yes, you did, or you wouldn't have called."

"Not since you've changed."

"I haven't changed."

"Yes, you have," he said. "I wouldn't recognize you on the street if it weren't for the mole on your temple. Check it for hairs from time to time. I read in my medical journal that hairs grow out of moles as you get older."

"I'm sorry about what happened, Peter," she said.

"I've almost forgotten myself."

"Bullshit."

"Yeah, well, take care of yourself and we'll talk to you soon." Peter replaced the receiver before Julia had an opportunity to speak again.

"Julia's turned into a fairy princess," Peter said to Bumpo when he had put down the phone. "I mentioned you and she said she can't remember anyone named Bumpo. It must be a name from a past life."

Bumpo told.

"Peter has had a bad enough day without fighting with you, Bumpo," Rachel said.

"I'm not fighting. I hate fights. I'm telling on him."

"I called Julia," Peter said when Rachel asked him.

"She didn't say she'd forgotten Bumpo, of course, and it wasn't kind to tell him that."

"Hell, Bam, face the music. She's forgotten us all. 'Peter who?' she said when I called. 'Peter Ustinov,' I said. 'Peter the Great. Peter, Peter, Pumpkin Eater.' I think I'm beginning to hate her."

Julia couldn't think of them sitting around the table at Rachel's, in the yard, in the library, in the white and maple kitchen of the glass shoebox. She couldn't think of them separately, recall the exact detail of their faces, the tenor of their voices. Thinking of them made her ill. She tried to imagine them as warm black bears, hibernating, thick fur against thick fur, together for the winter, living on food put up by Rachel. They would awaken in the spring after the ground thaw and greet her as if there had been no passage through a cold season, their memories frozen in ice, greeting her with the recognition of spring, their love for one another in the tight grip of a new bud.

Hal didn't say anything to Julia during rehearsals, but it was clear that his first choice for Alisssa was not developing.

"You don't seem to work well together," Julia said to him one evening after rehearsals when they were having supper together.

"No." He was distracted, chewing the yellow paint off a pencil.

"There are people I cannot direct. Who simply don't know what I'm after or can't find a character in themselves."

"You can direct me," Julia wanted to say. "I'll know exactly what you want me to do."

He rehearsed her often.

"Be more cunning," he'd say. "You're interested in the grandmother who kills husbands. Show it. You're wiser than that. Not so innocent and watch your hands, Julia. Your hands, your hands. Every time your hands react like birds flushed out of marshes."

Julia practiced restraining her hands.

"I'm nervous," she said to Hal.

"Of course you're nervous," he said. "I want you to be nervous. It's a good thing as long as you can get beyond it."

"I don't mean I'm nervous onstage," Julia said. "I'm perfectly comfortable onstage. I'd like to be there permanently."

"Don't be excessive."

"I'm trying to explain why my hands move too much," she said. "I'm nervous inside."

"I don't care why your hands move too much. I simply want them to stop moving."

One afternoon just before the opening in New Haven, when Julia was rehearsing Alissa, Hal stood on the seat of a theater chair and cheered.

"You've got her, Julia," he said. "The walk—the way you tilt your head, the tension. Terrific."

Offstage in *The Children's Garden* Alissa builds bonfires to dance around because she pretends she is a witch. Her father is dead; her mother remarried; she lives with her grandmother in a house where many children of past owners have been buried in the garden. Alissa insists on the bonfires, on pretending that she is a witch in self-defense. She is frightened that she will be murdered and join the children in the garden. All through the rehearsals as understudy until opening night in New Haven, Julia never thought about *The Children's Garden* except as it pertained to the character of Alissa.

Opening night was not a success. Backstage during the performance the mood was studied silence. Julia busied herself with the wardrobe mistress and getting candy for the stage manager. She could tell that the play was not going well.

Afterwards Julia remained downstairs with the wardrobe mistress, sewing the buttons on the back of Alissa's dress, which had popped when she bent down in the second act, stitching the grandmother's dress, which had been pinned together at the last minute because the actress who played the part was so thin, washing the thick makeup off Mrs. Laughlin's silk collar. The young woman who played Alissa passed the costume room and didn't stop to say good-night. She looked in, looked at Julia and their eyes met as though for the first time on a crowded bus, over a row of people without recognition. Later Julia was surprised that the young woman had not registered bitterness when she saw Julia because certainly bitterness is what she must have felt.

"How bad was it?" Julia asked Olivia, who played the part of Alissa's mother in the play.

"It wasn't good," Olivia said. She started to add something else but instead walked over to Julia and put her hand on Julia's cheek, leaving it there for a moment.

"Can you do that to me?" she asked, kneeling down so Julia could touch her face with her hand.

"See," Olivia said. "Your hands have gotten better." She took Julia's hands in her own. "But I notice you're awkward with gestures of love. Remember how your mother touched you without shyness when you were small." Olivia put her fingers to her own lips and then to Julia's in a kiss.

Hal Markus came down as Olivia was leaving. He kissed the older actress on the lips and they separated without speaking—a ritual with him after each performance, Julia discovered.

"Julia," he said, and she got up. He took her elbow in a firm grip, requiring attention, and said quietly, "You're on."

"What do you mean?" she asked.

"I mean, after tonight you're Alissa."

"You mean, for tomorrow?" she asked. "Is Alissa ill?"

"Alissa's fired," Hal said. "I mean, for as long as you can keep your goddamned hands from flying across the stage."

The company was staying in an old hotel down the street from the theater in New Haven and Julia had a small room to herself. It was next door to Olivia's, two doors down from Hal Markus'. Still awake at one, Julia heard the small gong on the clock at Yale University sound once and then at two, she heard it again. She got up, went down the dark corridor and knocked on Hal Markus' door. He didn't think twice.

"Julia," he said.

"How did you know?" she asked when he opened the door for her.

"I knew," he said. He had on a robe when he answered the door. He didn't seem to have pajamas on. She wanted to ask him if he wore pajamas to bed and had dreams before he got up in the morning. She wanted to know the small details.

"You can't sleep," he said.

He lay down on the bed on his back. "Look," he said. "You lie down on your bed with your head on a pillow like this, a pillow under your knees, like this. Don't close your eyes. Find something on the ceiling to study."

Julia knelt beside him on the bed.

"It's not exactly that I can't sleep."

"Well, it is exactly that I can't sleep with visitations at two in the morning. Go to bed."

"I want to tell you something first."

He sat up with a pillow behind his back, crossing his legs beneath his dressing gown.

"Please."

"Go ahead," he said. "I'll listen and then honestly, Julia, I want to go to sleep."

"All right," she said. "You know the bonfire part of the play. A few years ago my father was building a bonfire for a party we used to have every year on Boxing Day and he fell in the fire and was burned. That's why I can't sleep, because of what's in the play. and not that I'm nervous about it."

"I'm sorry," Hal Markus said.

"It seems that every play I'm in connects to my own life. That's why I left *Our Town.*"

"If a play is good, it should connect to your own life in some way or another. Use the connection, Julia, but translate it for the play."

"Have I told you about my father?"

"I don't want to hear about your father tonight."

When Julia went into her own room, Olivia was sitting on the bed in a man's plaid robe tied loosely around her waist. She was a tall, slender woman, serene but intensely personal, as though she required nothing of her relationships but the satisfaction of the generous gifts of herself to others.

She patted the bed. "Sit down," she said.

She helped Julia off with her robe.

"Hal is one of the best directors I have worked with," she said.

"But everything is for the play," Julia said.

"That's right." Olivia pulled down the covers, straightened the sheets. "Climb in," she commanded.

"I wanted to tell him about my father," Julia said.

"You can tell me about your father." But Julia wanted to tell Hal Markus, not Olivia, about her father.

Olivia covered Julia, turned out the light, sat down beside her on the bed and stroked her face, running her long fingers through Julia's hair.

"Do you have children?" Julia asked.

"I have a daughter," Olivia said.

"My age?"

"Younger. She's fourteen."

"I expect you're a wonderful mother."

Olivia put her fingers to her lips. "Shh." She brushed her fingers over Julia's cheeks, her forehead, the bridge of her nose, and when Julia woke in the morning, Olivia was gone and Julia was lying on her back propped with two pillows in a dusty room bright with sun.

In Boston the reviews were better; in Philadelphia the play opened on the tenth of October and Rachel and John came every night with one child or another, with Cally. One night Rachel came alone and brought flowers backstage. Olivia met her as she walked down the corridor from the stage door, took her to Julia's dressing room and closed the door. "So you can talk without the rest of us," Olivia said. Julia was grateful.

She and Rachel were awkward with each other. "There," Rachel said, handing Julia the flowers. "I hid them under my suit jacket in the theater," she said. "I didn't want to embarrass you."

"Don't be silly," Julia said.

"I didn't want people to know that you have so fat a grand-mother."

"Oh, Bammy," Julia said. But it was true. She didn't want people to know she had a grandmother, fat or not. When she left Radcliffe, she had carefully sewn the seams of her daily life to exclude the Howells. With their nightly arrival at *The Children's Garden*, the seams had burst at inappropriate places. Bumpo came the second night, at sixteen lost in his father's corduroy jacket; John was balding with wisps of white hair plastered to his pale skull like oiled duck feathers; Cally's legs in stockings looked like the appendages of plastic dolls; Peter had acquired an adolescent stance, his hips and shoulders tilted like seesaws.

Only Caleb was satisfactory. "It was a dumb play, but I didn't fall asleep," Caleb said, eating a handful of candy from the bowl on Julia's dressing table.

She wanted them to be the mannequins from the third floor at Bonwit's, perfectly dressed, spotless and unwrinkled in the colors of the season, unobtrusive in style.

"You know," she said to Peter. "You don't realize that we're kind of a weird family until you leave home."

The night before the opening in New York, Hal Markus took Julia home and walked her to the door of her apartment.

"I'm enormously proud of you," he said and kissed her on the lips.

That night, lying on the daybed in the window, decorated with the reflections of tiny lights from windows of the buildings next door and across the street, Julia could not sleep. She could not imagine a more perfect life than the one she had discovered.

Hal Markus did not tell her opening night that he was leaving *The Children's Garden* at the end of the first week to go into re-hearsal for a new play. Olivia and the rest of the cast assumed that Julia knew.

Opening night was like a wedding with flowers and champagne, promises of a long life together, embraces. The marriage, for it seemed to be exactly that, was for Julia a marriage into the family of *The Children's Garden,* unencumbered by the dark memories of her own blood family.

"I have never been so happy in my life," Julia said to Olivia.

It didn't last. Two days later Hal told her he was leaving.

"I warned you, Julia," Hal said as she walked down Broadway with him. "Directors leave."

"I know."

"You're too damned young."

"I know."

"I want you to be excellent for yourself."

"So you've said."

"I'm taking a taxi home."

"You won't be back to the theater?"

"I will stop in from time to time."

"Can I come with you now?" she asked as a taxicab pulled over.

"No."

"Please?"

"You have to rest."

"Just this once."

He hesitated on his way into the taxi, then stood back at the door and held it for Julia.

"Get in," he said to her.

They drove to his apartment in silence.

"I have nothing to eat," he said.

"I'm not hungry," she replied.

"I have work to do on the script of the new play."

"I'll be quiet."

"What do you plan to do?" he asked.

"Lie on your couch and rest," she said.

Julia lay on the couch, but she was restless with the desire of a young woman who does not understand the urgency in her body.

Hal got up finally from the script on which he was working at the dining room table. When he sat down beside her, she moved over, resting on her side.

He kissed her, opening her mouth gently with his lips, putting his hands underneath her white silk blouse primly tucked in at the slender waist of a black skirt. He unbuttoned her blouse, unhooked her bra and kissed her small breasts, licking the nipples with his tongue. She didn't know what to do. She had never made love before except to be kissed in high school in Washington and at Radcliffe by George Gibbs. He undid the waist of her black skirt and pulled it off, took off his own shirt, casually, as though he were considering a shower. He sat beside her on the floor, running his hand over her body with great gentleness, over her bare breasts, her stomach, across her pubic bone, her thigh, leaving her slip on while he kissed her belly and then pulling it off, pulling off her cotton knit underpants.

"A girl's underpants," he said to her sweetly, undoing her garter, unfastening her nylon stockings. And Julia lay there, allowing him everything. When he kissed her thigh, she lifted herself automatically to his mouth and he kissed the soft mound of hair and ran his warm wet tongue in the crevices of flesh. Then he stood, dropping his own trousers to the floor. She was embarrassed to look for long. She couldn't imagine that the tiny passage between her legs could accommodate that grand instrument. He kissed her between her legs with his tongue again and again until she softened against him as though she were a substance of different consistency and then to her astonishment he was inside her and raging, it seemed to be raging, such was the force of him on top of her, into a delirium beyond her control. She expected to die on the nubbly beige couch.

They lay together for a long time.

When he got up, he covered her with her black straight skirt, her silk blouse. She didn't look at him go into the bathroom with his clothes but dressed quickly while he was gone and was sitting at the dining room table when he came out.

She wanted him to touch her in a gesture of ownership, to brush the loose strand of hair out of her face. He looked at his watch, took her hand and walked out of the apartment with her. In the elevator he stood with his arms crossed over his chest, watching the descending numbers over the elevator doors light up. He hailed a taxi and the first one which passed pulled over. He opened the door for her and she crawled in.

"Good luck," he said through the open window of the back door as he shut it.

"Thank you," she said.

The next night, according to Olivia, Julia played Alissa with absolute conviction.

"You were fine," she said, walking home in a light rain.

"Thank God for Alissa," Julia replied.

Although Julia had told her nothing about Hal Markus, Olivia understood and took Julia to her own apartment, made a bed on the couch, covered her with a fat comforter and prepared hot chocolate for her. Then she sat beside her on the couch and told her stories.

"You are lovely to have me," Julia said.

"It's lovely having you. I don't particularly like to live alone."

"Doesn't your daughter ever live with you?"

"Sometimes," Olivia said. "For holidays."

"Why not more?"

"Her father was awarded custody." Olivia paused. "Because of my work."

"But she would have preferred to live with you?"

"No," Olivia said evenly. "She preferred living with her father." She leaned over and kissed Julia. "You make choices, darling. I made a choice for my work when I was divorced and so did

Beatrice make her choice. Now"—she pulled the comforter over Julia's shoulders—"go to sleep."

The Children's Garden closed in late spring, 1956, after a successful run on Broadway. Julia had worked hard. She had made Alissa her entire life and the cast of *The Children's Garden* her relatives.

During the winter Hal Markus, who had another play on Broadway, returned several times, but she never saw him alone and never called him.

"Each time I see you as Alissa, you're better than the last," he told her.

"I try to make every night the first night," Olivia said to Julia before the last performance. "Somehow, if I lose my innocence about the play, I lose the character."

"That's fine for plays," Julia replied.

"I have found it necessary for living, too."

"I want to be in plays because they end exactly as they're written to end. I want to be in them for the rest of my life," Julia said.

"Maybe we will both be in plays forever, darling, but you still have to learn to invent your own life offstage."

Julia sat in a chair in Olivia's dressing room, watching the older woman, whom she'd grown to love, in the mirror.

"I'm nervous," she said.

"Why is that?"

"About tonight," she said. "Will it be as terrible as I imagine when it's over?"

"Saying good-bye?" Olivia smiled, took Julia's hand and kissed her fingers. "Of course, and wouldn't it be disappointing if it were easy? If we just said good-bye and went off to our ordinary lives? What an empty way to go about our work."

The stage manager buzzed in Olivia's dressing room, indicating that the play was about to begin.

"Places," Olivia said and kissed Julia on the top of the head.

They didn't speak again until the curtain call was over and the company had embraced backstage, acknowledging the end of a life they had made together, as though the play were a venerable old woman whose loss to them, however great, did not diminish the life she had led, in which they were each richer for sharing.

"Hurry and change," Olivia said to Julia. "We're having a last good-bye at Sardi's."

"Time to go home with your mother, Alissa," Tom, the stage

manager said, echoing the play's lines, giving Julia a hug.

"I'm going to light the stage and dance around it till I fall," Julia said. "I hate good-bye parties."

"Alissa uses wild words in self-defense," Olivia said, lines from the play. "Now, hurry, my love."

Julia did not arrive at Sardi's. Olivia noticed immediately and walked back to the theater after her. Tom was just closing and locking the stage door when she ran across the street.

"Have you seen Julia?" she called.

"I haven't," he said. "No one's here."

"Let me check."

"I checked," he replied, but she patted his shoulder and went down the dark corridor, lighting the lights as she went, across the disassembled stage.

"You passed her," Tom said.

"Where?"

"There." He pointed to the seats in the orchestra.

"Julia." Olivia walked to the end of the stage. Julia was in the front row, shaking as if she were reacting to severe exposure.

"I want to stay here all night," Julia said.

"Have you taken something?" Olivia asked quickly. "You haven't done anything to yourself, have you?"

"Nothing." Julia held up her hands, which were quivering out of control. "Either I'm sick or I've lost my mind incompletely." She wrapped her trench coat around her shoulders. "I wish I could lose it completely."

Olivia covered her with a blanket from a daybed in a dressing room. "You carry her," she said to Tom. "I'll get a taxi." She grabbed another blanket on her way out, hailed a cab and took Julia to her apartment.

"This happened to me once at the end of a play, love, and I've seen it happen other times," Olivia said. "You're just spent." She rubbed her arms and legs until, very late, Julia finally fell into a light sleep. In the morning Olivia took her home.

"Home?" Julia asked.

"Home," Olivia said. "To your mother."

"No," Julia said, but she followed Olivia to her own apartment and watched her pack.

"You haven't another job right now."

"No, I haven't." Julia paused. "Do you think anything has happened to my mind?"

"I think you're just exhausted."

"You don't think I'll die, do you?"

"Not in the near future." Olivia laughed.

"I don't really want to go home," Julia said as Olivia put her in the back seat of a rented car, covering her with a blanket. "I suppose you know I hate Hal Markus."

"No, darling, I didn't know you did."

"I don't like my family either. They're so awkward it kills me to see them."

"I know," Olivia said, so full of feeling that Julia believed she did know.

Rachel met them. Olivia insisted she couldn't stay, that she must be back in New York by afternoon. Rachel wanted to send her off with a basket of jams and pies, small cakes and daffodils, but fussing in the kitchen, she couldn't find a basket, the strawberry jam had been opened, and the sponge cake was full of pinches from her own fingers. Finally, she grabbed the daffodils from the crockery vase on the kitchen table and handed them to Olivia with the water dripping from their stems.

"There," she said, "we're very grateful."

Julia was sitting in the room Rachel used as a study, on the bed that had been George Katz's. When Rachel came up with hot soup and toast, she was looking out the window.

"Does Mother know I'm here?" Julia asked.

"No, I was going to call her after I brought you this."

"Don't mention Daddy."

"It hadn't crossed my mind."

"It might, and if it does, don't let me know about it."

There was a cryptic entry in the family Bible in May 1956, a few weeks after *The Children's Garden* had closed.

"Is that all?" Rachel asked, looking over John's shoulder as he wrote.

"What would you add?"

"Don't be gloomy," Rachel said. "It's my turn."

"It's always your turn to be gloomy, Bammy," John said. Kissing her, he shut the book on his short entry of Julia's return, which read:

JULIA HAS COME HOME TO US—SO TO SPEAK.

INVENTED LIVES

WHEN I WAS GROWING UP ON THIS FARM, WE INHERITED OUR
LIVES FROM OUR PARENTS WITH THE TASK OF MAINTAINING
THEM IN GOOD ORDER, AS IF THEY WERE PERIOD FURNITURE,

John Howells wrote in the family Bible in September 1966, following a family celebration for Julia's twenty-ninth birthday.

"You're getting too serious with age," Rachel said when he read
her what he had written.

"One footstep in the grave, my love," he said.

"I'm thinking of going on a diet," Rachel said, thumbing through
the pages of a new French cookbook.

"A splendid idea. For the sake of personal pride I want you
slender at my upcoming funeral."

"For the sake of my future, also," Rachel said, sliding into the
small couch with him.

"That, too," John said, and in spite of her protests, he read her
the rest of the entry in the Bible. "You see," he said, "I am getting
old."

"What you're getting is longwinded," she said.

BUT THE SPEED OF CHANGE IN THIS CENTURY, THE FACT THAT
THE INVENTIONS OF OUR TIME COULD DESTROY US THIS VERY
AFTERNOON, DEFIES OUR EFFORTS. TODAY CHILDREN INVENT
THEIR LIVES. JULIA HOWELLS HAS INVENTED HER LIFE. SHE HAS
MARRIED PHILIP KENDALL, A WELSH PHYSICIAN, WHO IS SATIS-
FIED TO LIVE HERE IN DANIEL'S HOUSE AND RAISE BABIES WITH
JULIA. SOMETHING AT THE CENTER IS MISSING. I AM WORRIED
ABOUT JULIA HOWELLS, WHOM I LOVE, WHOM I LOVE, WHOM
I LOVE.

"I think I'll go on a carbohydrate diet," Rachel said. "I got so
light-headed on the protein diet that I went on last time I had to
eat cake."

"Did you listen to what I wrote, Bammy?"

"Of course I listened. I always listen."

"Well?"

"I don't know," she said. "Let's not talk about it."

"I'm thinking about selling the farm."

"You're always thinking of that."

"But we have to do something."

"That's why I'm going on a diet. If I had the choice of inventing my life instead of inheriting the dull neuroses of an ex-working-class Jew, I'd never have married and had children."

"You would have made a first-class madam."

"I'd like to have been an opera singer."

"You'd have been very good in the opera, Bammy, if only God had given you a voice."

"God!" She threw up her hands. "That's your trouble, John, and always has been."

John left the Bible open when he went outside with Rachel. Cally's children found it after they had done the dishes left from Julia's party.

"Have you read what Granddaddy's written lately?" Caleb asked Peter.

"Nope," Peter said and they read the last few entries together.

JUNE 8, 1959:   JULIA RECEIVES HER M.F.A. FROM THE YALE SCHOOL OF DRAMA, THE FIRST WOMAN IN THE HOWELLS FAMILY TO RECEIVE A COLLEGE DEGREE.

JUNE 9, 1959:   JULIA HOWELLS MARRIED PHILIP KENDALL, M.D., AT THE MAIN HOUSE.

JUNE 12, 1960:   THEODORE KENDALL, CALLED THEO, IS BORN AT FOUR IN THE AFTERNOON: 8 LB., 2 OZ.

AUGUST 14, 1962:   PHILIPPA KENDALL, CALLED PIPPA, IS BORN AT MIDNIGHT: 7 LB., 15 OZ.

"And they all lived happily ever after," Caleb said.

"Bullshit," Peter said.

"You don't think Julia is happy?"

"I think she's miserable."

"Honest?" Caleb leaned back on his chair. "She seems terrific to me."

"Seems, yeah," Peter said. "I'm glad I became a doctor."

Julia's birthday had been a hot, clear day and Rachel stayed with John in the yard to watch the end of it as the sun fell behind Daniel's house.

Through the trees they could see Julia in blue jeans and a bandanna, throwing a ball to Pippa, running after her bad throws; Theo, chasing his father around the side of the house, then Theo on Philip's shoulders, pulling himself up into the magnolia tree which was thick-branched and low, perfect for climbing children. They saw Julia lift Pippa, who buried her head in Julia's shoulder as though she were crying, but Rachel and John could not hear her. Julia put Pippa down and together they knelt, examining something on the ground which appeared to be one of the new kittens. Theo leaned over his mother's back, resting there with his arm around her neck. Philip had gone inside and returned with a glass, which he gave to Julia, who took it without looking up, and a Frisbee, which he tossed at Theo.

"Don't you think it's lovely to watch them?" Rachel asked.

"I think it's odd that Julia and Philip never touch each other," John said. "Have you noticed that?"

"I have noticed," she whispered into his neck, slipping her fingers under his belt, "that your pants are too tight."

"Oh, you have," he said.

"Come upstairs," she said.

"It's only seven o'clock," he said. "We had a very late lunch."

"Don't be so boring," she said, drawing him by the hand.

Upstairs, afterwards, they lay on their bed with the sheets thrown off.

"We haven't made love on a Sunday afternoon for years," Rachel said. She leaned over and kissed him on the chest. "I could make love to you every afternoon of my life."

"Apparently dementia is no deterrent." He took her face in his hands. "You know, my love, I'm glad you're going on the carbohydrate diet. The protein one makes your face break out."

There was a postcard on John's dresser from Bumpo in Colorado. He reread it when he got out of bed and placed it on the top of the stack of colorful ten-cent cards that Bumpo had sent regularly since he left college a year before. Each one read almost exactly like the previous one.

Dear Family,

It is knockout here in Dammer Dammer, Colorado. Only me and Skye who will love me forever and sunsets like you've never seen before. KNOCKOUT.

Peace,
Nat (Bumpo)

He signed all the postcards "Nat" with "Bumpo" in parentheses.

John stood at the dresser, filling his pockets with loose change, nail clippers, a watch whose strap had broken.

Often John and Rachel watched Julia from their bedroom window, playing with her family in the yard of her house.

"See," he said to Rachel, who had come to stand beside him. He pointed through the window, where she saw Philip carrying Theo on his shoulders and Julia with Pippa by the hand walk in the front door of Daniel's house.

"Something is missing between them."

"From where I'm standing, they are missing," Rachel said, squinting.

"Put on your glasses," John said, and then he noticed that she wasn't dressed. "For Chrissake, put on your clothes."

Julia had gone to Yale Drama School in September 1956, after *The Children's Garden* had closed. Rachel had turned to her at the Labor Day picnic given on the farm for the Home for Crippled Children in Doylestown.

"It's September," Rachel had said. "What are you going to do?"

In reply and to make up for the time she had spent as an invalid first in Rachel's house and then her mother's, Julia said she was going to Yale Drama School.

"Without a college degree?"

Julia shrugged. "I don't need one."

The next Tuesday Julia had left for New Haven with her clips from *The Children's Garden* in hand, with letters from Hal Markus and Olivia, teachers at the Neighborhood Playhouse. She was immediately accepted, although the director did say that she was only the second student to be taken without a B.A. and that he hoped at nineteen Julia was stable enough emotionally to attend graduate school.

"Dead emotionally," she said later to Bumpo, joining him in his bedroom which he had turned into a planetarium, painting the walls blue and the galaxy on the ceiling. He kept the shades drawn and spent most of the time he wasn't in school in his room facedown on his bed, trailing his fingers back and forth on the hardwood floor. If his family wanted to talk to him in those early teenage years, they sat in a rope chair in Bumpo's room, adjusting their eyes to darkness.

"Is that what's been the matter with you since you came home?" Bumpo asked.

"I'm dead and gone to heaven."

"I didn't think you believed in heaven," Caleb said, lying on the floor with his feet on Bumpo's back. "I thought you believed you died and were dead period."

"That's how I feel, but I'm obviously perfectly alive."

"Imperfectly alive," Peter said.

Julia had spent the late spring and summer in a nightgown, dressing only for occasional dinners at Rachel's. She lived in the Main House in George's room until one day in late June, as though she had planned it, she walked across the south fields to her mother's house, took some cookies out of the jar in the kitchen and climbed into her childhood bed.

She didn't read. She didn't see friends from school or talk to her brothers except the usual banter or to her mother, who seemed more than anyone to respect the changes in Julia. Cally never pressed.

"I don't know how you can stand to see her like that," Rachel said.

"It will pass. This summer is the first time in Julia's life that I have felt I understood her."

"What do you understand?" Peter asked.

"She's waiting," Cally said.

"For what?" Peter asked. "Christmas?"

"Don't be insensitive."

"What is she waiting for?" Bumpo asked, seriously concerned.

"Just waiting."

Every morning Bumpo brushed her hair. He went into her room early and brushed her long hair into shining while she lay on her stomach until Cally called them all for breakfast.

At Yale, Julia was outstanding. Her pieces were performed in the theater lab; she directed her own one-act plays and those of others; she acted and was considered not the most promising, as had been said of her before, but excellent.

"Technically perfect." Again and again she was told she was technically perfect.

"What a bore," she said once in her last year to Hal Markus, who had called her. They were sitting in her apartment on a couch together. Julia was curled into the corner, playing with the tail of one long braid, and Hal sat with his legs crossed at the knees the way she had first remembered him.

"I have no doubt that we'll hear about you, Julia," he said.

"When I'm nominated for a Tony in technical perfection."

"You were extraordinary in *The Children's Garden.*"

"I was lucky to start that way."

"Maybe not, because you've lost something. But it isn't uncommon to have a wonderful success too young and then get scared."

"I'm not scared."

"What are you then?"

"Alissa was the perfect part for me."

"That's not true either."

"I haven't felt the same way about plays since. I had a director and I wanted to be wonderful for him," Julia said evenly. "Maybe that's it."

"That's sentimental." They had never talked about what had happened between them during the time Julia was in New York.

"A common failing in second-rate actresses," she said.

"You haven't hit the source of what you can do, Julia, and if ever you do, either as an actress or a playwright, you will be very good."

"Fat chance," Julia said. "I'll get married and have children and watch TV movies at night in bed."

"You might fall in love."

"I have fallen in love."

"I mean really, so you stir up the center of yourself."

"I have really. It may be, you know, that all I can accomplish is technical perfection."

"Bullshit," he said and kissed her on the head.

"That's our family motto," she said. "Bullshit."

"What's it really like to fall in love?" Bumpo asked her after her graduation from Yale, the day before her marriage to Philip Kendall.

"Ordinary," she said. "I mean, just that, ordinary."

Julia had met Philip Kendall after a play he had seen at Yale in which she played the role of a ghost. He came backstage and introduced himself. He was a dark man, her height, fine-boned as the northern Welsh are, and weathered, with highly colored skin and untamed black hair, which he wore long over the collar of his jacket. He was a doctor. In the first month after they met, she moved into his apartment and they lived together as siblings, a relationship familiar to Julia and comfortable. Although they slept together, it was a simple, unexplorative act carried out like supper, a family meal, without danger of intimacy for either of them.

They developed a veiled life with each other, a relationship of courtesy and common understanding, like a marriage of thirty years after the old fights have been put aside, the passions filed smooth, the love, for certainly there was love, hanging on and hanging on.

She knew that Philip Kendall had a private life, but she didn't feel the urgent need of a lover to uncover it. They both realized that their careful life would allow secrets to remain undisturbed. Theo was born a year after their marriage, planned that way, because Julia wanted a child. They moved to the Howells farm, to Daniel's house, when Theo was eighteen months old and Julia was already pregnant with Pippa. Philip started a practice in family medicine in Doylestown, where he seldom had a more serious consideration than strep throat or grippe, occasionally pneumonia.

By September 1966, when Julia was twenty-nine years old, they had invented a life together.

At the beginning of September, Rachel put an ad in the local paper to rent the cousins' two fieldstone houses and the ad was answered by a group of college dropouts. They were peripheral members of the Students for a Democratic Society who went by single-syllable first names—Doug and Pat and Ralf and Max. They dressed in blue jeans and hiking boots and ate vegetables on principle.

"They don't work," John said to Rachel once.

"So?" she said. "Nor does Bumpo."

"That's a recommendation?" he asked.

"It's an observation," Rachel said. "Children today are concerned with the state of this country and they should be. They aren't so interested in getting ahead." Out of the stack of morning mail she handed John a new postcard from Andersonland, Colorado.

Dear Family,
    I've moved on to a mountain town outside of Boulder and it's
beautiful. Skye calls it paradise and says we'll never leave.
                                        Love,
                                        Nat (Bumpo)

"Is this validation?" John asked, leaving the postcard on the
kitchen table. "I've also noticed," he began again, "that they have
no sense of humor."

"Who?" Rachel asked.

"The goddamned people in the Cousins' Houses."

The group which had moved into the larger house in late September said that the other house would be occupied by a couple
traveling from California who were expected in October. They paid
two months' rent in advance on both houses and warned Rachel
that on weekends they would be entertaining a number of friends
from New York who would enjoy the country in the fall. However,
the people from the city who did visit regularly spent the weekend
inside the house, which could not, as Rachel pointed out, have
given them much change from their apartments. They never complained. When the stove broke, they bought a secondhand one.
When the small oak tree fell in the front yard, they chopped it up
for firewood and stacked it. Only when there was a grease fire in
the kitchen and the fire department was called did Rachel ever have
to go inside the house. And then Max hurried her out quickly,
saying there was no need, the fire was out and they'd been careless
with hot oil. Before she knew it, Rachel was standing on the front
steps. She had never rented to such independent people.

By chance, Julia became friendly with one of them. On fine afternoons in autumn she walked the farm with her children, gathering
leaves and pine cones, now and then walnuts. They often stopped
by the pond, throwing pebbles in the muddy water, Theo and Pippa
looking like the pictures of little boys and girls in old-fashioned
books at Bam's house, round-faced, red-cheeked, in Irish sweaters.

Often Julia dropped back to watch them from a distance, pleased
by the rich, gentle childhood she felt she was making for her children. She was lonely, but she filled the empty pockets of her life
with projects, pressed wild flowers, leaves ironed between waxed
paper, songs on the harpsichord in the study, clay made from flour
and water in the kitchen, finger painting on the kitchen floor, books
and books of stories, puppet shows.

She met Doug on one of her afternoon walks and their meeting became a ritual throughout the fall. She came to look forward to these encounters, to plan for them. Doug would join her and the children as they passed his house and they'd walk to the pond, through the woods and back to Daniel's house, often arriving just as Philip drove up in the jeep after hospital calls.

Doug was an ordinary-looking young man, with an air of studied poverty, pleasant, impersonal and informed, reminiscent of some of the young men with whom Julia had gone to high school in Washington: cautious, considerate and often dull.

"A slug," Peter said.

"He's not slimy," Julia replied. "He's just not very exciting."

"Mama says you spend every afternoon with him," Peter said. "I guess at this point in your life anything will do."

"He listens."

"What do you tell him?"

"A lot." She and Philip seldom had conversations requring intimacy and she had a few times found herself confessional with Doug for no other reason than that he was there.

"Terrific, Julia. Another point in favor of the new Julia Kendall," he said. "Spilling the family secrets to a Trotskyite, a late-blooming American revolutionary."

"He's not fiery enough for revolution."

"You misunderstand revolutionaries, my sweet." Peter hoisted Pippa on his back and took her into the house. "He's collecting information to use against you. A tedious statistician."

"I don't believe you."

"You never have."

"If that's so, why doesn't Bam get rid of them?"

"Bam likes this kind of situation. She should have been a chemist so she could have mixed liquid explosives in the safety of a laboratory."

They sat down in the kitchen and Julia peeled a banana for Theo and Pippa.

"What do you think they're doing here?"

"God knows," Peter said. "I thought Doug blankety-blank might have told you."

"Nope. I don't even know his last name. I always end up doing the talking."

Peter pulled a postcard from his jeans pocket.

"Here," he said. "Let me brighten your day with a word from Bumpo."

"Don't," Julia said. "I get them, too, once a week. I never read them."

" 'Dear Dr. Howells, Wow,' he writes, 'it's knockout to think you're a doctor already.' "

"Peter," Julia said. "Bumpo buys five postcards every week. He sends one to you and one to me and one to Caleb at Haverford and to Mama and to Bam. They're all the same and they break my heart."

Theo looked at his mother inquisitively.

"Honest?" he asked.

"It's a figure of speech," she said to him.

Theo watched his mother carefully.

Peter stuffed the postcard in his blue jeans pocket, kissed Pippa on the nose and started to leave.

"Do you remember when I called you in New York when Jimmy Bray got run over, while you were being a famous actress?"

"I remember."

"Why didn't you come when I asked you to?"

"I can't remember why."

"It was lousy," he said.

"Yes," she agreed. "It was."

"I wonder if all families just seem wonderful when you're a child."

"I'm hoping to do better," Julia said.

"Than Mama?"

"Yes, though Mama did the best she could."

"Dreamer." He brushed her hair out of her eyes sweetly. "And you were such a tough little kid."

"Bullshit," Julia said, and to Pippa and Theo's surprise and pleasure, she poured the glass of wine in her hand down the back of Peter's flannel shirt.

On the evening of the fifteenth of October, the night after the arrival of the black van from California, Philip returned from the hospital just as Julia was coming around the back of the house with Pippa and Theo and Doug. He didn't stop to greet them as he usually did. When Julia went in the house, she found him in the kitchen with a beer, spooning out a plate of manicotti which was on the top of the stove waiting to be reheated. His lips were white.

"I'd appreciate it if you'd have the children listen to records in Theo's room so that I can talk to you," he said, sitting at the kitchen table with his supper.

"Aren't we eating together tonight?" Julia asked when she returned from the children's room. In the years they had been married there was seldom an alteration in their routines.

"I have to go back to the hospital," he said. "Tell me about this Doug you walk with every afternoon."

"There's nothing to tell," Julia said.

"What has he said to you?"

"He's said very little."

"What has he asked you then?" Philip said, pulling Julia over next to him, leaving a hand on her wrist. "Certainly you don't walk around in silence."

"Well, no," Julia said. "Mostly he's asked about the family and what we're like, Mama and you and Grandfather."

"And you've told him everything, of course."

"There's nothing to tell," she said. Then: "I think you're jealous."

Philip put down his fork and looked at Julia in genuine surprise. "Jealous of what?"

"Why, of Doug!" Julia said, uncomfortable, squirming like a child under his direct gaze. "Of me and Doug what's-his-name."

Philip stood up, rinsed his plate and placed it in the rack. He ran his fingers through the shock of black hair, put his hands in his pockets.

"You are a newborn baby," he said to Julia. "You don't understand danger at all."

When he came back late that night, he slept in the guest room. Julia listened as he turned out the light; then she tiptoed down the hall and stood in the dark doorway. He was lying down, propped by pillows, visible in a bright moon. His arms were crossed over his chest, his long hair unkempt, and he looked to Julia surprisingly fierce and beautiful, as though he were in flight from the confines of the neat, transparent circle of their lives.

"You can come to our room," she said to him, wanting him suddenly.

"Of course I can," he said.

"I was glad to think you might be jealous," Julia said. "Even if you aren't. You're always so reasonable."

"I have learned to be," he said, putting an arm under his head.

"I've known you for eight years and you've always been reasonable."

"I learned before that," he said.

She sat down beside him on the bed and he moved slightly to accommodate her.

"What dangers don't I understand?" she asked.

"This Doug without a last name."

"Yes?"

"What have you told him?"

"How we live day to day. He's very friendly, Philip. Honestly. And boring. I can't imagine anyone so boring being dangerous."

"What questions?"

"What Bam does all day and Mama and how many days a week Grandfather works in the city and whether I'm simply a housewife. Unexceptional questions. And he plays with the children."

"I haven't liked them from the start," Philip said.

"Why didn't you say so?"

"This is not my house or my farm. One observes courtesies."

"You certainly can't be faulted for not being courteous."

"Besides, Rachel entertains herself by the repertory theater she puts in these houses. She hopes for high drama regularly, and people for whom to cook."

"She's a good woman," Julia said in Rachel's defense, but laughing a little.

"She's an exceptional woman, Julia, and often wise. Only in this case, I think not."

Julia lay beside him on top of the covers, her own head propped by a pillow, her arms as his were. She imagined that they would have looked like relatives to someone entering the room at that moment, related in their dark faces and wide-set eyes, the way their arms matched, their legs crossed alike, their fine cheekbones. She wanted to touch him, to confirm his familiar existence, but she did not for fear he would pull back as though she were an impostor and these last years, sharing the same bed, the same table, occasionally the same bath, had not altered the depths of their individual lives.

Julia knew Philip as a generous, occasionally witty man, even-tempered to a fault, whose time for each patient, for Julia and his children, was not defined by ordinary measures. He listened with such sympathy that people's sense of Philip Kendall after a personal conversation was actually a heightened sense of themselves.

If Julia were to make a list of what she knew about Philip, it would be short. He had been born in 1933, in North Wales, had moved to Holland with his family. His father had died there when Philip was eight, in circumstances related to the war which Philip did not discuss. His mother returned to Wales with her two young sons and died while Philip was practicing medicine there. His brother, a year older, was now a barrister in London and Philip was in constant correspondence with him, writing once a week, simple messages such as "All's well here. The lineup this week in N. Eastern U.S.A. is enclosed. Best, Philip." In the letter would be included the *Times* advertisement page of "COUNTRY PROPERTIES." In return he would receive from his brother, Arthur, a similar letter on professional stationery which would include "COUNTRY PROPERTIES" from the *London Times*.

"Are you going to buy a place?" Julia asked him once.

"Oh, no, darling," he had said. "I'm sure we won't buy a place."

"Then what do you do this for?"

"We always have, since were were boys in Holland," he said. "I think at one time, surely before I was thirteen, we did plan to buy a place in Wales and raise sheep, but that's long since been given up."

Julia had never met Arthur. He wrote her at the time of her marriage, a letter of great formality, welcoming her to the family and signed it "Yours, Arthur Kendall." She wrote back, signing "Love, Julia," and that was that.

Philip was considered a good doctor, responsible, not overambitious. He seemed to everyone who knew him, to Julia who should have known him better than anyone, to be a man at peace with himself, whose designs for his own life did not exceed what was possible and who therefore did not try, had no need to try, to alter the world as he found it.

Julia lay very quietly next to him. He was looking out the window, occupied with his own thoughts. Although she could not see his face directly, she knew by the set of his jaw, by a certain restlessness in his crossed arms that he was not at peace with himself. Unaccountably she remembered a sudden excitement when as a child she had looked under Cally's bed at Christmastime and found the presents in boxes stacked there. Although she could not identify the presents by specific names, just her discovery of their existence gave a new dimension to Christmas.

Without warning, Philip had become a mystery to her and she

wanted to take him on top of her, to feel him inside her, to know him specifically. This desire was new to her life with him and urgent. She did not touch him. She fell asleep, and when she woke up in the morning, Pippa was sitting on her stomach, unbuttoning the blouse in which she had slept. Philip was gone.

Philip Kendall was awake off and on all night. By sunrise he had decided to take matters in his own hands. He got up without waking Julia, dressed, took a toolbox from the shed and walked across the woods and lower field to the stone house. He expected the ex-students in the house to be asleep. Every blind was pulled and several windows without blinds were covered with paisley cloth. He knocked. When no one answered, he knocked again, once and several times, then announced himself. Doug answered in blue jeans without a shirt.

"I'm sorry to wake you," Philip said matter-of-factly, "but I have to check your downstairs bath. We are on the same system and occasionally yours collects the water. There's a release valve."

"Just tell me how," Doug said filling the doorway. "I'd be glad to fix it."

"Quite all right," Philip said in a cool voice. "I need to do it right away." And there was simply nothing that Doug could do, short of wrestling the small dark man to the floor because Philip pushed him aside and went in the house.

"Everyone's asleep," Doug said feebly.

"That's quite all right," Philip said. "I'll be quiet."

In the bathroom he pretended to do a number of things with a wrench and made a convincing amount of noise.

"Thank you very much," he said to Doug. He walked down the hallway, opened the front door and left, remarking that the water problem had been solved efficiently. He made one mistake, as he told John Howells later, because he was angry at this group of people. As he turned to pull the front door closed behind him, he met Doug's eyes directly, and his expression was not that of a physician turned early-morning plumber, anxious to get his toilet working so he could start the day.

When John and Philip came back to the fieldstone house with two officers from Solebury, the black van was gone, the front door of the house had been left open, the crates of rifles Philip had seen as he passed were no longer there, and the island in the middle of the kitchen where the sink was was full of chemicals which Philip recognized as useful only for the making of explosives.

"They may have left bombs," Philip said, shaken.

They found six inactive devices which the police took and decided that the rest of the bombs constructed during the six weeks the group had lived in the Cousins' Houses were in the back of the van. The group left clothes, a few pots, one stained sleeping bag and a box of pamphlets announcing the revolution.

Police in Newtown found the empty van late that afternoon in the woods behind the George School. An APB was put out, but the ex-students were never found. The following year Philip and John read in the *Times* about an explosion of a house in Brooklyn in which four young people were killed; one was Doug Bantrell and another was Max Heinz.

"We can sell the Cousins' Houses," Rachel said the afternoon that the black van left. "Just those and the land behind them. Then our land will make a triangle with Cally's house and Daniel's and the cemetery."

John raised his eyebrows. "That'll reduce your sideshow, Bam."

"It was a mistake," she said. "Don't make so much of it."

"I'm not, love."

"They seemed perfectly nice. Usually I like young people."

"Often I do, too."

"Anyway, I'm giving up. Perhaps we'll rent the small house next to Daniel's to very dull people who play bridge and don't drink and go to church. You can find them through the National Presbyterians."

"Oh, Bammy." John hugged her.

"I liked the Cares all right and so did you and actually the Volpones were wonderful. If only Mr. Volpone hadn't gotten caught, they could have been here for years."

John sat down at the kitchen table. "I was interested in Philip today," he said. "He surprised me."

"Did he?" Rachel asked, sitting down next to John with a pencil and a large sheet of paper on which to determine the division of land that very afternoon. "Underneath his gentle British manners, Philip Kendall is a passionate man."

"If he is, Bammy," John said, pulling her stool over next to him, "you would know it."

"I was thinking, just yesterday, while I was in your mother's greenhouse, that it isn't necessary for us to get old. For example, it's perfectly possible at our age to fall in love."

"I trust you mean with each other."

"Well, I suppose we could fall in love with anyone, but our lives would be simpler if we fell in love with each other. After all, you were seventy-two last summer, so we would be more sensible to fall in love with each other."

"I think you're right. I'm interested in your proposal as a long-term project."

"How did you know?" Julia asked Philip the night of the group's departure.

"I do not trust people like those," Philip said. "I expected something from the beginning." He was still nervous from the morning's discovery, rearranging the kitchen counter while they talked.

"Like what exactly?" Julia asked.

"They are people who believe that they are right without a doubt." He hung up his overcoat and sat down in the living room. "In Holland under the Nazis there were people like that."

For a long time nothing more came of this glance Julia had had behind the stage curtain, Philip Kendall out of costume, in street clothes, his hair askew. But a restlessness spread angrily in Julia like poison ivy in the fall.

That night, however, she made actual love to Philip as though she had met him for the first time and wished to make the night so memorable he would not want to leave her in the morning.

Later, when Julia looked back at those days in October, she recognized that Philip had been available to her as he had never been before, that she had allowed the moment to slip away, afraid to risk what she knew of a stationary marriage, set like a diamond in a high six-prong setting, whose glitter comes of reflected sunlight.

In November John sold the Cousins' Houses and ten acres of land with each of them. The sale left eighty acres, six houses, one of which was really a log cabin used by Pippa and Theo as a playhouse, a triangular piece of land, which included four acres of fields in crops, two large ponds, sixty acres of woods and meadows and the cemetery. It did not include, as Julia soon learned, the graves of the banished Lucy Tanner Howells and her daughter, Lucinda, which were located near the center of the acreage sold in November to the O'Tooles from New York City.

Julia went with Pippa and Theo to visit the new owner one afternoon in early November and they told her.

"I hope you weren't rude," Rachel said later.

"I'm too old to be rude," Julia said. "But I'm furious. They're our graves."

"Maybe we can make arrangements to buy them back from the O'Tooles. I'll ask Granddaddy."

"They even like the graves," Julia said. "They think it's quaint to have graves on your property."

John promised to speak to the O'Tooles.

"We'll dig them up, right?" Theo said.

"That's the only thing we can do," John answered. "We can't exactly buy back a piece of land in the middle of their property."

"Do we get to open the boxes?" Theo asked.

"That's an awful idea," said Julia.

"The first grade has a skeleton that's a girl," Pippa said. "You can take her apart and we get to play with the bones when we visit first grade."

"I think it's just dumb to dig them up if we're not going to get to see them," Theo said. "We could stand the girl skeleton next to Pippa to see who's taller and then we could sort of imagine what she'd look like with skin and blood."

The O'Tooles agreed reluctantly to give up their newly acquired graves but asked if they could come to the exhumation.

"Do they have to?" Julia asked her grandfather.

"Apparently they want to," John said.

"I'll combine this with a buffet supper to welcome the O'Tooles. A community affair. We haven't had one for months," Rachel said.

Julia called Peter and Caleb to tell them about the occasion, which was planned for the eleventh of November, a Saturday, so the children would be out of school.

"For Chrissake, Julia," Peter said when she reached him at his apartment. "I'm not going to take the time off from the hospital for the gravedigging."

Later in the week Julia received a Hallmark get well card from Peter. "Listen, darling," it said, "I'm more than a little concerned about you. If you don't take your theatrics back to the theater, you'll be institutionalized at thirty."

"Don't pay any attention to him," Cally said to Julia. "He's always been like that." She was making peach pies for the occasion, and hot bread.

Caleb said he would come. He took family occasions seriously. Although he thought it unusual to go home for a reburial of a couple of relatives who'd been dead one hundred years, most of the family occasions were unusual and he participated in them without fail and without necessarily understanding their significance. He did it because he loved his family and also because he had developed, in the years since he stopped wetting his bed, into a responsible young man who, as a junior at Haverford College, had made plans to become an architect. Besides, the occasion gave him and opportunity to bring home Rika, whom he hoped to marry the June after they were graduated.

Altogether there were seventeen people gathered at the oak tree beside Lucy Tanner and Lucinda's grave on a gray November morning just before lunch. The three O'Toole children stood solemnly with Pippa and Theo Kendall, drinking hot chocolate from paper cups. Caleb was there with Rika; John was there with Aiken, a farmer who had helped him for years. They'd been up at daybreak and dug two graves in the Howells cemetery far away from Dr. Thomas Howells, M.D., and his second cousin, second wife. Cally was there; Rachel, who had walked over with Julia through the woods; and the O'Tooles, who had invited Mr. O'Toole's bachelor brother and weekend guests from Connecticut, who they insisted had just popped in at the last minute.

It had been a fight for Rachel to persuade John to bury Lucy in the family cemetery. There was a note in the family Bible that said Lucy Tanner had been buried where she was by design.

"Everyone's dead," Rachel had said. "You can do what you want."

"That's just the point, Bam. If we don't honor these requests of dead relations, we can do anything we want. Nothing is sacred."

"Where do you plan to put them?" Rachel asked.

"Just outside the family cemetery there's a very nice place."

"In the cow dung?"

"We can put up a fence."

"If you won't put them in the cemetery, I insist we bury them outside the Main House in my rose garden."

"For Chrissake, Bammy, I'll have to put the bloody coffins on the tractor to drive them up through the woods. This occasion is crazy enough. Let's at least make it easy."

"I'm more interested in making it honorable."

Cally, too, had confused the issue because of Roger. Roger had died of natural causes in 1962, had been buried near the glass shoe-box, and every spring one or two of the dogs Cally had taken from the Humane Society dug him up.

"I don't know why Roger," Cally said to Rachel. "It must be because of his size. They haven't found the hamsters or the birds or the rabbits. The yard is full of animals."

"I suppose you want Roger in the family cemetery," John asked.

"That would be wonderful, if you wouldn't mind," Cally said.

"I mind enormously."

But John agreed to put Lucy and Lucinda in the family plot fearing that if he didn't acquiesce, he might be burying Roger in a similar ceremony.

Philip said he would not come. That under no circumstances on a perfectly decent Saturday was he going to spend his time witnessing the rearrangement of graves. But in the end he wandered through the woods into the clearing just as the second coffin was unearthed and brought by Caleb, John, Aiken and Mr. O'Toole's bachelor brother to level ground.

They were simple pine coffins, nailed shut, so light that Philip and Caleb could carry both of them. John followed, pushing the two markers in a wheelbarrow, and the rest of the group trailed behind.

"Are we going to open them up now?" Theo asked his father.

"Beats me," Philip said. "I'm unfamiliar with this ceremony. John?"

"I think we should," Theo said. "Don't you, Uncle Caleb?"

"Don't ask me, Theo. Bam knows about these things," Caleb said.

"I want to see if it's a girl skeleton," Pippa said.

"We know it's a girl, dummy," Theo said.

"Maybe not," one of the O'Toole children said. "Maybe it was a fake." But his mother hushed him and he didn't speak again during the ceremony.

John brought his shovel and stood next to the coffins.

"Rachel?" he said. "This is your idea. I'd like to put them in these holes and eat lunch."

"Let's look," Julia said.

"Mommy says we have to look," Theo said earnestly.

"Bam?"

Rachel said with great dignity, as though everyone assembled ought to know the protocol and unearthing dead relations were a common custom in the Northeast, "Of course. Caleb, will you pry open the tops, darling, and be careful not to break the lids?"

They took the lid off the smaller coffin first, pried it loose easily, and what appeared when Caleb lifted the lid, besides a small dense cloud of smoke, was a tiny skeleton covered with a blanket of dust. Caleb renailed the lid and with Aiken lowered the coffin into the smaller hole. Then he opened the coffin with Lucy Tanner Howells and what he found when he lifted its lid was a skeleton, facedown, of a woman who must have been extremely tall for her time. Without stopping to examine the skeleton, he nailed the coffin shut and with John's help lowered it into the ground beside Lucinda. John made a few embarrassed remarks, uncomfortable with the company of strangers at this ceremony, and led the group to the Main House, where Rachel and Cally had prepared a buffet lunch.

"My God," Julia whispered as they walked back through the woods after her grandfather. "Why do you think they buried Lucy Tanner facedown?"

"Punishment for her sins, I suppose," Rachel said.

That morning the postman had brought another postcard from Bumpo, longer than the previous ones, which the postman was reading himself when John appeared. It was addressed to John and read:

> Dear Granddad,
>   Bam says you may be selling part of the farm. Please don't sell it all without letting me know. Before long, I'll probably be back. I've moved to Oregon. I hitched out here last week when Skye split with someone she'd met in Dammer Dammer. I know you wouldn't have liked her anyway. She wouldn't have fit in. You'd love it here. The Pacific is knockout. Please remember not to sell the farm without letting me know.
>
>   Love,
>   Nat (Bumpo)

For the first time there was a phone number underneath his name, along with a new address in Wheelock, Oregon, c/o Mousers.

At dinner that night Philip Kendall agreed that it was, he supposed, unusual, for all he knew of American burial customs, that they had buried Lucy Tanner facedown, maybe disrespectful, unkind, even cruel. He agreed, as Julia persisted, but finally he had to admit that he honestly didn't give a damn if they'd buried her wrapped in the Union Jack.

Waiting for Love started that night in Julia's imagination, as she lay in the dark bedroom while Philip Kendall slept. It was a play about a young woman named Lucy Tanner and her husband, Dr. Kurtz, who is a Jewish physicist. The man with whom Lucy falls in love is a young German lawyer, a former member of the Hitler Youth. The child of their illicit union is Lucinda. The play is contemporary, circa 1965, and takes place in Cambridge, Massachusetts, in Dr. Kurtz's house. In the second act, Lucy dies in childbirth. During the third act, the German lawyer tries to reclaim Lucinda, who is two years old. She never appears onstage. In the end he must return to Germany because his mother is ill, leaving the physicist slowly starving Lucinda to death.

"What love are we waiting for?" Hal Markus asked on the phone after reading the first draft of Julia's play, written at a frantic pace.

"I'll retitle it," Julia said.

"No, leave the title as it is. Rewrite the play."

She worked every day from midmorning until supper, stopping only at three to pick up Theo and Pippa and take them to Cally's house, where Cally would have made cookies and applesauce or peach pastries and hot chocolate and the four of them would sit around the kitchen table, look out the window at fields with the last trace of maple on the trees and talk about the day. By four Julia would be back in her bedroom, working on the play.

She worked in a frenzy, finishing the second draft right after Thanksgiving. Often Cally fed Pippa and Theo and put them to bed in her house and Julia would not have dinner ready for Philip until after nine.

"A sense of balance seems to be foreign to your nature," Philip commented one night in early December.

"I thought you would be pleased to have me working again," Julia said.

"Of course," he said. "I think it's a good idea in moderation."

"There's nothing moderate about writing a play. You have to get lost in it."

"If that's the case—I don't know surely, I've never written plays— then I can only hope you won't write too many of them."

The play was conflagration; it consumed her.

* * *

When Hal Markus received the rewrite, he called Julia.

"It's technically flawless," he said.

"Oh, shit."

"Don't be upset. I think you should send it to Yale and have them do a part of it in a laboratory production."

"You think it will be terrible."

"Not necessarily. I think it lacks life because Lucy Tanner is a victim. Life in the theater comes of choice."

"I know what life in the theater comes of," Julia said. "Remember?"

Hal Markus sent copies of the script to Yale Drama School and to Olivia with a note that Julia had created the character of Lucy Tanner with Olivia in mind.

Shortly thereafter Julia received a letter from Olivia in New York:

> Dear, dear Julia,
>
> I have read *Waiting for Love* and think it virtually without fault in structure and timing. The characters are realized with great accuracy; the language is not only beautiful but moves the action forward with such little effort it is as though you've sewn the play with secret seams.
>
> Hal sent it to me saying that you had written the part of Lucy Tanner for me and I am overwhelmed with the sweetness of your thought, which makes it all the more difficult to write to you and say that I've thought and thought about it and know in my heart of hearts that I would have trouble playing the part of Lucy Tanner as it's written. I could go on and on and on and say for this reason and that reason, but I would so much prefer telling you in person. Please call.
>
> My love,
> Olivia

Julia did not call Olivia at all. A week later Olivia wrote one more note to Julia:

> Julia, my love,
>
> I've been thinking about the title *Waiting for Love*. It seems to me that Lucy Tanner would be more likely to go after love than to wait for it.
>
> I think of you. Love, O.

On the first of December Rachel told Julia that she and John would be going to Europe for Christmas.

"Why?" Julia asked.

"I've never been there," Rachel said. "John was invited by a client whom he has represented for years and so we've decided to go."

Julia wasn't listening.

"Who'll do Christmas?"she asked.

"You'll do Christmas," Rachel said, laughing.

"I can't imagine it," Julia said.

"What do you mean, lamb? You're very competent. You've been cooking since you were seven and it's simple. I get two turkeys and cook one the day before Christmas and one the day before that and Isaac sends us a Smithfield ham and your mother always does the biscuits. We'll do the pudding next Saturday and give it plenty of time to soak in bourbon and Lila will do the vegetables. Caleb will get a huge tree and we've been asking the same people for years and years. It will be splendid," Rachel said.

"Julia." She sat down beside her. "I'm surprised at you."

"It's not the stupid cooking, Bam," Julia said. "Any imbecile can cook. It's doing Christmas by myself."

Theo bopped Jason Titus on the head with the thick end of a baseball bat, unprovoked. "Bopped" was the first grade teacher's word and "unprovoked" was Philip's. The first grade teacher had used the word "premeditated," sounding each syllable as though it had been murder Theo had committed, when in fact, Jason Titus had not even had a mild concussion. The first grade teacher had called in the school psychologist and the principal for a conference with the Kendalls because they were, in the principal's words, "deeply concerned" about Theo.

When Julia pointed out that Jason Titus had not been seriously hurt, the school psychologist, who was not local and didn't know about the Howells' standing in the community, expressed his belief that the problem with Theo might lie with his mother, who determined the seriousness of a crime by the degree of brain damage it inflicted. Julia said she would speak with the first grade teacher and the principal. She would not speak with the school psychologist and left the conference room.

"That was extreme and rude," Philip told her later. She agreed it had been rude and that she didn't give a fuck.

"I don't want to talk about Theo," she said as Philip followed her into the house from the jeep.

"We have to talk about him," Philip said.

"No, we don't," she said, pouring a cup of very black coffee from the morning pot. "What is there to say? I have spent six years with Theo, all of my time, and if he is disturbed, as that man suggested, then I feel entirely responsible. I don't want to discuss it."

The principal used the word "disturbed" and didn't change it when Philip said that he had never, even in splendidly normal America, met someone who was "undisturbed." As we see it, the principal had said, Theo is withdrawn, does not relate well to his peers and has learning difficulties. He stands in the middle of the room, shouts, throws erasers. He taps and pops, hits and kicks, and otherwise interrupts the rest of his classmates, who have adjusted beautifully to the first grade. He is, in short, violent.

"He's not violent," Julia said. "I've never seen him violent at home."

The principal advised them that Theo was to be withdrawn from Downingtown Friends School until he had had a complete psychiatric examination and the psychiatrist would have to recommend that he was fit to return to school.

That day, after Philip had gone to his office, Julia drove to Downingtown Friends to collect Theo and all of the things in his cubby. Then she drove to New Hope with Theo and Pippa and parked next to the ice cream shop. At the toy shop down the street she bought Pippa a gingerbread boy to hang on the Christmas tree and Theo a tiny rocking horse carved out of wood. They went to the ice cream shop, where Theo had pink bubble gum ice cream, and they sat in the windows of Massey's Ice Cream Parlor and watched the tourists hustling down Main Street, buying and buying for Christmas.

"Why did you hit Jason Titus on the head?" Julia asked Theo.

"Because he's mean to me," Theo said simply.

"What mean does he do?"

Theo looked out the window, thoughtful, trying to think of the best way to make his mother understand.

"He doesn't do mean things to me," Theo said. "He has mean thoughts about me."

"You should never hit someone, darling, even if he is thinking mean thoughts," Julia said. "How do you know he's thinking mean thoughts?"

"I just do. I always know that."

"You look queer, like you're going to cry in the store," Pippa said to her mother.

"I won't do it again," Theo promised.

"It's okay," Julia said.

"It's okay for Theo to hit Jason?" Pippa asked.

"No, no, no." Julia took Pippa's plump hand going out to the car. "I forget what's okay."

When Julia put Theo to bed that night, she kissed him and whispered in his ear that she was sorry it had been a bad day.

"That's all right," Theo said to her. "I have trillions of bad days."

She turned out his light, opened his window slightly, put his clothes in the laundry basket.

"Anyway," Theo volunteered from his bed, "it's not your fault."

Philip had planned to tell Julia the very same thing. He was going to say at supper, after the children were sleeping, that she had to put too much of her own life into the lives of her children, that she could not take complete responsibility for their disturbances. When she came downstairs, he could tell it was the wrong subject. They ate in silence. Philip had never been able to fill a silence on his own and this evening Julia's temper defied conversation.

"I hate to hear you chew," she said once, and he made an effort to chew quietly, avoiding his salad.

"Anyone who can see us from the road is probably thinking to himself, What a romantic meal!"

"Unaware, of course, that I'm not allowed to chew it."

"I'm going to Mama's," Julia said, getting up from the table. "I can't stand to eat with you."

She wanted to ask Cally about Bumpo. Walking across the south fields with a flashlight, she could see Cally moving around the living room of the house and Lila, who had moved back to the farm, in the kitchen cleaning up. Cally still wore jeans and Nat's shirts, although she now had short hair which was curly and gray. She was heavy; not fat, but thick after years of relying on her shoulders and arms to move her. The living room was full of domestic animals, cats on chairs and ottomans and tables, three nondescript dogs lying on the rug and one curled on the couch where Cally had moved herself. There was a goat named Cynthia, who had replaced Roger and who now made goat sounds at Julia as she approached the front walk, butted her legs and followed her into the house.

"Get outa here, you goddamned goat," Lila called from the kitchen, but the goat paid no heed. It went instead straight to the kitchen and later, when Julia went to say good-night to Lila, she found her sitting on the kitchen counter in serious conversation with Cynthia.

"I thought you hated goats," Julia said.

"I hate this one," Lila said, "but she's too mean to kill, so we have to adjust to each other."

In the living room Julia sat in her mother's wheelchair. She had seen her mother all the time since she and Philip had moved back to the farm, but she seldom sat down in conversation with her and never came to ask Cally's advice, believing them to be such different women that her advice could not bear on Julia's life. This evening, coming in despair to talk to her mother, she was surprised at Cally's unexpected beauty in the soft light of the living room and at the sense of peace she felt just being there with her, watching her mother's untroubled face, for that was what it was. Untroubled. And here was a woman who had had, anyone would agree, more than her share of turned tables.

"You heard about Theo," Julia said.

"Theo told me himself," Cally said. "He told me another little boy was mean and so he beat him on the head."

"He's didn't say he's been kicked out of school, did he? I don't think he knows."

Cally raised her eyebrows. "Kicked out?"

"They say he's disturbed. They say—oh, shit, they say a lot of things about how he can't adjust."

"What is disturbed?" Cally asked.

"I don't know. They mean crazy, I suppose. Anyone different is crazy—like Bumpo. What did schools ever tell you about Bumpo?"

"I can't remember, darling. Bumpo didn't like school, and when he wanted to come home, he stuck his finger down his throat. They called me and I came and got him. I know it made them very cross, but the teachers always cleaned up, not wishing to be caught by the principal with throw-up on the floor. They were very stupid really. He managed to make himself sick regularly until the fourth grade."

"And you didn't worry?" Julia asked. "I mean, look at Bumpo

now. You didn't worry that he wouldn't adjust?"

"I didn't," Cally said. "Perhaps I should have and should still."

"Well, I worry all the time," Julia said. "Right now I feel entirely responsible."

"For his hitting the other little boy?"

"Yes. And being kicked out. For his disturbances."

"Well," Cally said, rearranging her legs on the sofa, "I do remember one way in which I felt responsible when I was young and when your father was well; until he was burned, I suppose." She looked at her hands while she talked. They were not delicate hands. They were thick and muscular, a worker's hands with square fingernails, clean but unattended. "When I met your father, I was seventeen and he thought I was very pretty. We never talked about how he thought of me because things turned so quickly, but I think he planned that we would do a lot together, go horseback riding, which I used to do quite well, and play tennis. He would go about town showing me off some, which is what men did then. When I got polio, I felt as if I'd let him down. I had been raised to believe that if you behave yourself, things will go very well." She folded her hands across her stomach, which was slack after babies and inactivity and lay like a pillow between her hipbones. "I was easy, which was the worst thing a girl in the South could be then. Your father had to marry me, and I got paid back."

"You didn't honestly believe all that, Mama."

"I did then," she said. "I was a child. I couldn't stand to think about what your father had lost by marrying me. There were many pretty girls he could have married."

"That's crazy."

"And it's crazy for you to feel responsible for Theo," Cally said.

"You don't still feel that way, do you?"

"No," Cally said. "I don't at all. I feel we made something wonderful of a life which surprised us and I also know what I didn't know then: that any life would have surprised us. We were very young." She took one of her fat tabby cats on her lap and scratched him between his yellow ears.

After Nat died in 1954, Cally lived two years alone with her sons and constant attempts by Rachel to take over everything. One afternoon, just before Christmas in 1956, Lila arrived with two suitcases and a footlocker and moved into her room, which had not been changed since she left it. Married life, she told Cally and the rest of the Howells, had not much agreed with her and, besides, Jimmy had taken up with a waitress at the diner. She was in no mind to share that black man with any woman, blue, white or yellow, who worked at the New Hope Diner.

She was glad to be back. It was as though she had never left. She kept her job in New Hope, got up early to make hot biscuits and coffee, to start supper so she could cook it when she came home. She fussed over Cally, rubbed her back and neck at night, sat up with her when she couldn't sleep, told her jokes and riddles. And as the year of Lila's return progressed, they began to giggle laugh again, to tell stories to each other as they used to do.

One night in April, a warm, breezy night, the air sweet and full of growth, Cally could not sleep and Lila came in.

"Cally?" she said. "You sleeping?"

"No," Cally said.

"Can't you?"

"Can't seem to."

"You want me to stay with you?"

"If you like."

And Lila undid the tie of her robe, took it off, slipped her thin gown over her head and lay with Cally.

For the last ten years their days had gone like that, two women whose lives together had begun in childhood, who could live separately in the same house, filling their own lives, but knowing the other's state of mind without any need to lay it out for examination. Some nights, without a word beforehand of arrangements, they came together in a secret but shameless communion.

"I expect Theo's generation is going to be as interesting as a box of macaroni," Rachel said to John, who was reading the *Wall Street Journal* in the library while she wrapped Christmas presents to be ready when she and John left for Europe the twentieth of December.

John put the newspaper in his lap. "I didn't hear you," he said.

"I was talking about Theo. Can you imagine how well your father would have done in school if he were going now? He'd be in the reformatory. In jail."

"Don't be extreme, Bam," John said. "We're making too much of a fuss about Theo. He'll begin to believe there's something the matter with him."

"My point exactly," Rachel said. "By the time he's twelve, dismissed from school for not fitting into the proper cubbyhole, he will certainly be emotionally disturbed."

"I thought things had been looking up since you lost weight," John said.

"I've always believed we have to anticipate the worst."

"I know you do, Bam." He kissed her neck. "I'm taking Theo to the pond to watch the last of the geese fly south this morning," John said.

"Be sweet with him."

"I am too sweet already with all of you."

"I'm sorry about your troubles," John said, taking Theo's hand, walking through the woods behind Daniel's house to the larger pond.

"Everyone is," Theo replied. "Everyone in the family."

"Do you like school?"

"I hate it. People are quite mean to me."

"I don't believe that, Theo. There are mean people, of course, but I have never seen a place where everyone is mean."

"That's 'cause you haven't seen my school."

"Perhaps." John paused. "I'll have to come to see it."

"It's too late," Theo said matter-of-factly. "I've been kicked out already. I heard Mommy and Daddy fighting about it this morning in the bathroom and Mommy threw the shampoo at Daddy and it broke all over the floor and then she cut her foot and yelled, so Pippa and I got to eat cereal without milk while Daddy fixed her foot." He swung his great-grandfather's hand and turned his head to look out through the trees around them. "I love the farm. I don't ever want to leave it."

It had been a warm fall, and the birds were late in their travels south. The days, like this day in early December, seemed to come from the earth, to rise out of the wet ground in a warm haze which hung on the trees and lower growth like a thick gauze curtain. As he walked through the woods, the view seemed to John, now, like a picture from an illustrated story of Rip Van Winkle, mist rising from the Hudson, altering the shape of things, blurring the raw color and sharp edges, a projection of an old man's dream for himself beyond the present waking moment.

He held Theo's hand tightly, so tightly he could feel choruses of pulses passing between them, as though they were insulated conductors of messages unrestricted by language. He remembered, out of a long distance, walking down P Street in Washington, holding the hand of Adelia, his first love. That was all a young man of eighteen could do with a young woman of appropriate family at the turn of the century in a southern town: hold her hand so fiercely that it stood for every unexpressed desire.

"You're squeezing me, Grandfather," Theo said.

"I'm sorry." John let go. "I was sending you messages."

"The messages pinched," Theo said and took his great-grand-father's hand again.

"I'm glad you like the farm," John said to Theo when they were settled in an old rowboat on the pond to watch the geese. "I want you to like school as well. It's important to get along there."

"That's what Mommy said."

"If you get in trouble for hitting in school, you will simply be known as the boy who hits. You won't be able to do the serious things you want to do."

"I want to burn down the school."

"Oh, Theo," John said and pulled the slight dark-haired child over on his lap. "Someday this farm will be your farm if it lasts that long and we last that long. If you're off hitting people and burning down schools, you won't have a bit of time to take care of it."

When John came back from his outing with Theo, there was a postcard of the blue-black Pacific from Bumpo which Rachel tried to rescue before John read it.

"You won't like it," she said to him. And he didn't.

> Dear Family,
>
>   Knockout news from Wheelock, Oregon. I have whittled a prairie dog out of white pine and sold it as a souvenir to the Prairie Dog Fast Food and Sleep-Over Chain to sell at the cash registers of their gift shops at $3 each. I get 1/6 of the profit of every prairie dog sold plus ownership of the patent, so starting next week, I'm hitching HOME—Hurrah! Hurrah!—to spend my lifetime at the farm watching the sunsets with Tuwilla and whit-tlng till I die.
>
>   Love,
>   Nat (Bumpo)

"Who is Tuwilla?" John asked.

"I imagine she's his girl friend."

"Tuwilla," John said, tossing the postcard into the wastebasket, from which Rachel retrieved it as soon as he had left, "Tuwilla and the Mystery of the Prairie Dog Chain by Natty Bumpo. I have a headache."

Julia left on the twelfth of December for New Haven to see excerpts of *Waiting for Love* done in the Laboratory Theater by the students of Yale Drama School.

She realized the play's failure after the first few minutes, sitting in the theater with the small audience of students.

"I know, I know, dammit," she said afterwards to the young student director, "first-rate technically."

"It misses," she told the students and actors after the production, "and I don't know why. I feel as if I have drilled a well and missed the source of water."

She walked to Peter's apartment, bad-tempered.

"I am, I suppose, a technically first-rate mother as well," she said to Peter that night at dinner after he had come home from the hospital.

"Don't come to me with your bad news. By profession all I do is deal out bad news."

"I'm sure there's good news, too, when you're a doctor."

"Not lately," Peter said.

He was not the usual Peter. Julia had noticed before he came home that the apartment hadn't been cleaned. There were clothes all over, newspapers read and thrown on couches, dishes in the sink, and the refrigerator was empty of anything but condiments and half a carton of sour milk. Peter, in the years since he had left home, had become fastidious; everything around him had an order. He scrubbed his apartment regularly, as though it were a surgeon's hands. He kept potted plants in perfect bloom and cuttings in tiny glass chemical vials in the kitchen window. When he went home for the holidays, he stayed at Rachel's because his mother's house was full of animal hair.

Julia went to the market across the street from Peter's apartment and bought lamb chops, green beans and a bottle of wine. She had stacked up the newspapers and was picking up his clothes when there was a telephone call from "Anne," the voice said, and if Peter wasn't there, he should call her when he was because she'd expected him last night for dinner, today for lunch and why was the phone busy all night and who, she finally asked, was she talking to.

"His sister," Julia said.

"Oh," Anne said. "Julia. Pete has told me about you. He's probably told you that we're engaged to be married."

"No," Julia said. "He hasn't told me that."

"Well," Anne said, "we were when last I was in touch with him."

"Your fiancée called in a fit," Julia said to Peter when he came in.

"I don't have a fiancée," Peter said.

"You hadn't mentioned one," Julia said, "but there is a girl named Anne who is suffering under that delusion."

"I was going to marry Anne," Peter said, absently kissing Julia on the head. "I'm not going to marry her now."

"Well, you ought to call and tell her."

"I guess I should." He took the phone off the hook. "I'm taking a shower," he said. "If you don't mind, leave the phone off. I don't want to hear from anyone."

"What about Anne?"

"She's the least pressing problem on my mind."

It was after midnight and snowing. Julia could feel the quiet on the streets that comes of a night snow, the sense of calm and the sense, which she gradually realized was what had woken her, of Peter in the living room. She got up, took the spread off the bottom of the bed and wrapped it around herself. She found him sitting in a chair in the living room, fully dressed.

"What are you doing up?" she asked him.

"Thinking," he said, and then he turned suddenly and faced her. "I am thinking I may have been responsible for a patient's death. Accidentally," he said. "I was accidentally responsible."

"Oh, Peter," Julia said.

"Be very calm," Peter said warningly.

"I am being calm," Julia said. "I promise."

"He was an old man who was recovering from a mild heart attack," Peter said. "Very old. Maybe eighty. I know that doesn't make a bit of difference, how old he was, but he was old and I gave him an injection which was meant for a patient with asthma. When I made the rounds at ten, he was dead."

"You know it was your fault?"

"I knew when I found him," Peter said. "I thought, Jesus, no one on this ward was expected to die, and immediately I remembered the injection and then that it was meant for the patient in Three-oh-nine. I've been sick ever since."

"Who knows?"

"No one knows. It's not surprising for a man that age who's had heart attacks to die." He was still sitting in the same position but turned now to face Julia, and automatically, as though he had beckoned her, she got up, sat on the floor beside his chair and put her head on his knees.

"I'm so sorry, Peter," she said.

"The trouble is I've been preoccupied. I should have known something would happen. Anne, the woman who called, is a woman I go to dinner with and shows and weekends in New Hampshire from time to time. I sleep with her, but I don't love her and I don't want to marry her. She's been pressing and pressing and pressing. All last week she sent flowers and telegrams and called on the phone and so, of course, I couldn't get her out of my mind and then I was overtired. You're always tired as an intern." He put his head back on the chair, covered his eyes with his arm. "Fuck it," he said. "There are no excuses."

There were, he told Julia, two choices. One, he could say nothing and live with it. He'd get away with that certainly because no one had the least suspicion. The other was to tell and be sued by the old man's family, be released from his internship, have to leave medicine, possibly go into research, raise plants and maybe sleep at night again.

Julia rested her chin on her knees.

"Well?" he asked.

"I don't know, Peter," she said. "It's a lousy choice."

"What I'd like to do is get out of here for a few days, come home for Christmas and think about it. I can't think here with Anne on my trail like a bloodhound in heat."

"Bumpo may be home for Christmas."

"I can't imagine Bumpo being much help in this matter."

Peter lay on the couch and Julia rubbed his back, aware that she had not touched him at all since he'd grown up, except for brief embarrassed hugs, a kiss on the top of the head. His back seemed enormous to her, the way her father's back had seemed when she was small.

"Things haven't been the same since Daddy died," Julia said.

"Don't be gloomy, Julia. I can't stand it."

The week before Christmas, Julia cooked. She made cookies, packed in pinch pots for the neighbors, and small cakes, strawberry and apple tarts for the volunteer firemen and ambulance drivers, the people in the Home for the Incurables, and mince pies and shoofly pies for their Christmas at the Main House, where they were celebrating Christmas as they always did, even though Rachel and John were in Wiesbaden. Rachel had left pages of lists which Julia followed. She made decorations for the tree with the children, with Theo mostly, who had not returned to school: strings of popcorn and cranberries, gingerbread boys with bright green ribbon, lines of gold and red ribbon with candy canes and sugar cookie stars. Together they sewed tiny lace angels that would hang on the balsam branches of the tree Caleb and Theo had cut in the woods. Cally taught the children carols on the piano in Rachel's living room. During Christmas Philip worked harder than usual, sometimes not returning until eight or nine at night from rounds at the hospital. He often left in the morning before dawn.

"Why is it that you seem to work so much harder at Christmas and holidays than other times of the year?" Julia asked one evening as they were eating dinner together. "Are people sicker?"

"No," he said. "In fact, I hadn't noticed that I was working harder. I'm sure the psychologist Theo sees would say I am escaping from something, but I'm not keen to examine it."

Julia did not press. She didn't particularly wish to examine it either. It was distressing enough to hear weekly from the psychologist that Theo had problems relating to other children, that Julia should provide him with frequent opportunities for playmates so that he would begin to develop friendships with his peers.

"I thank God that I grew up and raised Nat without paying a psychologist for daily information," Rachel said. "If the psychologists have their way, we'll go back to arranged marriages based on conditioned responses."

Dutifully Julia invited friends one at a time during the holidays to play with Theo and watched over them carefully so Theo had no chance to bop his playmate on the head. Not infrequently a mother would say no, her son could not come over, not on Monday or Tuesday, and Wednesday didn't look particularly good either, so Julia would know beyond doubt that the little boy had said he wouldn't play with Theo Kendall ever. No one invited Theo anyplace.

"It is not a tragedy," Philip said to Julia one night when she couldn't sleep for worrying over Theo. "It's not a failure on your part or Theo's. If there is blame to lay, it is on the people here who are only comfortable with manufactured children, mass-produced according to the ingredients listed on the label."

"Well, it's not a comedy either," Julia said.

"It is beginning to be, as these little, snotty-nosed boys who have adjusted so magnificently to the first grade come over one day at a time and play under your watchful eye. It's called black humor, very popular at the moment, my love. You should write a play about it."

Everybody told Julia that the Christmas dinner was splendid. Julia knew the food was good, the tree was as lovely as any tree decorated under Rachel's direction had been, and the singing seemed no different from the years that John had led it with his huge bass voice.

"It was wonderful, darling," Cally said, squeezing Julia's hand.

Peter, who had come for Christmas, still undecided about medicine, telling no one about the old man except Julia, called it a beautiful Christmas, the best he could remember, and Caleb agreed.

Only Bumpo, who had been away three years, remarked late Christmas night as they all sat in front of a fire in the library, Tuwilla on Bumpo's lap, that "something was different this Christmas."

"You're different," Peter said.

"It was more like something was missing," Bumpo said.

Julia knew that he was right.

She could not, as she had told Rachel early that December, make Christmas. Something was missing in her, as though in her travels she had lost some essential, precious garment. But on examination, she could not determine what it was that was missing, only the sense that it was gone.

Years later, when the Bible was in her charge, Julia read John's entry made after New Year's.

DURING THE TIME RACHEL AND I WERE IN EUROPE JULIA MUST HAVE DECIDED TO INVENT ANOTHER LIFE, BECAUSE CERTAINLY SHE'S LEFT THE ONE WE HAVE BEEN WATCHING HER LEAD FROM THE BEDROOM WINDOW OF THE MAIN HOUSE.

THE PURSUIT
OF HAPPINESS

JULIA'S PLAY IS A HIT ON BROADWAY. "WITTY AND WISE," WROTE THE REVIEWER IN THE NEW YORK POST. "A FIRST-RATE COMMENTARY ON CONTEMPORARY FAMILY LIFE IN WHICH COMMUNICATION HAS GIVEN WAY TO INTERPRETATION," "THE FUNNIEST, DARKEST PLAY OF THE SEASON," FROM THE TIMES. AND ON AND ON AND ON. WE ALL WENT TO NEW YORK, MARCH 4, 1972, EVEN CALEB FLEW IN FROM HOUSTON FOR OPENING NIGHT. WE FILLED THE SECOND ROW OF THE MUSIC BOX. AFTERWARDS, BACKSTAGE, I OVERHEARD THE PRODUCER OF THE PLAY SAY TO HER, "SO, JULIA, THIS IS THE MOMENT YOU HAVE BEEN WORKING FOR. YOU MUST BE VERY HAPPY." I COULDN'T HEAR HER REPLY. I DON'T BELIEVE SHE GAVE ONE.

John Howells wrote this entry in the family Bible sometime the week after March 4. Although no one could have anticipated it at the time, this was the last entry that he was to make.

Later Rachel reread the passage for signs of his dying, a summing-up of his living.

"What do you read between the lines?" she asked Peter.

"I don't read between the lines, Bam," Peter said.

But Rachel persisted. Again and again she read the last entry, a simple factual account except for the final observation.

On the late train ride back to Trenton after Julia's play everyone in the family was talking back and forth between the aisles except John.

"I thought the play was very funny," Peter said.

"It was about me," Theo said. "I was the hero, only Mama called me Joey in the play, so I wouldn't sue."

"Well, the namby-pamby father wasn't me," Philip said.

"Julia was probably thinking of me," Bumpo said.

"The play's invented," Caleb said. "I asked her and Julia said she made it up entirely."

"I think Julia's too thin," Cally said quietly. "She seems unhappy to me."

"She's tired," Peter said. "With this success, she's certainly not unhappy."

"What do you think, John?" Cally asked.

"About thinness or happiness?" John asked.

"Happiness," Cally said.

"I think Julia's learning about happiness," John said.

"You think she expected too much of this play?" Rachel wondered as Caleb was driving them back to the farm.

"She expected happiness of the play," John stated simply. He took her hand and kissed the end of her fingertips.

Julia made a new life in her work after Christmas of 1966. That winter she opened the log house on the Howells farm, set it up as a studio and wrote another play which wasn't produced. The following autumn she wrote a one-act play and was invited to direct it with another one-act play by Anne Sexton in an off-off Broadway theater. She moved to New York in January and stayed until the end of March, coming home weekends. She was asked to direct two plays in a summer repertory theater in Connecticut and she took Pippa for the six weeks she was away.

"Did you have a good time?" Philip asked Pippa on a long walk they took together with Theo the afternoon she returned with Julia from Connecticut.

"Boring," Pippa said. "Mama bought me ice cream every day but one for being good. Chocolate mint."

"Goody-goody," Theo said in disgust.

"We haven't got a marriage any longer," Philip said when Julia came home from Connecticut to spend the month of August on the farm. They were sitting on the lawn together in white slat chairs, watching Pippa and Theo run through the pasture behind the Main House. "What do you want of us?"

"I don't honestly know," Julia said.

She knew that she wanted to be left alone, but she didn't tell Philip. Her mind spun with living room sets with fine-looking couples making ordered lives for themselves and their children, bedroom sets for love affairs carefully arranged but not without mystery, final scenes before the curtain went down which put the story in perspective, gave it a design. In fact, just at this moment, watching the children in the field, Julia had fallen for a character she was inventing, a physician. Maybe he'd be British. Perhaps he ought to die before the end of the play; perhaps he ought to leave her.

"I wish that Theo weren't disturbed," she said as though that were in answer to a question Philip had asked.

"He's not," Philip said. "He's better."

"He may hurt someone tomorrow."

"Of course. Anything could happen tomorrow," Philip said.

Julia didn't move her hand, which rested underneath Philip's on the white wood chair, but she wanted to take it back in her own lap, put it in the pocket of her trousers.

At Yale the winter of 1970, Julia directed her new full-length play. It was about a couple and their five-year-old son, whose part was to be played by a full grown man, larger than the mother and father. Julia was away all winter, coming home only if Pippa or Theo was sick or for conferences with Theo's teacher at the public school, where he had developed a new difficulty. He refused to work. The principal suggested a special school if things did not improve. During the spring Julia returned to the farm and rewrote the play, called *Joey Boy*. In the play Joey Boy takes over his family, harassing his parents, ridiculing and beating them when they annoy him. In desperation, unable to talk to Joey Boy or each other any longer, they seek the help of a psychiatrist, first for one session a week, then two, then three and so on until it becomes necessary for the psychiatrist to move into the house with Joey Boy and his family. Finally he is required to transmit all family communication. A dinner table scene in the second act begins:

JOEY BOY: Tell my mother I don't like enchiladas.

PSYCHIATRIST: Joey Boy wants me to share with you the fact that he doesn't like enchiladas.

MOTHER: Joey Boy must eat one enchilada.

FATHER: Half.

PSYCHIATRIST: Half, Joey Boy.

JOEY BOY: No.

PSYCHIATRIST: Joey Boy is having a very negative response.

MOTHER: *(taking Joey Boy's enchilada and putting it on father's plate)* Please.

FATHER: I'll eat half.
(Mother finishes enchilada.)

In June 1971 Julia sent the play to Hal Markus. The day he received *Joey Boy* in the mail, he called.

"I know the play will go," he said.

"Do you think it's good?" she asked.

"Of course it's good," he said. "And I think it will go."

"Something's missing," Julia said. "It's not great."

"Every play should have a little love in it," Hal Markus said matter-of-factly.

"Oh, shit."

"Don't worry," Hal said. "It's going to make it."

Julia spent the summer at home, distracted, her mind running like a film strip at slow speed.

"Well?" she asked Philip when he had read the script for *Joey Boy*.

"It's amusing," he said carefully.

"Is that all?"

"What else should it be?"

"Serious."

"I suppose," Philip said. "Although I feel as if you're exploiting Theo in this play. That bothers me."

"He's not like Theo," she said. "Joey is powerful. He's ruining his parents' lives."

"They are letting him, love," Philip said.

Julia turned to face him at the kitchen table where they were sitting. "Do you want to separate from me? Is that what you're saying?"

"We've separated already," Philip said.

In September, after school had started, Hal came to the farm and spent a week going over the script with Julia.

"I can tell you have fallen in love like I did," Hal said to her one afternoon with an impish grin.

"What do you mean?"

"With your work." He laughed. "Remember how you used to complain to me about that when you thought I should be falling in love with you?"

Julia smiled. "Of course." She leaned back from the table where they were working. "And I am in love with my work, thank God."

At the beginning of February 1972, when *Joey Boy* went into rehearsals, Julia moved back to New York to an apartment belonging to a painter, a friend of Bumpo's from Dammer Dammer. She slept in his back bedroom with the window open because of the sharp smell of oil paints. His name was David Asher and he had cancer.

"Stage two, Hodgkin's," Bumpo told Julia. "In remission. It could reverse at any time," he added.

David Asher was a figure painter, full-sized nudes, mostly women, a few of himself. In his early twenties he'd already had a very successful show uptown. He worked hard.

"In a heat," Bumpo said, "because you never know."

During rehearsals Julia went home on weekends to the farm, but on Monday morning she took the early train from Trenton, picked up two pastries, two cups of coffee and went to David Asher's apartment. Usually he was just getting up and came to the door in blue jeans with oil paint spread in dark rainbows on them and no shirt. There was always a girl. Not his models. In the three months that Julia lived there he had two models, both young, fleshless, with small breasts and tiny mounds of pale pubic hair, like hothouse violets. They left each evening when the sun went down. But every morning at breakfast there was a girl or a woman, often older than he was. Julia seldom saw the same one twice. After breakfast David put on a shirt, washed his face in the kitchen sink and asked the woman to leave. At night, while Julia was reading herself to sleep in the bedroom behind the kitchen, she could hear David Asher making love.

He began work that spring on a self-portrait, a full-sized nude. Julia would return from rehearsals to find David painting in the living room in front of an enormous mirror. But what struck Julia in her present state of mind was that David Asher could stand naked and unembarrassed, reproduced three times in the room, no more revealed than a bowl of artificial fruit.

"He doesn't even know it's himself he's painting," Julia told Bumpo. "When he looks in the mirror, he sees an ordinary figure."

Bumpo shrugged. "I don't think you should be there when he's painting, Julia."

"You don't understand," Julia said. "I'm jealous of his detachment."

"Well." Bumpo sounded unconvinced. "He doesn't seem as detached as he used to be in Colorado. In Boulder he was painting landscapes. You know, mountains."

"Like the knockout pictures of mountains in the postcards you used to send us," Julia said with an edge.

"Yeah. Those," Bumpo said earnestly.

When Bumpo dropped out of college in 1965, his sophomore year, he told Julia it was because of nerves. "Drugs," Peter had said.

"What kind?" Julia had asked.

"Certainly grass. Probably anything that takes the sharp edges off the world for him."

Bumpo was away for two years, and apart from the postcards and occasional phone calls, no one in the family was in touch with him directly until he came home for Christmas in 1966 with Tuwilla.

He was a child. Except for the fact that he had made a lot of money from the Prairie Dog Fast Food & Sleep-Over Chain, he was a young boy who did not show his age.

"Don't make fun of him," Julia had warned Peter the first Christmas Bumpo had come home.

"Fun?" Peter said bitterly. "Is it comical that he's wrecked half his brain?"

"What do you think has happened to him?" Caleb asked.

"Twenty-five percent lobotomized," Peter said, "and in spite of that he's the richest nine-year-old on the East Coast."

"When I knew him," David Asher said, "he was taking barbiturates all the time. Once I had to rush him to the emergency room in shock and another time Skye took him. It's remarkable he made those prairie dogs and found Tuwilla."

"Tuwilla," Julia said in a dismay.

"Tuwilla's flimsy, but she loves him."

"There used to be something special about Bumpo when we were young."

"There still is, but the world is too much for people like Bumpo, Julia. He had to disconnect."

"Like Bumpo, you are disconnected," Julia said one afternoon when she had come to David Asher's early, finding him naked in the living room, arranging fresh red carnations in a crockery pitcher for the piece on which he was working.

"I found out I was dying when I was sixteen," he said matter-of-factly. He spoke of dying without drama, a fact of living no more invasive than headaches or broken bones. "There's nothing that seems to me worthwhile except painting. I don't have time for falling in love," he added. "Just fucking."

Julia lay in bed at night and listened to David Asher fucking, her mind crowded with Theo, Philip, whose private self tugged at her daydreams, John, who was getting old, and Rachel, compensating for John's years by spending long hours with him in the garden, with Peter, who had grown bitter since he had left medicine. It was too complicated to make a life in a family. That spring, before *Joey Boy* opened, she learned to fall asleep inventing characters for her plays.

On March 4, 1972, opening night for *Joey Boy* at the Music Box, after a week of successful previews, the Howells family organized to go to New York on the three o'clock train, to have dinner on the West Side, to meet Julia at seven. They had their tickets, second row center.

"I'm not going," Lila said to Cally, standing at the kitchen sink washing up the breakfast dishes. "Don't argue with me. I can hear it coming."

"I haven't said a word."

"I've a right to come to my own decisions." She shut the dishwasher door, shook out the dishcloth she'd been using and folded it over the tap.

"Is Caleb still asleep?" she asked.

"He didn't get into Philadelphia until after midnight. I was sleeping when he came in, so I expect he's tired."

Cally was at the table reading the personals for "PET GIVEAWAYS" when Lila sat down beside her.

"I ask you, what am I going to wear to the theater in New York City? My black slacks with tennis shoes?" She arranged her fingers around the coffee cup, tilted her head in Cally's direction and lowered her eyes. "My best blue jeans, or, sweet darling, you think I should wear my felt hat with peacock feathers, just so?" She pretended to arrange a hat across her brow.

"And nothing else," Cally said, looking up from the paper.

"I'll oil my body. Give it a sort of shimmering effect."

"You don't have to go, Lila. You can stay here. Julia would understand."

"I don't care about Julia, Miss Caroline," Lila said in her deepest black southern. "I care about you."

"Well, I care about you and I care about Julia," Cally said. She checked two listings in the newspapers, a neutered calico, four years old, who'd have to be put away if not adopted because the family was moving to Egypt, and a three-legged sheepdog with papers. She stuck the advertisements under the telephone with plans to call before they left for Trenton. Cally had agreed just last week, "no more animals for three months." It was a "four-legged diet," Lila said.

"I wouldn't worry about Julia," Lila said, going to her room.

Cally did. She felt as if she had let Julia down, unspecifically, simply by being a temperament which acceded to events with a kind of stubborn courage but without counteraction. The only genuine moments of understanding had been during Julia's slow recovery after *The Children's Garden* closed. She didn't feel that way with the boys. For no reason, Peter had not thought well of himself, but she did not hold herself responsible for that. Bumpo was by nature incapable of insulating himself against the world. Nothing Cally could have done would have saved Bumpo from the permanent alterations drugs had made in him. Sad as it was, especially for Julia, Bumpo was happy and innocent of his limitations. Caleb, like John Howells, was reliable as morning, uncomplicated by debilitating sensibilities. He expected to work hard, to be a good husband, a good architect, a successful and contemporary man.

"I don't know what to expect of Julia," Cally said once to Rachel in a rare admission of concern.

"Restlessness." Rachel did not hesitate. "Probably all her life."

"Wonderful," Cally said, discouraged.

"She could become quite a woman."

"She's thirty-five years old. She's going to have to resign herself to something before it's too late."

"Resignation is foreign to Julia's temperament," Rachel said. "Don't worry about her."

"I worry all the time. There she is off in New York, living weekdays with a painter of nudes, hoping to make a family on weekends."

"You know, Cally, I have always admired the fact that you don't impose on your children. I was never that way with Nat. Or you." She laughed. "I couldn't even bear to let you make a decision about paint color or wallpaper." She laid her hand on Cally's cheek.

Cally wheeled her chair down the hall to Lila's wing. The door was shut and as usual Cally knocked. Even after years of intimacy, they allowed each other absolute privacy.

Lila had on a blue tweed suit that had belonged to Rachel. It hung like a pup tent on Lila's slender frame.

"I reckon you like the 1950 hand-me-downs for colored help," Lila said.

"Why didn't you buy something, Lila?" Cally asked.

Lila sat down at the end of the bed. She took off the suit jacket, the white silk blouse with an open collar which had also belonged to Rachel, and sat in a beige translucent bra, the blue tweed skirt hanging on her hips.

"It's unnatural," Lila said.

"What is?"

"Everything when we leave this farm. I don't want to go tonight because it's going to be like Mama's funeral and I'll come home feeling like killing someone."

Melvina had died in her sleep in November 1969, just before Thanksgiving, of heart failure in the same room in which she'd lived for sixty years, where Lila had lived, in the servants' quarters of the Bouché family house in New Orleans. When Melvina had failed to have breakfast on the table Sunday morning, Mrs. Bouché had knocked on her door, entered when there was no response, and found Melvina lying on her stomach, her head turned to the wall.

"So Mama didn't get breakfast on the table Sunday morning," Lila said after Mrs. Bouché's call. "Because she was dead. Impertinent darky."

"Don't, Lila. It's Mother's way of hiding her feelings."

"She hides them real well, Miss Caroline. The FBI could search weeks and not come up with a trace."

They flew to New Orleans together. Cally stayed in her old bedroom, which hadn't changed since she'd left it, and Lila stayed in the room where her mother had died. The plans were to have Thanksgiving in New Orleans, after the services for Melvina, Wednesday at First Baptist, Bourbon Street. Lila went to the services with her aunts, uncles and cousins, all Melvina's kin. Even Lila's daddy, whom Melvina had supported for years since she'd left him, was there, a little drunk and weeping. The Bouchés arrived late at the church after the minister had begun a service which was long and noisy. Afterwards there was a supper at the pastor's house and the Bouchés attended, shaking hands stiffly with the next of kin, eyeing each other for signs of departure.

"I may stay," Cally said to her mother.

"Don't," Lila said. She was angry.

Later that night Cally found a check from Dr. Bouché in her purse made out for a thousand dollars to Lila.

"What should I do with it?" she asked Lila on the plane home the following Sunday.

"I'll take it," Lila said. She tore it up in little pieces and dropped the pieces in the bag for airsickness in the pocket of the seat in front of her.

"A thousand dollars for my mother's life," Lila said. "It's a good thing I don't carry a knife to funerals."

"I'm sorry," Cally said.

"We were born on different sides of the planet. I don't even know where we learned to speak the same language."

"From your mother."

"I suppose you're right, Miss Caroline."

"Don't call me that."

Lila raised her eyebrows, put her head back against the seat and turned away from Cally, but she didn't say anything more.

"I'll bring you the program of Julia's play," Cally said, leaving Lila's room, going down the hall to wake Caleb.

"Maybe I'll go to New York another time," Lila said, relieved. "Next week. Maybe next year. Julia will have other plays."

On the corner of Main and Second Street in New Hope, just across from the Bucks County Playhouse and next to the bridge over the Delaware River, was a shop called The Plant Shop, arranged inside and in fair weather on the street like a Victorian garden. There were wicker chaises, high-back chairs, intricate iron benches painted in white enamel, slat benches with black iron braces, and under a glass dome were baskets of fern, spider plants with baby spider plants cascading from the ceiling, begonias in flower, urns of spreading geraniums and grape ivy, small baskets of fresh-cut flowers by the dozen. In the back of the shop, behind the garden room, was a small and surprising jungle of rare oranges and magentas, scarlets, thick deciduous plants, cactus with tiny white and violet flowers, brashly beautiful offspring of a tropical garden. The shop belonged to Peter Howells and he ran it with only the occasional assistance of a graphic artist called Raphael who lived in the apartment above the shop.

Bumpo had bought the shop outright for Peter two years before, in the spring of 1970. He had, in fact, bought the entire building with two upstairs apartments, in one of which Raphael was already living. Peter eventually took up residence in the other.

"I have so much money from these prairie dogs I don't know how I'll spend it," Bumpo said when Peter protested. "There's nothing at all that I want." And it was clear that a pair of blue jeans, a flannel shirt, a jacket for winter was all Bumpo needed. He and Tuwilla had a vegetable garden and ate from it fresh in summer, canned in winter unless they went to Rachel's. They stayed at the farm except for periodic trips to New Hope to visit Peter at The Plant Shop, to get an ice cream cone, to go to a toy store, where Bumpo liked to look at toys for Pippa and Theo, so he said, but in fact, he looked for himself. He liked Erector sets and Lego, thought the colors of Lego were splendid. You could build anything with it, he said, and bought himself each new Lego set as it was manufactured. He liked tiny soldiers made of metal and painted in vivid colors. And kites. His own house on the farm was decorated with bright kites in the shapes of butterflies and beetles, bluebirds, peacocks with tail feathers in purple and royal blue. He liked board games particularly and sometimes in the afternoon he and Peter would drink wine and play chess or backgammon in the back of the shop where the tropical plants were kept. He had patented an idea for a board game called Wipe Out in which the challenge to the players is to avoid being poisoned by nuclear fallout by moving away from nuclear reactors located strategically on the board. He was confident that the idea would sell and had been working lately with a fantasy board game, Tuwilla's idea, called Princess in the Tower.

Bumpo seemed to be happier than any of the other Howells. He was wonderfully pleasant in the small world which circumscribed his life, with his family always, with shopkeepers and people on the streets in New Hope, with his lawyer, a distant cousin who had made fine financial arrangements in Bumpo's favor, with Tuwilla, who loved him openly like a kitten, rubbing against his back and side in public. Occasionally Bumpo thought of marrying her. But after Syke had left with the man from Dammer Dammer, he had lost faith in commitments other than blood. He even decided that if Tuwilla left with someone from New Hope, he could continue to live a satisfactory life in the house next to his mother, across from his sister and over the field from his grandmother. Peter had suggested Tuwilla and Bumpo not have children because of the possibility for genetic damage after Bumpo's years on drugs.

"I'm perfectly happy," Bumpo insisted to Julia when she questioned his way of life.

"I suppose," Julia said. He seemed a child to her, without concerns in a world unsafe for children. She found his open smile reminiscent of her father's, but less troubled, his enthusiasm for games and play, his unbounded love for each of the people in his family, annoying. "I can't imagine you'll be happy at sixty still playing games."

"Listen, Julia, you used to have a sense of humor. It left like a carrier pigeon when Daddy died."

"Well, I'd be worried if all I planned to do for the rest of my life was play, play, play."

"I'm having a wonderful time," Bumpo said.

"You're missing the whole twentieth century," Julia said crossly.

"Wipe Out is the twentieth century. At least part of it. I just prefer to play it than live it," Bumpo said.

And Julia realized he was right. That in many ways his mind was as fine as it had been when he entered Brown University, before he'd even smoked a single joint. Nevertheless, it irritated her to see him like a child.

Peter lived a quiet life in his apartment, visiting the farm only for Sunday dinners and to play with a basset hound he'd bought and kept at his mother's house. People in New Hope, townspeople, found Peter a regular subject for gossip. He was, at twenty-nine, remarkably handsome with a thick black beard and curly hair, carefully tended, tanned from hours of working outside, charming, and yet distant. He read from social history, philosophy, psychology and poetry. His customers, many of whom visited the shop to talk, regarded Peter as though he were an idea, uncomplicated by emotional dimensions. What really interested them, however, was to imagine his private life. Surely a man of such reserve was struggling with a private life. The customers of The Plant Shop were correct in their assumptions that Peter was unsettled. They simply misunderstood the reasons. They thought, for example, that he had left medicine because he had not excelled in that field and it was clear he was a perfectionist. In fact, he left medicine in 1967, the summer after his internship was over at Yale University Hospital, six months after he had killed the old man with the wrong injection and after he had accepted a residency in surgery at Georgetown University Hospital in Washington, D.C. In those six months of deep trouble, he had worked harder and with greater care than he had ever worked in his life. He became engaged to Anne, and although he didn't love her, not in the way he had dreamed of loving, he made plans, allowed her to make arrangements to marry in June, even to take a conventional wedding trip to Bermuda, a gift of her parents in Greenwich, Connecticut.

When the internship at Yale was over June 1 and he had packed his bags, the contents of his apartment in an old Ford van, with plans to go home for a week with his family and then to Connecticut for the wedding, Peter fell apart like a grocery bag wet at the bottom.

"I'm not getting married," he told Julia the first night he was home.

"The invitations are out. There are parties. We've been invited to two barbecues and a dance. It's in two weeks."

"I don't care if it's tomorrow. I'm not going."

And he didn't. He called Anne the following day. She said she was taking the next train down. He asked her not to come, but she did anyway and Julia picked her up in Trenton.

"I'm not going to be a doctor," Peter told Anne when she came.

"That's okay. I love you for yourself."

"Oh, bullshit," Peter said, exhausted by the accumulations of a troubled year. "I wish you'd go home."

She stayed two days. Peter talked to her the first day for a while, but he spent most of the day in the guest room in Julia's house with the door shut. He wouldn't sleep with her. That he said in front of Julia.

"I think he's mental," Anne said to Julia finally.

"Maybe he is."

"He says he's having a nervous breakdown," she said impatiently. "I really don't like nervous men. I mean, I never would have gotten involved."

Julia was sympathetic. On the way to the train Anne agreed that he had probably fallen apart in the nick of time. She was dead set against divorce, but a lifetime with someone mental might do her in. Before the year was out, Peter read about her engagement to a man from Princeton, Cottage Club, in the Sunday *Times*.

"You aren't having a nervous breakdown," Julia said crossly to Peter when she got back from taking Anne to the station.

"I don't want to marry her. And I don't want to be a doctor."

He asked Julia not to mention the old man, at least for the moment, and he moved back into Cally's house, his old room, until Bumpo bought The Plant Shop.

John particularly was disappointed, but he did not say so. There was such a fierceness in Peter's decision to leave medicine that no one in the family dared bring it up with him, except Julia, for fear they would learn something they did not want to know.

The people of New Hope guessed that Raphael was Peter's lover because they lived in adjoining apartments and neither seemed to have women companions.

New Hope was small and full of stories. Once Julia asked Peter, "You know what people are saying?"

"Sure," he replied.

"Well, is it true?"

"No, my love, but it's perfectly all right for them to talk about it. I don't mind at all."

"Do you like women?" Julia asked, trying to be offhand.

"I like women very much in the abstract," Peter said. "In actuality I like plants. Off and on the family. Theo most of the time."

Theo wasn't in school on March 4 because his tutor had told Philip Kendall, "Either he comes all day or not at all. We can't alter his patterns. That could cause serious trouble."

He had entered Kinkaid in October 1971, after he had been "released," according to the principal, from public school. On the sign bordered with ivy and surrounded by mature boxwood was written KINKAID SCHOOL FOR SPECIAL CHILDREN.

"It's a stupid idea to call them special children. All children are special," Rachel said.

John Howells was angry. "If these people treat Theo as peculiar, you can be sure he'll satisfy them by being so," he told Philip.

"In England Theo would be different and admired for it," Philip said defensively.

"Well, we're not in England," John said.

"Don't argue," Bumpo said. "Theo is going to be fine."

"He's not going to be fine," Julia said. "For Chrissake, Bumpo, everyone is not going to live happily ever after in spite of your wishing it."

John asked Julia to leave the table.

"I'm thirty-four years old," Julia said. "I can speak my mind."

"In your own home. Not in mine," John said.

Julia left and Philip followed her across the field to their house.

"The family is falling apart," Bumpo said at the table. "I can't stand it."

"As far as I can see, there's very little you can stand. We have a problem. When you have a problem, you try to handle it, which comes, I know, as news to you."

"I have made cherry cobbler from our own trees," Rachel said.

"One way to handle it is for Julia to stay home and raise her children," John said.

"Do you want ice cream? Vanilla. Homemade by Tuwilla."

"No," John said. "I don't want cherry cobbler either."

"Don't be bad-tempered, darling," Rachel said. "Mothers with Julia's drive don't stay home in these times."

"I am tired of this conversation about differences and specialness. These are the same times again and again. We don't need to burn down our houses every new generation in order to get on with the century." John got up from the table. "I wish you'd stop making cherry cobbler," he said to Rachel.

Rachel said to him in the kitchen after everyone had left, "You acted like an old man at supper, John."

"Which is what I am," he answered. "It's your turn now, Bammy. Do something about Theo. Julia, too."

"Your special nephew is here," Theo called to Peter, walking into The Plant Shop the morning of March 4. "Mad as a hatter! Crazy as a loon! Lost his brain on a Sunday afternoon."

Mrs. Alfonzo, shopping for plants, looked up from her box of pale pink hothouse begonias.

"He's very rude, isn't he," she said quietly to Peter, who was ringing up her purchase.

"I find him charming," Peter said pleasantly, handing Mrs. Alfonzo her change, which she counted twice before depositing it in her purse.

"Think Peter'd cheat you?" Theo asked.

Mrs. Alfonzo raised her eyebrows.

"We have different notions about charm," she said to Peter on her way out.

"Smitch," Theo said. "That's Pippa's word. She made it up for her first grade teacher. First-rate, don't you think?"

"I do," Peter agreed. "How many smitches do you know?"

"Well," Theo said. "That one. Tuwilla. Bam thinks it's 'cause she's pregnant."

"Terrific."

"She may have an abortion," Theo said.

"Who told you that?"

"Bumpo, of course." He sat down on the stool behind the cash register.

"Of course. Do you know what an abortion is?"

"Sure. Do you?"

"Yup," Peter said, dealing out cards for gin rummy, which they played when Theo visited the shop. "What other smitches?"

"Your old girlfriend. Remember?"

"Anne. A perfect smitch."

"Sometimes Mama."

Peter looked up. "Honestly?"

"Well, sometimes."

"I love your mother. She has troubles lately."

"Yeah, I know. Because of me."

"And others. You're not the only trouble in her life. But she's the best sister I could have asked for. We had a good time together and she was never, almost never, a smitch. Just funny."

"Well, she's not now," Theo said and looked at his cards. "So, I'm going to beat you as usual. You want to know what happened today with the psychiatrist?"

"Sure."

"Well, he wanted to know about me and Mama. Did Mama listen to me, did she play with me, do I remember her holding me when I was little. You think I was going to tell him that? Jeez, he's so dumb I can't stand it. 'No,' I said. 'No, no, no' to every question. If he'd asked me does my mother love me, which he was at least smart enough not to do, I would have said, 'No, buddy, bet your life she doesn't. Do you dye your hair?' "

Peter laughed.

"I think he does dye his hair," Theo said. "It's got purple tinges in the front. There." He put his runs down on the counter. "You're lousy today. The other thing he said. You know, the psychiatrist. It about killed me. He made his voice low and said, 'Tell me, Theodore'—he calls me Theodore—'how do you feel about your mother's play?' I said, 'Swell. It's about me and very funny. It's about you, too.' 'Me?' he said, very shocked, I could tell. 'Yeah,' I said. 'Only Mama gave you a different name and the guy who plays your part is real fat—even fatter than you.' I could tell he was upset because he asked me all about the play. 'Go see it,' I said. 'Mama may even get you a free ticket since you're my shrink.' I know he could've killed me. I could just feel it, but I said one more thing. I just looked out the window with this faraway look in my eyes, like I'm in a trance—real crazy." Theo looked out the window of The Plant Shop and rolled his eyes back. "Like that. And then I said—"

"You've got to stop it, Theo, or they'll never let you out of that school."

"Maybe I'll burn it down."

"Listen, if you do that," Peter said, "you'll be put in another one even worse."

"Thanks. I'll take that queen," Theo said. "Do you think you'll ever be a doctor again?"

"Maybe."

"How come you quit?"

"Because at the time I didn't think I was going to be a good doctor."

"Well, I think you're very good. If you got to be a psychiatrist, I'd go to you. I might even tell you the truth."

Peter picked him up and hugged him like a child smaller than he was, holding Theo's head against his shoulder. Sometimes with Theo, and only with Theo, Peter felt a surge of feeling near tears and then his nephew would wriggle away, as he did now.

"You're not going to get smushy, are you?" Theo asked.

Peter shook his head.

"Well, sometimes you are."

"Not much," Peter said and turned Theo upside down, holding him around the waist. "We gotta get ready to go to New York. Pronto."

John Howells was dying in unspecific but perceptible movements like a symphony in which the leitmotif is stronger with each repetition. He slept. He slept in the library with the drapes drawn and the windows closed during the summer of 1971. If Rachel found him there, she pulled the drapes and opened the windows in a temper.

"It's like a grave in here," she'd say. But when she left the room, he'd shuffle in his bedroom slippers to the back parlor, where there was no sun, or close the drapes again.

"I'd like to make an arrangement with you about your bedroom slippers," Rachel said to him earnestly one afternoon that summer, bristling with a kind of blind anger at the slow slap of his slippers against the hardwood floors. "I can't stand to hear your slippers in the middle of the day. It's as though you're ill."

"Buy earplugs, Bammy," John said.

"Then," she said quite earnestly, "I won't be able to hear the telephone."

"This has developed into a problem, my love. Perhaps we should separate."

"We're entirely too old to separate."

"Well, I'm too old to wear shoes all day in the house."

He slept after supper even when there were guests, although there were few guests because John was only interested in seeing his family. Rachel arranged for Tuwilla and Bumpo to entertain him after supper several days a week.

"He sleeps too much," Rachel said to Bumpo. "One of these days he's simply going to go off. Die by accident without ever intending it."

"What shall we do with him?" Tuwilla asked helplessly.

"Oh, talk. Play cards. Anything. Talk about the economic situation. It's his particular interest."

"I don't know about the economic situation," Tuwilla said.

"Anything. Teach him to play your nuclear disaster game, Bumpo."

John lost his temper after an evening with Bumpo and Tuwilla.

"What did you tell them?" he asked after the two had left.

"Nothing," Rachel said.

"You're lying," John said. "You've insisted they come up here to keep me awake after supper."

"It's not good for your digestion to sleep."

"Nor is it helpful to talk to Tuwilla about her vegetable garden or her unhappy childhood."

"She is sweet."

"And boring. I'd rather you cancel these arrangements."

"I'm afraid you'll get senile," Rachel said.

"I have noticed your concern, Bammy."

"And that you'll do what your father did. Pee in the drawers and so forth."

"I don't want you to worry about that. My father and I are temperamentally quite different."

He had a slight stroke in January which left him weak and another in February which affected his right arm. The second time the doctor told Rachel privately that John could continue to have small strokes or he could have a massive and final stroke at any time. It was difficult to predict with a man his age. When Rachel left the hospital with John the second time, her anger at his deterioration over the last six months was gone. She determined with an energy undiminished by years to make John Howells happy, as though it were 1914 again and she was a new bride who believed she could make her husband happy. She noticed that he stopped wearing his bedroom slippers after the second stroke in defiance of the slow surrender of his body. She kept flowers in the house, transformed each meal into a small and private ceremony, made a point of frequent conversations. His color improved, his interest in the small details of their life at the farm. He even admitted that he'd come to like Tuwilla.

John did not feel well the morning of March 4. He rose slowly and sat on the edge of the bed.

"Perhaps you shouldn't go," Rachel said.

"I'm going."

He went into the bathroom and shut the door. She sat in the bedroom and listened to him in the shower, half expecting to hear him fall. When he came out with a towel wrapped around his waist, she pretended to be reading *Newsweek*.

"Ah, Bam," he said, gently tugging her short gray hair, "you must be surprised to see that I didn't collapse in the tub."

"I wasn't worried."

"Bullshit, my love."

When Peter came in the kitchen after dropping Theo at his own house, John had just come downstairs.

"How's Theo?" John asked. "I saw you walking with him from the window."

"I don't think there's that much wrong with Theo."

"That his mother's return wouldn't cure."

"I don't even think that Julia's leaving made much difference. It's the school that's trying to convince him he's crazy."

"Take him out. Tell Julia to take him out."

"She tried, Granddaddy. The public school insisted that he stay until he is 'ready to adjust to a regular school.' "

"The longer he stays, the less possibility he will have of leading an ordinary life." John buttered his toast carefully, poured a second cup of tea. "Julia should come home."

In the library after breakfast, John brought up the subject of the family Bible with Peter.

"I have to think about who gets the Bible. But sometime I want to have a talk with you about medicine and your plans for returning to complete your work."

"I'd rather not talk about medicine, Granddaddy."

"Why not?"

"I may go back to it."

"I certainly hope so."

John Howells sat at the end of the second row, center aisle, next to Julia. Before the play began, he did not feel well.

"I'll take the aisle, in case I have to leave," he said to Rachel.

"How come I'm so big in this play?" Theo whispered to Julia after the curtain had gone up on Joey at center stage with a saucepan on his head.

"That's not you," Julia whispered. "It's Joey."

"Daddy said the play is about me."

"It's not biography. It's made up."

Bumpo laughed happily at all the lines, even the ones that were not intended to be funny. He nudged Tuwilla with his elbow and she laughed, too.

"Tell Bumpo to cut it out," Julia said to Peter.

"Julia says this is a very serious play, Bumpo, and you're not supposed to be laughing."

"Bumpo told me to," Tuwilla apologized too loudly.

"It's supposed to be comic, Tuwilla," Bumpo told her. "Peter always does this to me."

Philip did not laugh. He sat with his legs crossed, his elbows resting on his knees. Julia noticed that he was smiling from time to time.

"Don't you think it's a little funny?" Julia asked him at intermission.

"Of course."

"But you're not laughing."

"You said not to laugh."

"You're supposed to laugh in moderation," she snapped, showing her nerves badly for the first time that evening.

Pippa was sleeping on Cally's lap in the side aisle.

"What did you think, Cally?" Rachel turned to her daughter-in-law.

"I don't honestly understand it. Do you?"

"I'm not sure. It's comic. I understand the humor and maybe that's the point."

"Do you like the parents of Joey? They seem very silly to me."

"I don't like anyone in the play." Rachel turned and moved down the aisle to where John was sitting.

"Are you feeling better?" she asked him.

"I'm fine now. I must have been nervous for Julia, but obviously the play is wonderful. Everyone seems to think so."

"Cally doesn't understand it."

"Do you?" John smiled and patted Rachel's hand.

"In part. Julia says it's fashionable. That is why it may do very well."

"That's funny. I never thought of Julia as fashionable."

When Julia came back for the second act, she told her grandfather that she thought the play was a hit. Hal Markus had said you could sometimes tell by the spirit in the theater, which was high.

"You don't love it, do you?" she asked her grandfather.

"The play is very funny, but I don't love the people."

"I know. They aren't particularly warm. But that's kind of the point. It's an idea play."

"It's supposed to appeal to one's mind and not one's heart. Is that it?"

"Sort of," Julia said.

Theo told them to be quiet.

"The psychiatrist has high blood pressure. Is there an understudy?" Peter asked.

"Christ, Peter," Julia said.

During the second act Bumpo refused to laugh.

"You're so stubborn," Caleb whispered to him.

"Julia should have written a script for our responses," Peter said.

"Please shut up," Theo said loud enough for the row behind him to hear.

In the second act John was more conscious of his family than of the play. He liked the fact that they filled an entire row. Just their numbers gave him a sense of strength which had diminished in the quick rush of age this past year. He was particularly pleased at their differences from one another. Cally was dressed like an aging school-girl in a shirtwaist dress out of style, too tight at the midriff. Rachel wore a tweed suit and held a felt hat in her lap, a mink scarf around one shoulder pillowing her back. Caleb dressed to be adult. He had to select serious clothes to add years to his young face. Bumpo was in blue jeans, an old flannel jacket which had been his father's and was too large, his father's tie and a frayed oxford cloth shirt taken from his mother's closet, his hair in a golden braid down his back. He did not wear socks. Peter and Philip, both dark, with heavy hands shaped like clubs, dressed impeccably but without flair. Julia sat next to him, leaning forward, her elbows on her knees. She was uneasy and held her body rigid with the stiffness of mannequins. John felt a surge of adrenaline, a sudden need to continue in the world as he knew it, to be a part of the lives generated by these children.

He took Julia's hand during the applause at the end of the second act. "You know, darling," he said to her, "when it becomes fashionable to write plays for the heart, I hope you will do one."

The Howells stood on the stage set behind the closed curtain after the play. There wasn't enough room for them backstage at the Music Box. Theo peered between the curtains at the empty theater.

"Peter," he called, "look here."

The theater was dark; only the front rows of seats were visible.

"Isn't it strange that when the play is over, there's nothing left?" he said sadly when Peter had come up behind him.

"What did you expect to see? People sleeping in the aisle?"

"I don't know. I didn't expect it to look so lonely." He leaned his weight against Peter. "I want to go home. I hate New York."

"Are you coming with us?" Philip asked Julia when she finally had pulled herself away from the cast and producers.

"Home?" she asked.

"Of course," Philip said, impatiently, annoyed at the long wait backstage.

"I don't know." She felt unable to bridge the distance between her own family and the one she had created, uncomfortable with the familiar faces standing rather foolishly on a kitchen set, New York City, 1972.

"Make up your mind. We have a train to catch."

She took Philip's arm. "I thought I'd stay for the party."

"Fine." He picked up Pippa, who was sleeping against Cally's shoulder. "Let's go," he announced.

"Philip. You're cross, aren't you?" Julia kept his arm.

"Anxious. Caleb, would you hail a couple of taxis for us?"

"Please, Philip, I don't want you to be upset."

"Don't be falsely sentimental, Julia. It doesn't become you."

She walked out to the street with him. "Are you jealous?" she asked fearfully.

"Of your success? Lord, Julia, if you wanted to run for queen of England, I'd be happy to see you win. It's more complex than that. Besides"—he made an effort to be sweet—"this is not stage conversation."

She kissed them each good-bye in turn.

"I thought Joey was crazy. Not like me," Theo said, hugging his mother.

"Of course he's not like you." She bent down to Theo's height and kissed him. "Thank you for coming, lamb."

"I won't come again," Theo said without anger and climbed into the cab next to Peter.

"I hate for us all to go off and leave you, Julia," John said to her.

"I want to stay, Granddaddy."

When they had left, Julia walked back through the stage door, down the empty corridor, onto the stage set and stood for a few moments where her family had been standing. She looked through the curtains as Theo had at the empty theater and felt as he had, although she had not known their thoughts were alike, a sense of loneliness. For a moment she wished she had gone home with them.

Hal Markus found her on the stage with her head between the curtains, looking at the dark theater beyond.

"You're coming to the party?"

"That's why I stayed."

"You should feel wonderful." He took her hand.

"I do." She removed her trench coat from a hanger backstage, tied the belt around her waist.

"You're pensive." Hal put his arm over her shoulder. "Perhaps fame won't suit you after all."

She shrugged. "I expected to feel differently."

"You thought if the play was successful, everything in your life would be solved. I know. Bad mistake."

"I suppose I did think that."

"Think about the fact that it's a good play and it's going to do very well."

"It's an okay play," she said.

She left the party early. There was champagne and it made her quickly drunk. The cast was joyous, but she couldn't match their high spirits.

"You aren't going to wait for the early edition?" Hal asked, walking out with her to get a cab.

"Nope," Julia said. "I'm dead tired. Call me in the morning and read me the reviews if they're good."

The room spun if Julia lay down, so she sat up. David heard her and came in the bedroom in his blue jeans without a shirt.

"So," he said, "how was it?"

She slouched in a director's chair, her feet on the bed.

"Successful. Successful. Wonderfully successful."

"You don't seem exactly overjoyed."

"I'm pleased. I had too much champagne."

"I'll make you tea." He went to the kitchen. "So did all one hundred fifty closest members of your family come up?"

"Yup."

"Did they love it?"

"I don't think they understood it."

"Families are terrific that way."

"My grandfather said I should write with feeling," Julia said dramatically. "Philip was a drip."

"They came to see it, Julia," David said. "My father said he wouldn't bring my mother to my shows until I started painting people in clothes. My mother—he honestly said this to me in a heart-to-heart—finds the penis offensive." David lay down on Julia's bed. "God, it's late."

"Are you alone tonight?" Julia asked.

"Companionless," David said. "I can't stand it. It's giving me insomnia. Will you sleep with me?"

"Well," Julia said.

"Julia," he said, surprised, and then he laughed.

Julia had not thought once about sleeping with David Asher until that moment when he mentioned it in jest. She did not come to a decision or even give the question consideration. She stood up, slipped off her thin flannel gown and lay with him.

"Where're your breasts?" he asked, kissing her.

"Haven't got any," she mumbled into his shoulder.

"Too skinny?"

"Yup."

"You're sure you're a girl?" he asked.

"Pretty sure."

"Jesus, Julia, I never in my furthest dreams imagined this with you," he said, moving inside her. She came easily, before him, and thought with great detachment while they made love that this was the third man she had slept with and she was thirty-five. Not much for thirty-five. She tried to reconstruct David's face while he rocked facedown in her shoulder, but she could only think of him as a young man with cancer. Immediately she slept.

She woke up when Hal called with the reviews, which were outstanding.

"I told you so," Hal said again and again.

"Uh-huh," she said sleepily.

"Let's go to lunch."

"I can't, Hal. I'm going home."

"Home? I thought you were staying all week."

"I was. I changed my mind."

David was still sleeping, naked on the sheets, the covers thrown off. She sat on the end of the bed and woke him.

"David," she said, "I feel terrible."

"Oh, shit," he said waking slowly, pulling himself up against the headboard. "I hate remorse."

"It's just that I hadn't expected to sleep with you."

"Things happen," he said coolly, stretching and yawning. "Listen, Julia, don't feel terrible, okay? It didn't mean a thing."

"I know," she said sadly.

John Howells died on the tenth of June before breakfast.

"It's going to be a beautiful day," Rachel said to him from the bathroom, where she was doing her hair. A silver mist had lifted from the fields, the sky was an uninterrupted blue, and the sun, just over the horizon, had the gentle brightness of early summer. Rachel paused in dressing to open the bathroom window and lean on the high sill to watch the beginning of morning. She could see the strawberries at the end of her garden from the window. Some should be ready by today and she and John would have strawberries for lunch. Maybe with shortcake and cream.

She left the window open and put on makeup. She had started wearing makeup again, ever since they had bought a fluorescent light for over the bathroom mirror. In that light her complexion, a rich olive in other mirrors, was a tawny yellow. So she used blush. Then she decided on pancake, too, some mascara, and now it took more than half an hour by John's watch for Rachel to prepare herself in the morning.

"It makes you look like a clown," Pippa said to Rachel.

"Do you think so?"

Pippa nodded.

"I'm glad. One lives so long these days it's boring to always have to look the same."

Rachel noticed John first in the mirror. She was trying to catch her tiny eyelashes with a black mascara brush. He seemed to be looking at her and she smiled; then, with a sudden certainty, she realized that John wasn't smiling back.

"John." She turned towards him.

He was propped up in bed and his face, which had been directly forward, had fallen to the side against the pillow. His eyes were open and fixed. His hands were warm.

She called Philip, the ambulance, John's cardiologist, Peter and Bumpo in that order. Philip had gone to the hospital, so she left a message for him to meet her there. The ambulance arrived ten minutes after Bumpo, who had come as soon as Rachel called. Peter arrived with the ambulance. Cally, who had heard the sirens, came at once.

Rachel went back to the bedroom, slipped on a dress and sat with John. He was not dead. He didn't seem to be living either. His eye were marbles.

She took his hands. "I was in the bathroom looking out the window and I remembered the strawberries should be good by today." She patted his hand, rubbed his face, which had begun to take on the color of blue death. "You'll have to get better quickly because I was just planning to have strawberries for lunch."

Philip drove Rachel back from the hospital.

"It's not like him to die in the morning," she said absently. "He loved the morning."

Philip couldn't talk. He wanted to bring up the kind of conversation common in his profession, to say it was best John died quickly, didn't hang on for weeks, that he'd had a fine life, etc., etc., words he had used with grace countless times to families of patients who had died.

"I was in the bathroom. I'd just looked out the window at the garden. And then I went back to the sink and saw him in the mirror. Do you think the last thing John saw me do was put on makeup?"

Philip shook his head.

"It could have happened when I was looking out the window." She sat in the front seat composed. "He said, 'Good morning, Bam,' as I was going to the bathroom. My back was to him, and I didn't turn around. I think I said, 'Good morning, lamb,' but I don't remember. I didn't know it was going to matter."

Philip wanted Rachel to be silent or weep. "It doesn't matter," he wanted to say. But he realized that Rachel was establishing for herself the last scene of John's conscious life so she could re-create that moment exactly as he had experienced it, see it from the same angle of vision.

"I'm so sorry, Rachel," Philip said, and he pulled the car over four miles short of the farm, put his head on his fist on the steering wheel, and wept.

Weeks later he understood that the fracture of his carefully tended reserve had to do with a history of losses, the death of his own father. He had been raised by an English mother to act on death as a fact without residuals, to be filed away in a metal cabinet under *D*. He was expected to march through his daily life in even paces like a soldier indistinguishable from other soldiers, who can be counted on for bravery in the event of an emergency through strict attention to form.

He was raised with military commands: "Don't cry," "Be a man," "Stiff upper lip," "Be courteous," "Be moderate." But he was not surprised that when he wept for the first time in his grown-up life, it was with Rachel, who had never believed in his reserve as fact.

Rachel did not cry. Her sadness was too profound and permanent to be drained off in tears. She was an old woman, and although she certainly didn't want to die herself, she had known that when John died, she'd live her life out incompletely. They had been married fifty-eight years and had loved each other. She would keep the house, bring in fresh flowers, continue baking, cook Sunday suppers and make the holidays. Alone, she could try to recover John

Howells in the corners of their bedroom.

When Philip and Rachel arrived at the Main House, there was work to be done.

Julia was in New York for the week, making changes in *Joey Boy*. When Philip called, she said she'd phone from Trenton. She sounded businesslike, as though she had expected John's death that morning.

Caleb and Rika were able to get a plane out of Houston to Washington and then take a train to Thirtieth Street, Philadelphia, where Peter would drive in for them. Meanwhile, he picked up Theo at school.

"Will we see him?" Theo asked in the car going home.

"Nope," Peter said. "I'm sure Bam will have the coffin closed."

"Will they burn him?"

"No, Theo. I think he'll be buried in the family graveyard in a coffin like my father was."

"I'm glad. Everyone I know gets burned up."

"Who d'you know that gets burned up, Theo?"

"You know. Just everyone," Theo said.

Bumpo was in the garden telling Tuwilla about the Bible when Peter arrived.

"Tell Theo," Peter said. Bumpo handed Theo a fistful of early berries.

"We have a tradition that the oldest living person inherits the family Bible. You know the one that's been in the family since this guy named Caleb Howells brought it from Wales."

"I've seen it," Theo said. "Granddaddy showed it to me about a million times, only I liked the skulls beside it better."

"Yeah," said Peter, "I always preferred the skulls myself."

"Will Mama get the Bible now?"

"I doubt it. It always goes to a man to keep it in the Howells family."

"I think you'll get it, Peter," Bumpo said, spitting an unripe strawberry as far as he could.

"Maybe." Peter drew on the ground with a stick. "Only Granddaddy was upset that I quit medicine."

"If you got the Bible, you'd have to go back to being a doctor."

"How come?" Peter was drawing what looked like dogwood blossoms in the dirt.

"It just wouldn't be right to have a plant shop in New Hope. It's not sort of professional enough." Bumpo was filling the spaces around the strawberry patch with wet straw. "It's one way Granddaddy would get you back into medicine. He's not going to let any of us go easy, y'know."

"What about you?" Peter said. "It's your fucking plant shop."

"Me?"

"You're the economic structure of this family after all."

Bumpo picked a buttercup and put it behind his ear. Theo copied with one behind his ear.

"I suppose you're right," Bumpo said. "I was lucky."

"This country is full of luck," Peter said. "Oil and gold and trees. Jesus."

"Granddad never thought much of my prairie dogs. Not visionary enough."

"I think you're wrong. He thought your prairie dogs were okay."

"You know he hated Wipe Out."

"He didn't like the idea of Wipe Out. He honestly worried about those things. But he told me just last week that you'll probably make another fortune with Wipe Out—that the country's mad for violence. We can't get enough of it. Two bits, the Bible's yours."

Bumpo raised his eyebrows and motioned towards Tuwilla.

Peter looked at Tuwilla, who was at the far end of the garden, staking tomatoes and beans.

"Listen, Bumpo, you could be rich as Rockefeller. You'll start foundations. Hell. Think of it. The Bumpo Howells Memorial Foundation for Improvement of Plants and Animals, Living Things in General—on money made from Wipe Out. The future of this family is in cash, you creep, and you have it."

"You know, I wish you'd call me Nat or else Nathaniel. I've asked everyone to and they keep forgetting," Bumpo said quietly.

"It's hard to think of you as anyone but Bumpo."

Peter wanted the Bible. He didn't think about it often, but when he did, he thought of that inheritance as an acknowledgment, as a message of forgiveness from his grandfather. There would have to be a reason for him not to receive the Bible because he was the eldest son.

In the weeks before he died, John Howells had talked about the family Bible and the Howells land in the addled way of an old man who has his house in order but simply won't die. He asked Peter over several times for dinner, and each time he insisted that they talk about the twenty-first century. Theo would be forty in the year 2000, he pointed out. And if people continued to invent and discover new ways to run and destroy the world, was there even a point to imagining Theo and Pippa anywhere in 2000?

"No point at all," Peter agreed.

John Howells could not help himself. He wanted to plunge through time like an astronaut directed at the moon, to situate those lives he knew before he died.

He often had breakfast in the side garden with Bumpo in early spring, when the dogwood and azaleas were beginning to bloom, the sun bright but distant in the morning, cool enough for sweaters.

"I'd be grateful if you'd think of games that didn't wipe out the universe. You give people ideas," he said to Bumpo.

"People have those ideas already," Bumpo said. "That's why I invented the game."

"Sometimes, Bumpo, I worry about leaving all of you. When I was your age, there were illnesses from which people died mercifully and quickly, not in slow motion as they do today."

"It's okay," Bumpo said. "I mean it's an all right world, Granddad. Don't worry about us. We'll be fine. Don't you believe in God?"

"Do you?" John Howells asked, smiling at Bumpo, who at twenty-eight still looked like a boy.

"Sure. Tuwilla and I used to sit on our back porch in Dammer Dammer knocked out by the mountains and talk about God."

"I believe you had that conversation with another girl, Bumpo."

"Skye. You're right. But Tuwilla and I did, too. I mean we still do. I don't know if Peter believes in God. My guess is not—Julia either. But you do, don't you?"

"A lot of the time I believe in all of you," John Howells said.

The windows of the Main House were open top to bottom. Philip was on the phone in the library sending wires to friends and distant relatives. Cally and Lila were in the kitchen with Pippa, and Theo was following Rachel from room to room. It was just after noon. Rachel was dressed in an old white linen dress, thin and limp from many washings, but the dress had a certain elegance and was familiar. She had on black and white spectator shoes and a white cap. She stopped at the doorway of each room and looked. Occasionally she ran her hand over a table, checked her palm for dust, fluffed a pillow, picked up a scrap from the rug. The scenes she saw were not in the rooms she was inspecting but internal ones from memory.

"It looks well," she said to Peter, who had come in the library from the porch. "The house. Don't you think?"

"It looks fine."

"Flowers." She smiled slightly.

"I see. All over. They look lovely."

"Not funeral flowers. Can you tell?" she asked, putting an arm on Theo's shoulders. "They are from my own garden. I picked them yesterday." She added, "Before he died," as though her own flowers had opened with the morning sun in sweet and quiet defiance of John's death.

"You'd think a housekeeper had arrived this morning and tidied up," Rachel said to Peter.

"Mother and Lila were cleaning when I came in," Peter said.

"Of course. People will be coming by late afternoon. Philip has called everyone."

"Are you going to wear that cap when people come, Bammy?"

"You don't like it? I thought it might look formal, like afternoon tea."

"I've seen you in better hats," Peter said.

She took the cap off and handed it to Theo. "Here," she said. "Why don't you help Cally in the kitchen?"

But Theo didn't want to leave. He was interested to see how one behaved with death. He was watching Rachel for signs of catastrophe. He had imagined death in scenes more dramatic than this one and the ease of his great-grandfather's absence disturbed him.

Twice Rachel asked Philip to put down the phone and tell her about the *Times*.

"I've called. It will be in the *Times* tomorrow," Philip said.

"With a picture?"

"I didn't ask."

"There was a picture when Daniel died," she said.

She took Peter's hand. He realized immediately that it was a gesture not of affection, but of necessity.

"I'll be fine," she said to him, as though to convince herself. "Tell your mother I'm absolutely all right. But I need to rest so I'll be ready for the guests who should be coming this afternoon." Peter walked upstairs with her. "Tonight we'll have chicken with tarragon. Just the family. There's salad from the garden. Julia will be here by then, and Caleb with Rika. John has told me how I should arrange this evening for the passing of the Bible."

"I didn't know we were having that ceremony tonight," Peter said.

"Like the Jews. Buried before sundown. Well, sort of like the Jews. John gave me boring instructions for passing the Bible in case I might have forgotten the details from when Daniel died. Don't forget to pick up Julia in Trenton."

"Philip will."

Rachel went into the bedroom. The bed was still unmade, as it had been when she left with John that morning. She sat down on John's side, took off her shoes, unbuttoned the front of her dress, undid her garters and lay down on the sheet with the covers thrown back, her head on the pillow where he had slept.

Julia missed the twelve o'clock train. She was at Penn Station ten minutes early; she would not have had to run to catch it. She stopped at the newsstand to buy *Redbook* for exercises for summer and looked through "Milestones" in *Time* to see who had been born, divorced, married or died. She didn't recognize any names and put the magazine back. She bought a copy of the *Village Voice* and the *Times*. By the time she arrived at Gate 3 she was too late. She called Philip at the Main House and asked him to meet the next train. Then she sat down on one of the long wooden benches in the main room of the station, grateful for a place to sit, for the crowd milling around her like summer gnats, for missing the noon train south which would have sped her to Trenton and to Philip in a seersucker suit, and on to the Main House, where her family, seeming to number in the hundreds for the force of them, were waiting.

The train for Boston was called—Bridgeport, New London, Providence, Boston. Pittsburgh, Cleveland and Chicago. It occurred to Julia that she could go off in another direction. She could board the wrong train, be trapped in its run to a city north or west. She could get off in Cleveland, check into a hotel: Julia Howells, 109 W. 11th Street, N.Y.C. Lie in bed and read the "Personals" in the *Village Voice*. The family wouldn't hold up John's funeral forever while they looked for her.

She opened the *Times* automatically to the second section, turning from the back to the obituaries. Andrew Fortune had died of cancer at fifty-seven at Sloan-Kettering. He had been president of the Hammond Corporation, founded by his father in 1923. He had gone to St. Paul's and Yale and was divorced from the former Dorothy Brighton. There was one child, whose name wasn't given. Lacey Truesdale, who had written 103 gothic novels, had died at ninety-six in a nursing home in Middletown, Connecticut. She had never married. There were no survivors. The only other obituary was that of a German philosopher, Gunther Hermann, who probably had killed himself. He was only forty-two and had, according to the paper, died unexpectedly. He took up two columns with his degrees and books. Julia imagined John Howells filling two columns tomorrow, depending on who else had died. The article would say that he was seventy-nine, that his father was a four-term Democratic senator from Pennsylvania, that he had gone to Harvard, had founded an advertising firm, now the corporate firm of Howells, Hogan and Berger, that he had one son, deceased, four grandchildren, two great-grandchildren. He had no clubs or civic contributions. Even with a picture, he would take only a column, headed, perhaps, JOHN HOWELLS, AGE 79 or FOUNDER OF AD FIRM DEAD AT 79 or FORMER SENATOR'S SON, AGE 79. What son, Julia thought, can ever age to seventy-nine? She couldn't imagine Theo older than twelve.

If Julia cried, she would not be able to stop. Someone would have to pick her up off the railroad station floor. Call an ambulance. Search through her purse for identification. She wondered what a physician in an emergency room would do with a woman who could not stop crying. Anesthetize her? Would she cry in her sleep?

The one o'clock to Washington was called—stopping at Newark, Trenton, Philadelphia, Thirtieth Street, Wilmington, Baltimore, Washington, D.C. Julia lined up and followed the crowd down the steps of Gate 3.

Philip was alone. She saw him out the window even before the train had stopped. He had probably come alone so he could talk to her. Well, she didn't want to talk with Philip.

"How is everybody? How is Bam?" she asked once they were settled in the jeep headed from New Jersey to Pennsylvania.

"How would you expect everyone in your family to be?" Philip asked.

She had a sudden and true picture of her family. "Doing well," she said.

"They are," he said. "Especially Bam. They're anxious to see you."

"I don't want to have a fight about the fact I was in New York," she said.

"I appreciate that, Julia," Philip said.

She thought that he might take her hand. His own hand was lying on the seat between them. Hers were in her lap. He was handsome from the side, she noticed as if for the first time, with a fine straight English nose and high cheekbones. She had forgotten her attraction to him.

"Is everybody cross at me? What have they said?"

"Nothing. Your name hasn't come up. Only that you're arriving and so forth."

"Don't be bitchy," Julia said, resting her head on the back of the seat.

"I'm being honest," he said.

On the plane between Houston and Washington, Caleb didn't talk.

"I don't understand how you can just sit," Rika said to him, but Caleb could sit for a long time in the evening after dinner, on weekends, not consciously thinking. He did not by temperament attack his life with the intention of winning internal conflicts by taking the offensive. He went about his daily affairs portioning his energies like a banker, making safe investments. He was expected to become a good architect. His designs had won the attention of established architects at many firms while he was still a student at the University of Pennsylvania looking for a summer apprenticeship. He was not flashy. He was thorough in terms of detail, and content to perform small tasks on the designs of other architects, perfecting the process for invention without sacrificing his own angle of vision. He had designed an urban center in architecture school, conceived in human dimensions, like a medieval town, but open and light, solar-heated, taking into account a world in which wars can be fought in space and daily lives programmed by series of multicolored buttons. He was not social and found it difficult to engage in conversation with people other than his family unless the talk was specific and had to do with sports or his work. But he was well liked by people because he was unobtrusive and centered like a tree whose deep roots spread through several yards on the same city block. He was the kind of man who inspired affection based not on moments of intimacy, but on confidence. His family said he was like his grandfather. They both had a certain peace of mind, rare among the Howells, which came of a fundamental faith in themselves. They believed they could meet emergencies and people counted on them.

He was thinking about that when the pilot came on to say that they were flying over the Mississippi now, if everyone on the left side of the plane wanted to look out. Rika looked. She moved Caleb's arm, resting on her belly, a hard ball between her pelvic bones, the beginning of a baby.

"I always get excited crossing the Mississippi," she said to him.

He smiled at her. She could tell he hadn't heard what she had said or the pilot.

"Do I look old?" Caleb asked suddenly, turning to Rika so she could examine him for age.

"You look twenty-six," Rika said simply, touching his cheek with her hand. He had grown into a slender, rather elegant man, extremely tall, fair-skinned with sharp features, long-faced with close eyes, a strong chin. He could have been forty. He had the kind of looks which go from youth to age in a single change.

"I am twenty-six," he said. "But I think I look much older."

Rika shrugged. "You look your age to me." And then she glanced at him quizzically. "I like the way you look, Caleb, if that's what you mean."

"It's not." He laughed.

He doubted that Rika would understand his state of mind. She was the middle child in a large Quaker family. Her father, Dr. Mundel, was a professor at Haverford College; her mother painted miniatures, not for sale. Their world seemed to operate according to the logical theories her father talked about in philosophy classes.

"They're a perfect family," Caleb said to his own family after he and Rika were engaged.

"Perfect Quakers," Peter said. "They communicate silently through the inner light."

"Shut up, Peter," Bumpo said. "I'll marry Rika. I'd love a family that didn't fight."

"She hasn't the stamina to marry you, Bumpo," Peter said.

After the engagement had been announced, the Howells were invited to Sunday dinner with the Mundels at Haverford College, where they lived. After a plain dinner without wine, the Mundel girls entertained with chamber music. Rika played the flute.

"That was very nice," Peter said on the way home. "I wish we'd thought of getting together a string quartet when we were growing up."

"It would never have worked," Rachel said.

"You can always tell a family that's harmonious. They make music together," Bumpo said sadly.

"Watch the sunset, Bumpo, and shut up," Peter said.

As the plane from Houston descended over northern Virginia, dipped down to the Potomac and onto the runway on the Virginia bank of the river, Caleb was thinking about his responsibility for his family. Perhaps, he was thinking, he should move east again, join a firm in Philadelphia, even live on the farm.

"It is a strange feeling not to have men in the generation of my family older than mine," Caleb said to Rika. "I have my brothers, but that's different."

"You have Julia," Rika said.

"Yes," Caleb said. His sister, whom he often thought of as a mother, seemed years older to him than Rika. He wanted to see her immediately. He was impatient with the hours of travel ahead of him before he would be home.

Julia met Rachel just as she came out of her bedroom after a rest, dressed in her white linen dress and now a white turban pinned together in the front with a cameo.

"Do you think it looks foolish?" Rachel asked.

"I think it does," Julia said and hugged her grandmother. "Oh, Bammy."

"Don't, lambie. We must be brave."

"For whom?"

"For each other." Rachel held Julia at arm's length. "You look dreadful. You should start using cream on your eyes or they'll wrinkle like cotton."

"I've been working hard."

"And forgetting to sleep."

She took Julia into her bathroom, sat her down on the toilet seat. "You must have makeup," she said. "Caleb will think you're dying when he comes."

She put on blush and liquid powder under the black circles. "Take your hair down," she insisted.

"Who is coming for dinner?"

"Just us. Do you have anything white?"

"White? You mean a dress?"

"Anything. A blouse. Do you remember when I told you that in India they wear white for funerals?"

Julia took the pins out of her hair and brushed it.

"We're not in India, Bammy," she said.

When they went through the bedroom, Rachel nodded towards the unmade bed. "There," she said, and Julia understood. "I haven't had the heart to make it."

Rachel sat at the head of the table in John's place, Theo and Pippa on either side of her. The table was set for a holiday with fresh flowers and linen place mats. Lila and Cally had been cooking since noon. Although no one was able to eat much, there was a general mood of excitement which even Pippa noticed.

"It seems like we're not sad enough," Pippa said.

"That's why we pass on the Bible," Peter said, "to keep from being too unhappy. Like in England. The king is dead, long live the king."

"That's pretty dumb, as usual," Theo said.

"My guess is Bumpo gets the Bible and he has to promise no more dope forever," Peter said.

"I don't use dope any longer," Bumpo said. "I even take vitamins." He looked at Tuwilla for confirmation.

"And if Peter gets it, he'll have to go back to medicine," Caleb said.

"He already is," Theo said. "He's going to be a psychiatrist for children like me."

"You're perfectly normal, Theo," Philip said. "It's almost boring how normal you are."

"No, I'm not," Theo said absolutely. "You know that."

Caleb announced that Rika was having a baby in November.

"Stand up, Rika," he said. "You can almost see it if she stands straight."

"Oh, Caleb," Rika said, embarrassed.

"We all stand up and have our stomachs examined at family dinners, Rika," Peter said. He stood up. "See. Mine is perfectly flat. No evidence of a baby."

Pippa laughed. "Boys don't, dummy."

"Mama's had her tubes tied so she can't," Theo explained.

"Is that so? You didn't tell me," Bumpo said.

"When?" Cally asked, surprised.

"This is inappropriate conversation," Philip said.

"I haven't," Julia said, ignoring Philip.

"Julia," Philip said.

"I was thinking of it," Julia said to Rachel.

"My family tends to be very private," Rika said quietly, finding an ally in Philip.

"A remarkable quality. I had forgotten there were families like that," Philip said.

"I bet it's Caleb," Bumpo said. He had been sitting pensively resting his chin in his hand.

"What's Caleb?" Pippa asked.

"Caleb who gets the Bible."

"I think it might be," Caleb said simply.

"You won't be disappointed if it's not, Caleb?" Peter asked.

"Of course not," Caleb said. "It's not a prize."

"It's a responsibility," Rachel said.

She took the letter from her lap. It was a business envelope with "JOHN HOWELLS, INC., 551 Fifth Avenue, New York, New York," printed in the upper-left-hand corner.

"Have you read it?" Theo asked Rachel.

"No," she said.

"When did he write it?"

"In the spring. He kept it in his sock drawer."

She opened the letter and read it first to herself, intending to read it out loud. Peter, who was sitting close to her, could see that it was brief.

When Rachel looked up, she was crying.

"I'm sorry," she said. "I can't read it." She passed it to Julia. "You read it."

Julia opened the letter dated March 1, 1972.

DEAR JULIA [John Howells had written], WRITE THE LOVE STORIES AND TELL THE TRUTH ABOUT THEM. WITH LOVE, G——.

INHERITED LIVES

JOHN HOWELLS DIED JUNE 10, 1972, AND LEFT THE FAMILY
BIBLE TO HIS OLDEST GRANDCHILD, JULIA.

"Age thirty-five, black hair, small mole on her right temple, ordinary height, skinny," Peter said after reading Julia's entry in the library of the Main House the week after his grandfather's death.

"And a girl," Bumpo said from the couch, where he was lying with the Sunday *Times* sports section across his stomach.

"Without noticeable breasts, but a girl nevertheless," Peter said. "I can see the Bible is going to become a fascinating document under your care, Julia, if this entry is any example."

The children had come to the Main House for breakfast as one or the other of them had done every morning since their grandfather had died.

"I don't mind the evening," Rachel had said without a trace of self-pity, "but I find the mornings difficult. Such a long day ahead, you see."

It hadn't been necessary for her to say anything else. They had come. Caleb and Rika ate their meals at the Main House until they returned to Houston. Theo and Pippa came each morning, sometimes in pajamas. Even Cally came.

Rachel made biscuits and spoonbread, sliced strawberries from the garden and peaches, which she served with thick cream. By ten o'clock, when they had left to go home or to work, she had a kitchen full of dishes to attend to. On the mornings that everyone came, it could take her until noon to clean up.

"Read Julia's entry out loud," Bumpo said from the couch.

Peter did. "You see?" he said.

"Brilliant," Bumpo said.

"My very thought," Peter said.

"What else is there for me to say?" Julia asked.

247

"Since you're the one in charge of this book, I want to put in my request for a better story when I die. I want my contributions to the general welfare listed, my generous spirit and sense of humor, good looks retained into middle age. Listen, Julia, you're a writer by profession. You can do better."

"Mama's an actress. She just writes plays for fun," Theo said.

"Well, she can make the Bible into a play. 'Inherited Lives'—a new family comedy by Julia Howells. It can open with a narrator offstage speaking: 'It grieves me to report that Nathaniel Howells, alias Bum-po, the Prairie Dog King, died this morning choking on a peach pit while stoned in his grandmother's living room. He has left his fortune to the Boys for Jesus Commune in Dammer Dammer, Colorado.' "

"That is not funny," Bumpo said.

"You're absolutely right. It's deeply serious. I'll start again," Peter said. " 'It grieves me. . . .' "

"Don't. All the stories you make up are so gloomy. Besides," Bumpo said, "I don't smoke dope any longer."

"Yes, you do," Pippa said, sitting down on Bumpo's feet. "You did when Tuwilla was at the market the other day and you made me promise not to tell."

Julia closed the Bible, put it under her arm. She called good-bye to Rachel, who was in the kitchen.

"Mad?" Peter asked her. "Are you just going to take your Bible and go home?" Peter followed her out, down the front steps of the Main House and over the hill to Julia's house. "You are cross," he said, linking arms with her. "I'm sorry, Julia."

Julia pulled away, in no humor for gestures of affection or apology.

" 'Write the love stories,' Grandfather says to me. You read that. What, for Chrissake, do I know about love stories?"

Philip had told Julia a few nights after her grandfather's death that he might go to England and take the children. They had been sitting in the kitchen, sharing a bottle of wine. Philip was drinking moderately, as he always did, and Julia, even before the conversation about England, had drunk too much.

"For Theo," he said reasonably. "In England eccentricities are better tolerated." He nervously ran his forefinger over the rim of the wineglass until it sang.

"Theo is sick, Philip." Julia poured another glass of wine. "I don't care how wonderfully tolerant the English are; he'll be sick there, too."

"That's not the point entirely." Philip took the bottle, corked it and put it away.

"You'd like not to be married to me any longer," Julia said, sensing she had lost him already, long before this night. It seemed to her that it was better to choose the ends of unions than to have them come upon you abruptly. She longed for a detachment like Bumpo's, to ride out the days as he did, five feet off the earth in a drug-induced dizziness with pigeon dreams of flying.

"I'd be very happy to be married to you, Julia, except we are only married in name." He leaned across the kitchen table hoping to engage her attention.

"What do you mean? We sleep together," Julia snapped.

"Oh, that. Yes, indeed, there's that. You've drunk too much wine and it's given you a bad temper."

"I had one already," Julia said, getting up and pouring the rest of her wine down the sink.

"Do you remember how cross you were at Harold Markus when I first met you because he was married to his work?"

"Yes." Julia sank down on the bench across from him. "But now that I'm older, it makes sense to me that he should have fallen in love with directing. He knew he couldn't make his life work out for him."

"But surely you can understand that it's not a good arrangement to be married to someone who prefers her love affair with work to her love affair with you." When Philip was angry, he looked at her directly with an intensity that seemed practiced for such occasions. It frightened her.

"I understand," Julia said quietly, wishing to end the conversation, wanting the early formality of their lives together as a protection against this new and unsettling honesty. "I wish sometimes you weren't so very sensible, Philip. It would be refreshing if for once you'd do something surprising, like take off your clothes and run naked all over the farm."

"Oh, you do," Philip said, getting up, shutting the windows for the night, locking the back door. "I might win you from the theater by running naked? I had no idea it would be so simple."

Julia woke Philip in the middle of that night. "I can't sleep," she said. "I don't know if I've even been to sleep yet. Do you know what time it is?"

"Four-fifteen exactly, darling."

"Do you think it's odd that Grandfather left the Bible to me?"

"Not at all. I expected it absolutely."

"Don't you think it was invasive of him to send me that letter charging me to write the love stories?" She leaned towards him in the dark.

"Not at all. It was quite like him." Philip propped the pillow behind his head, preparing for a night of wakefulness. "He was a thorough man. He didn't want you to mistake your responsibility." He rearranged the covers, spreading a sheet over Julia with great gentleness.

"Fat chance," she said, turning on her side, away from him. "I haven't anything to say about love stories."

"That's good news," Philip said. "Then you can go back to sleep."

The summer after John Howells' death Julia often sat on the wide porch at the back of her house, facing away from Rachel's. From there she could see the children playing in the creek. In the evening, when Philip came home from the hospital, he asked about what she had done that day. There was something accusing in the way in which she replied, "Nothing," as though he had had some responsibility for the day's failure. As an answer to Rachel's questions about whether Julia was writing, Philip rolled his eyes until the blue pupils disappeared behind the lids.

He had come to the Main House to have lunch with Rachel, part of the regular but unspoken plan among the family that Rachel would always have someone for whom to cook a meal. The arrangement was casual. Philip would call Peter in the morning to say, "I have a couple of free hours at lunch. I think I'll stop by Bam's." To which Peter would reply, "Swell. And tell her if she'll make that veal dish tomorrow night, I'll come for supper with some heather for her garden." The plan kept Rachel in the kitchen all summer.

"Death is unacceptable to Julia," she said to Philip that afternoon.

"She finds her satisfaction in lives she can arrange with her pen and direct herself," Philip said.

"I'd do that, too, if I had the choice," Rachel said, folding warm peaches in a crepe. "I don't think Julia has ever recovered from Nat's death."

Peter was honestly worried about Julia. She never went to The Plant Shop that summer, but one afternoon, when Raphael was minding the store, Peter visited her on the back porch of her house.

"I thought you were going to write a play this summer," he said.

"I'm writing one in my head," she said. "It's about a woman at the bottom of her life."

"That should be jolly. *Self-Portrait in Gray*, you could call it. I notice you've been practicing to play the major role."

"Don't make fun of me, Peter. I've lost my sense of humor." Julia had on a T-shirt of Bumpo's that said CHILDREN ARE FOR KEEPS, running shorts and sandals. She wore her hair pulled back in a braid and no makeup. Like an adolescent, she never changed clothes that summer. Her present sense of herself was tied to such repetition.

"How did you ever get over that old man in the hospital in New Haven?" Julia asked suddenly. They had not discussed the death of the old man since Peter left medicine. It was a closed issue. No one except Julia knew about it.

"I didn't," Peter said.

"But you get along very well. You work, you go out. You're even funny."

"But I'm not a doctor."

"You are a doctor. You could practice any time you wanted to."

"Sure, Julia. You too, you know. You could be a director or an actress or a playwright or a mother and wife. Or all of them at once. You can even be a Bible historian. Think of it. I don't know why you're in such a blue funk this summer."

"I don't want the damned Bible," Julia said.

"Give it to Pippa then. She can draw pictures in it."

"I can't even write except in my head."

"Well, if you continue to think of the woman at the bottom of her life, she might materialize right on this back porch and you won't even have to make her up."

"Shut up, Peter. I've already told you about my sense of humor."

"Do you think Julia shows signs of having the kinds of problems that Mama used to have?" Peter asked Rachel when he came for dinner, bringing the heather for the garden.

"No," Rachel said. "Julia is as sane as most people I know. Too sane."

"Well, it's certainly a bore to see her rocking on the back porch, retired from living, inventing this goddamned depressed woman for a new comedy she's thinking of writing."

"I have faith in Julia," Rachel said.

"As a writer, yeah, me too."

Rachel poured wine for both of them, filled his plate with veal in tarragon.

"Ah, Bammy," he said, kissing her loose-fleshed cheek, "Julia needs to spend more time cooking."

"Absolutely." Rachel smiled. "And she needs to fall in love."

"Maybe I'll get her together with Raphael."

"I was thinking of Philip," Rachel said, tossing a spinach salad.

"You're always so conventional, just when I'm beginning to have hopes for you."

"I'm being serious. Ever since your father died and that stupid affair with Hal Markus, she has reminded me of my mother, who was in an accident when she was your age and never got in a car again. She was afraid to learn to drive herself and she would never trust another driver with the controls. And then my father's death . . ."

They talked until the candles had burned down to the candle-sticks. Peter helped Rachel with the dishes because when she got up, she was swaying with more wine than she had drunk for years.

"You don't think Julia's like Hannah, do you?" Peter asked in the kitchen while he was drying the glasses, unwilling to drop the subject of his sister, on whom all of the Howells children had counted as a barometer for their own living.

"She's like me and your mother, probably even Hannah. When she was small, she used to pretend to be Lucy Tanner all the time. But like Hannah in her dying? Not a chance, Peter. You know Julia better than that."

Unsatisfied, Peter asked Philip, who refused to be engaged in personal conversation about his wife. One evening in late July, Peter went to talk to Cally about Julia. The children seldom spoke to Cally about problems. They had more faith in Rachel and they were worried that their concerns might break her, although she had been well for years. When Peter arrived at his mother's, Cally was distracted with a situation of her own.

"Jimmy Zimmer has come back for Lila," Cally told Peter.

"That's nice for Lila," Peter said.

"I suppose. He's a no-'count man but perhaps he's better than no man."

When Peter mentioned his concern about Julia, Cally shrugged. "There are worse things than depression."

* * *

Jimmy Zimmer had arrived unannounced, expecting Lila to be so overjoyed at seeing him that she would leave with him that night. She wasn't displeased that he'd come back.

Lila and Jimmy had talked in her bedroom for hours. They'd drunk beer, filling the wicker wastebasket with empty bottles, sitting across from each other on twin beds with a fan on so Lila's skirt billowed around her fine legs. While they talked, Cally was working in the garden, as she always did after lunch. When she was finished weeding, she called Lila to help her back in her wheelchair. Because of the noise from the fan, Lila couldn't hear her. When she finally got help, not from Lila, but from Theo, who had come over to visit, Cally was in a bad humor.

"Jimmy just walked in the front door and hollered for me as if he owned the place," Lila said that night at supper in the kitchen. "Some surprise."

"I suppose," Cally said.

"I thought he'd gone for good," Lila said.

"I doubt Jimmy Zimmer does anything for good," Cally said coolly. "Are you going to leave with him?"

Lila used her fork as a baton to gesture, slapping it against the palm of her hand.

"He didn't insist," she said. She was distracted and that annoyed Cally, guessing at Lila's thoughts.

"Just a friendly call?" Cally asked. "He wants to keep in touch every decade or so?"

"He's had troubles," Lila said.

"Poor man," Cally said with uncommon bitterness. "I wouldn't know about troubles."

Lila stood up from the table and took Cally's plate.

"You through?" she asked, not waiting for an answer. She cleared the rest of the dishes. "I didn't issue an invitation for him to come here," she said, her back to Cally.

"I presume he had an invitation before he left this afternoon."

"Don't be fresh," Lila said.

Cally wheeled out of the kitchen and into the bedroom while Lila did the dishes. When Lila came in, she was already in a nightgown.

"I was going to bathe you," Lila said.

"I don't need help." Cally lifted herself on the bed. "So, when does he want an answer?" She threw off the covers and leaned against the pillow.

"I am his wife, you know," Lila said.

"Just go," Cally answered.

"He was only with that waitress for a short time and then he was injured at work and on unemployment."

"It sounds like a great opportunity for you, Lila." Cally turned out her bedside light and closed her eyes. "Do you mind letting the dogs in and tying Cynthia up before you go to bed?"

Lila shut the bedroom door. "I'm not that goat's nigger, Miss Caroline. I'll let in the dogs."

When Cally got up the next morning, Cynthia was tied to her usual stake. That day, and the next, she and Lila lived together in silence, like shadows of each other, attached at the base. They ate at the same table, although neither of them was hungry. The second day Jimmy Zimmer called. Cally could hear some of the conversation from the kitchen, where she was attending to three baby wild rabbits Philip had unearthed with the tractor earlier in the week.

"I don't know," she heard Lila say. "I simply don't know, Jimmy. Give me some time."

There was more conversation which Cally didn't hear, but she certainly heard Lila shout, before she slammed down the phone, "I'm no one's fucking nigger, you hear?"

When Lila came out of her bedroom, she was dressed in a pale yellow sundress that made her skin look blue-black, high-heeled patent sandals and a straw hat with ribbons. She looked beautiful, as Cally had remembered her from girlhood.

"I'm going to town."

"New Hope?"

"Doylestown."

Cally didn't ask if she were going to see Jimmy Zimmer or when she would be back. But when it was eight o'clock and Lila wasn't back, Cally called Julia and asked her to come over.

"You have had that same terrible-looking T-shirt on all summer," Cally snapped when Julia came in. "Do you need clothes?"

"Same shorts and sandals, too, Mama," Julia said, ruffling her mother's hair, surprised at Cally's temper but not responding to it. "Do you have something cold to drink here? It's murderously hot."

"Mint tea, and milk, of course." Cally's voice was strident. Her spirit had altered since morning. It crossed Julia's mind that Cally might be ill again. She couldn't remember the signs.

"You look wonderful, Mama. You must have been out all day. Your face is so tan." She poured two glasses of mint tea and sat down at the kitchen table across from her mother's wheelchair.

"Don't be unnaturally pleasant," Cally said. "I feel awful."

"How?" Julia deliberated. She thought about asking Philip to come over.

"Sick at my stomach," Cally said. "I haven't eaten properly for three days." Cally seldom mentioned her physical state. It was a matter of privacy.

"Maybe you should see a doctor."

"I don't need a doctor," Cally said. She was crying.

"Mama." Julia reached over and took her hand.

"Lila's husband came here, and he wants her to go back to him," Cally said.

"Maybe she won't." Julia held both of her mother's hands in her own.

"I think she has. I think she went back to him today. She took the bus to Doylestown and she hasn't returned. She's never done that," Cally said. "And he's been gone for twelve goddamned years. I hate him. I honestly do."

"Mama." Julia thought she would have to call Philip or take Cally home with her tonight. "Even if Lila does leave, you'll be fine. You've lived alone before, and Bumpo's here, and me and Peter. Caleb's even thinking of moving back. And now Bam's alone, you could move into the Main House with her if you didn't like staying alone."

"You don't exactly understand," Cally said, calmer, withdrawing her hands, wiping her eyes.

"Of course I do," Julia said. "Lila has done everything for you. I know you'd miss her, but we could sort of organize a team to help like we've been doing at Bam's."

Cally reached over and brushed a strand of hair out of Julia's face.

"I know you'd all be wonderful," Cally said quietly, looking past Julia at the window, into the dusk of nine o'clock. She sighed deeply, as though the confession she was prepared to make had been planned for a more appropriate moment than this one but could not be avoided. "What you don't understand is that I'm in love with Lila."

Even before Cally had spoken, she had heard a noise out front, the door open, and then the soft lilt of Lila's voice speaking to Cynthia. "Get lost, goaty girl," she said.

Julia didn't say what came immediately to mind to tell her mother which was: "Of course you love her. We all do. She's like a member of the family." Later she was glad there hadn't been the opportunity to prove that Cally was right and she hadn't understood at all.

Replaying the scene in her mind while she tried to get to sleep that night, Julia remembered that Cally's face had betrayed her when Lila walked in the kitchen.

"Philip?" Julia said, lying next to him. He replied with a groan. "Do you know what Mama told me tonight?"

"I haven't a clue," Philip said.

"That she's in love with Lila."

"That's very nice," Philip said.

"I mean in love. Like an affair. Do you think that's true?" Julia asked.

"I'm a very simpleminded man about matters like these. I honestly can't be of any help."

"I think that's what Mama told me," Julia said.

Cally had wanted Julia to truly understand what the loss of Lila would be, not to make light of it, and so she had told her daughter a real secret. Julia turned on her side away from Philip, full of a compassion foreign to her because of its long absence from her life. There, in the house where she'd grown up for all those years, her mother and Lila had been living an unsuspected life. She was not shocked or even, she decided later, surprised. Cally suddenly came to life like a child's dream of dolls who carry on at night while everyone in the house is sleeping.

"If Lila honestly leaves Mama, I'll kill her," Julia said fiercely.

"Wait until tomorrow, Julia. It's worth a second thought," Philip said.

The next morning Julia printed "Inherited Lives" on the first page of a yellow spiral notebook. She would write about Cally, not for the stage necessarily, although certainly that was the form it would take, but for herself.

Before she started to work, she went over to Cally's, where her mother was working in the garden.

"Are you okay?"

"Fine," Cally said.

"Lila's not leaving?"

"Lila's leaving for a month or so, but not for good. At least not now."

She didn't mention what she had told Julia the night before and

Julia didn't bring it up. But they were both aware of a common understanding, something they had not had to bind their lives in the years of Julia's growing up.

After Lila came home from seeing Jimmy Zimmer in Doylestown, she and Cally had sat in the kitchen, talking until after midnight. She wouldn't go with Jimmy, she said. That was decided. But she'd like to leave for a while. She needed to think about the life she had chosen.

"Sometimes I feel I'm at the same place as my mama, keeping a white man's house. No change in fifty years."

"It's different," Cally said.

"Certainly your mother and my mother didn't have the same working relationship as you and I do." Lila's voice had an edge.

"It's really different."

"I confess it is," Lila said. "But these last couple of days I've felt like a colored woman."

"Because Jimmy told you that you are."

"Jimmy simply said what I'd been thinking. Besides, you wouldn't want me to stay unless I chose to."

"Of course not. We've been together without a break for a very long time. Why don't you take a trip or go home?"

"I was thinking that. I ought to go visit my relatives, see if any of them has fallen for a white woman."

Cally didn't smile.

When Lila put her to bed that night, Cally took her face in her hands. "I love you," she said.

The next week Julia and Pippa went to meals at Rachel's. Cally had left for New Orleans to stay with her parents, who had been ailing for years, but they wouldn't sell the house and they wouldn't die. Peter had closed the shop and gone to New Haven to speak with some of his former medical professors. He had taken Theo with him.

"Of course," Julia had said when Peter asked if Theo could go with him. "Theo would love it. But why?"

"For company."

"Are you sure that's all?"

"Certainly," Peter had said, but it wasn't true. He wanted to talk about Theo to a professor of psychiatric medicine with whom he had worked when he was at Yale. And he didn't have confidence in anyone else taking care of him. Julia was not accountable for daily things, and Philip . . .

"What is going on with Philip?" Peter asked Julia before he left. She shrugged.

"You mean, because he's working so hard?" she asked.

"He's never home and he hasn't worked a fourteen-hour day since I've known him."

"Perhaps he's met someone," Julia said flippantly.

"You're kidding, I suppose."

"I don't see him to ask him. He's been working like this since June."

"Shit," Peter said. "I'm ready for this summer to be over. Everyone in this family is behaving like an adolescent."

It actually had crossed Julia's mind that Philip had met someone else, but her own mind was with her play. The facts of her life seemed like details she had read in a book of short stories which had a temporary but unimposing reality. If she thought about Philip, she recalled that for nights now, maybe even weeks, she'd been asleep when he came home. She didn't know when they had last made love.

"Is everybody ill lately? You're at work half the night," she said to Philip the next morning.

"The heat," he replied.

"You know, you haven't kissed me for a long time."

"It's been too hot for anything." He was looking out the window.

"No, you've been home late."

"You've been distracted all summer," he said.

"So have you," she said.

Bumpo went with Peter and Theo on the same train to New York on the twenty-fourth of July. He was wearing Peter's seersucker suit, which was too large and out of date, and a shirt of his grandfather's, which was too small, although a tie concealed the fact that it didn't button at the neck. At the last minute, as he was getting on the train, Julia realized that he was wearing shoes and no socks.

"You can't go to New York for a business meeting like that, for Chrissake," she said.

"Too late," Bumpo said, as indeed it was. Julia and Pippa waved good-bye from the platform in Trenton. Bumpo was going to spend several days in New York with his lawyer, an accountant and the manufacturers of Wipe Out, which had been distributed in December 1972 and hit the country like a tornado, leading the game market lists in numbers sold, beating old favorites like Monopoly and backgammon. Julia waited at the station with Tuwilla, who was taking a train from Trenton the same morning but in the other direction, to Washington to attend her brother's marriage in a Hare Krishna house where he had been living in unparalleled bliss, Tuwilla's words, since the late sixties.

"The farm is empty except for us and Pippa," Julia told Rachel at supper.

"And Philip," Rachel said. They were eating a cold supper on the patio at dusk. The fields beyond were dotted with fireflies, which Pippa was collecting in a glass mayonnaise jar the lid of which was full of holes punched with an ice pick.

"Wherever Philip is," Julia said.

"Are you worried?" Rachel asked.

"Perhaps," Julia said. "I wouldn't blame him if he has met someone else. I haven't been a particularly good wife these last two years, since before *Joey Boy*."

"I wonder what a good wife is," Rachel said. "I think I had a good marriage, but I certainly would have failed the tests for being a good wife." She picked the black olives out of the salad and ate them with her fingers. "I wanted to be married and that, of course, is necessary at the beginning."

Rachel had looked lovely since John's death. She took great care with herself, did her hair daily and seldom wore the foolish hats which had been her custom in her married years. She dressed for dinner and wore makeup all day, as though she were at any moment expecting company or preparing to go out. Julia found herself looking at her grandmother with the interest she might have had in a stranger, at the texture of her skin, her hazel eyes which became flecked with yellow in the sun, at her fine, distinguished nose which would have done as well on a man, at the way she gestured when she spoke and the way she walked, like a woman who thought of herself as beautiful.

"I have been wondering why you dress so well since Grandfather died," Julia said suddenly.

"Survival, my lamb," Rachel said. "I didn't have to work so hard at it when he was alive."

"Mama didn't change that I know of when Daddy died. At least in terms of how she looked."

"She had all of you children and Lila."

Julia looked up. "Lila?"

"Lila has been with your mother for years."

"Helping Mama," Julia said cautiously. She wondered if Rachel knew. She couldn't imagine her mother telling Rachel or that her grandmother at seventy-six, part of a different century, could guess at such a relationship.

"Your mother loves Lila," Rachel said simply, and it wasn't appropriate for Julia to pursue the conversation without risking the confession of Cally's secrets.

That night and the others that followed while the farm was deserted, Julia and Pippa helped Rachel clean out John's closets and his study upstairs off the bedroom. They found boxes of Daniel's which John had kept, and even of Thomas'. Julia sorted through the boxes and found a number of things that had belonged to Lucy Tanner, a lace handkerchief in tatters, a baby shawl, drawings of bearded men and round-faced women in buns drawn in brown ink on yellow paper and signed "L. Tanner," a locket with a strand of black hair.

"We should have Boxing Day again," Rachel said, "before we drown in all this memorabilia."

Julia looked up from the floor, where she was sitting amid open boxes and letters, old documents and photographs. No one in the family had mentioned Boxing Day since her father had died. At least not in terms of a revival.

"I couldn't stand it," Julia said.

"Perhaps I couldn't either, or maybe I've just gotten so old my senses are dulled. That happens, you know." She pushed a box away. "Boring letters from Thomas to his second wife. Your grandfather kept everything. Even receipts." She took down a new box. "I liked Boxing Day, you know. It was typical of this family to borrow a custom from another country and change it." She had found a book kept by Lucy Tanner and had opened it.

"Can you read this?" she asked, handing it to Julia. "The writing is very difficult."

"I can read the dates," Julia said. "In fact, I can read a lot of it. 'I have had no word of Robert for months. I sent him a note when I knew of the baby which said, "Our joy will be flesh." It is possible he misunderstood. His wife may have read the communication first. Were it not for this child, all the life would be gone out of me.' "

Rachel found a picture of Lucy, taken in the late 1800's, long after the portrait over the mantel in Daniel's house had been painted.

"She looks Indian," Julia said. "Very dark and strong-featured."

"The Howells disapproved of her. Daniel used to tell me she was very sensual."

"There were a lot of Roberts?"

"I doubt it. I have always guessed that Thomas had a surgical approach to the human body. I think, too, she must have loved Robert. I understand that he was brought to the farm during the war, when Thomas was serving as chief surgeon for the Union forces in Pennsylvania. He was separated from the Confederate forces and was brought with another soldier, who apparently died. But Robert stayed on at the farm, hidden in the old barn behind the Main House, according to Daniel. They carried on what was described by your grandfather as a lurid affair, but I assume it was lovely. When Thomas came back, she was pregnant, obviously not with his child, and he restricted her to the farm. Daniel remembered her wandering the upstairs rooms of the Main House in a temper and he maintained that as a mother she was loving only with Lucinda. Here." She gave the diary back to Julia, and the photograph. "Keep them with the Bible. The rest of this junk—Thomas' medical journals about the hernias and gouts of Bucks County—we'll give to Philip."

"Did you ever have an affair?" Julia asked.

Rachel stalled to think of what she wanted Julia to know of her life, what stories she wanted to die with. "Not an affair in the sense that Lucy did. I never loved anyone else but your grandfather."

"I slept with the painter where I lived in New York. Only once. I don't know why I did it."

"Well," Rachel said, "there aren't reasons for everything. If there were, it would be tedious to live."

Her name was listed in Philip's medical records as Andrea De-Laurentis, age twenty-eight, divorced, full-term pregnancy, child deceased. One abortion. Address: Box 826, New Hope, Pennsylvania. No telephone. Occupation: painter. She came to Philip's office with a tubular pregnancy in 1970 and the medical report mentioned that Philip had sent her to the head of obstetrics at the University of Pennsylvania Hospital, who in turn sent in a customary report to Philip after the surgery was complete. He remembered her immediately when she came to see him at the end of June 1972 because she was tall with dark red hair, brown eyes, deep-set, no freckles—not beautiful but striking—and she dressed like a southern Irish farm girl. The new medical information indicated exhaustion, lethargy, depression, no appetite, mild headaches, a sensitive stomach. When he lifted her white patient's robe and pressed her belly in the center, she winced. He sent her to the laboratory for a series of blood tests and made an appointment to see her the following day. The diagnosis was infectious hepatitis. When she came to his office the next afternoon, he held a hand mirror up for her to look at the yellow cast to her eyeballs, the definite change in the color of her skin.

"I hadn't noticed," Andrea said. "I work all day in my studio and never pay much attention to the way I look."

He wanted to say something very foolish like "You ought to," but he restrained himself. He told her to get plenty of rest, to come back at the end of the week, that he'd have to check her often in the next month.

"Is she *that* sick?" his nurse asked after she had made four subsequent appointments for Ms. DeLaurentis.

"Yes," Philip replied, although the hematology report had not indicated a severe case.

Philip went home with Andrea DeLaurentis occupying every corner of his mind. He watched Julia walk naked to the bathroom and wondered how she would look with full breasts and red hair. He had a dream, maybe even a waking dream, in which Andrea came to him suffering from serious depression. To compensate in kindness, he made love to her on the examining table, bolting the door to the corridor with the instrument sterilizer.

At the end of the week Andrea said her depression was worse. She had suicidal thoughts in the evenings, particularly if she had worked all day.

Philip asked her a number of questions. She thought they had to do with her health.

"Were you married long?" was one of the questions.

"Two years," she replied.

"Both pregnancies then?"

"No," she said. "Only the first, a baby who was born with a congenital heart disease. He died when he was six weeks old."

"I'm so sorry," Philip said. He wanted to weep. He could never recall having such an emotional response to a patient. It was worrisome.

"Afterwards we separated. That happens sometimes to a marriage when a child dies, so I understand."

"I know," Philip said, nodding his head.

"It happened to you?" she asked.

"Not exactly." He paused. "Well, in a way, I suppose. I have two children, both living," he added nervously, unable to go on with confessions of a failed marriage. "The tubular pregnancy?"

"I don't know whose child it was. After I was divorced, I lived differently than I ever had before."

"I see," Philip said quickly.

"And now"—she laughed—"I'm practically celibate."

"Well, that's not good for you."

"I suppose not."

"You are alone then much of the time?" He closed the manila folder.

"I have friends, of course, but my family is in Providence and there's no one in particular. You don't think I'm developing psychological problems, do you? I mean, your questions."

"Oh, no," Philip said professionally. "The depression is due entirely to hepatitis, but you shouldn't isolate yourself too much."

That afternoon she asked him not to call her Miss DeLaurentis. Just Andrea.

Or darling, he thought.

He suggested she make her appointment the following week for four-thirty.

"All the four-thirties are booked," the nurse said.

"Then make it five. Any day but Friday."

"I leave at five," the nurse said.

"I know. I'll lock up."

"I thought you hated five o'clocks."

"I've changed my mind."

The following week Andrea arrived early. He kept her waiting on the examining table with her starched white robe tied at the back while he finished with the rest of his patients.

"Miss DeLaurentis is in Room three," his nurse said, not altogether pleasantly.

"Very well." He did not look up.

"Are you ready for me to leave now?"

"You may leave now," he said brusquely, ignoring her implications.

"Hello, Andrea," he said in his deepest voice when he entered Room 3. He had decided on a paternal approach, authoritative and gentle. It seemed to suit him. He guessed she would like it also.

He took the sheet off her legs and lifted them one at a time, bending her knee toward her abdomen. They were long, slender legs, newly shaven, softened with cream. Philip had never noticed the legs of a patient before, the feel of taut, muscular flesh beneath his hands.

"Hurt?" he asked. Her head was turned away from him towards the wall.

"No," she said.

He laid both of her legs flat, covered them and lifted the front of her surgical robe, pressing her stomach, checking for internal swelling.

She nodded.

"There?" he asked.

"Yes."

"That's normal for hepatitis," he said.

He sat her up and listened to her chest and back with his stethoscope. Her hair was very long and he had to lift it.

"Here," she said, reaching back to hold her hair herself.

"I have it," he said. "Relax."

She did. She relaxed against his chest.

"I'm so tired," she said. He checked her eyes with a light.

"Still depressed?"

She nodded.

"You're getting too thin." He ran his hand down her side. "You'll lose your beautiful breasts." He didn't say that.

"Get dressed," he said. "I'll talk to you in my office."

In his office he told her that he was taking her to dinner. "Just to El Pino's on Main Street," he said, his heart beating so fast he felt like exploding. "I have to be at the hospital for rounds at seven-thirty."

At El Pino's they ordered veal. No wine. Philip had to work and Andrea couldn't drink with hepatitis. He wanted to order a fine bottle of champagne and drink it down quickly so that full of heat and courage, he could take Miss DeLaurentis to his office and make love to her, kiss her lips which were large and full, kiss the pale nipples of her breasts.

"Good night," she said to him. "Thank you for dinner."

"Thank you," he said, following her out of the restaurant.

"I may see you next week or if I feel better, I'll cancel and see you in two weeks."

"I need to keep a close check on you, Andrea," he said, trying to sound casual. "Keep the appointment next week."

* * *

Philip had begun to think about his family, particularly his mother, which was surprising. He had never loved his mother. But in the month of July, lying awake at night with his eyes closed, pretending Julia was Andrea DeLaurentis with her red hair spread out like a silk scarf on the pillow, he thought about his mother differently from the way he had as an adult. She had been a distant woman, rather lovely, like unsigned paintings of the aristocracy, refined and conventional, self-contained and undemonstrative. Sentimentality annoyed her, particularly in regard to her husband or her sons. He remembered her cheeks and hands as cool, never damp, her lips narrow as thread, disappearing with age. They seldom touched. Their conversations were formal and instructive on her part. In fact, he had no reason to think of her, but something about Andrea DeLaurentis—or else his overwhelming feeling for Andrea —brought on a state of mind suggesting a fact or a wish, he didn't know which, from his childhood.

The following week Miss DeLaurentis canceled her appointment. His nurse came into his office specifically to tell him.

"She must be better," he said, knowing that his nurse had guessed at his disappointment.

The tests he took the next visit showed she had developed mononucleosis. He was not surprised since he had frequently seen patients with both infections, but he was ashamed of his great pleasure when the tests were positive. She promised to get more rest and to make an appointment once a week faithfully through the rest of July and August in the four-thirty time slot. Philip couldn't construct a reason to take her out to dinner again.

He spent Saturdays in New Hope, hoping to catch a glimpse of Andrea DeLaurentis, "shopping," he told Julia, who was hard at work on *Inherited Lives*. She had decided to include the women in her family and was reading the Bible for clues to the characters of Lucy Tanner and Hannah Howells.

"Shopping?" she asked.

"A diversion while you're working. I like to watch the people on the street."

She didn't believe him. He had never liked to watch the people before. He hated crowds and had never gone to New Hope on weekends, especially in the summer when the tourist season was in full swing.

One evening too hot for sleeping, Julia and Philip sat in the living room reading. When Julia looked up, Philip's book was sitting open on his knees and he was staring straight ahead.

"Who are you thinking about?" she asked him.

"Patients," he said.

"What one?"

"I have several I'm concerned about."

"What does she look like?" she wanted to ask. "Is she like me?" But she didn't ask anything, simply picked up her book and continued to read. She was not anxious for confirmation. She had felt Philip slipping from her all summer slowly, like the change in temperature when the earth moves away from the sun. If she forced the issue now, they would have to stop their present lives together and make new arrangements. Julia wasn't ready for that. She wanted this moment, in spite of its limitations and Philip's preoccupations, to last, at least until she finished *Inherited Lives*.

Philip saw Andrea DeLaurentis in The Plant Shop in late August. He had stopped by on one of his Saturday outings to visit Peter and there she was in white shorts and a blue knit shirt with her hair in braids on top of her head. She was buying a hanging basket of wandering Jew and four geraniums. Her back was to him when he came in. In fact, if Peter had not called out at that moment, Philip would have ducked into the pharmacy next door and lost himself in the latest *Time*.

"Phil," Peter called. "I thought Theo was with you."

"No," Philip said, standing at the screen door, preparing to back out of it. "Theo's with Julia and Cally today, buying presents for Pippa's birthday."

Andrea recognized his voice and turned around.

"Oh, hello," she said. "I never expected to see my doctor leading a regular life."

"Oh, yes, I do lead a regular life," Philip said awkwardly.

"You know Philip?" Peter asked.

"He's my doctor," Andrea said.

"He's my brother-in-law," Peter said.

"Peter's really a doctor, too," Philip said, suddenly embarrassed by the fact that Peter was a merchant selling plants to Andrea.

"Who?" she asked.

"Peter."

"Oh, you," she said, turning to Peter. "I just shop here. I didn't know his name."

"That's what I meant. I thought you should know he is a physi-cian."

"Well, that's very nice. Thank you. I'm glad you're a doctor," she said to Peter in a voice too sprightly for kindness. "I'm a lot better. When I see you this week, I hope you'll tell me I'm fine because I've been invited to the Cape for two weeks."

"Yes, I hope."

"Well, bye," she said, inspecting a fig tree on her way out the door.

"Bye," Philip said. "Jesus. I don't know why I said what I did, Peter," he said after she had left.

"Flustered by redheads."

"It could be."

Peter did not mention the red-haired woman with geraniums to Julia, but he found himself wondering at Philip's unfamiliar awk-wardness that afternoon.

Theo spent days during the summer at The Plant Shop with Peter. He worked, watering and weeding the plants. He played games and went to Dockets to pick up two chocolate sodas with chocolate ice cream in the afternoon, and he also spent time in back of the shop striking matches. There was a yard and patio behind the greenhouse and at first, Peter wasn't aware of what Theo was doing. He simply assumed that Theo was involved in one or another imaginary game until one afternoon, while he was in the greenhouse, he smelled smoke. He found Theo sitting in front of a small fire on the back patio.

"What are you doing?" he asked, still carrying the yellow roses he had been in the process of clipping.

"Want to see?" Theo said. He took a pile of sticks and paper and began to build, in the manner of a log cabin, a building, carefully constructed with spaces for windows.

"Are you going to be an architect like Caleb?"

"Nope," said Theo. He took a pack of matches from his pocket and lit the pile of sticks. There was a quick, high fire.

"I just like the fires," Theo said.

When Peter mentioned the fires to Philip, Philip said that he used to do exactly the same thing when he was a boy. It was damn lucky that the house had never burned down. Julia told Peter she was at the end of her rope with Theo. Together they went to the Kinkaid School for Special Children, where Theo had been. They said he should return. He wouldn't be allowed to burn matches there. He wouldn't be able to have them, of course. The psychiatrist in Philadelphia whom Theo had seen every two weeks at the insistence of the Kinkaid administrators said, "It's good for him to act out his aggressions with these small fires. We'll just keep an eye on him."

"I hate psychiatrists," Julia said.

"I'm thinking of becoming one."

"Is that supposed to change my mind?"

"No, Julia, it's supposed to confirm it."

In late summer Theo regularly burned small buildings made out of twigs and paper behind the greenhouse. Peter had to admit that Theo always built his fires safely on the brick patio and he never made large buildings, content with small fires. But he was still worried. Moreover, Theo, who had been boldly honest, no longer told the truth. He was charming but untruthful.

"Theo's not telling the truth," Peter said to Julia in desperation at the end of August. "He can't even tell the truth about simple things. He says such things as we had crow pudding for supper last night and makes up stories about your shooting crows."

Julia laughed.

"I don't think it's funny."

"I know. It's unfunny, I suppose. I think we should talk to Bam about it."

"It's been a bad summer for us all with John's death," Rachel said. "Everyone is distracted. Poor Theo."

In the daytime Theo spent hours with Peter or Rachel, who was putting up vegetables and fruits from the garden, or with Julia on long walks in the evening after Pippa had gone to sleep.

"Your grandfather believed that if we treat Theo as abnormal, he'll grow up to be just that," Rachel said.

Julia agreed.

"We can't ignore the fact that he's making these fucking fires all the time," Peter said.

"I wish you wouldn't use that word in anger, Peter."

"Bumpo says it forty times a day."

"Never in anger," Rachel said, lifting a sterilized jar from the pan of boiling water on the stove.

Bumpo was famous. In early September *Time* magazine came to do a feature story on the creator of Wipe Out. *Fortune* contacted

Bumpo's lawyer and *Redbook* and *MS.* wanted to do stories on the "New Couples," using Bumpo and Tuwilla as one of their subjects. Except for *Time*, Bumpo refused. At first, he turned down network television.

"It's a wonderful opportunity," Rachel said.

"To make an ass of myself."

"Wipe Out would sell millions."

"Already it's selling millions. Besides, I don't believe in television."

"God, Bumpo, you watch it six hours a day," Peter said.

"That doesn't necessarily mean I believe in it. Anyway, I'm too nervous to be on TV. As soon as the cameras moved in, I'd have to go to the bathroom."

On the day in August that the reporters from *Time* magazine came, Bumpo overslept. Rachel had ordered the grass cut, had brought fresh flowers from the garden, had requested a cleaning lady from Doylestown to do a thorough job on Bumpo's house.

"You made Tuwilla cry," Bumpo had said to his grandmother when the cleaning lady came. "She works hard to keep the house up."

"I'm sorry, Bumpo. I want everything to be perfect. We've never had *Time* magazine visit the farm before."

"I wish we weren't having them now."

"Bumpo's still sleeping," Tuwilla said to Rachel when she arrived at their front door at nine.

"Tell him to get up. The reporters will be here in half an hour." Rachel was carefully dressed in a black linen suit with a printed blouse tied in a loose bow at the neck and black patent low-heeled shoes.

"What are you going to wear?" Rachel asked Tuwilla, who was in blue jeans and a peasant shirt. Tuwilla looked down at herself.

"This," she said. "I've gotten fat and my other pants don't fit."

"I hope you're not pregnant," Rachel said, unable to help herself. Her self-reproach came too late, for Tuwilla was crying again. "I've been so nasty since John died. People are going to start wishing that I'd die, too." She rearranged the roses on the mantel, put a pot of zinnias on the coffee table. She opened the windows in the living room. "Tomb living. I can't bear it."

Bumpo came downstairs in jeans, zipping up the fly, and without a shirt.

"I think they're here," Rachel said to him.

"I haven't eaten yet," Bumpo said, following Rachel into the kitchen, where she had carried their unwashed dishes from the night before. He took a doughnut from the refrigerator and poured a cup of coffee.

Theo and Pippa came in the back door.

"Is that what you get to wear for the magazine?" Theo asked. "Mama wouldn't let me wear jeans. It's like the family is running for President."

"It's a question of being embarrassed nationally," Rachel said.

Tuwilla came downstairs in a dress with her long hair loose and wrinkled from braiding. "Will this do?"

"You look beautiful," Pippa said.

"You do, Tuwilla," Rachel agreed.

Peter came in the back door, singing, "Mine eyes have seen the glory of the coming of the Lord/He is trampling on the vineyards where the grapes of wrath are stored."

"I thought you were going to be at work this morning," Rachel said crossly.

"And miss this fine opportunity to cash in on Nathaniel Howells' fame? You look terrific, Bumpo. Let me draw a heart on your chest with some of Bam's orange lipstick."

"It's red lipstick. Absolutely Red, it's called."

"How about it? An Absolutely Red heart?"

Julia came in with Cally.

"They've just arrived," she said.

"Oh, my God," Rachel said. "Put on a shirt, Bumpo, please." Bumpo wasn't there.

"Where is he?" She looked desperately at Tuwilla. "Please get him."

"He's in the bathroom," Tuwilla said helplessly.

"He's the grand old Mr. Touchdown,/A hero for all time," sang Peter, leaping across the floor with a make-believe football in the crook of his arm. "He can kick and pass and throw,/And is the fastest runner we will ever know."

"Sit down on the couch. You're making everyone nervous, Peter," Rachel said.

"It looks to me as if everyone is already," Cally said pleasantly.

"I'll go meet the reporters," Rachel said, arranging herself.

But it was too late. Pippa and Theo were racing over the south fields, Pippa hard on Theo's heels, and just as Rachel got to the front door, Theo threw his left leg in Pippa's path and she flew to the ground.

"Oh, Jesus," Rachel said. "Julia, you'll have to do something quickly."

Pippa was sitting on the ground where she had fallen. When she saw her mother coming, she wailed loudly. "I hate Theo," she said as Julia lifted her to her feet, examined her skinned knees. "Look at my dress. He threw me down in the mud."

"Welcome, gentlemen, to the Howells family farm which has been in the family for almost two hundred years and let me take this opportunity to introduce you to the subject of your interview, my dear brother, Bumpo, the Wipe Out King." Whereupon Peter threw open the door to the downstairs lavatory, revealing Bumpo sitting on the toilet, his elbows on his knees, his chin in his hands.

"Shut the door, Peter," Bumpo said.

When Rachel returned with the people from *Time*, Bumpo was still in the bathroom, but Tuwilla had given him a T-shirt, purple with white letters reading WIPE OUT and surrounded by flowers and butterflies in many colors, which she had embroidered for his birthday.

"Hello," Bumpo said, tucking in his shirt as he came into the living room, where a photographer and two reporters were standing.

"Is that the only shirt you have, darling?" Rachel couldn't resist saying.

"Yup, the only one," Bumpo said.

The photographer was very kind about taking several group pictures of the family on the couch in Bumpo's living room before the reporter, who seemed to be in charge, said in some agitation, "Now we'd like to speak with the principal. If your family is around, you might be uncomfortable."

"Doesn't bother me at all. I like to have them around," Bumpo said. "Anyway, you might like to talk to them. Peter's a lot better with words than I am. I mean I have a terrible time expressing myself. You won't quote me. My grandmother'd die. Here sit down." He motioned to the couch.

The article in *Time* created a folk hero. The gentle, leftover hippie, "least likely to succeed" in the George School yearbook, college dropout, living on a compound with several generations of his family, millionaire inventor of Wipe Out, a game which has captured the spirit of the time.

"Jesus," Peter said when the article came out. "Are you that rich?"

"I guess. I don't know."

"Well, if you are, we can all afford to be emotionally disturbed forever."

After the article about Bumpo in *Time*, Rachel called the chairman of the board at Friends and asked that the school take another chance on Theo. There was a promise in her request, if only in terms of timing, that the school would have reason to be pleased to have Theo back.

"I think this kind of barter is a bad idea," Peter said to Rachel when she stopped in The Plant Shop one afternoon and told him about it.

"It was the only thing to do," she said. "Theo must be in a regular school. Is he here?"

Peter motioned to the back of the shop. "Can't you smell the matches?"

Rachel sat down on a stool next to the cash register and absently snapped the browning flower heads on a pot of begonias.

"How much did you promise the good Quakers?" Peter asked.

"Nothing, Peter."

"Bumpo's income is national property now. They know they'll be golden for years. What's one screwy child against a promise like that?"

"Theo's not screwy," Rachel said.

"Maybe not forever, Bammy, but at this moment, it's not your Joe Average twelve-year-old sitting on my patio, burning down twig and paper houses by the hour. And you know I love him. I'd give my eyeteeth to be able to say he's just like every other boy I know."

"Have you talked to Julia about it?"

"A lot. We talk about Theo all the time."

"And so she's writing a play," Rachel said bitterly.

"Which is what Julia does when her heart is broken, Bammy. You know better than any of us."

Julia began *Inherited Lives* with Lucy Tanner. She went through the Bible and copied in her own hand all the notations about Lucy, as if by that act something of the lost spirit of Lucy could be recaptured.

LUCY TANNER MARRIED DR. THOMAS HOWELLS, MAY 26, 1845, AT THE BUCKINGHAM FRIENDS MEETING.

LUCY TANNER, DAUGHTER OF A HALF CHEROKEE AND A WHITE WOMAN FROM CHESTER COUNTY. THE FATHER WAS A TANNER AND SOLD HIDES FOR A LIVING UNTIL HE WAS KILLED AT THIRTY-THREE. LUCY TANNER IS MORE STRIKING THAN THE PLAIN WOMEN OF BUCKS COUNTY. SHE HAS BLACK HAIR AND BLACK EYES BUT DOES NOT HAVE THE COMPLEXION OF INDIAN WOMEN. SHE IS NOT PLEASED WITH WOMEN'S WORK IN THE KITCHEN AND SEWING AND HAS ASKED HER HUSBAND, DR. HOWELLS, IF SHE MAY GO WITH HIM ON HOUSE CALLS. HE HAS TOLD HER SHE MAY NOT.

OFFSPRING:

ROGER HOWELLS b. 1846 d. 1846.

WALKER HOWELLS b. 1848 d. 1910 IN WASHINGTON, D.C., KILLED BY A STREETCAR

ELIZA HOWELLS b. 1850 d. 1852 OF THE FEVER

CHRISTIANNE HOWELLS b. 1852 d. 1900 OF PNEUMONIA AT THE FARM

DANIEL HOWELLS b. 1854 d. 1944

LUCY TANNER HOWELLS HAS SETTLED TO THE BUSINESS OF RAISING CHILDREN, THANKS BE TO GOD. T.H., M.D.

ON BOXING DAY, 1859, LUCY TANNER, DRESSED LIKE A GYPSY, DRANK PORT AT DINNER AND RAN AFTER HER HUSBAND AND BROTHER-IN-LAW LIKE A MADWOMAN WITH A BALL OF FLAMING CLOTH. IT WAS WRITTEN UP IN THE PAPER, NAMES INCLUDED. T.H., M.D.

THOMAS HOWELLS SERVED DURING THE WAR AS SURGEON FOR THE UNION FORCES IN PENNSYLVANIA AND SPENT THREE YEARS OFF AND ON AWAY FROM HIS LOVING WIFE AND CHILDREN, EXCEPT FOR OCCASIONAL HOLIDAYS. T.H., M.D.

MAIDA b. 1870 d. 1870 BORN DEAD

LUCY TANNER HOWELLS d. 1870 IN CHILDBIRTH

LUCY TANNER HOWELLS WAS A DARK BEAUTY WITH BAD BLOOD FROM THE INDIANS WHICH CAUSED HER SINFUL ACTS OF A MOST UNFORGIVABLE KIND. SHE DIED AT FORTY IN CHILDBIRTH AND THE CHILD PASSED TOO. T.H., M.D.

In early September, Julia finished *Inherited Lives* and took it to New York, to Hal Markus.

"Hello, hello." Hal kissed Julia on both cheeks. "You have circles under your eyes."

"I've been working nonstop."

"You need makeup."

"I have makeup on. Blush. So I wouldn't look yellow." She looked in the mirror in his foyer. "I look fifty. Don't you think?"

"At least." He gave Pippa a hug.

"I brought Pippa along so if I died of exhaustion on the train, she could identify me to the conductor," Julia said, hoping it sounded like a small joke. In fact, she was serious. Writing the play had exhausted her brain. She was a cadaver with the blood drained out. She could die easily.

"Don't look at me like that," she said in response to Pippa's gaze of concern. "I was teasing Hal. I brought you along for company."

"You want me to read this while you wait?" Hal asked, taking the manuscript from her. "I don't ever do that."

"I know it's very silly."

"A newborn. You don't trust me with it unless you're in the next room." He ruffled her hair. "I hope it's worth it. I had planned to take a shower, get my hair trimmed and buy a new shirt this afternoon."

"It's the only good thing I've done."

"You were a good actress."

"Since *The Children's Garden.*"

"What about *Joey Boy?*"

"*Joey Boy*'s slick," Julia said. "Do you want me to make you a sandwich while you read?"

"If the play is good, I can make it through without a sandwich." He went into his bedroom and shut the door.

Inherited Lives is the story of an actress who lives in her dressing room at the Booth Theater, where she has been playing the role of a charming but dangerous widow, who disrupts the lives of the young men in a small town. The actress, Alice Steward, never leaves the theater, even her meals are brought to her there by the stage manager. Although successful in her work, she is fearful of the ordinary world, which she has left because of a failed marriage and a dead child. It is a play about love. The events take place in the dressing room of the theater in a single evening, during which Alice is visited by the four generations of women preceding her own who married into her father's family. Each of these women moves into her dressing room with a bedroll and some clothes, personal possessions of other sorts. Each one stages for Alice her own love story. At the end Alice is crowded out of the dressing room where she has been living for eighteen months by these inherited lives, and just at dawn she leaves the Booth Theater, sustained by the love stories she has witnessed.

"Well?" Julia asked, getting up when Hal Markus came out of the bedroom.

"It's wonderful," he said.

"I'm so glad." She hugged Pippa in joy.

"When can we start?" he asked.

"Do you think Olivia will play Lucy Tanner? She'd have to leave *Singing for Money*."

"I don't know, but I'll call her this afternoon."

He sat down at the table and began to make notes for directions on a legal pad.

"I want to direct," Julia said.

"Oh," Hal said, surprised. "I thought you meant for me to direct. I thought that's why you brought it to me to read."

"No," Julia said absolutely. "I wanted you to read it and to consider producing it."

"I don't produce plays; you know that."

"I know you haven't, but you could."

"I'm a director first and last, Julia."

"I had hoped you'd consider it."

"It's not an easy play to direct," Hal said, turning the legal pad facedown, lighting a cigarette, putting his feet up in the corner of the chair where Julia was sitting.

"You're cross," she said.

"I'm not cross. I'm merely giving you my professional response. It's not a play for a novice. You're trying to dramatize an internal event in the mind of a character, to sell the audience on the fact that this neurotic actress—I mean, she's got to be neurotic living in this goddamned dressing room—then comes through an evening of visitations reborn."

"She's not neurotic," Julia said.

"She's got a problem."

"I thought you liked it."

"I do like it, for Chrissake. I just don't think you should direct it."

Julia got up and went to the kitchen, took an apple out of the refrigerator and stood at the counter, cutting the fruit in careful sections.

"Well," Hal called from the living room.

"I haven't changed my mind," she said. "I want to try it."

"You'll be able to get the backing because the play's good and *Joey Boy*'s a hit."

"But it may not go?" Julia asked, peeling a second apple for Pippa.

"It's a very chancy play."

"Would you consider producing it?"

"If it's under your direction? Maybe, let's say maybe."

"Terrific," she said. "That's terrific."

"You ought to go into games like your famous brother, Julia. That's a very safe line of work." He kissed her, patted Pippa's head. "Watch your mother on the train, Pippa, and promise you won't call if she gets into trouble."

"What trouble?" Pippa asked.

"He's making it up," Julia said.

"Well, at least I'm glad you're finished with that play," Pippa said in the taxi to Penn Station.

"Me, too," Julia said.

"This has been a terrible summer. Everyone, even Daddy, has been acting like strangers, like we ought to introduce ourselves at dinner. Have you noticed Theo lately?"

"I have. And I guess I haven't, too. What have you seen?"

"He plays with fire all the time."

"I did know that. Peter has been watching him."

"I kind of wish he weren't coming back to Downingtown next year." She followed her mother through Penn Station, down the steps to the Metro to Trenton.

"Why? Because he gets in trouble so much?"

"That and because I'm afraid that people will tease him because he's different." When they were seated, she leaned against her mother's shoulder. "I still love Theo, of course, but it's very hard to be his sister."

"And his mother."

"Poor Theo," Pippa said. "You should have him take soccer. Boys who do sports have a better chance."

Theo would not take soccer.

"Try it," Julia said to him in mid-September after the first week of school.

"I have tried it," Theo said. "In the Kinkaid School for Special Children, back when everyone thought I was so special, I tried it. I hated it then and I hate it now."

Theo was lying face down on Julia's bed, pretending to draw figures with a stick on the Mexican rug.

"What do you like?" Julia asked, turning from the mirror where she was fixing her hair.

"Nothing at school."

"But, Theo, you have to. You have years more at school. It's foolish to hate it."

"I'm crazy," he said offhandedly. "That's what Miss Barnes told the principal yesterday and I happened to be nearby and overheard."

"You're absolutely not crazy, Theo. Put that thought out of your mind."

"It would be easier to put it out of my mind if people like Miss Barnes stopped putting it in there."

When Julia called in a fit, Miss Barnes said Theo was lying. "Not telling the truth" were her exact words. She said she would never use the word "crazy," even if it were so, she added.

"Did you make that up about Miss Barnes?" Julia asked.

Theo shrugged.

"Well?"

"I have a lot of things to think about."

"I called Miss Barnes. She was very cross about it. You have to tell me the truth, Theo. I was embarrassed."

"Sometimes I forget the truth if I'm thinking of other things."

"What are you going to do about Theo, for Chrissake?" Peter asked Julia, stopping by her house on his way for lunch with Rachel.

"God knows," Julia said. "Philip's no help, he's so distracted."

"Why don't you stay away from New York this year? Be at home. Do the play next year."

"Maybe I should." She was sitting in the kitchen, drinking a beer and cutting up eggplant and zucchini and tomatoes for dinner. "Goddammit, Peter, I gave all of my time to Theo when he was small"—she slammed a knife through the center of a fat yellow onion—"and it doesn't seem to make a bit of difference."

"I know. But, Julia, I'm worried."

"I can make something of this play, Peter. But I have no control with Theo."

"I understand."

"You think I'm wrong."

"How can I say that to you, Julia? I'm getting like Bumpo. Sometimes I hate to be grown-up."

"I suppose I think I'm wrong," Julia said, but she went on with the play.

In late September Olivia called to say, "Yes, absolutely." She was thrilled to do the new Lucy Tanner. Hal agreed reluctantly to try his hand at producing and by the first of January he had successfully raised the money to open March 1, 1973, at the Booth.

Theo even seemed to be better. His first-semester grades were passing. He won the main role in the school play of *Tom Sawyer*, and the psychiatrist in Philadelphia, whom Theo saw regularly, remarked to Philip that Theo's self-image had certainly improved.

"I'd like to take Theo's self-image and cram it down his throat," Philip said to Julia. "In England . . ."

"Go to England, for Chrissake," Julia said.

"The point is to raise Theo in England."

"Fine and I'll keep Pippa here," Julia said.

"It's worth considering."

That argument was as close as Julia and Philip came in the winter of 1973 to an honest appraisal of their marriage, but before anything else could be said, Julia went into the bathroom, locked the door and read the *Times*.

Hal Markus came to the Booth several times in the weeks of rehearsal before *Inherited Lives* opened. Julia had moved back into the apartment with David Asher, but she spent at least fourteen hours each day in the theater, pursuing every detail like a laboratory scientist, hoping by such attention that the play would begin to take on a life, which it had not done yet. The play dragged in the middle. There was a certain monotony to the love stories. The young actress who played Hannah was whiny in the part. Her suicide was a relief. She couldn't seem to give the role dignity.

"Fire her," Hal Markus said.

"She may work out. I'm meeting with her alone every day."

"You can't take that chance," Hal said, sitting next to her in the front row during the opening scene.

"Olivia is wonderful," Julia said.

"Of course, but she's not going to compensate for the martyred mother bleating all over the stage like a lost lamb."

At the end of the play, when Alice is ready to go out into the world again, the script called for a quiet but clear transition in the character of Alice from the world inside her dressing room to the world outside. She takes off the clothes she wears for her role in *Black Widow* and puts on street clothes. She takes down her hair. She examines herself in the full-length mirror with growing boldness and then says good-bye to the women who have come to inhabit her dressing room with her.

"Trash," Hal said the first time he saw the scene played. Julia didn't reply. When he looked over, her cheeks were wet.

"Listen, for Chrissake," he whispered to her. "No time for an Achilles' heel in this business."

"What am I supposed to do about you taking over my job?"

"Kick me in the crotch," he said, giving her hand an affectionate pat. "Tell me to get out of the theater. Have me arrested."

Julia stood at the edge of the stage when the final scene was done. "It is a serious scene. You're playing it like a song-and-dance routine."

And they played the scene over and over every day until Alice, in a temper at herself, kicked the full-length mirror and it shattered.

"Well?" Julia asked Hal that afternoon.

There were only eight days left before the previews.

"I don't think I ought to come anymore."

"Nor do I," she said. She put her arm through his and walked him to the Forty-fifth Street door. "It's harder than I'd thought."

In the last week of rehearsals the play seemed to come together.

"I think it's going to be good," Olivia said happily. "Honestly. And I love Lucy Tanner. We aren't willing today to be satisfied like she is with a great love that cannot last. Always we want to control our lives. That is more important to us than love. As soon as you love someone, you have automatically given up that control."

"You're right," Julia said, resting on the couch in Olivia's dressing room during a lunch break. "When I was reading the family

Bible, I was astonished at the courage of their love stories. And I am trying to keep my hand on every lever as if that is possible. I wouldn't even let Hal direct this play."

"It's your play. You should have a chance at it."

"You think so?"

"Absolutely."

"Even if it fails?"

"Of course. This play isn't the last. You'll write others."

"Do you consider the failure of a play when you're working?" Julia asked.

"Never. Or I'd doubt the character I play."

The Howells planned to attend opening night March 1 at the Booth, all of them except Caleb, because Rika had given birth to a daughter in early winter.

The cast was optimistic.

"Be cautious," Hal told Julia.

"I am," Julia said. But even Hal agreed that the previews had been good.

It occurred to Theo at the last minute to set fire to the Main House. He was already dressed to go to opening night of *Inherited Lives* and was tossing a tennis ball aimlessly against the front porch of his house when he decided offhandedly to get a can of gasoline used for the tractor from the shed, pour it along the base of the kitchen porch and light it. Later he would say reasonably that he had chosen the Main House because no one was there. Bam and Cally had gone to New Hope to pick up Peter and Lila. His father had gone to get Pippa from her dancing class. Only Bumpo and Tuwilla were around the farm and they kept their house like a cocoon, with the shades drawn and doors closed and the lights off, a musical cocoon with the stereo playing all day. So they didn't notice the fire until it was blazing like a child's drawing of the sun in orange and red. Too late. Just as Rachel was driving up the driveway with Peter in the front seat and Cally in the seat behind him.

"Oh, Christ," Peter said, the first to see.

Rachel stopped the car and put her head on the steering wheel. "I can't look," she said hoarsely.

"Drive on up the drive. Move over. I will," Peter almost shouted.

"The car might blow up if we get too close," Cally said.

Peter got out of the car and ran up the hill. Halfway to the Main

House, Peter intercepted Theo running towards him.

"Did you do that?"

"It's so bright," Theo said. He was crying. "I had no idea."

Bumpo and Tuwilla were standing on their front porch, frozen there.

"I called the fire department," Bumpo said to Peter as he ran up to the porch.

"I called them," Tuwilla said.

The four of them stood on the porch of Bumpo's house and listened to the beginning of sirens in the far distance to the north and then another set of sirens from the west.

"I said it looked like a terrible fire," Tuwilla said. "They're sending engines from Doylestown and New Hope."

"You can't even look at me, can you?" Theo said to Peter quietly. "Just turn to me."

"Right now I can't," Peter said.

Through the curtain backstage Julia could see the empty seats in the second row, second section, where her family should have been seated. Midway into the first scene, while Lucy was speaking, she went to the telephone by the stage door and called the Main House. The telephone did not ring when she dialed direct. The operator who came on said it was disconnected.

"My family isn't here and their phone has been disconnected," she whispered to Hal.

"Things happen. Don't worry," he said.

"I know things happen. What do you think I should do?"

"The audience looks good," Hal said.

"I'm so worried."

"It's going well, Julia."

"I mean, about my family."

"Call one of your brothers," Hal said.

"Jesus, I didn't think of that."

There was no answer at Cally's or Peter's when Julia called, but Bumpo answered after several rings at his house.

"Where are you?" Julia asked.

"There's been an accident," Bumpo said. "A fire."

"What's happened?"

"Theo."

"Is Theo dead?"

"Let me put Peter on."

"Is Theo all right?"

"Julia?"

"What's happened, Peter?"

"Theo will be all right."

"I knew something was the matter."

"We didn't think you'd notice that we weren't there or I would have called."

"Tell me."

"Theo set fire to the Main House just as we were leaving."

"Bam?"

"No one is hurt. But the kitchen wing of the Main House is burned to the ground."

"You're sure everyone is okay?"

"Yes."

"I'm coming now."

"There's no need to. Everyone's here. No one's hurt. Bam's upset, and Theo. Shit. I knew something like this was bound to happen. How's the play going?"

"I have to leave," Julia said to Hal.

"You do?"

"Tell everyone I'm sorry."

"What, for God's sake, is up?"

"Theo set fire to my grandmother's house."

"Is everyone all right?" He put his arm tight around her shoulders. She nodded.

"Stay then, Julia."

"There's nothing more for me to do here."

"This play is your baby," Hal said, shaking his head in disapproval.

"I have to go home."

Weeks later, Julia wrote in the Bible:

ON THE NIGHT OF MARCH 1, 1973, WHEN "INHERITED LIVES" BY JULIA HOWELLS OPENED AT THE BOOTH THEATER FOR THE FIRST PERFORMANCE OF ITS THREE-NIGHT RUN, THEO KENDALL SET FIRE TO THE MAIN HOUSE AND THE KITCHEN WING BURNED TO THE GROUND.

PLACES

THE STORY BEGINS AGAIN MAY 1, 1973, AT THE HOWELLS FARM
OUTSIDE SOLEBURY, BUCKS COUNTY, PENNSYLVANIA. IT IS COLD.
THERE'S A FIRE IN THE DINING ROOM AT DANIEL'S HOUSE, WHERE
ALL OF THE CHILDREN ARE SITTING AT BREAKFAST, LOOKING
OVER CALEB'S BLUEPRINTS FOR REBUILDING THE MAIN HOUSE
WITH AN INSTITUTIONAL KITCHEN FOR "THE FARM," AS BAM
INTENDS TO CALL THE RESIDENTIAL CARE FACILITY SHE HOPES
TO OPEN THE FIRST OF SEPTEMBER.

"For odd people," Rachel had said. "Elderly and teenagers.
They'll look after one another."

"Why don't you establish a place for ordinary people? We have
plenty of queer ones around the farm already," Peter said.

"Self-defense," Rachel said simply. "I'm getting old myself."

BUMPO IS PLAYING ON THE FLOOR WITH THEO. THEY ARE WORK-
ING OUT PLAYS FOR "ALL CLEAR," A GAME FOR SURVIVORS, A
SEQUEL TO "WIPE OUT." PETER IS ON THE TELEPHONE WITH THE
HEAD OF PSYCHIATRY AT YALE, MAKING FINAL ARRANGEMENTS
TO BEGIN A RESIDENCY IN JULY. RIKA IS NURSING CHRISTIANNE.
TUWILLA, WEARING THE NEW BUMPO T-SHIRT, DISTRIBUTED BY
ARCHER GAMES, MAKERS OF "WIPE OUT," IS LISTENING TO BAM
DECORATE "THE FARM."

"Sunny and cheerful," Rachel said.

Tuwilla nodded absently.

"What do you think?" Rachel asked. "Should we have private
rooms or two together? A teenager and an elderly person."

Tuwilla shrugged.

"Jesus, Bam," Theo said. "Not together."

"An odd teenager and an odd elderly person. I hope I get to
spend the night," Peter said, putting down the telephone.

285

"We'll have some plain old people, won't we?" Tuwilla asked wistfully.

Rachel raised her eyebrows. "You don't have any recommendations for the kitchen, do you?" she asked.

"No, I guess not," Tuwilla said.

"Good. I have been thinking about it for weeks. I want it white."

"Fine," Tuwilla said, understanding the nature of her agreement to be Rachel's assistant in the running of The Farm. "I like white very much."

CALLY IS OFF ON A TRIP TO FRANCE WITH LILA, STAYING TWO WEEKS IN A VILLAGE IN THE SOUTH OF FRANCE ON THE SPANISH BORDER WHERE THE BOUCHÉS ORIGINATED.

"A honeymoon," Peter said.

"Don't say that," Caleb said, uncomfortable about the relationship between his mother and Lila, which had become acknowledged in the family after Lila's return.

"That's what it is, Caleb," Peter said.

"I think it's perfectly lovely," Rachel said.

Peter rolled his eyes.

"Are you going to write about it in the Bible, Julia?" Caleb asked.

"Julia should write about it in French—a language more delicate than our own," Peter said.

"You know, Cally could be alone and instead, she's with someone she's known all her life," Rika said quietly.

"Exactly," Rachel said.

"The Owl and the Pussy-cat went to sea/ In a beautiful pea-green boat./ They took some honey and plenty of money,/ Wrapped up in a five-pound note," Peter sang, dancing with Pippa.

THE ONLY CHARACTER MISSING FROM THE FAMILY PLOT IS PHILIP KENDALL, WHO LEFT THE UNITED STATES ALONE ON MARCH 4, THREE DAYS AFTER THEO BURNED DOWN HALF THE MAIN HOUSE. HE HAS BEEN GONE TWO MONTHS WITH NO WORD EXCEPT AN OCCASIONAL POSTCARD INDICATING HIS WHEREABOUTS AND A NUMBER OF CALLS TO THE PHYSICIAN IN DOYLESTOWN WHO HAS TAKEN HIS PATIENTS TEMPORARILY AND A CABLE WHICH ARRIVED LAST NIGHT STATING: "I WILL BE AT THE FARM SOMETIME LATE THE EVENING OF MAY 2. PHILIP."

"Worried?" Peter asked Julia quietly.

"Yes," she replied.

"Perhaps Philip's coming back for good."

'Maybe he is."

"Is that what you want?"

"I don't know, Peter. Either way worries me—if he comes home for good or doesn't come home at all."

Pippa leaned over the table between Peter and Caleb. "Don't you have the feeling that something's about to happen—with Caleb building half a house for Bam and Peter being a doctor again and Bumpo being famous all over the world and Daddy coming home maybe forever?" she asked.

"Maybe not forever," Theo said, lying on his stomach playing All Clear.

"PLACES," Julia wrote at the end of the scene set she had written for the May 1 Bible entry.

"Oh, shit," Peter said when he read Julia's entry. "I see you are writing us into a play in the Bible. The curtain is about to go up on the dancing bears and trained elephants and poodles in gathered skirts," he announced.

"On us."

"That's what I mean," Peter said, hugging his sister's slender shoulders.

Philip came the next day, before Julia was prepared for him.

"What would you have done to be ready? Put on a tiger costume?" Peter asked her in the kitchen while Julia made coffee for Philip, who was in the living room with his children.

"I would have done something. Fixed Pippa's hair and made the beds. I would have found a way to have Bam out of the dining room, along with the plans for her infernal home for strange old men."

"Welcome home to the dining room set—a little worse for wear—of Howells' domestic tranquillity." Peter took sweet rolls out of the oven for Philip, who had flown all night.

"Did you see Theo with Philip?" Julia asked putting coffee on a tray.

"He hasn't spoken to him, has he?"

"I imagine Philip will find silence another example of Theo's eccentricity considered perfectly normal in England."

"You are a wreck, Julia," Peter said lightly, putting his hand against his sister's cheek. "In this state of mind, you could fall in love with the jackass, if you're not careful."

"He's not a jackass, Peter. He's a very good man."

"No. More like a second-rate burro. Divorce him quickly."

"Irreconcilable differences?"

"Neglect. Inadvertent cruelty. The list is endless. We should thank God for the advances of modern technology. Personal relationships are a thing of the past like wringer washing machines and garbage pails. A generation or two from now, people with very large heads will look back on love as we do the minuet, a sweet and rather silly dance." He took Julia's hand, raised it above his head, struck a mannered eighteenth-century pose and bowed. "Minuet, madame?"

"Go to hell, m'sieur."

In the dining room, Caleb was explaining the division of the Howells land to Philip. "We'll divide the property with separate deeds. Bam will keep twenty acres, the Main House and her garden, the barn and the greenhouse and the larger pond."

"I'm starting a home called The Farm, a very dignified sort of place—residential."

"For retarded women over seventy," Peter said, coming in the room.

"That's not it at all. It's going to be a place for elderly people who are lonely and teenagers who have run away from home. There'll be room for twenty people once the wing is rebuilt."

"You said they had to be peculiar or you wouldn't let them in."

"I don't want boring people who talk about what the world is coming to or who go to church excessively. Otherwise, I'll run a very democratic place."

"The Farm is a tax break for Bumpo—nonprofit corporation," Peter said, setting down the coffee and sweet rolls in front of Philip. "If Bumpo keeps getting so fucking rich, we're all going to have to get into good works."

"We'll give Bumpo this ten acres with the graveyard."

"I hate the graveyard," Bumpo said. "It gives me nightmares. Let's give it to the church."

"Why would the church want our dead relations?" Peter asked.

"From the road they will seem to give the place an increased membership."

"Then perhaps Julia and you can have the graveyard," Caleb said to Philip, drawing a light pencil line across the blueprint at the back of Daniel's house.

"They don't need the graveyard," Theo said from the floor, where he was arranging the blue, yellow, red, and green survivors in a colorful pattern on the rug. "They're getting a divorce."

Bumpo pretended to concentrate on All Clear. Rika left the room, carrying Christianne. Julia met Philip's eyes directly with her own.

"We are?" she asked quickly, thinking the subject of divorce had been planted intentionally by Philip with Theo.

"That's a very good question," Philip said wryly, crossing his legs, leaning back in the chair. "It's clearly one we'll have to discuss as a family. Sit down, Julia."

"Don't be unkind."

"I'm not at all. Peter, perhaps you should begin. Is it a question of divorce we're raising or has that question been settled and we're here to discuss when? By consensus, of course, like all good Quakers."

"Today," Theo said. "Why not today?"

Pippa looked as if she were going to cry.

"I'm leaving." Bumpo gathered the pieces of his new game in a cardboard box with "Ken-l-Ration" written on the side. "Everyone here knows I hate fights. Come on, Tuwilla."

"There isn't a fight," Tuwilla said quietly.

"There's going to be. In one second."

Julia sat down at the table next to Caleb.

"Theo and I are going to go clean out the small pond for swimming this summer," Peter said.

"Why today?" Theo asked.

"It's a very good day for it, Theo." Peter took hold of his shoulders and pushed him out the porch door in front of him.

"It's an amazing family that can supply an in-residence shrink for its emotionally disturbed progeny," Philip said, finishing his coffee.

Caleb rolled up his blueprints. "Well, we'll talk about this later. I have the whole thing planned to divide the farm so each family will have its own house and some land."

"Each family that lasts."

"Well, sure. You know, that's kind of your business, not mine."

"You're a visionary, Caleb. That's an original observation in this group."

Rachel was left standing at the dining room table. She was shorter than she had been when she was younger, but at full height she was still an impressive figure.

"In our family there has never been a divorce," she said directly to Philip.

"I am filled with the pioneering spirit. Perhaps you would prefer I commit suicide."

"Don't, Philip," Julia said quickly.

"Come, Pippa. The whole strawberry patch is in flower and we need to put on a ground cover," Rachel said, reaching for her great-granddaughter's hand.

"Bam has been living with the children and me since the fire," Julia said after Rachel had gone.

"Wonderful. How many are there in residence? Have the retarded people begun to filter in?"

"They aren't retarded, Philip."

"And certainly Bam wouldn't allow them in if they had been divorced."

"There were few divorces when Bam grew up. Of course she doesn't believe in it."

"That's a little like not believing in syphilis."

Julia put her legs up on the opposite chair and leaned back, taking a sweet roll and munching the brown sugar corners. She was aware of a new self-consciousness, a sense of herself in duplicate as though she were reflected in a mirror to her immediate right. Her pulse raced in her wrist and she was blushing. She wanted to write lines for Philip to deliver—"You are lovelier than I remembered," or "I'm so glad to be home," or "We were both at fault. Let's begin anew"—but she did not allow a soft line in her face to give her away. Self-protectively she assumed an expression of severity. "Welcome home," she said quietly.

Philip moved into the downstairs guest room where Daniel had died, by day a study. He didn't unpack. Instead, he spent his first afternoon home helping Peter and Theo clear the pond for swimming.

"We will have to bring up the subject of Theo's pyromania," he said that evening, sitting in a large comfortable chair by the fireplace. "That's why I came back."

"I thought it was why you left," she said.

"That, too," he said sharply. "Theo has had an extraordinary hold on my adult life."

Julia took the pillows off the couch and made a bed while Philip watched her. For dinner, she had put on a light silk dress printed with daisies. Since no one dressed for dinner at the farm any longer, Philip was touched by such a gesture in a woman who had never bothered with the way she looked. She had worn her hair brushed back in a ribbon, the way it had been when they first met.

"I don't think Theo's a pyromaniac," she said, sitting on the made bed.

"Perhaps not, but he is unusually fond of fires. Thank you for making my bed."

"Oh, that's all right." She arranged her dress awkwardly, crossing her legs. "Do you want to talk about Theo now?"

"Not tonight."

"Then tomorrow. Whenever you like. Good night." She walked across the room. "Do you want brandy, Philip, or a cup of tea?"

"Don't be excessive, Julia."

"I'm being pleasant," she said.

"We'll talk about Theo in the morning."

The night Theo had set fire to the Main House Bumpo had met Julia at the train in Trenton and on the way home he had played the radio at top volume.

"Please tell me what happened," she asked when she got in the car.

"You'll see, for Chrissake."

"Please, turn off the radio," she asked him.

"Turn it down," she asked again.

"Bumpo."

"My nerves are done in, Julia. Finished. This night has been the worst night of my life."

"Worse than Daddy?"

"Be quiet."

"I mean it, Bumpo. You're driving me crazy."

"Theo."

"He is not crazy," Julia said. "I suppose you're blaming me. My son, my fault."

"I didn't say that."

"You implied it, goddammit."

"Listen, Julia, it's not a regular sort of thing to set fires to houses, you know, and it's got me very upset."

"What does Peter say?"

"Nothing to me. He's been with Theo since the fire."

"Where's Philip?"

"I don't know."

"You don't know?"

"Maybe he's in his room or in Doylestown. He was there when

the fire engines arrived and then he disappeared. Pippa's with Bam and Tuwilla, and Mama and Lila have been trying to settle the goddamned zoo at their house, which has been barking and howling since the fire started. It's been a terrible night. I want to move back west, where I don't have these troubles."

"Try paradise, Bumpo. You've got a clean record and could get in easy."

When they reached the house, Philip was sitting up in bed, fully dressed, reading a medical journal about cat viruses transmitted to humans. He put the journal aside when Julia walked in the bedroom.

"You ought to give this article to your mother. It says that they've isolated eight different viruses transmitted by cats to humans and in four of them you develop diarrhea and your hair falls out."

"Philip."

"I want to make it perfectly clear that I'm not discussing the fire tonight."

"You have to."

"How was the play?"

"How should I know? I left in the first act."

"But you're the director. How can you leave your charges?"

She had a sudden urge to slap him, accomplished before she had a chance to reconsider. He did not alter his expression while she stood watching the distorted reproduction of a hand surface on his face.

"If you want to discuss the fire, your family is hovering like vultures around the kitchen table at Bumpo's. Theo's there, too, I assume."

"Oh, Philip. This is all so bitter." Julia went out on the small porch off her bedroom from which she could see the back of the Main House. The air stank of smoke. The kitchen wing of the house protested with squeaks and small crashes as it settled into its new condition.

"What does it look like up close?" Julia asked.

"Like a half-burned-down house."

"That's all?"

"In this family you would expect something unusual when a house burns down. A remarkable transformation to some higher form of being. Gnomes and princes. I regret to say you will find a burned house in the morning in which, in the kitchen wing, only the appliances and bathroom fixtures are recognizable."

She went to Bumpo's house. Peter met her at the door. Pippa came out and took her hand.

"What about Theo?" she asked.

"It was my fault," Peter said. "The signs have been there all year. He was going to burn something."

"Of course, it's not, Peter. Where's Bam?"

"Bam is in mild shock. She's lying on Bumpo's bed, listening to rock music, which Bumpo has been playing so he won't crack up in the confusion. She'll be fine. After she lies down for a while and gathers her forces, she'll begin designing a new fucking house."

Theo was sitting in Bumpo's kitchen, peeling an orange with great care so each section of peel had a design which fitted into an orange puzzle he was making on the counter. When he looked up at Julia, his eyes were blazing.

"No one was hurt," he said.

"I know." Julia instinctively put her arms around him.

"Why are you doing that?" he asked, resisting her.

"Because I feel so bad for us, for you, Theo," she said.

"I'm fine," Theo said crisply. "It's not the worst thing I could have done."

All night she and Peter sat up in Bumpo's living room.

The next morning Theo brought the review from the *Times* to Cally's, where everyone except Philip had assembled for breakfast. He had left early for the hospital. Theo was in high spirits, his best self, warm and good-tempered, as though the burning of the Main House had been a temporary release.

"Do you want me to read the review, Mama?" Anesthetized, she had almost forgotten. Yesterday was a lifetime behind her.

He read: "*Inherited Lives*, written and directed by Julia Howells, opened at the Booth last night with high hopes. Here is a new play by the successful creator of the dark and witty *Joey Boy*, which has had a long and prosperous run on Broadway. We were cheering for Julia Howells and we expected a great deal. Not surprisingly, we were disappointed.'"

"What does he say is wrong?" Julia asked.

"He says, 'The character of Lucy Tanner, played by Olivia Reynolds, is the most perfectly realized of the five women in the play. The fault is in the direction. *Inherited Lives* is a difficult, elusive play, internal in concept. Ms. Howells needed a first-rate director, which she has not yet become.'"

"Hal should have done it."

"That's what the review says," Theo said. "I'm sorry, Mama. Maybe you can write another play."

Philip was packed to leave for London three days after the fire.

"Why?" Julia asked, sitting on the edge of the bed, watching him collect his toilet articles.

"I've made arrangements for Dr. Andrews to take my patients for a while. I'll be staying with Arthur, at least at first."

"That doesn't tell me why you're going."

"I don't know why." He sat down beside her. "When I woke up the second morning after Theo started the fire, you were downstairs on the telephone with Hal Markus and Pippa was in my bathroom brushing her hair. Theo was sitting on my bed in his pajamas, watching me wake up with that look of his. He asked me was I still angry with him. I said, 'Plenty.' I told him to get dressed for school. He said that he doubted the school would be willing to keep him now, but he got dressed. We said good-bye to you, still on the telephone, and I drove them to school. Theo asked me what I was going to do about Bam's house and I said, 'Go to England.' It was automatic. On the way to the office I made plans to go."

"Are you running away from us?" Julia asked.

"I haven't the slightest inclination to analyze it."

She didn't try to detain him. She took him to Trenton to catch the train because he didn't want her to drive him to New York. Just before the train came, he told her he was sorry *Inherited Lives* had closed. She kissed him stiffly and watched him, after they had parted, struggle through the aisle with his luggage as the train moved north.

Peter was cross at Philip. He told Julia that Philip had chosen the wrong time to leave the family, that he lacked character.

"That's not true," Julia argued. "I've been awful for years. Besides, can you imagine what it would be like to marry into this family? Like marrying an elephant."

"A circus elephant." Peter laughed. "If Philip was going to marry a Howells, he should have known he was taking his chances on sordid developments."

"You mean like the fire and Bumpo?"

"Bumpo's the new folk hero of this country, Julia. He makes Paul

Bunyan look like a dwarf. America loves him. He's the lost soul in us all."

Bumpo was going to run The Plant Shop when Peter went back to Yale to do a residency in psychiatry.

"Why, for Chrissake?" Peter had asked him. "You don't need to do anything except lie in bed and listen to rock music. Make up games."

"I'm tired of games," Bumpo said. "The only new idea I've had for weeks is a plant-growing game. The guy who accumulates the most rare and living plants wins. I figure the board will be pretty, full of tropical flowers. When people aren't playing, they can hang the board on a wall in the family room."

"Who has a family room?" Peter asked.

"Everyone in the suburbs. It's the people in the suburbs who play Wipe Out."

"In the family room?"

"I suppose."

The fact was Bumpo liked to sit in The Plant Shop and sign autographs. After the story in *Time* and follow-ups in other media, the manufacturers of Wipe Out had distributed Bumpo T-shirts and Bumpo bumper stickers and smile faces with sticky backs for notebooks and doors and mirrors and girls' shoulders.

When Bumpo wasn't around, Julia and Peter talked to Caleb about him. After the fire, Caleb had set up a drawing board in The Plant Shop so he could work on plans for the Main House and for the house he was building with Bumpo's help on the land adjoining the Main House, now called The Farm.

"A retirement home," he said. "I won't stay in Houston forever, and if we're going to have builders on the place anyway, they may as well do both jobs."

"Just like you, Caleb, to plan for your retirement at twenty-eight," Peter said.

"I found out from Bam that we wouldn't be able to do any of this if it weren't for Bumpo, you know. Grandfather's money went quickly to support Mama and us after he sold the business."

"I would have thought you'd be the one to make money, Caleb. Maybe Peter. But never Bumpo," Julia said. "It still makes me sad to see him."

"How come? He's happy," said Caleb.

"He doesn't know half his brain has flown the coop," Peter said. "Once I talked to him about the kinds of dope he was using in Colorado and he doesn't remember a quarter of it. He's goddamned lucky not to be an eggplant."

"I'm not so sure," Julia said. "A lot of people I know would trade places with Bumpo in a second for a chance to be on the farm with Tuwilla and vegetables and board games."

Not only autograph seekers searched Bumpo out at The Plant Shop. Some people came just to talk to him. They wanted to tell him everything about their true loves, their fathers, their affairs, their sense of inadequacy, their fears.

"We're so much alike," they'd invariably say.

"For Chrissake, Bumpo. You should be doing the residency in psychiatry this summer."

"No, Peter, I could never make it through school. I just listen. People like that."

"People are paying sixty dollars an hour lately for listening."

"But it's different. They'll tell you more if they know you never made it through school."

Rachel had recovered from the fire quickly, as Peter predicted she would. She had only one relapse in late May when she read in the Doylestown paper that George Katz had been shot by his estranged wife. On principle she never read the obituaries and would have certainly missed George's if it hadn't been on the first page of the second-section local news. There were no survivors.

"It upsets me that there's no possibility for a continuation of the line. All the rest of his family died in the war," Rachel said.

"If I remember correctly from Grandfather, that is a blessing, Bam. His line wasn't worth continuing."

"I liked him quite well. And I'm upset that the few possessions of his I've kept through the years were burned in the fire."

In quiet protest, Rachel went to bed for the day.

Caleb designed the brochure for The Farm. The facility was supported by the Nathaniel Howells Foundation for Projects in Social Welfare, established specifically for The Farm, although it was likely, according to Bumpo's accountant, that it would create other projects in the years to come.

Caleb drew a picture of the Main House for the front of the brochure.

"We must do the leaflets on ragweed paper," Rachel insisted. She wrote the copy:

> The Farm is a residential facility established in 1974 to provide a home for children between the ages of twelve and eighteen and self-sufficient elderly people who would benefit from and co-operate in a family structure.
>
> > Rachel Howells, Director.
> > Willa Howells, Assistant.
> > THE FARM
> > Box 21
> > Solebury, Pennsylvania.

"I don't like the name Willa," Tuwilla said.

"It's a lovely name," Rachel said.

"But it's not mine," Tuwilla said.

"You'll learn to like it much better. I'll have everyone call you Willa so you'll get used to it. Tuwilla sounds like the name of a flowering tree."

"Don't you call me Willa," Tuwilla said to Bumpo.

Bumpo promised.

"My name isn't Howells either," Tuwilla said after she had agreed to be called Willa.

Rachel raised her eyebrows. "It should be," she said.

"What she means is we should be married," Bumpo said.

"But we aren't and Howells isn't my name."

"We'll just get married. It'll clear up a lot of problems."

They were married in late April at the county seat, the site of John and Rachel's wedding.

"It wasn't very romantic," Tuwilla said later to Bumpo.

"Weddings never are," Bumpo replied matter-of-factly.

"When I die, The Farm will be yours," Rachel announced to Tuwilla after the wedding.

"I may not want it," Tuwilla confided weakly to Bumpo.

"Bam won't die," Bumpo said with certainty.

"Sometime."

"Nope, never."

"I expect John would be upset if he knew I was turning the Main House into The Farm," Rachel said one night at supper shortly be·fore Philip returned from England.

"He knows," Bumpo said dreamily.

"Oh, shit," Peter said.

"Life after death, dummy," Theo said.

"I know, I know," Peter said.

"Maybe he'd feel better about it if I made The Farm Quaker."

"He gave up being a Quaker before he married you," Julia said.

"You'd go crazy running a Quaker place, Bammy. All those moments of silence," Caleb said. "I think you're just going to have to feel guilty for turning Granddad's house into a welfare office."

"You misunderstand," Rachel protested.

"He can't do anything to you when he's dead," Pippa said.

"That's not exactly true, Pippa," Peter said. "For example, your poor mother is supposed to spend the rest of her days writing love stories and either she has to invent them or lie in the Holy Bible about the history of the Howells family or else, poor chick, she has to find some real ones. So you see the Power of the Dead. Whammo."

Philip was up and dressed before dawn on the morning of May 3. He was in the process of building a fire in the study, reading old newspapers he had missed before he wound them into a tight ball for burning.

"I see Athalia Drew died while I was gone," he said to Julia when she came in.

"I didn't know her," Julia said.

"She was the owner of a bookstore in New Hope."

"Your patient?"

"Yes. She had cancer of the pancreas. Very quick. They must have forgotten to tell me when I called the office." He knelt down to build the fire. "It's as bitter as England here."

"What would you like for breakfast?" Julia asked.

She was dressed in a long skirt, a heavy sweater, her hair piled loosely on top of her head.

"I have had breakfast, Annie Oakley," Philip said. She was pleased that he had noticed her costume.

Julia fed the children and walked them to the end of the drive to wait for the school bus.

"My father's back," Pippa said joyfully as she hopped up the steps of the school bus.

"To get a divorce," Theo said under his breath.

"What happens in our family is not a public affair," Julia said to Theo.

He raised his eyebrows.

"Don't ruin Pippa's pleasure in having Daddy here."

"Short-term, like all pleasure," he said caustically.

"That's better than nothing," she said.

"See you tonight, Mama." He followed Pippa up the steps. Occasionally, since the fire, he had kissed his mother good-bye. He did this morning, turning on the bus step and kissing the top of her head.

Since March he had been doing extremely well in school. He had participated and his relationships with other children, although distant, were unremarkable. Since Philip had left, there hadn't been a single letter from a parent requesting Theo's removal from the seventh grade.

The school knew about the fire. Philip had called Downingtown the following morning and told them. By late April, six weeks after Philip had left for England, the principal made a call to Julia full of compliments about Theo. "He's very smart," she said, "but I think it would be wise for you to have another series of psychological tests done on him to see where he might go when he finishes eighth grade here." In fact, she insisted.

So Julia and Peter took Theo to Johns Hopkins University Hospital in Baltimore for three days of brain scans, encephalograms, Rorschachs, a Thematic Apperception Test, the Minnesota Multiphasic Personality Index Test, an IQ test and several private sessions with a group of psychiatrists. The tests showed that he was extremely bright, verbal, thoughtful, perceptive, with a sharp, if somewhat bitter, sense of humor.

He told Peter that he'd come through the tests as mildly special, nothing extraordinary.

"Tough luck," Peter had said. "I know you hoped for better."

"Better than I had hoped," Julia said.

But the psychiatrists cautioned against false optimism. There was the fire, they said, and a history of difficulties in school. Theo had not indicated that he was capable of establishing relationships.

"Why not?" Julia asked.

"I don't know why not," one of the psychiatrists said.

"We have a large family; he is surrounded by people who love him."

"I'm sure he is."

"Do you think it has anything to do with the fact that I've spent so much time away these last two years?"

"Not necessarily. It doesn't seem to have affected your daughter," the psychiatrist said. "He feels a genuine kinship to your brother Peter. His feelings for you are ambivalent, which is not unusual for a twelve-year-old boy. He is alienated from his father. But of course, he lied to us much of the time. He tried to figure the intention of our question and to create an answer which suited him. He invented Theo Kendall for us in self-defense. He doesn't want anyone, and certainly not strangers, to know him well."

That night Peter stayed to talk at Julia's.

"Well?" Julia asked.

"What did you expect for a thousand dollars from a group of men whose comic fluids dried up at birth?" Peter asked. "The first Book of Revelation?"

"They didn't give the worst news we've had."

"They're not in the business of good news. I thought the visit was successful as those things go. We now have an impartial report on Theo to send off to high schools and to file under Strange Development of the Howells Family Brain," Peter said. "There. Yours to keep, my love." He handed her a small brown portfolio including all the tests and a four-page written report marked "Theodore Kendall, April 21–23, 1973." "The brain in a manila folder. Future generations won't apply for jobs without their brain scans in tow."

Julia turned on the light beside her chair and studied the report of the brain scan which pointed out that Theo's brain was asymmetrical, "cockeyed," Peter said, but in the range of normal. The Minnesota Multiphasic Personality Index Test indicated that Theo did not relate to his peers, that his communication with others was cerebral, not emotional, that he resisted touching or being touched, that in short, love was understood as a concept, but not experienced. In contradiction, the report indicated that Theo had an abnormally strong reaction to loss.

"What a committee of dunces," Peter said, reading over Julia's shoulders. "How the fuck can Theo react to loss if he doesn't know how to love?"

Julia leaned back in her chair and closed her eyes. "I don't know."

"There is no evidence of trauma or damage which would impair the development of emotional responses. We can either assume that Theo is emotionally immature or that the area of his brain which logs feelings is not operational."

"Oh, shit," Julia said. "Read me a story from Grimm."

"I guess we just live with the fact that we're raising a child with missing parts," Peter said.

"Did you find out if Theo's cuckoo?" Pippa asked that night when her mother tucked her in bed.

"Of course he's not." Julia laughed. "No more than Uncle Bumpo."

"That's what Bumpo said. He said you were having tests done on Theo to see if he was cuckoo. That if the tests had been around when he was little, he would have been sent to a funny farm. Bam got mad."

"No wonder. It's not true about Theo or Bumpo."

"Bumpo was just a regular, normal crybaby when he was growing up," Peter said, leaning over to kiss Pippa good-night.

When Julia came back to the house on May 3 after seeing Theo and Pippa off on the bus, she removed the folder from Johns Hopkins University from the file cabinet and brought it to Philip in the living room.

"Here. Since you've come home to discuss Theo," she said, handing him the folder.

"Or our marriage." Philip looked up from the paper. "They are the same subject."

Julia sat down in the armchair across from Philip and watched him read the report. His hair was longer, wilder, since he'd been away; his cheeks were still flushed with the high color of a rainy climate; and his eyes, which she recalled as gentle, were not soft, but scorching. She wanted to turn away from him. He had aged in two months—well, as men of sharp features and fine bones tend to do, but perceptibly. There was an alteration in his presence that made him a stranger. Julia was alarmed by the awkwardness of a situation set askew by her strong desire for him.

The look he gave her when he had finished the report set aside further conversation. He went to the telephone and called his office. When he came back, he pulled up a footstool and sat down next to Julia.

"How long do we have to talk this morning before your relatives or some of their social projects join us?"

"Did you see Bam leave?"

"She's gone. I know because she wanted to tell me a horror story about a man she knew who'd been divorced and miserable for years. I expect she made it up this morning. The other was about bran. She wanted to know my medical opinion about bran. She has, as I'm sure you know, gone into bran with her usual excess."

"See, you have missed them." Julia laughed.

"I have missed everyone, of course. One doesn't get by fourteen years in this family unaltered; that isn't the question."

"What are your plans?" Julia asked, stalling for time.

"I don't have immediate plans. I'll go into my office this week and try to reach a conclusion with you. It makes no sense to drag things out week after week, and it's not fair to the children."

"Let's talk about Theo first," Julia said, sensing that Philip's next statement in a prepared conversation was divorce. For reasons she didn't understand, the thought of Philip's leaving for good was giving her the same symptoms as stagefright, a fierce tightness in her chest, her heart and stomach beating double time like a metronome.

"So what about Theo?" Philip asked.

"You read the report."

"These reports are becoming as familiar to me as the disaster section of the *Inquirer*. This one was more thorough and disastrous."

"No psychiatrist has ever mentioned Theo's sense of loss."

"You paid these blokes more money. They had to come up with more information."

"You don't believe it?" Julia asked. She was feeling physically sick, perspiring. Her mouth was dry. She moved away from the fire and sat on a hard-back bench, on the other side of Philip.

"I believe them. I have a profound sense of loss and so do you. He inherited that, like his English nose and flat bottom, from his father."

"Ours came of living, Philip."

"That's true, but I think children inherit a parent's sense of living as though it were genetic."

Julia stood up and walked around, willing her heart to slow down, which it would not.

"Are you all right?" Philip asked.

"I don't feel well. I feel peculiar."

She went to the kitchen and washed her face, telling herself it was stupid to have heart seizures over someone who wanted to

leave her. The water did nothing. She took an aspirin. "Oh, fuck,"
she said aloud and rehearsed all of the aggressive words she knew.

"If you leave, will you take Theo?" Julia asked, returning to
the living room.

"I hadn't thought so," Philip said.

"You'd go back to England, wouldn't you?" And in England,
you've often said, eccentricities like Theo's are common."

"We both know Theo can no longer be considered eccentric."

"Emotionally upset. I'd think that would be common in England."
She was feeling worse, as though she might catapult over the couch.
She'd never had real stagefright like this before.

"I haven't said I'd go back to England. I don't necessarily think
I would."

"Because the patient of your dreams doesn't want to go?" Julia
asked.

"Who is that?"

"You tell me," Julia said.

"I know," he said slowly, and he smiled. "You mean a young
woman who is a painter in New Hope. Andrea DeLaurentis."

"I suppose that's who I mean.''

"She was just that, Julia, a woman of my dreams. When she got
well last September, I had another patient I dreamed about who
was married, the woman with cancer of the pancreas—Athalia Drew.
I recall that in my dreams of her, I imagined her well."

"I am supposed to believe that?"

"You've seen people in the last stages of terminal cancer. Of
course I was dreaming."

"And what about Andrea, the painter?"

"Pipe dreams," he said. "There was nothing between you and
me any longer and so I dreamed about other women to get by. It
was a lame approach, not admirable, but typical, I expect, of a
British physician skittish about living."

"I thought . . ." Julia began.

"I know what you thought."

"It made me sick," she said quietly. "I hadn't realized until
today how often I had thought of you with someone else."

"I'm glad you expected the worst of me."

When Caleb came in with Christianne in a back pack over his
shoulders and the blueprints of The Farm under his arm, Julia

was lying on the floor of the living room with her legs propped up against the fireplace and her eyes closed.

"What's up?" Caleb asked.

"Your sister's had a heart attack," Philip said in mock seriousness.

"You're joking, right?" Caleb walked around Julia so he could look at her straight on. "You look okay, Julia. I mean you look pretty good for lying down."

"It was a case of stagefright," Julia said.

"What was?"

"She fainted," Philip said.

"I think I hate you," Julia said.

"Me?" Caleb asked.

"No, me," Philip said. "You are lovely," Philip said, leaning over her with a grin. "I wish we had this moment met."

"We can pretend. You seem to be better at that than I would have thought," Julia said.

When Caleb walked in the back door of Bumpo's house with Christianne, everyone was working in Bumpo's kitchen.

"Julia fainted," he announced.

"Fainted?" Peter asked.

"Dead away. She was on the floor with her feet up when I walked into her living room."

"Fainting is not like Julia," Peter said.

"Under tension, Nat used to faint. That is actually how he was burned on Boxing Day when your mother was in the hospital," Rachel said.

"Julia's not like Daddy. She has never fainted before."

"Who knows? She has his eyes," Rachel said.

"Oh, shit, Bam," Peter said. "It's her stupid marriage."

"Marriage is a two-sided situation. I believe in no-fault divorce," Bumpo said.

"The Howells don't divorce," Rachel said.

"Which is why I won't get married," Peter said.

"You haven't even made a stab at it. People in town think you're in love with Raphael."

"Maybe I am, Bumpo. God just hasn't revealed the fact to me yet."

"Your generation is afraid of relationships. You want daily pleasures but nothing enduring," Rachel said.

"That's an honest response to facts. Nothing does endure," Peter said.

"Of course not," Rachel said, matching paint colors and wallpaper for the remodeled section of the Main House. "But we can't live that way."

"I do. Happily, happily ever after, believing in nothing. Plants. I believe strongly in plants," Peter said. "What do you believe in, Bam? Surely not God. Good works?"

"I don't believe in good works. They occupy my mind. I believe in what exists between two people. That's all. That's enough."

"I still have more confidence in plants," Peter said.

Caleb sat down on a chair beside his brothers.

"Did Philip have affairs? You said he had a woman patient," he asked Peter.

"I don't know if he *had* a woman patient. He was interested in one."

"That sort of thing makes me furious," Caleb said.

"It would. God, Caleb, you've got so much honor you might survive nuclear fallout."

"I bet Julia's had a bunch of affairs. Actresses have a reputation for being loose," Bumpo said. "I read an article recently."

"She's your sister, Bumpo," Caleb said. "She's not an actress."

"Who knows? How do you know what I do? I may watch pornographic films in the basement while everybody's at work."

"You don't. I'd know that. I make a point of checking on you every few hours," Tuwilla said.

"You don't know what I'm thinking about. I may be imagining I'm head of an architectural firm redesigning Houston since it was wiped out."

"I love Life Truly/Deed I do/Wipe Out's the only thing to do," Peter sang.

"Do you have imaginary girl friends?" Tuwilla asked.

"Twenty-eight or -nine, I forget," Peter said.

"None," Bumpo said.

"Chicken," Peter said.

"I'm making the point, if you'd ever listen to me, that we know the surface of each other and nothing more," Bumpo said.

"It's the chance for something more than the surface of each other that keeps us going, lamb."

"Then you believe in love, Bammy," Peter said.

"I do," Rachel said.

When Julia walked across the field to Bumpo's, the family was still working in the kitchen.

"The romantic heroine approaches alone," Peter said.

She opened the back door.

"A lively group." She entered the silent room. "You've been talking about me, right?"

"Pros and cons of your marriage," Peter said.

"Are you all right, lambie?" Rachel asked.

"Caleb told you."

"He did."

"I used the old approach to saving a marriage. The battered bride faints," Julia said lightly.

"Did it work?" Bumpo asked.

"Of course, dummy. I'm a good actress."

"Honestly?"

"We're still on the subject of Theo. This afternoon we have to go see his teachers. Could you pick up the children at the bus, Peter?"

Peter followed Julia out of Bumpo's house. "Are you leaving now?" he asked.

"In a few minutes. Philip is changing. Why?"

She sensed that Peter wanted to detain her. He stopped, leaned against a tree, pulled a leaf off and stuck its stem in the corner of his mouth.

"Would it be better between you and Philip without Theo?"

"How do you mean?"

"Would your marriage be better?" he asked, and Julia was surprised at his seriousness.

"The problem of Theo is inextricable from our marriage."

"I would like to have him," Peter said simply.

"Have him?"

"I'd like to take him with me to New Haven when I go for my residency. I'd like to raise him because I think I know him pretty well and because I love him."

"I know you do, Peter."

"I thought it might be easier for you and Philip," Peter hedged.

"I doubt it. Theo is a handy target for other things wrong between us."

"I wouldn't expect you to say yes immediately. I just thought I ought to tell you." He started to walk away. "I doubt I'll ever marry if that's a factor in your decision."

"I'd be surprised if you did."

He grabbed her nose. "I'll get the kids this afternoon. Have a nice time with your divorce, Julia. I'll send flowers either way."

She was grateful for his quick recovery.

Peter had thought often about taking Theo. He daydreamed of trips they'd take together in New Haven, of skiing weekends in Vermont, of movies and dinners they'd cook together, places he would show Theo, things he would teach him to do. He was reasonable and knew it unlikely that Julia would even consider the possibility. But he wanted Theo. More times than not, he felt that Theo was his by nature. When Rachel mentioned just this morning the mystery between people, he knew that tending plants was a poor exchange for his great need for a son like Theo. Not like Theo, but Theo himself. It was, of course, too much to ask of Julia.

"Marry," she would say if he insisted. "Have your own son."

"You don't understand, Julia," he would have to reply. "I could have a son like Bumpo, like Caleb, like the family of my fictitious wife. I want Theo."

Philip had been home from England for ten days and he was still in the guest room. He had not unpacked his suitcases and to all appearances he was ready to leave at any moment. There was the question of his practice, the matter of Theo, financial details, all more complicated than he had anticipated. It could take another week. Maybe two. Meanwhile, the family, as Philip would have predicted, continued to discuss the marriage among themselves.

Just knowing Philip would be getting up when she came down to cook breakfast for the children caused Julia to wake every morning with new springs of energy, like the fresh rushes of water unsettling the still surface of ponds in the deep thaw of April. She didn't exactly want him in the room they had shared for years. His presence in the house was sufficient.

"Sufficient for what?" Peter asked.

"I don't know," Julia said. They were putting the final touches on The Plant Shop, advising the contractors who were beginning to build the dome for Bumpo's tropical jungle.

"It is crazy. I have a sense of well-being, although he's going to leave. He says he is."

"Has it occurred to you that his leaving brings your peace of mind?"

"No," Julia said.

"Do you fight?"

"We talk about Theo."

"That's all?"

"That's all we've talked about so far."

At the beginning of the third week of Philip's return he came home at noon on Monday from the office to find Julia outside at the Main House. It was a warm day, bright and clear, pleasant enough to eat out of doors. Philip and Julia went to a small inn on the Delaware River for lunch. No one was there. They sat at a table next to the river staring at its swift dark surges. Julia felt like a child at her first carnival, overwhelmed by the tinsel-bright chances for pleasure around her, wary, too, that she may have misjudged the promises of pleasures. She didn't want to talk. Her opportunities for the day going well seemed better without conversation, so she looked at the river with purpose. She sensed in Philip a resolve at a moment when it seemed to her indecision was the wiser course to take.

"Thinking of scripts?" he asked her.

"No. I haven't had an idea for a new play yet."

"I'm sorry I never had a chance to see *Inherited Lives*."

"You can read the play."

"That's never the same. Anyway, you've changed since you wrote that play."

"For the better?" she wanted to ask. "Are you pleased?" "Are you honestly curious any longer about what's going on in my mind when I look at the river?" "Do you ever think about making love to me?"

The waiter brought pâté and French bread, a carafe of wine. She was grateful for his interruption.

"Peter spoke to me last week about wanting Theo to live with him. That is at least some solution," she said distantly.

Philip touched her wrist. "We're not going to talk about Theo," he said.

"All right. Later then."

"We have talked about him all we can."

"What do we do then?" Julia asked, safe with the subject of Theo, uncertain of the ways in which the afternoon might develop without his protection.

"We don't give up loving him. What choice do we have? If those stupid cells the Hopkins doctors mentioned aren't going to develop, we can't will them there or plant them or shock them into existence."

Julia turned away from the sun, took her hair down and tied it behind her head in a rubber band.

"I suppose the question is: Without Theo, what is there to say?"

They ate in silence. Philip drank wine like water.

In the jeep going home the wind whipped between them, the side flaps of the windows slapping the car metal like belts and the black road in front of them winding like ribbon. He had to look carefully ahead and not at Julia in order to avoid an accident.

She put her hand on top of his. "I suppose all that can be said of us is the fact registered in the Bible: 'Married, June 9, 1959.'"

Philip turned into the Howells farm. They drove up the road past the Main House, now under construction, past Bumpo's house, where Tuwilla was staking peas and young tomato plants, into the driveway of Daniel's house.

"It might add some interest to future generations if we could say: 'Divorced, 1973,'" she said.

She got out of the car and walked around to Philip's side, where he was fussing with the gearshift.

"I love you, Philip," she said.

Later they lay on the cool sheets of the bed they used to share, their heads pillowed in the curve of one another's legs, silenced by the sweet victory of recovery.

At the beginning of June, Philip was still in the guest room, using his suitcase as a bureau drawer. Eventually Julia anticipated he would move his clothes upstairs, resettle in his old room. There was never a decision to remain together such as the one they had made to marry. What happened between them was the same slow expansion of the heart as that which comes with the birth of a new child, an expansion which grows in spite of accidents and reversals and, like children, is treasured for the short life of that worth loving.

Julia told Peter that Theo was going to remain with them at the family dinner she gave in late June to celebrate Peter's return to medicine.

"So Philip is staying," Peter said.

"For the moment."

"What's this? Another trial run? The Summer of Our Marriage. Shit, Julia. You could write another play."

Peter was mixing whiskey sours, chipping the ice with a hammer on the kitchen table. He filled a tray with glasses and the pitcher of whiskey sours and carried it to the porch, where Rachel and Caleb were working on a wicker table. Caleb was saying that he thought some of the land ought to be sold.

"I hate strangers. They'll put up new houses," Bumpo said from the hammock where he'd been lying all afternoon half-asleep. He and Tuwilla had had a fight about the Howells. There were too many, she said. She always felt overwhelmed and so she had spent the afternoon in her bedroom writing letters to her mother in Colorado and her brother in the Hare Krishna house and her father in Oregon. She might come to the dinner party for Peter and she might not.

"There is nothing the matter with new houses," Caleb said. "I'd design them myself with the intention of fitting them into the landscape."

"Sounds awful. Glass houses full of strangers. If that happens, I'm moving back to Dammer Dammer in September."

On the lawn, Pippa played with Christianne. Cally braided Rika's long hair to get it off her neck in the dense and surprising heat of dusk.

Philip and Theo were in New Hope buying a gift for Peter. On a glass table set for supper, Lila was reading the Howells family Bible, occasionally whistling a low "Shiiiit." Then she'd lift her head. "Cally, did you ever read this?" and she'd read aloud a story about Hannah or Lucy or Rachel.

"Good news," Peter said, coming in with drinks, putting the tray down on a table next to Bumpo. "Philip's not moving to England."

"He's staying here with Julia?" Rachel asked.

"That's right." Peter passed out the drinks.

"Knockout," said Bumpo. "And they lived happily ever after."

"I don't really think Julia's marriage is our concern," Cally said quietly. "It's difficult to have a private life in this family."

"It gives me great pleasure to announce the opening of *Private Lives*," Peter said, "a new tragicomedy by Julia Howells about a couple in America the Beautiful, who meet and marry and fight and fall in love."

"And live happily ever after," Bumpo said. "Write that down in the Bible, Julia."

Julia stood in the doorway, watching the pageant of her family celebrating their daily lives as if there were an inviolate order to the scene on the screened porch. On the lawn beyond, Pippa was inching along the grass, generously imitating Christianne, fat with baby flesh, struggling forward on hands and knees.

"The Howells lived happily off and on until they died," Julia said from the doorway with a quick bow, and Peter leaned over Lila and entered Julia's speech in the Bible dated June 30, 1973, and signed, P.H., M.D.

BOXING DAY, 1976

Julia wanted to celebrate Boxing Day in 1976. Rachel was extremely pleased, but she tried to conceal her excitement for fear that as the time approached, Julia would change her mind.

"You think I'll chicken out," Julia said to Rachel one afternoon when they were baking turkeys and fruit breads days in advance in the fine new kitchen Caleb had designed at The Farm.

"Not exactly," Rachel said cautiously, "but I am surprised."

"And happy, too, I can tell." Julia hugged the soft dough of her grandmother's thick waist. "For old times' sake."

"We enjoyed ourselves." Rachel smiled.

"And still do," Julia said, dumping raisins and chopped pecans into the rich honey batter. "I want to do Boxing Day for my children—a made-up Howells holiday to repeat in their own lives if they wish. Besides, if we have Boxing Day, everyone will have to come home for Christmas."

And everyone did. Caleb and Rika came from Houston, to which they had returned in the fall of 1975, after The Farm had opened and Caleb had completed his own small house on the land behind Daniel's.

"For my retirement," Caleb continued to maintain, although in the back of his mind, safe from Rika's investigation, he planned to come home in a matter of two or three years. Rika was pregnant on Boxing Day with a son they would name Nathaniel, born on March 11, 1977, who, with his sister, Christianne, would grow up on the Howells land in Solebury, where Caleb would come to be known in a small circle as a conservationist who protected the land from shortsighted developers, a good architect, accountable and honest.

Peter came for Christmas week from Philadelphia, where he was a psychiatrist at the Family Center for Adolescents associated with the University of Pennsylvania. He had moved to Philadelphia in 1975 after a short residency at Yale. In the fall of 1976 Peter bought an old Victorian town house in West Philadelphia because Theo was coming to live with him. Together Peter and Theo had spent the fall sanding the wood floors to their natural color, stripping the wallpaper, taking up wax-layered linoleum from the kitchen.

It had been Julia who finally agreed that Theo should live with Peter. She and Philip had moved to England in late spring, 1974, to try it as a home and with the secret hope that Philip would be right about eccentricities. He was not. If anything, in Britain Theo was worse. He began to leave school early for pubs, where he could be served at fourteen, to ride motorcycles at dangerous speeds, to favor town girls in Caenarvon with stiff beehive hairdos and broad rumps.

"We're going to have to leave," Philip said one day, making arrangements with two Welsh school friends, whom he had joined in the practice of medicine.

"Will we go to London?" Pippa asked.

"We'll go home," Philip said.

Theo thrived with Peter. Weekends he often went to his parents' house and even Pippa remarked on her brother's peace of mind. Julia did not recover from her sadness about Theo, but she was glad for Peter and Theo, which was sufficient.

When Julia and Philip returned from England in the fall of 1976, Julia had gone to New York with a new play, which was opening off-Broadway under her direction the first of the year.

"*The Summer of Our Marriage.*" Peter laughed when Julia told him the title. "Is it another tragicomedy?"

"It's about Bam's Farm, according to Pippa," Theo said.

"Jesus, what would you do without us, Julia?" Peter asked.

The Farm drove everybody crazy, even Cally. It was successful with a waiting list of old people and teenagers, a very happy place to live, according to the reports submitted to the foundation of which Bumpo was president. But the old people occasionally fell on the narrow back stairs or developed intestinal problems from Rachel's rich cooking or had spats with each other during social hours after supper. One teenager was pregnant when she arrived and another sailed from the second-story window as Mercury with winged feet, deluded by LSD.

"Close the place," Peter said after the winged Mercury was safely in the psychiatric wing of the University of Pennsylvania Hospital.

"We can't," Cally said. "It would break Bam's heart."

So the family established a routine for each of them to help.

Julia invited everyone she could think of to Boxing Day. Old friends, distant relations, teachers, shopkeepers. She put up posters in the towns of Solebury and New Hope. BOXING DAY AT THE HOWELLS', the posters said, BRING YOUR BOXES OF ACCUMULATED JUNK TO BURN ON THE BONFIRE, A COVERED DISH, A BOTTLE OF WINE. SKATING ON THE POND IF IT'S FROZEN.

The pond was frozen. Julia was up early the morning of Boxing Day in the kitchen with Peter when Pippa and Theo came downstairs in jeans, heavy sweaters and skates tied over their shoulders.

"Daddy's already up trying out the pond," Pippa said. "I can't remember ever skating when I was little."

"We haven't had a cold spell like this for years," Julia said.

"I know," Pippa said, taking a doughnut from the oven. "Even the weather changes when you grow up."

Julia woke Caleb and Rika, gave Christianne cereal and was ready to leave herself when Bumpo arrived in Nat's old letter sweater from Yale and a knit cap pulled down over his forehead so he looked like a gangly adolescent girl with his long blond hair.

"Jesus, I can't wait for this day to be over," he said, collapsing on a wooden chair, stretching his legs out so Peter had to step over him to put away the breakfast dishes. "Bam is reborn. She made Tuwilla get up at five to help the goddamned teenagers pack their boxes to burn."

"What did you expect?" Julia asked, pouring him a mug of coffee.

"Wait'll you see Bam in her raccoon coat and red bandanna. You'd think we were having a costume party for the exhuming of dead relations," Peter said.

"What does that mean?" Pippa asked.

"Ghosts," Theo said, drinking orange juice straight from the pitcher.

"Lo and behold, you light the bonfire, toss on the boxes, and Ghosts," Bumpo said, shaping apparitions with his hands. "*You might think it's just smoke, but you'll be wrong.*"

"We can have the bonfire by the pond," Caleb said, coming downstairs, blueprints under his arm.

"On the south side field where there aren't any trees," Bumpo said.

"Yeah. I wasn't planning to extinguish the forest."

"You can't be too careful," Bumpo said, closing his eyes. "This holiday is a terrible idea."

"Bumpo, get the truck with the wood, pick up Mother and shut up," Peter said. He handed a pair of skates to Bumpo. "Ask Lila if she'd like to try these."

"Lila won't skate," Bumpo said. "Me neither. I have the feeling that as soon as I get on the ice, there'll be a miraculous thaw."

Julia walked with Peter and Pippa down the path in back of the Main House, still called the Main House by the family in spite of Bam's insistence on The Farm. Theo was behind them, carrying Christianne on his shoulders, and Caleb was helping Rika.

"Why don't you leave the blueprints at home, Caleb?" Peter called back.

"He's planning to move the pond fifty yards to the south," Theo said.

"He's going to design a contemporary bonfire," Pippa said, putting her hand on her mother's shoulder as they descended the hill to the pond.

Through the bare white birch trees Philip was visible skating close to the bank. And Rachel, in her bandanna, was moving like a small brown bear on her hind legs towards the truck where a disgruntled Bumpo was unloading kindling. They walked into the clearing just as Philip sailed across the pond on his bottom.

"This is not my kind of holiday," Lila said, wrapped in a blanket.

"I think it's lovely, Julia," Rachel said. "I'm so glad we decided to invite everyone."

"People are coming by caravan from New York," Bumpo shouted from the back of the pickup truck. "Julia put the fucking posters all over the subway."

Julia knelt down next to her mother, put her arms on Cally's knees. "Do you mind, Mama?" she asked.

Cally brushed Julia's hair back. "Mind Boxing Day? I always thought it was a silly holiday before your father was burned. And I still do."

Julia sat with Pippa and Peter on the exposed roots of an old black oak and put on skates.

"I'm glad you decided to do Boxing Day again," Peter said.

"You've always had a black view of life," Bumpo said. "Am I supposed to light this thing now, Julia?"

"People aren't coming till twelve."

"Light it anyway for us. There's plenty of wood," Caleb said, getting on the ice. "And it's cold as a snake."

"Be sure to stand back," Rachel instructed. "Check the wind."

"I'm standing back," Bumpo said. "One more step and I'd be in the pond."

Bumpo observed the fire with his hands on his hips. He lifted the sleeve of Rachel's coat and checked her watch. "Shit. Fourteen more hours of this day. I can't stand it."

"When the teenagers come, you must watch your language," Rachel said.

"Don't worry, Bammy, I'm going to bed in half an hour and sleep through the day."

Bumpo climbed down the bank onto the pond and began to skate in his shoes.

With Pippa, Julia skated to the middle of the pond. The morning sun was halfway up, over the hills beyond the farm, at the right angle for shadows.

"Look," Pippa said, putting her arm around Julia's waist. "Our shadows fill the pond." Julia looked. There Caleb was skating carefully with a large-bellied Rika, and Theo was bending over Christianne, pushing her in front of him like a stroller, Bumpo was walking across the pond, imitating Peter with exaggerated movements of grace, and Philip was lounging on the bank. Rachel and Cally and Lila were at the edge of the pond, planted like boxwood, their shadows merging with the fire which had no fixed shape but an irregular and changing blackness on the surface of the ice.

"In the spring, you know, when the pond is settled, you can see your face in it," Pippa said to Julia.

It was November, just before Thanksgiving, that Julia had decided to do Boxing Day. She had been reading through the Bible in the hopes of finding the idea for a new play in the way she had found *Inherited Lives* when she came upon John Howells' entry on miracles after her father's death. And like the sudden revelation of photographs when the faces surface in fluid and are clear as life, Julia understood the miracle.

She had wanted to tell someone immediately the great news of her discovery. As a mother she had wanted especially to tell her children. But instinctively she knew she could not explain a mystery to children that she had only just come to understand herself. She would do Boxing Day instead.

"Do you believe in miracles?" she asked Peter, grabbing his hand as he skated by her.

"I love miracles. I think you ought to make an in-depth study. Write a miracle play."

"I'm being serious, Peter."

"I have an announcement," Peter shouted, making a dramatic turn on the ice. "Julia is writing a miracle play."

"About saints?" Bumpo asked. "What does Julia know about saints?"

"Julia is writing a miracle play about us."

"Do we all get to play our own parts, Julia?" Caleb asked.

"I refuse to play the foolish brother," Bumpo said.

"It's a terrific part, Bumpo. It could be the best. The trick is playing it well," Peter said.

Cars were beginning to arrive, pulling off the main drive onto the south fields, where Peter had put up signs for parking. Tuwilla was walking down the hill from The Farm with the teenagers and heartier residents. Small children spilling out of the parked cars were running across the field ahead of their parents.

"Oh, shit, I'm going to bed," Bumpo said.

That night, after the festivities and the cleaning up, the Howells children lay around the living room of Daniel's house, half sleeping in exhaustion, talking very little. But there was in the room a wonderful spirit of accord that must come to soldiers in the trenches after a long volley has been survived—a company knowledge that the treasure of living comes in moments and is prized because the moment does not last.

"Jeez," Theo said, his feet on the fireplace next to the screen. "Half of America came."

"A sampling of the nation, Granddaddy would have said. The one percent cross section," said Peter.

Bumpo lay on the couch, still in his knit cap pulled down over his eyes.

"You know, Jules, I thought I was going to hate today and it turned out fine. As good a day as when we were little. As good as Bam used to make."

Julia leaned against the fieldstone fireplace. She wanted to write something grand in the Bible. Equal in promise to the first entry of Caleb Howells, to the entry on the miracle of her father's life. She wanted to respond to John Howells' command for love stories.

WE DID BOXING DAY AGAIN. DECEMBER 26, 1976.